Chasing Morgan

T0050554

Chasing Morgan

Book Four: The Hunted Series

JENNIFER RYAN

AVONIMPULSE
An Imprint of HarperCollinsPublishers

Excerpt from *The Governess Club: Claire* copyright © 2013 by Heather Johnson.

Excerpt from *Ashes, Ashes, They All Fall Dead* copyright © 2013 by Lena Diaz.

Excerpt from *The Governess Club: Bonnie* copyright © 2013 by Heather Johnson.

EPub Edition OCTOBER 2013 ISBN: 9780062305961

Print Edition ISBN: 9780062305978

HB 05.25.2023

*To my husband and children for your continued support
and taking this journey with me.
To my wonderful editor, Amanda Bergeron, for your
amazing talent. This book and my writing are better
because of you. Thank you for your continued support
and encouragement.
To all the fans of The Hunted Series.
All of you make this possible.*

Chapter One

One year ago . . .

MORGAN'S FINGERS FLEW across the laptop keyboard propped on her knees. She took a deep breath, cleared her mind, and looked out past her pink-painted toes propped on the railing and across her yard to the densely wooded area at the edge of her property. Her mind's eye found her guest winding his way through the trees. She still had time before Jack stepped out of the woods separating her land from his. She couldn't wait to meet him.

Images, knowings, they just came to her. She'd accepted that part of herself a long time ago. As she got older, she'd learned to use her gift to seek out answers.

She finished her buy-and-sell orders and switched from her day-trading page to check her psychic website and read the questions submitted by customers. She answered several quickly, letting the others settle in her mind until the answers came to her.

One stood out. The innocuous question about getting a job held an eerie vibe.

The familiar, strange pulsation came over her. The world disappeared like a door slamming on reality. The images came to her like hammer blows, one right after the other, and she took the onslaught, knowing something important needed to be seen and understood.

An older woman lying in a bed, hooked up to a machine feeding her medication. Frail and ill, she had translucent skin and dark circles marring her pain-filled eyes. Her pain washed over Morgan like a tsunami.

The woman yelled at someone, her face contorted into something mean and hateful. An unhappy woman—one who'd spent her whole life blaming others and trying to make them as miserable as her.

A pristine white pillow floating down, inciting panic, amplified to terror when it covered the woman's face, her frail body swallowed by the sheets.

Morgan had an overwhelming feeling of suffocating.

The woman tried desperately to suck in a breath, but couldn't. Unable to move her lethargic limbs, she lay terrified and helpless under his unyielding hands. Lights flashed on her closed eyelids.

Death came calling.

A man stood next to the bed holding the pillow like a shield. His mouth opened on a contorted, evil, hysterical laugh that rang in her ears and made her skin crawl. She squeezed her eyes closed to blot out his malevolent image and thoughts.

Murderer!

The word rang in her head as the terrifying emotions overtook her.

Morgan threw up a wall in her mind, blocking the onslaught of disturbing pictures and feelings. She took several deep breaths and concentrated on the white roses growing in profusion just below the porch railing. Their sweet fragrance filled the air. With every breath, she centered herself and found her inner calm, pushing out the anger and rage left over from the vision. Her body felt like a lead weight, and lightened as her energy came back. The drowsiness faded with each new breath. She'd be fine in a few minutes.

The man on horseback emerged from the trees, coming toward her home. Her guest had arrived.

Focused on the computer screen, she slowly and meticulously typed her answer to the man who had asked about a job and inadvertently opened himself up to telling her who he really was at the core.

She replied simply:

You'll get the job, but you can't hide from what you did. You need help. Turn yourself in to the police.

None of her personal information appeared on the website, and she'd put a lot of time and effort into keeping her identity and location a secret for reasons of her own. He'd never find her.

A chill ran over her, despite the warm sun on her skin.

She put through the charge and tried to erase the vision from her mind. She'd told him to go to the police. Nothing more she could do. She didn't have any proof a crime had been committed. You couldn't make accusations against people based on a vision. Even if she went to the police with what she knew, they wouldn't take her seriously. She'd learned that the hard way.

The help she provided Tyler and the FBI was different. Her unique link with Tyler allowed her to assist him with some of his cases. Tyler had nothing to do with this man. She could ask him to investigate, but why would he? He had a hard enough time believing what she told him about the cases he was working on. She didn't want to have to convince him all over again that what she saw was real and true. It hurt to have to convince him every time, despite the ample proof she'd given him on multiple cases. After all this time, he should believe her—believe in her.

She didn't want to think about Tyler right now. He'd be in Colorado today. Close. Their connection that much stronger, and the harder he'd ignore it and push her away. Maybe she should give in and go see him.

Why couldn't he stay in San Francisco?

It wasn't time for them to meet again. She sighed and tried to put him out of her mind. Not possible. They were connected on an elemental level, and had been for a long time.

Why did things between them have to be so complicated and difficult?

Dealing with her customers was simple. They went to her website and clicked on the link to ask a question. She charged fifteen dollars for requests she answered. If she couldn't answer the question, or wouldn't answer, she didn't charge and sent a standard reply, telling the person she couldn't help.

Either the person believed in her enough to pay the fifteen dollars, or they didn't.

Sure, they had to accept her terms and conditions. After all, what she "saw" was open to interpretation and the result may not be what the customer expected. In short, if they didn't like the answer, they couldn't shoot the messenger.

She specifically informed customers to beware what they asked, and how they asked it. You may get the answer to a question you hadn't intended.

If you suspected your spouse of cheating on you, don't be surprised if she confirmed it, and that the other person was your best friend. She wouldn't lie, or tell you only what you wanted to hear.

In a few cases, she simply refused to answer. People often wanted to know when they were going to die and how. In her opinion, this kind of information did more harm than good. It usually altered the course of a person's life, and she didn't want to be responsible for changing one's fate and destiny.

One thing she knew for certain, life had a pattern. Mistakes are repeated until the lesson is learned. Knowing something ahead of time didn't necessarily mean you could change the outcome. Some things were meant to be and nothing could stop them from ending the same way she saw them, even if the path that led to that end took a detour first. That wasn't to say the course of the future couldn't be altered. It could. She'd done it several times. For Tyler's family, she'd do it again.

Chapter Two

JACK'S GAZE LOCKED on her as he made his way out of the trees, across the wide expanse of pasture and to the house. He'd spotted her sitting on the porch with her laptop. The rain of golden hair drew his eye. Thick and slightly wavy, her hair dropped almost to her waist. The color so bright, the sunlight seemed to glow out from the mass of waves.

"Hello, Jack."

How did she know his name?

Her voice threw him again. A sultry voice from such a fresh face. She looked to be in her early twenties. Probably five-foot-seven, she had a slim build and curves made to keep a man up at night. Her skin was lightly bronzed from days spent in the sun, and her striking blue eyes reminded him of the color of a clear, clean azure sea.

It struck him that he also saw a lifetime of wisdom in those eyes.

She has an old soul.

He hadn't known what that really meant until now. As he looked at this young, vibrant woman, her eyes spoke volumes.

Nothing else to say to describe her. Some sort of essence emanated from her he couldn't name. Words wouldn't do her justice. He wondered what such a beautiful woman was doing living in the middle of nowhere—seemingly alone.

"Um, hi. I'm Jack Turner. I own the Stargazer Ranch that borders your property. Uh, we're neighbors." He shifted nervously in the saddle. Not like him at all, but something about her unsettled him.

"Howdy, neighbor." A strong, sturdy man. It made her secretly laugh to see him a little out of sorts with her. She knew a lot about him, impressions from Tyler of his good friend, Jack. She hadn't expected him to be discombobulated by the sight of her.

Her casual country joke brought out a smile. She laid the computer on the table and poured a glass of ice tea from the tray. He never took his eyes off her as she came off the porch and walked to him with the glass. His penetrating gaze unsettled her.

"For you. You look a little hot. Have some iced tea."

She handed him the glass when he came down off the horse. Interested in the beautiful animal, she took his head in her hands and gave him a scratch behind the ears and under the leather bridle. The horse bent to her and laid his head to her chest. If he were a cat, he'd have purred.

"He usually doesn't take to people. In fact, he only responds like that with my wife, Jenna." He took a deep sip of the cold drink before adding, "He likes you, though."

"He knows a good thing when he sees it. Blue loves your wife because he knows she needed him at one time, and now he trusts her. She's kind to him."

"How'd you know his name? Do you know my wife?"

"Sort of." She stepped back from the horse and looked at the tall man standing beside her. A good man, dedicated to his family and his ranch. He was happy. That came to her clearly and washed away the last remnants of the murderous vision. She wished she had that same feeling in her own life. Jack had everything he wanted, his wife, his children, his family of friends, and love.

Again, she thought of Tyler and pushed his face out of her mind.

"It won't be long now before you have a new baby. Your wife is well."

Your wife is well. Not a question, a statement. Something about this woman wasn't quite right. Jack felt like he knew her, but he'd never seen her before in his life. Unforgettable, he'd never forget her.

"Yeah, she's fine. We're excited about the baby. Our boys are looking forward to it."

"I bet they are. They're the spitting image of you and your twin brother. That little Sam was named appropriately. He's just like his uncle. Matt. Now, he's the serious one. He'll take after you. He has a deep love for animals, especially the horses. He'll carry on the tradition your wife set up for the ranch. He and your nephew, Jacob, will tend the ranch much like you and Caleb tend it now. You've made a good life for your family. It's something to be proud of."

How did she know about his family?

"Have we met before? Are you friends with my wife?"

"No and no," she said with a smile. "I moved in almost a year ago. I pretty much keep to myself. I like it here. It's quiet and beautiful. You can't beat the trees and the blue sky. I like the land and the expanse of it. You know what I mean."

Rambling, it had been a long time since she'd had someone to talk to. She needed to remember that while Jack and everyone else in Tyler's family were like old friends to her now, they'd never met her.

Jack took another long sip of his tea and tried to figure out how she knew so much about him and his family. *You know what I mean.* Again, not a question.

She looked normal. She didn't seem like some kind of psychotic stalker. Maybe she knew about Jenna's wealth and that she ran Merrick International. Maybe she had some plot to get money from Jenna.

She chuckled. "I'm not after Jenna, or her money. You can rest easy, Jack. I mean you no harm."

Surprised and confused, had he spoken his thoughts out loud and not realized it?

She turned the conversation and his thoughts. "You came to see me for a reason. It's quite a ride over from your ranch. What can I do for you, Jack?"

He shook his head and stared down at her. Unexpected in every way. He felt like he stood on quicksand, sinking fast. Like she knew the joke and the punch line, and the joke was on him. He didn't like the feeling.

"I came to ask if I could work out some sort of agreement with you to use your land."

"Yes."

He kept talking right over her. "I've expanded my breeding program, and I have a lot of horses I need to spread out. I have enough pastureland, but your land isn't being used for any animals. I thought maybe I could rotate the horses from my acreage to yours, leaving mine to recuperate between switches."

"Yes," she repeated.

"I'd pay you for the use of your land. We can negotiate a price."

"Okay."

"My men or I will have to come and check on the horses and bring them feed. I'll be sure to set up a water source. Basically, you won't have to do anything. I'll take care of everything the horses need. You aren't using the land, and I don't believe they'll bother you."

"You said that already. And, I said yes. Go ahead. Bring them over."

"You're sure?" he asked, surprised she'd agree so easily.

"I'd love the company. I hope you won't mind if I spoil them by giving them apples and carrots once in a while."

"No. That's, yes. You can give them some treats. Are you sure?"

"Yes. It's no problem. It gets lonely out here sometimes. The curse of living in the boondocks. It's my own fault really. I don't do well around people. Too many emotions flying around," she said and waved her hands in the air like a whirlwind. "I like it here though. When the property came up for sale, I couldn't resist," she said with a secretive smile. "I'm meant to be here."

"It's a great place," he agreed.

The three-bedroom house was in great shape. The last owners had updated the kitchen and bathrooms and added on a wide wraparound porch that stretched from the front of the house around to the back into a deck that looked out over a wide expanse of lawn and lush gardens. From the front of the house, Jack saw the roses blooming in a profusion of colors. This woman took care of her home and land. He had no doubt the horses would be safe here with her.

"Why don't you like other people?"

"I like them fine," she answered with a shrug and scratched Blue's nose. "I just have a hard time coping around strangers. You're the first person I've had here, since I moved in. It's nice to have company, especially a nice man like you. You have good energy."

Sometimes she sounded like a crackpot, but she enjoyed watching Jack get confused and irritated.

"Relax, Jack. You can bring the horses. The fee you're thinking of is okay with me."

"Huh?"

"You'll need to shore up a few of the fences. I've let them go, since I moved in. I'm fine with you taking the cost of the repairs out of the monthly fee, since the improvements will be to my land. I only have one request. If you aren't the one to come and check on the horses, then I'd like it to be Caleb. I think it will be okay if it's just the two of you. I'd like it if you or Caleb wanted to stop in and say hello once in a while. But no one else. I don't like strangers."

"You don't think of Caleb and me as strangers?"

"I know a lot about the two of you. For instance, I know you have to get home because you're expected at Sam's place for a family dinner. You'll decorate cupcakes with the children. Sam and Tyler will be home today."

"Sam won't be here for another week, and Tyler doesn't usually come with him. How do you know about them? About dinner?" He took a step toward her. Those all-seeing blue eyes gazed up at him and a soft smile spread on her pretty face. Her hair softly swayed in the breeze like a living thing.

"I didn't get your name. Who are you?" His tone demanded her answer in no uncertain terms.

"I'm Morgan."

Everything in him went still. He hadn't expected this. It all became clear. He finally understood how she knew about he and Jenna, Caleb, the kids, Sam . . . and Tyler.

"You're Tyler's Morgan."

She laughed with a self-deprecating smile. "Tyler's Morgan," she said softly. "Tyler wouldn't claim me to save his life. What is it you guys like to call me? Oh, yeah, the psychic ghost. I have to say, I don't really care for the nickname. I'm no ghost, as you can see. I don't usually talk to ghosts either. I know that was your next question."

Stunned, he stood speechless and a little scared. Psychic, she knew things about all of them. Things Tyler sure as hell hadn't told her. They hardly talked, and when they did, she only called to offer a clue to one of his cases. Tyler had only seen her once. Several years ago, she'd stopped Tyler in a restaurant and told him to find his sister and saved her life by sending Tyler after her. Since then, they'd only spoken on the phone.

Tyler was obsessed with finding Morgan.

"You and Caleb can't tell Tyler where I am."

"How'd you know that's what I was thinking? Can you read my mind?"

She laughed. "Not really. Not like you think. You're easy to read. Tyler's your friend. He'd like nothing better than to find out where I've been all this time. He's frustrated with me."

"Angry is more like it."

"Exactly. It isn't time for us to cross paths. Not yet. We weren't supposed to meet when we did. His sister should have died in that explosion. I couldn't let that happen. It would have devastated him."

"He is close to her," Jack confirmed. "I can't imagine losing my sister or brother."

"She took a path she wasn't meant to go down. I had to correct it, or Tyler wouldn't be where he is right now. He wouldn't have been there to help Sam with Elizabeth. She was a victim of circumstance. She and Sam will have a good life together."

"You know that?" he asked with skepticism and hope all tied up together.

"They're meant to be together, like you and Jenna. Cameron will have his dream for a family come true very soon. You and Sam will have a good time watching him stumble through the process. In the end, he'll make the right decision because she's the woman intended for him. She'll already know it. He'll take some convincing."

"You know about Cameron, too?" Cameron worked for Jenna at Merrick International. They were all friends and close as family.

She put her hands in the back pockets of her jeans and looked up toward the setting sun. She had all the confidence and certainty she needed. "I know about Tyler's family."

"Yes, but how do you *know* all this?"

She gave him a cocky smile. "Do you want to talk about psychic and paranormal phenomena? We could have a really good debate about how I do the things I do, and how you don't really believe I'm capable of seeing the past and the future."

"I don't know what I believe. I know you've helped Tyler and Sam a number of times. They say you're always right."

"I'm right about dinner tonight. Sam and Tyler aren't expected, but they'll arrive just the same. How do I know that? I just do. I see it. I always know where Tyler is. It's like seeing a map in my mind, and wherever he is there's a pinpoint of light. That isn't exactly how it is, but it'll give you a reference for how I know."

"Does he know you're aware of him all the time?"

"Tyler is too concerned with the fact that I give him

information I pull out of thin air, and he doesn't know where I am. He hasn't considered the bigger picture. He's obsessed with finding me, but I don't think he's actually considered what he'd do once he had me in his sights. His feelings about me are all jumbled up. The only thing he really knows is that it unsettles him that I can do something he can't explain or accept."

Jack smiled mischievously. "He has a thing for you. We all think he's half in love with you already. A one-minute conversation changed his life. You changed his life."

"Yes. And soon I'll do the same for you. In order for that to happen, you'll have to keep my secret. I mean it, Jack. You and Caleb can't tell him I'm here, or that you've seen me."

"Why not? What harm is there in the two of you finally seeing each other again? I think you and Tyler could be great together."

If only that were true. Unfortunately, their meeting would be tumultuous. She couldn't see it all clearly, but she understood when they finally did come together, his case would drag her into a dark and dangerous world. She couldn't tell Jack all of that. He might give her the benefit of the doubt, and he did doubt, but he wanted the best for Tyler. She did too. She wanted the best for all of them.

"It's important, Jack."

His eyes narrowed with suspicion. Okay, not a good enough explanation.

"What if I told you that if you tell Tyler where I am,

harm might come to someone in your family? Someone you love could be hurt. Would you risk it just so you wouldn't have to lie to Tyler?"

"Is something going to happen to someone in my family? Have you seen something? Who's going to be hurt?"

She ignored his concern and his questions, though she knew his feelings ran deep.

"Would you risk it, Jack? Because I won't. Not even so I can see Tyler now, instead of on a future date I can't pinpoint."

"I'd never risk my family. Who's going to be hurt?"

"I won't tell you that."

He dropped the glass in his hand. It shattered on the gravel drive.

His anger came fast and swift. She'd known he'd be upset about any threat to his family, but she hadn't anticipated his actions. He grabbed her by the arms, lifting her from the ground so they stood face-to-face. His eyes narrowed and filled with rage. The anger washed over her like the heat of a wildfire and took her breath away.

"You'll tell me who's in danger, and you'll tell me now." He spaced out each word to make sure she knew he meant business.

"Jack . . . Put . . . Me . . . Down."

She struggled to assert herself, even though she looked like every ounce of energy had drained from her body. Afraid to let her go, her skin turned translucent and the deep blue of her eyes faded and dulled. It looked like he'd hurt her, and he'd barely touched her. She'd wilted like a flower in the desert heat.

He set her back on her feet gently and kept his hands on her arms to hold her steady. He brushed a hand over her golden hair. "I'm sorry. Are you okay?"

"I'll be fine."

She took a step away and erected a wall to block the remains of his anger. She never thought she'd need one between them. She'd made a mistake in not remembering his love of his family and his overwhelming need to protect and keep them safe. She wouldn't make that mistake twice. Out of practice dealing with people in person, the computer allowed her anonymity. Maybe a little too much anonymity.

"Listen. Just tell me what you know about my family. I need to know. I have a right to protect what's mine."

"Yes, you do." Feeling stronger by the minute, Jack's concern replaced his anger.

"Then, tell me who it is."

"It won't help you to know."

"I'm not playing games here, Morgan. I want to know. Now."

"It's complicated, Jack. Let me lay it out for you this way. Everyone's life flows in a line like a river. We're born and we age. There's no going back to the beginning, or changing the past. The future is the only thing we are capable of changing because it hasn't happened. There's a process to life. Every action has a reaction. If you do or don't do something, that action can affect the future. In the case of Tyler's sister, an event changed the timeline and sent her down another path, one she wasn't meant to take."

"Okay. So you fixed the line and put her back on the right path by telling Tyler to go and get his sister."

"Right. Simplified, but right. She wasn't meant to be in that house when it exploded. The future she might have had before being there changed. Tyler saved her, and now she has a completely new future."

She had to take another deep breath to help clear the last shimmers of Jack's anger from her system. "The vision I have of your family's future has an event where someone will be harmed." She left it vague. She didn't want to tell him she saw someone shoot his little boy. That would only send his anger into overdrive again. "In the vision, I intervene and prevent the person from being harmed."

"How do you prevent it? Why not just tell me? Then, I can make sure the event doesn't happen at all."

"It doesn't matter how I prevent it. I can't be specific enough about the vision to say, 'Don't go here on this day.' I don't know which day it is, and it's an event that happens in your family often enough to make it difficult to say exactly when it will happen."

"Either you're deliberately trying to confuse me, or you're being vague to piss me off."

"I'm not doing either," she snapped.

She couldn't get Tyler to accept what she did and the things she saw. It shouldn't surprise her Jack remained just as skeptical.

"I'm simply trying to explain the event I see is something you do all the time. I can't pick out a specific enough time to tell you when it will happen, except to say that on this occasion I'm there to stop the person from being harmed." She put her hand up to stop him from interrupting again. "Now, if you tell Tyler where I am, you change the timeline. The event I see happening will still happen, but I might not be there at that time because you've changed things. You see, the event happens on a day that Tyler and I meet again. In the vision, he isn't expecting me to be there. That, I know for sure."

"So, you're saying if I change things now, it could change things then."

"Exactly. You don't like lying to Tyler, or keeping secrets from the people you love. But you can't risk one of your family members getting hurt. Right?"

"I'll make the deal, if you swear the person won't be harmed."

"I can't promise. What's meant to be will be. I can only tell you in my vision I keep them safe."

She had to make him understand. Just because she saw something in the future didn't necessarily make it absolute. "We're talking about a future event. When I see the vision it's only the truth so long as none of the events leading up to it aren't altered. The future isn't written in stone. I can only promise that if I show up at the event in the future, and it happens the way I envision it, I'll stop the person from being harmed."

"Then how do I know my meeting you now hasn't altered that future already?"

"Because I knew you were coming today because you want to put your horses on my land." She gave him a brilliant smile.

"You did?"

"Yes. I also know that Sam and Tyler are on their way. Go home to your family. Leave the future to fate. Let life happen."

His frown deepened. He didn't quite believe her, but he couldn't ignore her prediction either.

"Go home. Have your family dinner with everyone. Decorate cupcakes and enjoy the evening. Things are as they should be. Tyler will wait. It's how it's meant to be. He isn't ready to see me. He hasn't figured out what he wants from me, besides to ring my neck for not doing what he wants, when he wants it."

He took a deep breath and accepted he couldn't change a future he couldn't see with a slight nod. "Will you be all right here alone?"

"I'm fine. I'm not alone. I have Tyler, whether he likes it or not. I hope I have you, too, Jack. I hope we can be friends."

"We are."

Struck by his certainty, it had been a long time since someone simply accepted her for who she was. She stood on tiptoe and kissed his cheek. "Thank you." Her voice cracked, despite her valiant attempt to hide her emotions. "I can't wait to see the horses."

"You're welcome at the ranch anytime you want to visit. Jenna would love to meet you."

She smiled. She'd be a part of their lives soon enough.

They had their own living to do for the time being. "We'll see. Like I said, I don't do well around people."

"Let me clean this up for you." Jack indicated the broken glass at their feet.

"I'll take care of it."

"Sorry about that."

He boosted himself up on Blue and stared down at the striking woman who'd kept them all guessing for years. She wasn't what he'd expected. He didn't think she was what Tyler would expect either.

"I won't tell Tyler, or anyone else, you're living here. I'll bring the horses myself and take care of the fences and water. I'll be the one to check on them. If I have to send someone else, I'll tell him to stay clear of the house. Is that okay?"

He wouldn't involve Caleb. He didn't want to make his brother-in-law lie to the family too.

"That's fine."

"Do you have everything you need?" He looked around again at the house and the SUV parked in the driveway. The car wasn't new, but it looked well maintained.

"I'm fine, Jack. I work from home, so I'm here most of the time. Don't worry about me. I've gotten along for a lot of years on my own."

"Okay, then. Oh, about the money?"

"The amount you have in mind is okay with me."

"You know the amount?"

She gave him a cocky half grin and winked. "I sure do."

"Tell me what it is."

"Goodbye, Jack." She'd let him question that for a while. It would drive him crazy wondering whether she really knew or not.

WITHIN THE MONTH, Jack arrived several times with small herds of horses. In the end, there were more than twenty-five beauties in her pastures. She visited with them often. Jack spent time working on the fences, and she enjoyed hearing about what Tyler and Sam were up to. It was strange getting information about Tyler from someone who knew him personally. Everything she learned about him came as glimpses from his mind. She still didn't understand the connection between them, but she'd learned to accept it. She wished Tyler would do the same.

The first month the horses arrived on her property, Jack came to pay her for the use of the pastureland minus the amount for the improvements to the fences and water lines.

He gaped at her when she caught him lying about the amount.

"This isn't the agreed-upon fee. You know it and, more importantly, I know it. You just wanted to see if I'd say anything, or if I'd know. Shame on you, Jack," she said and tried not to laugh.

"Oh, come on. I just wanted to see if you were pulling my leg, or if you really did know what I was thinking."

"I know. It's okay." She didn't really care about the

money, but he handed over another hundred dollars. She accepted it and his juvenile behavior. Used to it, people questioned her all her life about whether she really had a gift, or if she was simply lying.

"How's the baby?"

"Beautiful like her mother. Come to the house and see her."

She would love to see the baby. She wanted one of her own and a family like Jenna and Jack had created. Not in the cards. Her future remained uncertain, shrouded in a thick fog she couldn't see past. Frustrating as hell to see other's so clearly, but not her own.

Her future rested on the outcome of seeing Tyler again . . . and beating the evil waiting for her.

"We'll see."

"You won't come, will you?"

"It's not time yet. You're going to California tomorrow."

Jack smiled. A last-minute trip, Jenna had some work to do at Merrick International. "Yeah. Want to come? You could see Tyler."

"Not yet. Timelines, Jack. This trip you'll spend time with Cameron. He's got quite a journey ahead of him."

"Yeah? I hear he's got a new woman in his life. I hope Emma likes her."

She concentrated on Cameron, his daughter, and their life. The woman in his life now swirled Cameron's future into chaos, sweeping up his past and obscuring his ability to see things clearly. The second woman had the ability to bring him into the eye of the storm where everything was

calm and clear. There, he'd find the future he wanted—
for him and Emma.

"Emma won't like the woman who's there now. She'll
like the second one."

Jack knew she wouldn't tell him anything more. He'd
reluctantly accepted that about her over the last month.

"I'll see you soon." He slid back into his truck, shaking his head, and left her alone on her porch, an angel
with golden hair and a smile on her lips.

"I can't wait to see Tyler's face when he sees you again."

Chapter Three

Present day . . .

"I HATE PAPERWORK," Tyler grumbled and grabbed the coffeepot, pouring himself a second cup. Might as well have an apple-raspberry turnover from Decadence to go with it. The food would be good, even if the coffee was several hours old and probably tasted closer to motor oil.

Ever since his partner, Sam, met and married Elizabeth, he'd gained ten pounds and spent an extra day at the gym each week trying to keep from gaining ten more. The fact that she owned and ran two of the best places to eat in the city didn't hurt. He often ate at both places. Most of the time it was so he could see her and his other friends. They just happened to be Sam's family, his twin brother Jack, along with Jack's wife Jenna and their three kids. Cameron Shaw was another friend and part of the group. Jenna was the CEO and Cameron the president of Merrick International. Cameron had recently married Martina Fairchild.

All his buddies were married with children.

Being the odd man out didn't sit well with him. He wanted what they all had, a family.

The only steady woman in his life was simply a voice over the phone—and strangely, as he believed, in his mind. His psychic ghost. She floated into his life without warning, gave him some clue to a case, and then she disappeared into thin air. Well, not even that, really, because she was just a voice. A really sexy voice. She kept him up nights thinking about her and the sultry tones that haunted his dreams. He didn't want to analyze too deeply the fact that he sometimes thought he could actually hear her talking to him in his mind. Or admit it to anyone else.

Haunted, like a ghost occupies a house. Somehow a piece of her lived inside of him.

Morgan. God, she was in his head. A chance meeting in a restaurant more than five years ago started him down the road of the longest relationship he'd ever had with a woman. If you could call it that. The fact that he'd only seen her for maybe five minutes and spoken to her in person for less than a minute didn't really matter. She left an indelible print on him. About five-seven, blond hair down to her waist, and long legs. He could almost feel them wrapped around him, so vivid were some of the fantasies he had about her.

She'd burrowed deep into his psyche. He thought about her all the time. Sometimes she was a blessing, and other times a curse. Mostly he blamed her for things in his life that he couldn't seem to get right. If he had a bad date, it was because he spent the night with the woman wondering if she was like Morgan. Were they similar or different? If Morgan were there, what would they talk about? What would they do together? Would he kiss her? Take her to his bed?

He thought about her at work. Every case he took, he wondered whether she'd call with a clue. Over the past year, his need to hear her voice grew to a gnawing hunger.

At a low point, in need of someone to comfort him, she'd call out of the blue. It could be late at night, or in the middle of the day, but she'd know he needed a shoulder to lean on and a friend's ear to bend. She'd listen, and then remind him he wasn't alone. Every time they spoke she reminded him of that simple fact. She might not be with him physically, but she lurked in the shadows of his mind.

It was a comfort and a curse.

Loneliness grew in his soul like a vine, wrapping itself around everything in his life. Watching his friends and their happy family lives took its toll. He wanted so much to have the kind of life Sam, Jack, and Cameron enjoyed with their wives and children.

Instead, he sat in his beige walled cubicle typing out the latest reports for the case that Morgan had helped them solve. The walls were closing in on him. He stared across the aisle at Sam's back as he wrote out other reports. The constant clicking of his partner's fingers on the keyboard drilled into his head and made the splitting headache that had taken hold hours ago pound with every tap of the keys.

He took in his life, sitting in his cramped cubicle next to his partner, eating his partner's wife's outstanding food, drinking stale coffee, and wondered why he couldn't make a relationship with a woman work.

Doo, do, do, dooo—

"You really need to change the ring tone on your phone, man." Sam smiled.

Tyler frowned at the thing.

"I'm just happy I finally figured out how to get the thing to stop beeping every time I have a message. Why can't they make a cell phone that's simple? Punch in the number you want to call and it goes through. What do I care if it can access the Internet or play music? I have a computer and a radio to do those things. It just makes the damn things more expensive and more difficult to use."

Doo, do, do, dooo—

"Answer the damn phone and make it stop that ridiculous ring."

"Reed."

Happy to hear the voice on the line, he tipped his head back and silently swore at himself for forgetting to call her.

"I'm working. I can't come over now."

Tyler rolled his shoulders and rubbed two fingers at his temple. He'd been working nonstop for more than two weeks. He hadn't seen or taken Maria out on a date. He'd missed more than one of her calls. More nights than he could count, he got home too late to return her call.

"I'm sorry I haven't seen you in the last couple of weeks. We made the arrest last night. I just have some paperwork to finish and there's a press conference in . . ." Tyler glanced at his watch. Not much time left before his meeting with his boss, Agent Davies, about the press conference. "I've got twenty minutes to finish the reports and see my boss before he makes a statement to the press. Once that's done, I can go home."

He sighed and ran his fingers through his already disheveled hair. Exhausted, he hadn't slept more than three or four hours a night for the past four days. He needed a decent meal and twelve straight hours of sleep. Either he saw Maria, or got some sleep. If he wanted to make a relationship work, he needed to work to make it a relationship.

"How about I pick you up in about two hours and I'll take you out to dinner at Decadence at the Merrick Building. We'll have a nice dinner and spend some time together."

She let loose a happy squeal, telling him he'd made her happy enough to forgive him—this time.

"I'll call you when I head out."

Sam had this same conversation several times with women he'd dated. That is, until he'd met and married Elizabeth. One in a million, she understood his work and the long hours he put in. She never failed to surprise him. When he walked through the door, she'd kiss him like it might be the last time, and they'd share their time together like a precious gift. He'd almost lost her more than once, and they both knew his job was dangerous. The time they shared together was something neither of them took for granted. When he left for work, she respected his passion and dedication to his job. She'd worry, but he could count on that kiss and her love when he got home.

Listening to his partner talking to his latest girlfriend reminded him again how lucky he was. He hoped Tyler would find someone as special as Elizabeth, someone who understood the kind of man Tyler was and what it took to do a job that took his total focus and dedication.

"Yeah, the case will be on the news. I think it's going national." She congratulated him for solving the case and getting the recognition he deserved. He appreciated it, but corrected her assumption. "I work undercover. I won't be on TV. I'll call when I'm on my way to pick you up."

They said their goodbyes and he smiled, anticipating spending the evening with her. Things between him and Maria seemed easy, uncomplicated. They'd enjoyed each other's company for the last four months.

Right now, he didn't know if it was for the moment or forever. Maybe he lacked that something that made women want to stick it out with him and make it work. He could even go so far as to say that the women he chose were just substitutes for the real woman he wanted. So far, he hadn't found the staying kind.

It all came down to his job. Maybe it would forever keep him alone.

A whisper of Morgan's haunting voice floated through his mind. *You're not alone.*

Her voice, forever reminding him that she was with him, and yet nowhere near him. He asked her more times than he could count where she lived. A hundred other questions she either gave him vague answers to, or outright refused to answer. Like banging his head against the wall, trying to get any personal information from her only ended with a headache.

Any time he suggested they meet, or she should come to San Francisco, she always gave him the same cryptic reply, "It's not time. Not yet."

Not yet? What the hell was she waiting for?

Well, he'd gotten tired of that not yet and took it for what it probably meant: never.

He threw a pencil across his desk and went back to typing his reports, ignoring the ghost in his head and the bone-deep need to pull her closer. Or worse, answer that voice with another plea for her to come to him, only to be denied with another *not yet*. A man could only take so much rejection from the same woman.

Still, he needed her. Another thing he didn't dare admit to that voice, her, or even himself most of the time.

Chapter Four

TYLER DIDN'T HAVE time to analyze the fact that he counted on that sultry voice at times like these when he was tired and feeling like life wasn't going his way. Sometimes he actually truly believed she had a connection to his thoughts and feelings.

"Reed. Get your head out of your ass. We have a press conference in fifteen. Let's break this case down to the facts for public consumption," Agent Davies ordered.

Tyler shifted his thoughts back to the job at hand. His personal life could wait. That's what he kept telling himself anyway. If he didn't find some kind of balance between his personal life and the job soon, he'd burn out and have nothing waiting for him on the other side.

"Public consumption, huh. Well, then it breaks down like this. Anthony Delgadillo is an asshole and the public should cheer his arrest. Think the sound-bite guys will play that on the ten o'clock news?"

Agent Davies frowned. "Probably not. Sam, what's your assessment on the arrest?"

"I completely agree with Tyler. The slimeball is an asshole, and the public should be happy to see him behind bars."

"All right." Davies sighed. "You're both tired and punchy and just want to get out of the office and go home. Sam, I know you miss your wife and baby girl. Tyler, you look like you could use a week's sleep. Bear with me for a couple of minutes." He glanced at both men. "Now tell me what you want the director to hear about this high-profile case on the ten o'clock news."

"Well, there's a whole other story," Tyler began. "The director should know that two of his finest agents worked their asses off to bring down a notorious thug, who's been using the port of San Francisco to traffic prostitutes. The aforementioned slimeball asshole kidnapped, raped, and forced twenty-six women to be his prostitutes, personal playthings, and punching bags. The women from San Francisco were all single women who were snatched from their apartment buildings upon their returning home from work. The women who weren't abducted from San Francisco were from the Las Vegas and Reno areas. Thanks to Detective Rasmussen and Detective Stewart from San Francisco PD, and with the cooperation of the FBI, the suspect and his accomplices have been arrested. The streets of San Francisco are safe for single, twenty-something females. Since several of the slimeball asshole's clients are high-profile, wealthy men, the media will make a spectacle out of the case. We'll have to watch that their names aren't leaked to the press, but we all know they'll get hold of the names. Hell, they probably already have them."

Satisfied with Tyler's assessment, Agent Davies added, "Don't forget about Morgan. She nailed this case for us. We'd have never found the guy if it weren't for her help."

Tyler didn't want to bring Morgan into the conversation, especially when they were talking about a press conference. He hated that he had to tell one of the detectives about her because the detective refused to work with them without knowing where Tyler got his leads. He made a judgment call and divulged the fact that Morgan tipped them off to the name of the ship in port.

"Morgan isn't part of the public consumption part of this conversation. We promised never to put her name out there, or link her with the FBI. If you do, you're taking a chance she'll never help us again. She made that very clear. But, yes, without her help, this case was going nowhere fast. Detective Stewart won't thank us for that. I'd watch him during the press conference. He's out for the glory. He didn't like sharing his case with us, or the fact that we used a psychic to solve it."

"Don't worry. I have no intention of outing her, or making the FBI look less than reputable by using a psychic to solve our cases. Besides, the only information we have on her is her name. The public wouldn't be able to find her. You haven't found her."

He didn't need reminding that all his efforts to find her were for naught. The damn woman didn't want to be found. It nagged him.

"Don't bet on it. The press can be relentless when they want something uncovered. Besides, we don't need to know anything about her, except she's always right. She's proven herself over the last five years. She has a better track record than any other psychic the agency has ever used. It makes you wonder what she could tell us if she worked more closely with us on our cases." He thought about it often, which only intensified his irritation with her.

Agent Davies wrapped things up. "Okay, so Morgan is out of the press release. That's a given. We'll give the credit to the detectives and the cooperation between the police and FBI on the case. End of story. They'll have their sound bite, and we can all call it a day. I've pretty much got the outline for the charges and the official statement. We'll take some questions, which I'll field to the detectives.

"I'm ready to get this over, press conferences and reporters are part of the job, but not my favorite part. Let's get this done. You guys hang out behind the reporters and keep your mugs off the news."

Tyler and Sam would rather do their paperwork than go to the press conference. Davies liked having them there in case the facts of the case were presented incorrectly. Davies could find them behind the crowd and confirm or deny whatever the press came up with in the way of facts with a nod from them.

Tyler just wanted this day to be over. It couldn't get worse.

Chapter Five

TYLER AND SAM hung out at the edge of the gathering
crowd outside city hall for the press conference. All in all,
it appeared the mayor's office and the public were happy
to see another dangerous criminal taken off the streets.

Tyler worried about Detective Stewart. He'd seen the
detective off to the side talking confidentially with a bar-
racuda of a reporter by the name of Janet James. Well
known for getting the inside scoop and spinning facts
for sensational sound bites. Not uncommon for her to
stretch the truth and elaborate on details to get the rat-
ings she needed to land the news-anchor job she coveted.
So far, the only thing she'd landed was the reputation for
sensationalizing news and turning it into tabloid fodder.

Tyler stayed alert and on edge. Agent Davies delivered
his statement to the press, finishing up with thanks for
the chief of police, the detectives, and the FBI agents who
participated in the investigation. Tyler cringed as the

press erupted, shouting questions at Davies. One after the other, Davies answered without revealing pertinent facts from the case.

Detective Stewart stepped forward to answer a reporter's question regarding the timeline of the abductions from the first woman kidnapped to the last. Tyler's gut had warned him to watch out for Detective Stewart, but he never saw this coming.

One mistake, trusting in the wrong person, and Tyler's world crashed down around him.

"Detective Stewart, isn't it true that you were against calling in the FBI? In fact, the SFPD was close to solving the case when the FBI took over." Janet smiled for the camera and at the detective. Their earlier conversation had been a strategy session for working out the questions she'd ask and the responses he'd give. Tyler's gut turned over.

"The SFPD worked diligently to solve this case. We collected a lot of evidence before the FBI joined the team," Detective Stewart answered vaguely.

"Is it true the final details of the case came from a psychic the FBI brought in to help with the investigation?"

Tyler took a step toward the detective about to give away Morgan and ruin his and the FBI's relationship with her. She'd made it clear. Don't give out her name, or acknowledge her involvement with the FBI. Ever.

Now, because Detective Stewart was pissed about sharing the spotlight with the FBI, he was going to tarnish the FBI's reputation and ruin their relationship with Morgan in the process.

Sam grabbed Tyler before he took another step toward the podium. "Just wait. He hasn't said her name. It's well known the FBI uses psychics on occasion. Maybe he'll make it look like we exhausted every tool at our disposal to bring down Delgadillo."

"The FBI did bring in a psychic," Stewart answered.

"Detective, didn't this psychic lead you to the ship in the San Francisco port that housed the abducted women?"

"The psychic provided the FBI with the name of the ship. She indicated that we would find the missing women onboard. As I understand it, she's quite accurate and works closely with Agent Reed."

The blood drained out of Tyler's face and his whole body went slack and cold. He stood dumbstruck. Stewart couldn't possibly be outing *him* and Morgan to the press.

Agent Davies tried to intervene, but the reporter and the detective were on a roll and the detective refused to give up his position in front of the microphones without a fight and stood firm.

"So you admit this *so-called* psychic actually predicted the correct name of the ship where the women were held?"

"That's right. Agent Reed assured me and my partner that Morgan provided legitimate leads on multiple cases and is a tool he and the FBI relies on extensively. Agent Reed met Morgan in Texas, and she was instrumental in saving his sister. We were confident, based on the FBI's recommendation, and those of Agent Reed, that the information from Morgan was reliable."

At the linking of his name and Morgan's to the press, Tyler heard Morgan scream *No!* in his mind so loud and with such anguish that he actually grabbed his head from the pain. Sam's hands clamped onto his arms, and he dragged him away from the crowd, down the street to their car. He couldn't think for the searing pain and pressure in his head. It took several minutes for the pain to subside. He stopped Sam's progress and turned back to city hall and Agent Davies trying to end the press conference.

"I've got to go back. He's got to be stopped. Didn't you hear her yelling?" He shook his head to try to clear away the pain. The pressure in his head made his nose bleed. He swiped his hand across his face, smearing the blood more than removing it.

"She didn't want her name to get out to the press. She didn't want anyone to know she was helping the FBI. Now everyone knows. They know she's been working with me." He rubbed at the sides of his head to try and ease the last of the throbbing ache.

"She sounded so scared," he said miserably.

The press conference continued, and Janet James's next question almost sent him to his knees.

"I understand this psychic, Morgan, also directed the FBI and yourself to several of the 'clients.' In short, she named names. That's quite a gift if she can link these men to the prostitution ring."

"Morgan provided several names of wealthy, well-connected men linked with the abducted women."

Detective Stewart implied the entire case had been

built on Morgan's predictions. If the public thought the FBI could charge these individuals with a crime based on a psychic's word, the FBI would look like a laughingstock. This case was turning into a media nightmare, and Stewart fed the frenzy.

Davies physically nudged Detective Stewart from the podium. Although it appeared he simply took up the space where Stewart had been, Stewart knew the score. The FBI replaced him again. Davies didn't care and addressed the press and the gathering audience. He looked out across the faces to the rear and spotted Tyler and Sam well away from the crowd. Sam held Tyler up. He had a firm grasp on his upper arm and Tyler looked stricken. Blood ran down his face and onto his shirt. The worst possible situation, he wondered if Morgan would ever help the FBI again. He considered the number of cases that might go unsolved if she didn't.

"The FBI set up a sting and arrested the individuals participating in the solicitation of a prostitute. The individuals arrested, no matter their financial standing or personal connections in the community, were arrested based on the evidence and their breaking the law. We also freed the women from their abductors, and criminal charges have been filed against those individuals. Let me emphasize that the FBI, in conjunction with the SFPD, worked diligently to uncover the *evidence* to bring these criminals to justice. I would also like to inform you that while the FBI *on occasion* uses psychics to aid in an investigation of a case, they only play a small role. While Morgan provided the FBI with information, the FBI and police bear the responsibility to prove the charges."

Janet James, ever aware of the camera on her, gave her most serious look. "Agent Davies, please provide Morgan's full name. I'm sure the public would love to know who this woman is and how she can pick names out of thin air and link them to criminal activity. It makes one wonder what other abilities she might possess."

"Neither the FBI nor the SFPD have any further comment about Morgan and her association with the FBI."

Before Janet James made any further comments or questioned him further, he thanked everyone for coming, stepped away from the podium, and went directly to the chief of police. He leaned into his ear and made it clear that outing Morgan, the use of a psychic, and Stewart's assertion that the FBI's reputation was less than impeccable was incomprehensible. He wanted Stewart's ass.

A simple press conference had turned into a ticking time bomb for the FBI. Resigned, Davies wasn't going home any time soon and headed back to his office to meet with Tyler and Sam. No doubt they'd be waiting for him.

Chapter Six

SAM DIDN'T KNOW what to do about Tyler. He'd gone from devastated to angry to quiet since Morgan's name went out to the press. He steered Tyler to the car and shoved him inside. Sam didn't like the blood coming from Tyler's nose, or that it took several minutes and every fast-food napkin he scrounged up to stop it.

"You're bleeding all over the place."

"My fucking head is killing me."

Tyler stared blankly out the windshield throughout the entire ride back to the office, disturbing Sam.

They sat in the parking garage for nearly five minutes with no indication Tyler intended to move. Ever. "We're here, get out." Sam gave Tyler a shove to get him moving.

They took the elevator up to the fifth floor in silence. Sam kept an eye on Tyler as he made his way to his cubicle and dropped into his seat.

He stared at his desk without really seeing it. Sam

didn't understand why Tyler took this so badly. No one could possibly find Morgan without knowing her last name. Even they didn't know it, or where she lived. They'd considered trying to find her on several occasions. Tyler always stopped at the last minute. He didn't want to jeopardize the tenuous relationship they had with her. He had a gut feeling that if he found her without her permission, it would ruin things between them, and she'd disappear from his life.

"Man, come on. Talk to me. Tell me what happened."

Tyler heard Sam like an echo in the chasm of his mind. If he'd had any doubt before, or more accurately denied the obvious, he couldn't anymore. No more Morgan. In some awesome way, she'd become a part of him. And now she was gone. He couldn't explain it. He just knew she wouldn't speak to him in his mind anymore. She wouldn't call with a clue on one of his cases. He'd lost her today, and he had no idea how to get her back. He didn't know if he wanted to get her back. The loss of her felt like a death, her presence in his mind replaced with a grief so deep it rocked him to the core. He didn't know whether he could live through her coming back, and maybe losing her all over again. It hurt too much. More than he thought possible. He cared for her more than anyone else in his life—except maybe his sister.

"She's gone. She knew her name was linked to me and given out to the press. I heard her."

Tyler's monotone voice shifted Sam's concerned expression into something more disturbed.

"What do you mean, she knew? How can she be gone? She wasn't here. Was she?"

Sam must have felt as out of his element as Tyler did whenever Morgan was involved. Something strange happened. The bloodstains on his shirt and sleeve reminded him of the excruciating pain when Morgan tore away from him. He couldn't come up with a better explanation for what happened, leaving him raw and hurting.

"I listened to that arrogant asshole tell the press everything about how we solved the case. He gave them my name and Morgan's. He told them we'd met in Texas. She screamed in my mind so loud, my head felt like it might explode. One minute she's there, and the next . . . she's gone."

He turned from his desk and faced Sam standing in the opening to his cubicle with his shoulder braced on one side and his arm stretched across to the other.

"I've never really explained my connection to her. Sometimes she calls just to talk. I've told you that before," he rambled.

Sam stood up to his full height and crossed his arms over his chest. Tyler's words might have been difficult to believe, but it didn't make them any less true. Tyler couldn't explain it. It just was.

"What I haven't told you is I'd think about her and want her to call, and she would. Whenever I needed to hear from her, she called. And sometimes she was just a whisper in my mind telling me what I needed to hear." He didn't add she'd tell him he wasn't alone. He was now.

Utterly, desperately alone.

"She's gone. It's as if she was inside of me, and now I'm empty."

At a loss, Sam opened his mouth to say something, but stopped and closed it with a frown. Next, he tried to make Tyler feel better. "Maybe this isn't as bad as we think. I mean, what does the press really know? We used a psychic and her name is Morgan. You met her in Texas. That isn't a lot of information to go on. It isn't like they're going to find her and plaster her face all over the news. Stewart made himself look like an idiot. The only thing he accomplished was telling the press the police had done all the real investigative work, and we came in and used the word of a psychic to take over their case and tie it up like a bow without any evidence. You know it will all come out in the wash."

Tyler remained quiet and seeped in his own thoughts—or lack thereof, since Morgan refused, or couldn't, answer his silent plea to come back.

"The police chief is probably ripping Stewart a new one right now for blowing your cover. Davies will make sure his ass gets handed to him on a platter," Sam coaxed.

"That's something, at least." Tyler shrugged. "I know the case is sound. The press doesn't have any more information on Morgan than we do. What I can't explain is why it upset her like that? I also can't explain that I know in my gut that somehow we've opened up a can of worms, and those worms are rotten. I think we just put her in danger. I don't know how to fix this, or how to protect her from something I can't even explain." He kicked his desk drawer in frustration.

"Why do you think she's in danger?"

"I don't know. It's a feeling. Remember when we were working the Silver Fox case, when you met Elizabeth?"

Sam would never forget that case. He'd met the love of his life and almost gotten her killed, twice. "What's that got to do with now? The Silver Fox is dead."

"Remember the message from Morgan to you? *Mind your back.* Not *watch your back*, but *mind your back*, and that funny feeling you get creeping up your spine when something isn't right. Right now, I'm minding my gut. Something isn't right."

"You're creeping me out. Hell, you're starting to sound like her."

"Yeah, well let's hope I'm not any more psychic today than yesterday. I hope I'm just overreacting to that asshole giving out information that has nothing to do with the arrests we made last night. Maybe I need a good night's sleep. I'm completely wrung out."

He put his hands over his face and scrubbed the heels of his palms over his eyes.

"Shit." Sam ran his hand through his hair, looking as frustrated and drained as Tyler felt.

"My sentiments exactly." Davies came up behind Sam. "Let's move this into my office."

Once they closed the office door, all the men took a moment to gather their thoughts and mentally review the scene that had played out on the steps of city hall.

Davies took the lead to get him and Sam back on track. "This case is officially closed. The press surrounding Morgan will die down. In the end, it isn't a big deal that the FBI used a psychic to solve the case. The evidence will stand up in court. Period.

"The press may have Tyler's name, but they will not show his face on TV. His cover remains sound.

"Tyler, I can see you're upset about Detective Stewart showboating it today with the press and outing you and Morgan. In retrospect, I'm sure you'd agree there isn't really any damage done, except that we looked like we couldn't solve this case without using some rather extreme measures."

"Morgan isn't an extreme measure. She's come through for us on more than two dozen cases in the last year. She's always accurate. She's never let us down."

Not like he let her down. She'd come through for him so many times, both on a case and in his personal life. She'd saved his sister and he couldn't do the one thing she'd asked of him.

"She asked us not to use her name. Ever. End of story. I screwed up, and it's cost us. She won't help us again."

"What do you mean? No one could possibly find her with so little information to go on."

"We gave out her first name, the fact that I met her in Texas, that she's a psychic, and she can name names. Granted, she only saw the men's faces. If they weren't such public figures, she wouldn't have known most of their names. You and I both know she saw a lot more faces that she couldn't identify. The press doesn't know that though. They think she can simply name an offender in a case and we make the arrest. The implications of this go beyond the fact that we've lost Morgan, or that the press may or may not be able to find her."

Tyler was right, and Davies reluctantly admitted, "We've already started receiving phone calls from all kinds of people asking to talk to her. A number of law enforcement agencies submitted requests for her help on cold cases and missing persons cases. Then there are the nuts, calling for everything from asking her to help them get rid of a ghost to contacting aliens."

"You see. This is just the beginning."

"This will die down in a few days. The press will move on to another story and the fact that the FBI uses a psychic will be just another story in the trash pile."

"Used."

"Used? What?" Davies looked at Sam, who'd been sitting quietly watching Tyler out of the corner of his eye.

"We used a psychic. She won't help us again."

"Did she call you? Is she angry about her name going out to the press?"

"She didn't have to call me. I heard her loud and clear. Angry about the press conference, is a matter of opinion. The sound she made, well, it made me think she was more terrified than angry."

Tyler felt ragged and tired all the way to his bones. He slumped in the chair, wishing to go home, fall into bed, and bury himself under the covers.

Davies sighed with frustration and confusion. "You aren't making sense. Did you talk to her, or not?"

"Nope. I just know."

Davies let go his frustration on a ragged sigh. "Sam, help me out here."

Sam leaned forward, bracing his forearms on his thighs and faced Davies. "What my partner isn't telling you is that he heard Morgan scream in his mind. The next thing I know he's grabbing his head like he'd been shot, he's bleeding from his nose and saying she's gone. Gone, as in from his head. And apparently, from us."

"Thanks, Sam," Tyler said and stared up to the ceiling. "Now he'll have me seeing the mind-benders on a daily basis and riding a desk for the rest of my life. This day just keeps getting better."

"No one's going to the mind-benders. Even the thought of seeing the agency shrink sends a chill up my spine."

Tyler agreed. They were always trying to get you to tell them about your feelings. He wasn't about to dump his feelings on a stranger, who wanted to analyze everything from his upbringing to his choice of job and his need to control things.

"So, you think she won't help us again."

"No. I don't. We . . . I gave her my word. She wanted to remain anonymous. Only the three of us know she worked with us. That is until I gave her name to those detectives. Stewart just wouldn't bend on knowing where I got the amazingly accurate leads. I should have made something up. I should never have told them about her."

"Stewart should have kept his mouth shut," Sam snapped.

Tyler appreciated Sam's anger.

The door to the office opened and Agent Davies's assistant peeked in. "I know you didn't want to be disturbed, but there's a man on the line claiming to be Morgan's father. He's demanding to talk to Agent Reed. Do you want to take the call?"

All three men stared at the woman standing in the doorway like she'd just announced the president was on the line. Actually, they wouldn't have been this surprised to get a call from the president.

Agent Davies recovered first. "We'll take the call. What's his name?"

"He won't give it. He's extremely rude and agitated. The operator sent him to me when he refused to give any information. They thought he might give me a name if he felt like he'd get a chance to talk to Agent Reed. No such luck. He refused to speak to anyone but Agent Reed."

"Put him through. I'll put him on speaker, if you don't mind?" Davies asked Tyler. At Tyler's acceptance, he opened the line to Morgan's father.

"This is Agent Reed. To whom am I speaking?"

"I'll tell you, you motherfucker, when you tell me where my daughter is. You can't hide her from me. I have a right to know where she is."

Tyler wanted to follow his gut instinct and hang up and never accept another call from this guy again. He didn't know who the guy was, but Tyler meant to keep him away from Morgan at all costs.

"Well, now. With that kind of attitude, you can bet your ass I won't give you her location."

He wanted to know the guy's name and how he fit into

Morgan's life. Why didn't her father know where Morgan lived?

"You better tell me, Reed. I'm her father and I demand to know where she is."

"How do I know you really are her father? What's your name?"

The man paused for a moment, telling Tyler without words he did have something to hide.

"James Weston. Now, where's my daughter."

"So Mr. Weston. You're from Texas, right?" Tyler needed more than a name to run down information on the guy. He needed a place to start and a state would get him closer. He'd met Morgan in Texas, but neither she nor this guy had a Texas accent. Morgan's sounded more East Coast. This guy's was even more pronounced. Tyler imagined Morgan had lost part of her accent after leaving wherever she'd lived before Texas. He didn't even know if she still lived there.

"Morgan was born in West Virginia. I live in Niles now."

"Niles Canyon? You live here in California?"

"I just said that. Now, tell me how to contact my daughter. Is she living in San Francisco? Maybe somewhere outside the city in the Bay Area?"

Davies typed the pertinent information into his computer and waited while the search went through on James Weston of Niles, California. They'd know everything about him in a few short minutes.

"We'll get to that. I'm not convinced you are who you say you are. So, your daughter is Morgan Weston, huh?" Tyler hedged.

"You and I both know she doesn't go by Weston. Her mama kept her last name. It's some kind of family tradition. My ass. I don't know any women who wouldn't take their husband's name. Still, she wouldn't marry me without keeping it. I loved her, so I let her have her way, that time."

As if she hadn't had a say other times. Tyler found that an odd thing to say. Weston's tone told him this man expected to get what he wanted without question. Apparently, he'd wanted Morgan's mother, and he'd conceded the last name in order to have her. Probably the last thing Morgan's mother ever got Weston to concede to her.

Tyler wouldn't be surprised to find a few domestic disturbance calls to the Weston house. Maybe Morgan's mother even filed charges of domestic abuse against her husband. Something Tyler had seen many times in his career. He could talk to a man like Weston and know just how the scenario played out between him and any woman he had in his life. Tyler wondered where Morgan fit in the picture. Had Weston abused her in some way, too? The thought made him sick.

"So what name does Morgan go by?"

"Her mama went by Standish. We may have been married before God, but that woman came from Satan. She bore that demon of a daughter. Should've known right off she came from a long line of witches. She put a spell on me. Every single one of them Standish women was the devil's spawn."

Tyler looked to Sam and Davies for some kind of support or understanding of this guy. One second he spoke like any normal man wanting to find his daughter, even if he did it in a hostile tone. The next second, he was spouting off about spells and the devil. He was talking crazy, and they had no way of knowing if he was telling the truth or lying.

"So, Morgan's a demon witch who comes from a long line of witches. Well, let me just scroll through my contact list and give you her address. I'm sure she'd love to hear from you."

Tyler rolled his eyes. This guy couldn't be for real. If he was, Morgan probably had a good reason for hiding from him.

Davies read the files popping up on his computer. He turned the screen so Sam and Tyler could see.

James Weston, recently released from prison after serving twelve years of a fifteen-year sentence for voluntary manslaughter. He'd killed his wife, Fern Standish. Another notation stated Morgan Standish had been the key witness during the murder trial.

Tyler scribbled a note to Davies for him to get a copy of the police report and court transcript. He wanted to know exactly what happened to Fern Standish and just what part Morgan had played in sending her father to jail.

Davies pointed to the screen and Tyler stared in disbelief as he looked at a picture of a young Morgan Standish. She looked to be about twelve. No mistaking her. He'd never forget those blue eyes or that golden hair. When he'd met her, he assumed she was eighteen or nineteen. According to the records, he'd been right. Now twenty-four, she had a Texas driver's license. The photo was about seven years old. She looked so young.

"It's none of your business if she wants to see me or not. I have a right to know where my daughter is." Impatient, his voice grew louder.

If Morgan's testimony cost James twelve years of his life, Tyler didn't need to guess why he wanted to find her. Revenge.

"Just tell me how to get in touch with her. That's all I want."

"Her last name wasn't given out. So tell me how you know it's the same Morgan."

"It's her. No one but Morgan could pick out those men and name them. She's better than any so-called psychic out there. She's seen things since she was just a little bit of a thing. Used to scare me sometimes the things she knew. She can do things too. She can get into your head, hear your thoughts, crazy things like that. More too."

The *more too* interested Tyler. He already knew she could read his mind. He wanted to know what else she could do.

Sam's hand locked on Tyler's arm. The stunned look on Sam's face as he stared at the computer screen disturbed Tyler. He read the information on Morgan. An open cold case, the police considered her a missing person. She'd gone missing after the trial. No one knew if she'd been kidnapped, or simply left on her own.

Tyler's chest ached. Twelve years old when she disappeared, he thought about the first time he'd met her and the fact that she looked like a student with her backpack.

They'd met in a restaurant while he finished his meal and she'd just ordered iced tea and a bowl of soup at the table beside him. He considered her order and appearance and realized she might have been on her own for more than five years before they met. He wondered what she'd done, and where she'd lived for those five years. He couldn't imagine what she'd been through. He didn't want to imagine it. He didn't want to think about her alone and on the streets at such a young age.

Time to get *Dad* off the line, so they could do some research. What could they do about Morgan? She'd asked them not to give out her name, and now they knew why, at least partially. She was hiding from her past.

"Listen, Weston, why don't you give me your number, and I'll get back to you with Morgan's information. I'm not giving out her number without talking to her first."

"All I want is her phone number. If she doesn't want to talk to me, she can hang up. Either way, I'm her father, and I want to talk to her."

Tyler wasn't about to give him anything. He didn't know how to contact Morgan. Her calls always came through with a blocked number. He'd never had a reason to dig any deeper. If Weston got the number he'd be able to find her, or at least come close. You could find out just about anything about a person using the Internet. Tyler planned on doing a little research himself using the FBI's resources and the Internet once he got rid of Weston. They already had all the information they needed on him. Davies had spent the last few minutes digging up everything on Weston and his troubled past. They needed to know about Morgan.

"I hate to tell you this"—actually he didn't—"but I won't give out her number to you or anyone else. The next time she calls, I'll let her know how to get in touch with you. We'll just leave it up to her."

Probably never going to happen, even if by some miracle he did hear from Morgan. No way she'd want to contact her father. After all, she'd sent him to prison. He couldn't imagine Morgan's devastation, losing her mother by her father's hand.

"The next time she calls, huh. You don't know how to get in touch with her." James laughed. "She's crafty, that one. You probably have no idea what she's capable of doing. I'll just bet you're looking up information on me and her. You're probably more interested in her though. You'll be lucky if you find anything on her after the trial. That girl lit out as fast as she could.

"Maybe you'll get to her before I do. It won't make any difference. You talk to her; you tell her I'm coming for her. Well, on the other hand, she probably already knows and this is all for nothing. You have a good night, Agent Reed."

He hung up before Tyler responded, his sardonic laughter ringing in Tyler's ears.

Chapter Seven

THEY SORTED THROUGH all the information they gathered on James Weston and Morgan Standish for two hours. Tyler learned more about Morgan in that short period of time than he had in the five years they'd talked on the phone, and it shamed him.

Weston hadn't been an outstanding parent. He hadn't even been a good parent. Seven domestic disturbance calls on record. Tyler could only guess how many times the cops weren't called to the Weston-Standish home. Morgan had been sent to a foster home for a few weeks when her mother ended up in the hospital for minor injuries and psychiatric evaluation. Morgan's mother had become severely depressed in the end and hadn't been able to properly care for her daughter.

Morgan's juvenile records were sealed. Davies offered to get them. Tyler declined. None of their business, they certainly didn't have any reason to dig up her past. They'd already gone beyond the point of decency, justifying their actions because her father had called and essentially implied a threat to Morgan. He'd already killed her mother. They only wanted to make sure Morgan was safe.

That's what Tyler kept telling himself. He just wanted her to be safe. Somewhere in the back of his mind, he had his doubts.

"Look what I found," Sam said from his cubicle across the aisle. "I searched the Internet for anything on 'Morgan' and 'psychic.' I found a few interesting sites that have a lot of information about her."

Tyler got up from his desk and stood behind Sam and read over his shoulder several of the bookmarked web pages.

Tyler read silently about the court case in which she testified for the prosecution against her father. Vilified in the press, they called her a witch and talked about her ability to see things. They made her sound crazy and delusional. He read an account where several rocks had been thrown at her outside the courthouse where she testified. Police had to aid in getting the crowd to stand back, so the star witness could enter the building. Harsh treatment for a young girl in this day and age.

The trial had been sensationalized because Morgan's father and his attorney had gone to the press and made Morgan out to be crazy, psychic, and possessed by the devil. Every religious zealot and crackpot showed up at the courthouse to rid their community of the devil's demon.

"Small towns," Sam said. "They made her out to be the

bad guy, even though her father killed her mother. She saw it all happen. She told the police where to find the weapon. She didn't see him get rid of it, but she knew. We both know how she knew where to find the knife."

Tyler nodded. "She saw it in her mind, or however she does what she does. Twelve years old and people are yelling 'Witch!' and throwing rocks and all she wanted is justice for her mother. On top of it all, her vicious father sent those close-minded, intolerant jackasses after her. I can't imagine what that did to her."

"I'd say it did a lot," Sam said sadly. "Look at the next article. She went missing the day the trial ended. Her father hadn't even been found guilty or sentenced, and she'd already taken off. People speculated one of the crackpots outside the courthouse had kidnapped and killed her. That seemed to be the consensus for a while. Then, nothing. It looks like the cops just tossed her file into the cold case pile. I'll bet they didn't do more than wait to see if a body turned up. When it didn't, they forgot all about her. No one wanted to deal with the strange girl who saw things." He looked up at Tyler as he read the article. "It's sad. None of them understood her, so they made her the villain. There's hardly anything about her father and the murder. They were all fascinated with her. They made her into some sort of sideshow freak."

"No one cared enough to remember she'd witnessed her mother's murder," Tyler said, disgusted. "They gave up on her. No one helped her. They tossed her into a system that didn't want to deal with someone different. They treated her like a freak instead of a scared little girl."

Tyler shook his head in disbelief. "Twelve years old, Sam, and look what a town did to her."

He felt sick.

Doo, do, do, dooo—

"You really need to change that thing," Sam teased. He closed out the web pages with the news articles and Tyler answered his phone.

"Oh, God, Maria. I'm sorry. There was this big blowup at work. I've been stuck in a meeting with my boss and digging through information on a case."

Today turned into a rotten day, and he thanked his lucky star Maria didn't lay on the guilt trip because Tyler had forgotten their date. He grinded the heel of his hand into his tired eye.

"Yeah, it's been a bad day. I promised dinner at Decadence, but it's too late. How about I pick up a pizza and come to your place? Yeah? I want to see you, too. Okay. Let me tie up some things here, and I'll be over within the hour. Yeah, I can't wait to see you."

He hung up and realized he did want to see her. He hadn't made anything work out with Morgan today, but he could try to salvage the tenuous relationship he had with Maria. He needed something good to hold on to, and the only thing he had was her.

Morgan was gone.

If he wanted to have that elusive wife and kids, he needed to make it happen. Maybe he could fill the emptiness after Morgan's abrupt departure from his life with a real woman, one that he could talk to, touch, and have a real life with. He'd been putting off other women because Morgan had always been in his head and on his mind. Now that she was gone, he decided it was the perfect time to put the rest of his life in order. He'd start with Maria.

"I have to say, I'm surprised she isn't pissed off. She seemed pretty understanding."

Tyler had to admit, it surprised him too. Every other woman he'd dated would have broken up with him, or at least yelled and called him every dirty name in the book. He appreciated Maria's easygoing nature even more.

"Maria liked the idea of spending a quiet evening together at her place. Maybe she's one of those rare women who understands that sometimes, as hard as I try, I can't be at her beck and call. She said she just wanted to see me, and if that meant she had to wait another hour, she was fine with it." Tyler's spirit felt lighter already. He had no way of making things up to Morgan, but he could make things right with Maria.

What's Morgan doing? Is she okay?

He stopped that train of thought, mentally disembarked, and boarded the new train that lead to Maria and a real relationship.

"Yeah, I guess. Before you take off, check this out. I don't know if it's Morgan's, but I think it's a safe bet to say it is. I think this is how she earns a living. I guess we could check her taxes and find out where she works . . ."

"No. We have no reason to invade her privacy like this. Having her father call and finding out about her past . . . I don't know, it feels like I've betrayed her," Tyler said.

"You mean *we*. You and I are partners. She may contact you, but you and I are in this together, whatever happens. Her father has no way of finding her."

"I wish I felt the same way." He looked at the website Sam had pulled up and his gut twisted when he saw the image of a woman with her arms outstretched and white light, like the light of a star, shining from her silhouette. The image rocked Tyler back on his heels. Morgan. Her long flowing hair, the hint of the outline of her face turned to the side. The shape of her body illustrated in the outline as the light radiated out of her form.

Strange and ethereal and beautiful all at the same time.

He'd only seen her briefly, but she'd haunted him ever since.

Morgan, his psychic ghost.

"I tried to send a message over the website, but when you click on the link to ask your question, there's a message that pops up and tells you the site isn't taking requests at this time. I wonder how many people found this site after the press conference. At least, there's no personal information on the site, no name, address, phone number, nothing. This could be anybody. She must have shut things down with the message if she was getting bombarded with requests."

"Maybe," Tyler said, his eyes locked on her image.

"According to the site, she accepts all questions and inquiries. She states clearly, if she can't answer, you don't have to pay. If she can, she charges fifteen dollars and sends you an email with your reply. There are no horoscopes. I find that odd. All the other sites I looked at have some sort of fortune-telling platitudes. Morgan deals in simplicity. Either she can answer you, or she can't. According to all the testimonials, she gave out accurate and precise information. She doesn't offer up some broad answer that could mean the same thing for any number of scenarios. People talk about how she knew things that no one could have known."

"I'm not surprised. She never gave us something we couldn't use. She may not have known the specific case the clue went to, but she was never vague enough that the clue fit any case."

Tyler gave her credit where credit was due. "She could have said it's a white guy who's average height between the ages of twenty and forty. She never did. She'd always give an accurate description."

If the guy was white, twenty-seven, with dark hair and green eyes, that's what Morgan told them. Specific. She only called on cases that she could help. She never promised to try on other cases. He liked that about her.

No way did she help them so she could prove something to them, or anyone else. She didn't do it as a gimmick, or to draw attention to herself. She did the opposite. He, Sam, and Davies were the only ones who knew just how much help she'd provided. He should have never let Detective Stewart coax him into giving up his source. Why didn't he keep his mouth shut like he'd done on the other cases? Why did he talk about Morgan this time? And to a man who only wanted to prove the FBI incompetent and out to take credit for the bust?

"Yeah, she's amazingly accurate. So, what do you think? Is this her website?" Sam asked.

"The image of the woman on the first page is her. She added the white light to obscure her identity."

He'd know her anywhere. He stared at the webpage again and simply sighed. He couldn't fix this. Frustrated, there was more wrong with this than he could see. He couldn't call her and find out what scared her away, or warn her about her father. She'd made herself clear. She wanted to be left alone. She'd left him alone. And it pissed him off. This whole damn mess pissed him off.

"I gotta go. If her father calls again . . . I don't know. Get rid of him."

"We have enough information to locate her," Sam said.

"Why? Why would we do that?" Tyler let his anger show. Sam raised an eyebrow, a look of concern coming over his face. Tyler was usually the calm one in the room when everyone else was falling apart.

"To let her know her father's looking for her. To tell her we're sorry her name went out to the press. So that we can ask her to continue helping us when she can."

Maybe you can tell her you're in love with her, and you're miserable without her, you dummy. That's what Sam really wanted to say. He held his tongue. Tyler was in no mood to hear it, and Sam didn't want to start a fight. Tyler held on to denial about his feelings for Morgan. It ate him up inside and Sam had a feeling he traveled the road to ruin by trying to make things work with Maria. She was just a poor substitute for Morgan. They all had been. He wished Tyler would finally come to realize that himself.

"You assume she doesn't already know all that. Nothing has changed. Her father can't find her. If he could, he'd have done it already. As far as her helping us, I don't think she will. At least, not any time soon. You didn't hear her horrible scream. It's more than the press conference. I think she knows this will lead to something else," he said without really thinking it through. "Whatever," he said, frustrated. "Leave her alone. It's apparently what she wants. It's what she's always wanted."

With that, Tyler left. He turned his back on Sam and all the Morgan business and headed out to be with Maria.

Sam called after him. "Don't you think it's odd that her father lives here and heard the press conference? Don't you think it's odd that it upset her they connected her name to us? What do you think she knows that we don't?"

Sam threw his pen at the cubicle wall. With a bounce, it fell to the floor. Tyler was long gone and neither one of them could sort this out, or get Morgan off their minds. Frustrated and angry with Tyler, Sam grabbed his stuff. Time to go home to his wife and get the kiss waiting for him.

Chapter Eight

MORGAN WOKE UP on the sofa feeling drained and empty. Her throat and eyes hurt from crying herself to sleep. She didn't know the time, or even care. She just wanted Tyler back. The gaping hole inside her hurt with a pain she hoped to never feel again, but dreaded she might live with the rest of her life.

"Tyler." His name was a plea, a prayer that he'd come back to her.

Morgan closed her sore eyes, calmed herself with a couple of deep breaths, and pictured Tyler in her mind. She used all her talent to push her consciousness into Tyler's, to find the connection they once shared and feel whole again.

Like anyone else she tried to read, she caught vague impressions. Something strong shrouded him. She couldn't push through, but she tried. She called out to him, hoping he'd answer. "Tyler."

For a moment, she became one with him. He sat on an unfamiliar sofa, a pizza box lay open on a coffee table, and the TV brightened the otherwise dark room. Barely awake, he sat in a daze, not really seeing or hearing anything around him. He didn't notice her intrusion on his quiet solitude. Everything about him felt different. The hurt and pain matched her own. She wanted to erase it, but didn't know how. Even now, the connection to him seemed so tenuous and fragile. It took everything inside her to stay with him.

His voice broke the silence for the first time. "Make it stop," he thought.

She knew just how he felt. She wanted this agony to cease and for them to be together and joined once more in their intimate connection.

A woman called Tyler's name, and just like that a door slammed on her, blocking her out of Tyler's mind and sending her consciousness back to the reality of her spot on her sofa with a massive headache to go with her loneliness.

She opened her tear-filled eyes and stared at the cold, dark room and realized he didn't want her anymore.

Her fault. She'd kept things between them on a purely professional level. Every time he pushed to deepen their relationship, she balked and evaded, despite how much she truly wanted to be with him. He didn't understand why she did it. She never told him a little boy's life hung in the balance and she could not, would not jeopardize him for her own selfish desires. Telling him would have complicated things further. He'd understand soon. She hoped.

Her gift had cost her so many things in her life. She'd given them up willingly so she could be who she was, but losing Tyler hurt. Today, she thought her gift more curse than anything. One day soon, she'd see Tyler again, but she didn't expect a warm welcome. More than their connection had been damaged; their friendship and whatever else they might have shared suffered. She didn't know if Tyler would ever forgive her for sharing her gift and taking it away.

Maybe she should call him. She immediately thought better of it. The raw pain ate away at both of them from the small glimpse she'd gotten. They needed time. She'd try again tomorrow. Maybe then he'd let her in.

She didn't know what she'd do if he didn't, because she needed him to survive what came next.

Chapter Nine

DAMN THAT PSYCHIC witch. If it weren't for her, he wouldn't be here. He didn't like the little shop filled with pewter dragons baring their sharp teeth and claws, their crystal eyes staring at him. No matter which way he turned, they followed him. Accusing.

He clenched his sweaty palms. What if she knew his real reason for being here? Would she do the reading, or call the police and have him arrested? The longer he waited for her to speak, the more nervous he became.

He scoffed at the little potion bottles on the table near him. One for love, wealth, health, and wisdom. As if purchasing a glass bottle of some stupid liquid with a cork in it could bring you love, or make you a fortune. Not likely.

Little leather pouches hung from silk cords you could wear around your neck to ward off evil, or bring harmony to your aura. Glass and stone spheres in every color imaginable sat atop ordinary pedestals, and some so ornate they were more interesting to look at than the spheres. Candles made the colored glass orbs sparkle and cast eerie lights in the dark room.

The overwhelming scent of sandalwood and jasmine incense really bothered him. Hot and stuffy, the scents filled the air in the small room to the point of suffocating him. He sniffled and wiped his running nose on his sleeve.

The woman, wrapped in a long purple flowing hooded robe decorated with astrological signs, sat across from him chanting some sort of nonsense. The large clear crystal ball sitting on an elaborate stand between them mirrored everything in the room in inverted reflection.

Suddenly, she stopped and stared across the table, her gaze penetrating and intrusive. A bead of sweat made a track from his hairline down his temple until he wiped it away from his cheek.

"Do you have the donation?"

Donation, my ass. She wanted payment before she told him what he wanted to know. A simple question. He needed a simple answer. He passed over the twenty-dollar bill and wiped the sweat from his brow again. His shirt stuck to his back.

"Ask your question of the universe? Madam Sarina will provide your answer."

"Does she know who I am? Can she find me?"

If Morgan saw that man take those women and identified the ship he kept them prisoner on, she could see him. He had to stop her—and all the others—before he ended up on the news too.

Not a lot to work with, but Sarina had been doing this gig for a few years and made decent money selling her trinkets and passing out contrived information to those seeking answers. Some came looking for fun and a cheap thrill. Others were desperate.

Desperate didn't begin to describe this guy. If her instincts were correct, he wanted to know more than he asked. His eyes constantly moved over the room, and he shied away from the dragons on the shelves. He seemed to be afraid of the answer he expected to hear.

She didn't know which answer would satisfy him and make him leave. She had an overwhelming need to get him away. Slight in build, short for a man, nothing particularly threatening about his appearance, but something about him made her apprehensive. His presence, something in his eyes, those always-moving eyes were dark and shadowed with something she couldn't name. When she looked at him and those eyes, she thought of death. A chill ran up her spine like someone stepped on her grave.

That had nothing to do with being psychic or seeing what others couldn't. She wasn't gifted in that way. She read people well, and her innate interest in others created the perfect job for her. With a little help from some books on body language and how to tell if someone was lying, she was pretty good at figuring out what people wanted to hear. When she couldn't read them, or the question was too specific, she winged it and made up an answer general enough to cover most anything.

She didn't care what they asked, whether for themselves or someone else. She made sure they had a good experience in her shop and they left satisfied. On rare occasions, she even told them she just didn't know. When that happened, they sometimes were upset, but most of the time they were content with her honesty. Better that than insincere, vague answers.

On this particular night, the customer wouldn't be satisfied with *the universe has left your answer clouded in mystery*. He wanted an answer to his question. And for him, this was serious business. She hoped she said the right thing. Because the guy looked like he held onto his patience and sanity by a thread.

"Madam Sarina is in contact with the spirit world. They want you to be more specific. Who do you want to know about?"

"Morgan. Does she know who I am? Is she going to cause trouble for me? She gave me the information about the job, didn't she?"

The guy leaned so far forward on his chair she thought he might topple it and the table. Intent on her, she got caught up in those eyes. Usually, she'd drag out the reading and give the customer a good show. Not tonight. Tonight, she wanted this guy gone.

"She gave you the answer you needed."

"She did. She was right. She's always right. It's the other. Will she tell?"

She didn't know what the 'other' was, and she didn't want to know. This guy wanted to keep his secret. Better to tell him what he wanted to hear. Maybe then he'd be satisfied and leave.

"She told you what you needed to know. The spirits assure me she doesn't have anything else to tell. She won't cause you any problems."

"You said she doesn't have anything else to tell. That's because she already knows. She knows. Do you know too? Can you see what I did?"

She had no idea what he meant and shook her head no, leaning back to put some distance between them and the dangerous vibe that made her want to run.

He leaped across the table and grabbed her around the throat and they both fell to the floor. The chair and table toppled, and the crystal ball clattered across the floor. She gasped for air, choking, and desperately tried to call out for help.

"Can you see what I did?" He squeezed harder and slammed her head against the wood floor. Her feet kicked and scuffed behind him. "Can you?"

She stared into his dark eyes, saw the madness and her own death. She didn't know what he'd done before; it didn't matter, he was going to kill her now.

She'd worked more than fifteen years in the psychic-reading business without seeing anything. She hadn't seen her own death coming. Maybe this was her due for cheating all those people into believing she saw something they didn't.

The world around her turned black as her killer's eyes.

Now she can't tell.

He'd rid himself of the psychic, Madam Sarina. He'd get rid of all the psychics. A clear purpose took hold inside of him. He'd kill all the psychics. He'd eliminate

Morgan. Then, none of them would see. There'd be no one left to tell.

He slipped out the back door and into the acrid-smelling alley behind the shop. Garbage cans overflowed. Foggy, the eerie smoke-like mist swirled around him as he quickly made his way down the dark alley. The streets weren't very busy in this part of town at this time of night. More homeless people than tourists or residents. This part of town catered to the keep-to-yourself-crowd rather than to people who were likely to notice him leaving an alley in a hurry and report a suspicious person in the neighborhood.

He made his way to his small, cramped apartment above a bank of storefronts. Old and musty, most nights it smelled of fried duck and ginger from the Chinese restaurant downstairs.

Quiet, no one bothered him. That's what appealed to him.

He tore off his jacket just inside the door and sat on his old faded brown plaid couch. Sagging in the middle, worn fabric, but it was his. He could sleep on it, eat on it, and do whatever he pleased without anyone telling him to keep his feet off the furniture.

His mother had ruled his world and nagged and fretted over every little thing he did until he couldn't take it. He'd taken care of her during her illness. She'd suffered and made him suffer for it. Every ache and pain caused by the cancer had worn away what little happiness and love she'd had for him, until she'd become even more temperamental and accusing. She'd blamed him for ruining her body, her life, and leaving her in writhing pain. Of course, before the cancer she'd blamed him for every man who'd ever left her. She'd blamed him for not being strong enough, smart enough, or enough of anything and everything.

He leaned his head back against the couch and gazed up at the dingy ceiling and thought about how powerful he'd felt with his hands around Madam Sarina's throat. He'd been enough then. Enough of a man to take her life. He'd silenced her. She'd never tell his secret.

He pulled his head away from the couch and looked down at the coffee table and the phonebook open to the listing of San Francisco psychics. He'd start with them. He'd rid himself of the seers. Then he'd be safe. He'd find Morgan too. Once he found her, he'd make her pay. His mother always accused him of never seeing anything through. He'd see this through.

Morgan started this. He'd finished it.

He picked up the pen next to the phonebook and scratched out Madam Sarina's shop. The Psychic Eye wouldn't be open for business tomorrow.

For the first time in his life, he felt calm, almost happy. He tossed a frozen dinner into the ancient microwave and set the timer. He'd eat and he'd plan. His mother had always told him, if he only made a plan and followed it through, he could accomplish anything. Maybe, just maybe, she'd been right on that one point. He knew what he had to do. He had a purpose.

Chapter Ten

A WEEK AFTER the press conference, Tyler realized he hadn't accomplished anything at work. At first he found himself waiting for that sultry voice in his mind. When he didn't hear it, he got angry. His head wasn't in the game, and Sam had to cover for him more times than Tyler wanted to admit. Sam finally had enough and told him to take a few days off, get his head clear, and get back on the job. Tyler would have normally told Sam to take a hike off a cliff and mind his own damn business. But in this case, he found the vacation idea tempting. More so when he factored in Maria and a trip to Hawaii.

A few days turned into ten, but he'd needed the time off and to prove to himself he could make a relationship with a woman work.

He and Maria hadn't bickered in all of those ten days. They would talk over dinner, or spend a quiet evening enjoying the food with few words between them. If she preferred he kept the conversation away from the topic of his job and the many horrors he saw on a daily basis, he couldn't blame her. His type of work didn't fascinate everyone. Frankly, he was tired of talking about it himself. He lived it every day. He could keep work and his personal life separate.

Sam called him several times the last couple days of his vacation. He ignored every call and message. Whatever had been going on at work, he didn't want to know. Sam had told him to clear his head, and just when Tyler took his advice, Sam tried to suck him back into work.

When they returned late Thursday night, Tyler asked Maria to stay with him at his apartment. Afraid of breaking the spell, sending his life back to the way it had been, he didn't want to go home to an empty apartment and an empty bed. It wasn't even the sex. The island vacation proved they didn't need to make love every night. Just being together was enough.

At least that's what he thought, until his first day back at the office when he walked down the aisle to his cubicle and caught Sam kissing Elizabeth. They clung together so tightly that every inch of her pressed to him. The intimacy of the embrace struck Tyler in the heart. Nothing else around them mattered. Caught up in their love for each other and their desire to express that love blocked everything else out.

He hadn't realized he'd stopped outside his cubicle and stood staring until a high-pitched voice brought him back to his senses.

"Up. Up. Up."

Little Grace held her arms up to him and waited to be picked up. He obliged the angel and kissed her soundly on the cheek. She patted his shoulder and laid her head on his chest for a rest while she sucked her thumb. She smelled of baby powder, soap, and just sweet baby.

"Hi, Gracie. Did you miss Uncle Tyler?"

She didn't answer, and based on the weight of her head on his shoulder, she was pretty well on her way to a nap. He snuggled her closer and held her tight as Sam and Elizabeth broke their embrace. A soft blush colored Elizabeth's cheeks. Beautiful as always, the swell of her belly reminded him the second addition to their family was on his way. He felt the familiar pang of jealousy. He almost wished he'd been the one shot and drugged in front of her house. Maybe then she'd be kissing him and the baby girl in his arms and the one on the way would be his. Sam's happy life would be his. It wasn't, though. Elizabeth belonged to Sam in a way that transcended their simply being married. They were connected to each other. You could see it, feel it.

He glanced at Sam and ignored the disgusted glare. "You got her. Can I keep this one?" He indicated the sleeping Grace in his arms.

"You can't have either of them. If you weren't holding my daughter, I'd deck you."

Sam turned to his wife and kissed her again. Long and soft and so full of love that his heart ached. He hadn't seen her in three days and he missed her. "I'll see you tonight. I hope."

He ran his fingers lightly over Elizabeth's cheek, down

her neck, and over her shoulder and down her arm. He hated to leave her. He'd only gotten to see her and Grace for a few minutes in between meetings, and now he had to leave. They had to come all the way to his office so they could see him. He felt badly that Elizabeth had finally given in and come after him.

She never complained about his job. Pregnant and feeling needy, she wanted him to take care of her. Sure she could take care of herself, but hormonal and tired, she deserved a little pampering when she was carrying his child. Not so much to ask. At least normally it wasn't. This case involved someone he knew. He couldn't ignore it, but unfortunately that meant he'd ignored his wife and daughter.

Elizabeth had enough this morning and came to get her man and a little loving for her and their daughter. He'd already kissed his daughter. His wife held his attention and made him want to go home and crawl into bed with her. He might just have enough energy to make love to her before he slept more than the three or four hours he'd gotten every other night of the last week.

He kissed sleeping Grace on the head and rubbed his hand softly over her back.

He'd been happy Tyler had finally taken a vacation. He'd been mildly irritated when Tyler ignored his first few calls. That mild irritation had a good week to build to an all-out fury when Tyler hadn't returned a single message all weekend, especially since Sam knew Tyler returned home last Thursday.

Almost ten o'clock on Monday morning and Tyler

had finally come into the office. Sam had been at work for hours. Yeah, he wanted to deck Tyler. It wouldn't do any good, but he'd feel a hell of a lot better. He'd settle for leaving him in his dust and in the dark.

"Was it something I said?" Tyler joked.

"More like something you didn't say," Elizabeth scolded. "Like hello when Sam called you the first, the fifth, or the tenth time." She couldn't help the anger in her voice. She'd missed Sam over the last few days, and Tyler had shown up and ruined Sam's mood.

"I was on vacation. Can't a guy even take a few days off without his partner calling him every day? Sam's good at his job. He didn't need me for anything."

"Is that what you think? He'd call you on your vacation about something as trivial as needing your advice on a case." She rubbed a hand over her growing belly and took a breath. She didn't need this agitation in her condition. Her daughter was also sound asleep and bound to wake up if she heard her mother yelling.

"What's the matter then? Is it Jack or Jenna? One of the kids? What's the emergency?"

"Morgan is the emergency. At least, she is to Sam. Have you forgotten about her? More than five years of her helping you and you turn your back on her just when she needs you. She saved your sister. After everything she's done for you, you can't even pick up the damn phone when Sam calls to find out if there's a problem."

His heart jolted. Worries and questions filled his mind. "Wait a minute. What's wrong with Morgan? Has Sam heard from her?"

"No. He hasn't. He's been trying to find her. She covers her tracks better than anyone Sam's come up against. Every time he thinks he's close, he hits another brick wall.

"I don't know all the details," Elizabeth went on. "Sam is reluctant to talk about what's happened. What I do know is this case is really getting to him. He needed you. And you were too busy sunning and funning in Hawaii to pick up your phone and give Sam five minutes of your time."

"I'm sorry, Elizabeth. I am. I'm here now. I'll help Sam with whatever case he's working."

"This isn't just a case. It's about Morgan. This is about the Psychic Slayer."

That got his attention. Every instinct in him went on high alert. The instinct to protect Morgan flared. Vacation or not, his mind just shifted into full FBI mode. "Excuse me? The Psychic Slayer. What the hell is that?"

"Keep your voice down. Grace is sleeping."

He stroked his hand down the back of the little bundle in his arms. Completely at ease, she softly breathed as her mouth worked on her thumb.

"The Psychic Slayer is the name the press gave the maniac going around San Francisco killing all the psychics. I don't know all the details, but I know he started the night of the press conference when Stewart gave Morgan's name to the reporters. Since then, he's committed four more murders. All of the women were psychics. At least, they claim to be. They work in various shops around the city giving readings and such. The newspapers are vague about the details.

"Sam got involved after they discovered the third victim. It seems Detective Stewart and his partner Detective Rasmussen didn't think the FBI, particularly you and Sam, would be interested in the case. Sam's been butting heads with them for more than a week. The fourth murder happened Saturday night at a street fair. The psychic gave palm readings in one of the booths. They found her strangled with her tongue cut out and her eyes glued shut. The press says there are no witnesses or leads on the case. Sam remains closemouthed about everything. He's worried about Morgan. Enough so, that whenever he isn't working on the four murders and aggravating the two detectives, he spends all his time trying to locate her."

"Did Sam tie Morgan directly to the murders somehow? Or is this all some crazy's idea of getting back at psychics because they heard the FBI uses psychics to solve cases at the press conference?"

"You'll have to talk to Sam. I only know what I've read in the papers and the little bit Sam mentioned about trying to find Morgan. He wouldn't work this hard to find her if it wasn't important."

She picked up the paper from Sam's desk and threw it on Tyler's desk in front of him. The headline said it all.

THE PSYCHIC SLAYER STRIKES AGAIN!

Like a dramatic headline out of a comic book, only this was real.

"Do you really think the murder of four women, all claiming to be psychics, doesn't have anything to do with

Morgan? If you do, you're in denial about more than the fact that you care about her."

"You don't even know Morgan."

"I know you," Elizabeth snapped.

He couldn't deny that. He and Sam were close. Elizabeth fed him as often as she fed her own husband. He spent a lot of time talking with Elizabeth at the restaurant. A very good friend, he counted himself lucky to have her in his life.

"What makes you and everyone else think my feelings for her run any deeper than they would for any other colleague I've worked with for years?"

He wanted to get up out of his seat and pace. He couldn't. Grace was sleeping and it took everything he had to keep his voice down. He didn't know why Elizabeth got after him. Well, he did. He'd let Sam down, and Elizabeth wouldn't stand for anything to happen to Sam. "I'm seeing Maria. We just spent ten days in Hawaii, and she stayed at my place all weekend. Things are going really well between the two of us."

"I'm not buying it. I know what love looks like. If Sam and I had spent ten days in Hawaii together, you can bet Sam would be smiling like a clown and tired to the bone from lack of sleep. You, Tyler, do not look like a man who just spent the last two weeks in bed with a woman.

"I remember when Sam and I got out of the hospital and we were finally alone. You remember the two of us. We were constantly kissing and falling into bed together. The beginning is always the best part of a relationship. It's that time when you can't keep your hands off each other.

Tell me you and Maria never left your room in Hawaii. Tell me you didn't even have time to sightsee."

Tyler turned away as Elizabeth's words hit home. Tyler didn't want to lie or admit his relationship with Maria wasn't like that for them. They weren't hot for each other every minute. He expected most couples went from hot bunny sex to lukewarm lovemaking after they'd been married for a long time. Seeing Sam and Elizabeth kissing had changed his mind on that as well. He didn't mind his and Maria's tepid sex life—much. They didn't have to be locked in sweaty, hot sex every time they were alone together. Right?

"We had a great time. There's a lot to do and see."

"You're trying to make a relationship out of a friendship. Maria's a nice woman. She'll probably make someone a good wife. She just won't make you a good wife. She's too mellow, and she hates your job."

"Elizabeth . . ." Tyler started to interrupt.

"Let me finish. The lack of passion and fire between you will wear on you. You're too vital of a man to last long with a woman like Maria. Worse would be if the two of you stayed together for years. You'll be miserable. You already are. You just don't see it."

She patted her belly again and looked right at Tyler, so that maybe what she said would sink into that warped mind of his. "I worry about you. It's sad to think the hottest thing on that island was the volcano and not you and some woman tearing up the sheets.

"You're a gorgeous, sexy, strong man. Yeah, maybe this is the hormones talking, and the fact that I haven't seen my husband in three days, but I never thought you'd settle for anything less than a woman who could spark a fire in you both physically and mentally.

"Life with Maria is easy. She'll spend her time making things nice for you. You two could have a nice, normal, dull life together. I always thought you were the kind of man who wanted a challenge. I always imagined you'd find someone who made you work for it, since most everything comes easy to you. Look at the last several years of your life. A handful of women have warmed your bed. There's probably a hundred who'd line up outside right now for the chance to be with you. None of those women ever got to you like Morgan gets to you. I never thought you'd settle. You aren't a quitter. I wonder why you gave up so easily on Morgan. Did you ever once ask her out on a date?"

Thinking about Morgan stirred up too many complicated feelings. One thing was clear, Morgan had set the boundary and any time he tried to cross it, she backed off.

"Admit it, you're hot for me. You're just waiting for me to say the word and you'll dump Sam. You, me, and the angel here can take off together."

"You're an idiot. I'm actually starting to feel sorry for you. You didn't listen to a thing I said."

He hated upsetting her. He didn't like the fact she was right about some of it. Okay, maybe most of it. It sucked being the one to look bad in front of your friends.

"I listened. Things between Maria and I are good. I want someone in my life I can count on. I want a normal home life."

"I guess I'm wrong then. Maria will certainly give you comfortable and normal."

He didn't like the way that sounded, or the way she'd said it like he'd settled for less than he deserved. "I want what you and Sam have. I want a wife and kids. I'm getting too old to keep up with the dating scene, and I'm tired of it. This job takes everything I have. I don't want to keep putting myself out there and coming up with just another woman warming my bed. This time I want her picking out the sheets."

"Is that what you think Sam and I have, a nice, comfortable, normal life? Is that what you think Jack and Jenna have, or Marti and Cameron? What we have is a great love between us. We have a bond and a deep passion for the person we're with. Is that what you feel for Maria? Because if you do, then I'm completely off base. I just want you to be happy like Sam and I are. You know, I still get weak in the knees and light in the head when I walk into a room and see him. He still makes my blood run hot when he kisses me. Don't get me wrong, we have our comfortable and normal, but it's built on a foundation of love and passion. Tell me that's what you have with Maria and I'll congratulate you. You'll never hear me say I want more for you, more than you apparently want for yourself."

Elizabeth cared deeply for him and knew speaking her mind wouldn't damage their relationship. Maybe he and Maria weren't like Elizabeth and Sam. They could still build a life together and make it work. He'd spent a lot of time thinking about it and decided that maybe he wasn't one of the lucky ones who'd find that hot, passionate love that all of his friends had managed to find. Maybe the fire between him and Maria glowed more like an ember than an all-consuming flame. At least it was something to build on, and not something that would flash and burn itself out.

"I know what you and the others have is something special. It's just not in the cards for me. I'm happy with Maria. Things are fine."

No Tyler, they're not, but you'll keep trying to convince yourself. Won't you? Elizabeth took her daughter and kissed Tyler's cheek. She hadn't gotten through to him. No one could. Set on his course to destruction, he wouldn't be detoured.

"I left an invitation on your desk. We're having a family dinner at the restaurant at the end of next week for Marti and Cameron. Kind of a baby shower. The baby is due in a few weeks. I thought it'd be nice to have a celebration and give them a few gifts for the baby. It'll be a nice opportunity to get everyone together. I assume you'll bring Maria with you."

"Yeah, we'd love to come. It isn't often we all get together. At least, not everyone at one time. I'm looking forward to it. Do we know if the baby is a boy or a girl?"

He'd have to buy a gift. Maybe he and Maria could do it together.

"No. They wanted to be surprised. They're worried about Emma. She's excited about the baby coming, but she's afraid something bad will happen to Marti, since her mother died after giving birth to her. Emma hasn't been sleeping well, and she constantly follows Marti around, making sure she's okay."

"There haven't been any problems with the pregnancy so far, have there?"

"No. Cameron is understandably nervous, but everything is fine so far. Marti says she feels great. The doctor assures them there's nothing out of the ordinary."

"Okay. Maybe I'll give Cameron a call and check on things. I haven't talked to him in a while. Maybe I'll take Emma out on a dinner and movie date, so Cameron and Marti can have time alone together before the baby comes."

"I'm sure they'd appreciate it. Emma does love her Uncle Tyler."

"I like the kids," he said and kissed Grace's chubby cheek. "All of them."

"You'll be a great father someday. You're a natural with them."

"I hope so. I'd like a family of my own. Watching all of you guys . . . Well, you make it look easy."

"It's not easy. It's love. I hope you have that, too, Tyler." She picked up Grace and turned to leave, but swung back around to him. "Bring Maria by the restaurant for dinner one night. I'd love to see the two of you. I'll make you a triple chocolate cake."

Always looking out for him, the invitation signaled a truce. She'd back him up, no matter his decision. She'd be the first to congratulate him if he married Maria. He could count on Elizabeth to make her feel welcome in their family circle.

"Your triple chocolate cake is my favorite. We'll be there. I don't know exactly when, though. I want to catch up on things with Sam. It looks like we'll be in deep with this new killer on the loose."

"Come in any night. The cake will be there, and so will I."

"You always are." He stood and put his hand on her shoulder and gave her a squeeze. "Thanks."

"You're welcome. I just want you to be happy."

"I know." It's what he wanted for himself. He kissed her on the cheek and watched her and Grace leave.

"You lucky bastard, Sam," he muttered and went to find his friend. If he still had one.

He better be ready to duck.

Chapter Eleven

TYLER WOKE UP this morning ready for work. Now he'd had a run-in with Sam, had his life examined and shoved in his face by Elizabeth, and found out someone was killing psychics.

His fault. He'd given Detective Stewart her name. Stupid. Everything inside him always warned him to protect Morgan. He hadn't said anything to Elizabeth, but since Morgan's abrupt departure, he'd been thinking about her and the emptiness she'd left in his mind, his life, his soul. Part of him was missing. He thought the vacation with Maria would help him put the whole thing out of his mind. Instead, he'd lain awake in the dark hours of the night thinking about Morgan and that emptiness he couldn't seem to fill. Spending time with Maria helped with the worst of the emptiness, but it remained. He didn't think it would ever go away.

Morgan had always been at arm's length and beyond.

Different from any woman he'd ever met. It wasn't just that she had a sixth sense, or whatever the proper term for what she did. She had always been so genuinely interested in him. She asked him how he was, never satisfied with an *I'm fine*. He counted on her. She had been there for him every time he needed her.

She didn't want to be in his life anymore. He'd have to accept that. His own damn fault.

Something Elizabeth said kept nagging at him. She'd asked him if he'd ever simply asked her out on a date. No, not really.

In the beginning, he'd tried to change the nature of their relationship. He'd gone from getting messages from her to their speaking to each other directly. Hard-won progress when Morgan controlled the relationship, keeping her secrets to herself and never opening up about anything. She refused to answer any of his numerous questions.

Why? It had always bothered him.

The more he thought about it, he realized the only personal things they talked about involved him. He'd given up asking her about her life, except to ask her questions about how she saw the things she saw. He'd turned into a selfish asshole, taking everything she offered and giving her nothing in return but a lot of grief over her gift. She was there for him when he needed a little pick-me-up, or when he just needed someone to talk to. She'd call and he'd dump his load on her. He wondered if she had anyone to count on like he had counted on her. She'd certainly never had him. It hit him hard. Maybe he'd given up too easily and let her get away with distracting him from getting too close.

It bothered him that he didn't know if she had friends she confided in, or maybe even a boyfriend. Or husband. That thought made his chest go tight. She'd have at least told him that much.

He hated analyzing things after the fact. The many things he didn't know ate at him. The thing is, he wanted to know everything about her, but she didn't want to tell him for whatever reason and it hurt.

Morgan left him. Her choice again. Not his.

Too late now to make things right with Morgan, he needed to concentrate on his future—with Maria.

Elizabeth hadn't been gone five minutes before Agent Davies yelled at him to come into his office. Tyler hadn't even managed to sort through the stack of files on his desk, or look at the Psychic Slayer evidence and information.

"Are you going to get your head back in the game, or is your brain still on vacation?"

"I'm here. I need to catch up on the new case Sam is working on. I don't know all the facts, but I'm curious as to why Sam's hell-bent on finding Morgan."

"She's the key to this case. All the women were psychics in some fashion or another. They worked in local shops giving readings, providing spiritual guidance, and telling people's fortunes. Not exactly the same as Morgan, but our guy seems to be eliminating them, so that they can't talk."

"What do you mean, so they can't talk? What do they know?"

"The profiler we brought in suspects he's cutting out their tongues and gluing their eyes shut so they can't see or talk about what he's done. The profiler believes the guy committed some terrible act. Probably murder. He probably committed this act some time ago, got away with it, and now believes the psychics can see what he did and will tell the police, and he'll be arrested. Since the murders began the night of the press conference where Detective Stewart stated Morgan could not only see the crime, but name names, the profiler believes this instigated the murderer to start his crime spree.

"He strangled victim number one in her shop. They struggled, and she ended up dead. The others were planned. Our guy came prepared to kill them. In each case, it appears he pays for a psychic reading and strangles them. He's escalating. The last three were butchered as I described."

"Well, I see how this ties in with our using Morgan, but you said it directly relates to her. How and why?"

"Sam checked your voicemail while you were on vacation. Our guy called and left you a message. We have a recording of his voice. The tech guys are trying to see if they can determine where the call originated, and if they can isolate anything in the background to give us any kind of clue."

"What was the message? What don't you want to tell me?"

Sam walked in the door. He'd had a hell of a couple of days and didn't feel real generous toward Tyler.

"He wanted to thank you for letting him know she's

in San Francisco. He pretty much said that he's going to rid the city of all the seers, so they can't tell. Tell what, we have no idea."

Sam sat in the chair next to Tyler facing Davies behind his desk. He sighed, tired and a lot disappointed he'd cut his visit with Elizabeth short this morning.

"Do you think he knows her?" Tyler asked.

"At the very least, he's talked to her. Maybe through her website. Which I've confirmed does belong to her. The site is tied to her credit card. The bills for the credit card are sent to a post office box in Texas. The post office where the box is located won't give us any information on Morgan without a warrant. The only thing I could get the clerk to tell me is that she doesn't pick up the mail there. It's forwarded. He wouldn't tell me where. I don't have enough to get the warrant. She isn't a witness or a suspect in any ongoing case. I don't have a legal reason for the post office to tell me where the mail is forwarded, and if they have any information on Morgan we can use.

"I've been trying to find Morgan because I don't know if she knows there's a threat against her. Actually, there are two, if you count her father, who's called twice since you've been gone. I also don't know if she's living anywhere near San Francisco. For all we know she could have a shop here like the other women. This guy could find her before we do."

Sam rubbed his hand over the back of his neck and slapped his hand down on his thigh. "You'd think with all the technology we have at our disposal we could find one woman. If she wasn't hiding from her father, it might be easier."

"If you haven't found her, this guy won't either," Tyler said.

"Yeah, I guess after everything she's done for us, we should just leave her in the dark. We don't owe her a heads-up that there's some nut out there who may or may not know her, who wants to kill her." Disgusted, he glared at Tyler. "Oh yeah, and let's not forget her father is looking for her. I'm not so sure his intentions are all that good. Hell, he may be the one killing all the psychics for all we know."

"Have you talked to him?"

"Nope. He's gone, too. We haven't been able to find him. His place is in a rural area. There's a barn with some horses, but Weston hasn't been around the few times I've gone out to question him. The neighbor says he's been feeding the horses, but he doesn't know where Weston went, or when he'll be back. He says Weston takes off all the time."

"So we don't know if he's our guy or not. Either way, he wants to hurt her. I know it."

"Did you ever once ask her where she lives? Did you ask her what she does for a living? Did you ask her anything personal about herself that didn't have to do with her being psychic? Did you ever talk to her like your friend, and not some informant on a case?"

"Sam, I . . ."

"Did you ever ask her how she was? Did she need anything? The woman has been living on her own, since she was twelve for all we know. Her father killed her mother and she witnessed it. Her hometown press vilified her, so much so that she took off. At least, that's what we think. How do we know what really happened? Maybe some whack-job from her hometown kidnapped her and kept her for his own entertainment for years."

Tyler's face paled and he pulled away from him.

"Obviously, you hadn't thought of any of this. You're too busy being hurt that she left you. Too busy being angry she's different than everyone else, and you didn't know what to do about her. You want her . . . don't shake your head . . . and at the same time, you want to shove her away. Maybe you've done just that.

"The thing here, Tyler, is that we don't know. We don't really know anything about her. What we do know, now, is there are one, and probably two men, who want to find her and possibly kill her. You want to be pissed at her because she's different. Fine. Be pissed. It doesn't make you any better than those people from her hometown who threw rocks and called her a witch."

"I'm not pissed at her. And she's not a witch."

"No. She's just a woman. You're angry with her because she left you after the press conference. She left, and it pisses you off that she's gone and you have no idea how to get her back. I'll bet you've spent every day since telling yourself you don't want her back. You're better off without her. Now, you can move on with Maria, and you won't have Morgan in your head and on your mind. Except she is, and you can't escape. And that pisses you off, too."

Damn if Sam didn't know him really well, too well. He couldn't deny anything Sam said. Doing so would only prove to Sam just how deep his denial ran about everything.

Angry she'd left, she hadn't leaned on him after her name went out in the press. She hadn't trusted him enough to make things right. Now look what happened. He hadn't been there for her in the past, so how could she rely on him now. She'd given him her time, her gift, and her reassurance. He betrayed her by giving out her name. He should have told Stewart to go to hell and accept the information they had without question.

Sam read his mind as usual. "I know what you're thinking. She didn't come to you. She didn't trust you enough to tell you about her past, or her father. If she knew these murders were going to happen, she didn't tell you. She just cut herself off from you."

Sam stood and looked down at Tyler. "You know, I've been thinking about that day and her vanishing act from your head. I wonder if she left you, or if you pushed her out. Maybe it's a little of both. She got upset and left, but you won't let her back in. I don't know how it works, or how she does it. I do know we need to find her. So, open up that mind of yours and call out to her, think about her calling you, do whatever it is you used to do that made her call you when you needed her. We need her now. She needs us."

Sam turned to leave when his cell phone chimed, letting him know he had a text message. He read it and turned to Davies. "I have to go to Colorado." He glanced at Tyler. "The autopsy for Shannon McKay, aka Mystic, is in an hour. Be there. Look for yourself what this guy is doing to these women. Then, imagine it's Morgan on that cold slab because we didn't warn her."

Tyler didn't need to see the dead woman. The minute he found out about this case, he'd been terrified the next victim would be Morgan.

"Maybe she already knows," he said without looking at Sam.

"You think it works like that? If it did, then why doesn't she call and solve every case we work? It would save us a hell of a lot of time and manpower. Hell, we could just have her solve all the world's problems.

"People are dying. This guy specifically called you about Morgan. You may think she's better off wherever she is because we can't find her; so neither can her father, or this maniac. Well, that's not good enough for me. It shouldn't be good enough for you."

"It's not good enough for me. I want her safe, and if I knew where she is, I'd protect her with my life. It's my fault she's in danger and I'd do anything to take it back, but I can't. So, let's work the case and find this bastard and stop him before he gets close to her."

Sam's cell phone rang. He punched the talk button and listened.

"The jet is on the runway waiting to take off. You'll be home tomorrow morning," Jack said.

"What's going on? Is it Jenna? One of the kids?"

"No. Don't say anything to anyone. Morgan wants to see you. Only you."

Stunned, Sam dropped back into his chair, rocked by the news.

"How do you know this?"

"I'll explain later."

"I'm leaving right now."

"Come to the house. I'll take you to her. I mean it, Sam, don't tell anyone. It's important."

"You have my word. You will explain this to me when I get there." He hung up before Jack gave him excuses for keeping secrets.

When Sam stood, Davies shouted, "Where the hell do you think you're going? We're in the middle of this mess."

"I'm sorry. It's an emergency. The jet is waiting at the airport. I'll be back tomorrow morning." He headed out the door before anyone stopped him.

Davies looked to Tyler. "Do you think something's wrong with Jack, or his family?"

"I don't think so. It's got to be something else." Tyler shrugged. He and Sam could probably use the space right now. "I can handle things until he's back tomorrow. I'll go to the autopsy, get the details, catch up with the detectives at the SFPD, light a fire under Detective Stewart, and I'll go from there. I'll catch up by tonight, so Sam and I can hit the ground running tomorrow morning on the same page."

"You didn't mention trying to find Morgan in that speech."

"She's definitely a priority. He's right. I'm pissed at her for leaving us in the lurch like this. We could use her on this case. If she'd been less difficult about keeping things on her terms, we might actually have her phone number. Instead, we're wasting time trying to find her."

"Isn't that why she left the messages? To keep you from making demands and asking a lot of questions about how she did what she did. It seems to me, over the last two years the two of you had settled into a routine. She'd call with the clues, and you'd take them and run with them. I know you've talked a few times personally. Makes me wonder what it is about her you're afraid of that you never pushed her for her number or to meet in person."

"I'm not afraid of her, if that's what you mean. Why the hell is everyone on my case about her today? First Elizabeth, then Sam, and now you. You let me know how you feel about a psychic dogging your every move and talking to you in your mind after she's been doing it for the better part of six years. Then, you tell me how you feel after you've gotten used to hearing her in your head, and she up and disappears on you in the blink of an eye."

Davies smiled across the desk at him, but Tyler ignored the look, knowing he'd given away too much information.

"Sam mentioned you could think about her and she'd call you. Do that."

"I can't. She isn't in there anymore."

"So you say. Do some deep breathing, meditate, chant, whatever. Anything, for god's sake, to get her to call you."

Tyler rolled his eyes and stood. Like he hadn't already tried that a dozen or more times. "I'm going over to the medical examiner's office. I'll check back with you later."

"Ignoring it won't make it go away," Davies yelled after him as Tyler left his office.

How could he ignore her when she consumed his every thought? If she hadn't called him by now, she wouldn't. He'd find her another way.

Chapter Twelve

SAM CALLED ELIZABETH on his way to the airport. "Sweetheart, can you meet me at the airport with Grace? Jack sent the jet. I need to go to the ranch for a meeting."

"But I thought you were in the middle of a case. Why are we going to the ranch?"

"I have a lead on the case. I'll meet someone who lives near the ranch. We'll stay overnight, and you and I can spend time together."

She met him at the plane with Grace an hour later. They spent the time on the flight snuggling on the couch and playing with Grace. Family time. Exactly what Sam needed to recharge. They flew to the private airstrip Jenna had built several years ago. It saved time rather than flying into the small airport more than an hour away from the ranch. This way, they were only ten minutes away. Grateful for the short drive, the lid on his boiling anger rattled by the time the plane landed.

Sam didn't worry about leaving Elizabeth at the ranch while he went to see Morgan. She'd enjoy seeing Jenna and the new baby. Willow was only a few months old and Elizabeth could fuss over her with Jenna while he went to see Morgan.

They drove to the ranch in the spare SUV Jack left at the airstrip. He, Elizabeth, and Grace walked in the front door of the family home and greeted everyone. He made it clear to Jack why he was there. "Let's go. Now."

"Nice to see you, too, brother. You can't even say hello to your sister-in-law and your niece."

He'd seen them all a few weeks ago, but Jack was trying to get him to calm down. He walked into the Great Room and stood in front of Jenna and Willow. They made quite a picture rocking in the old family rocking chair. Jenna, always stunning, seeing her with little Willow curled up on her chest sleeping took his breath away. He loved his wife and daughter, but he had a special place in his heart for Jenna. He always had.

"Hello, beautiful." He leaned over to kiss Jenna on top of her head. He whispered to his niece, "Hello, mini beautiful."

Elizabeth found Sam's greeting for Jenna and Willow sweet. He turned to mush around them. Jenna had encouraged Sam and her to get together. She'd helped her open her restaurant in the Merrick Building. They'd become sisters over the last couple of years. She already had two brothers, so it was nice to have a sister. Sam needed to take a breath. He'd been running on empty for too long now. Jenna had a way of calming him when no one else could.

Jenna took Sam's hand so he couldn't walk away. "Hello, Sam. I'm glad to see you. Jack surprised me a little while ago. He said you two have something to do, but he won't tell me what it is. What are you two up to this time?"

"Is Jack going with you to see the person involved in your case?" Elizabeth asked.

"Yeah, he knows someone who might know something about the murders. We've got to go." He pulled away from Jenna and kissed Elizabeth and his sweet baby girl, Gracie, and headed to the door. "Let's go, Jack."

Jack smiled at his wife and Elizabeth. "Looks like it's time to go."

They left the house and their confused wives behind and walked to the stables. The women would be fine. They had a one-year-old, the twin boys, a baby, and Elizabeth's pregnancy to talk about and keep them busy.

"Why are we going to the stables? Do you have to check on the horses before we go?" Sam asked.

"No. We're riding over."

"Over to where?"

"Next door." Jack sidestepped to avoid the punch he thought Sam might throw. Sam only glared, fists at his sides.

"It'll take about forty minutes to ride, but I figure you need time to let your anger subside. You can't see Morgan if you're angry. She can't handle it."

One of the ranch hands waited by the stables with two saddled horses. Sam mounted his horse as Jack got up on Blue.

"Are you telling me Morgan lives next door to you?" Sam asked angrily.

"Didn't I just say that?"

"I ought to kick your ass for keeping this secret. How long has she lived next door?"

"A little more than two years. Do you remember the house and property that came up for sale down on Sycamore Drive? Tyler wanted to buy it."

"Yeah. It sold before he had a chance to make an offer on the place."

"Morgan bought it. To be fair, I didn't know she lived there, until about a year ago."

"You've known for a year how to find her. You know what happened a few weeks ago with the press conference and her leaving Tyler. Why would you keep it a secret that you knew how to get in touch with her?"

"Because she asked me to. No one, except me, knows that she lives there. I mean it, Sam. No one knows. She's there alone. I found out she lives there by accident. I wanted to see if the new owner would let me put some horses in the empty pastures. I went over to ask, and I found her. At first, I didn't know it was her, but she sure as hell knew me. She knew things about the family. When she said her name is Morgan, I knew it was her."

"Tell me about her. I mean, we all know she's psychic, but what's she really like?"

"She's nice. She's sensitive. I mean it, she won't be able to deal with your anger. I made a mistake when I met her and I got upset. It's a physical thing for her. She literally wilted before my eyes. I've seen her several times since. If

I'm happy, you can see she's happy because I am. If I'm a little off or down, she responds to that." Sam shot him a skeptical stare. "Look, I don't know exactly how it works with her. I just know she's different. You can't go in there with your emotions all over the place, or your anger out of control."

Sam took a calming breath and looked around them as they rode through a large open field of green grass with the forest bordering their progress. Peaceful, the green of the land and the clear blue of the sky. He loved Colorado. He came here when he needed to recharge. He and Elizabeth stayed at the lake house as often as they could manage. This is where they spent their vacation time. He could see why Morgan had chosen to move here. He loved the calm tranquil setting too.

"I'll do my best to keep myself in check. Why does she want to see me?"

"I told her about the murders last week when I saw her. This morning, she asked me to contact you and ask you to come. She didn't say anything more."

"You had to tell her what happened."

"Yes. She didn't know anything about it."

"So, without her connection to Tyler she didn't know I was working on the case."

"I don't know about that. She doesn't really talk about what she can do. She's quiet most of the time. She asks about the kids, you and Elizabeth, everyone. It's like she's been a part of the family. I kind of think of her that way. She's like a sister."

"Tyler will be pissed when he finds out every time he's

been here over the last year she was next door. He was so close to her."

"Do you remember when you came home early and brought Tyler with you when Elizabeth took maternity leave?"

"Yeah, Morgan helped us wrap up a case early. Tyler decided to come for a short visit."

"That's the day I met her. She told me you two would come home early. When you actually showed up and surprised everyone, I was completely stunned. I didn't believe her. Not until I saw you both walk through the door."

"So, she's the real deal," Sam said, amazed.

"You know she is."

"It's different having her predictions and clues come secondhand through Tyler. It's another thing to meet her and have her do it in front of me." Sam shook his head.

"Are you nervous?" Jack laughed. "Sam Turner, FBI agent, nervous about meeting a woman."

"I'm just not sure what to expect," Sam said and meant it. He'd spent a lot of time thinking about Morgan. He knew things about her that Jack didn't know. He didn't want to make a bigger mess out of things with her than they already had. He didn't know how she'd feel about him digging in her past and finding all the buried skeletons.

"She's just like anyone else. See." Jack pointed to the woman kneeling in the garden as they came out of the trees and made their way across the wide pasture. "She's just a woman."

"Just a woman, my ass. That is one gorgeous woman. Are you kidding me? That's Morgan?"

"Yep," Jack said with a wide grin.

"No wonder she's been haunting Tyler ever since he saw her five years ago. No man could forget her."

Jack smiled and dismounted Blue. He tethered Blue to the low fence surrounding Morgan's garden and waited as she approached.

Sam sat mesmerized by the angel coming toward him. That's all he could think. She looked like what he imagined angels looked like in heaven. Her softly waving gold hair blew in the breeze. Her amazing blue eyes held him in place. Not very tall, but he felt her presence. Maybe it was a trick of the light off her hair, or sun-kissed golden skin, he wasn't sure, but he thought she glowed.

Ordinary in every way, and extraordinary in so many. She wore simple worn blue jeans, a bit of dirt staining the knees, and a white blouse. She carried a pair of gardening gloves. Ordinary. Slim, but no mistaking the womanly curves, from the swell of her breasts in the open collar of her shirt to the slight flare of her hips.

She walked toward him, completely unaware of her appeal. The swing of her hips and the hint of a smile on her soft, full lips could bring a man to his knees. And then she spoke and her sultry voice made him think of hot nights and soft, smooth blues.

"I don't haunt Tyler. I'm not a ghost. Like Jack said, I'm just a woman." She smiled as she came out of her garden.

Sam looked from Morgan to Jack and shook his head to clear it.

"She does that," Jack said referring to Morgan knowing what they'd talk about on the ride over. "It's kind of creepy. You'll get used to it."

Sam dropped down from his horse and approached Morgan. He did something she never saw coming. He wrapped his arms around her and held her to his chest tightly and whispered into her ear. "I am so happy to meet you. I've waited a long time to say thank you. Thank you for helping me with Elizabeth. Thank you for helping with all the other cases."

"Oh. Well. Damn. Elizabeth is a lucky woman." She held on to Sam because it felt good to let someone be close. It had been a long time since someone hugged her. Her eyes got misty, and she had to take a breath to calm herself. "You think she'd mind if I keep you?"

Sam chuckled. She held on to him like she had no intention of letting him go. "I think she'd like me back, but you can borrow me for a little while. We have a lot to talk about."

"I know." She reluctantly let him go and took a step back. "Come in. I have iced tea and brownies made."

She led the way up the wide porch and through the screen door. She loved the way it banged shut after the men came into the house. She spent all of her time alone, and company was a treat. She'd seen Jack off and on over the last year. A busy man, after checking on his horses he usually headed back to his own home and family. He stopped to talk to her whenever he could, and she appreciated his time and company.

She really liked the horses. They made the property

less lonely. She liked hearing them whinny and nicker in the pastures. She took them treats and petted them as often as she could. She was working up the courage to ask Jack to teach her to ride. She could get her own. She'd buy one of the horses from Jack. The black one with the white line on his nose and head. She liked him and secretly named him Blaze.

Surprised again, Sam liked her home. Pretty, like Morgan, simple and charming. The entry opened into a large family room that adjoined the kitchen and dining area at the rear of the house. A set of glass double doors went out the back to a deck and patio beyond. The family room had a large river-rock fireplace with a chunky wood mantle. A large vase of flowers sat on the mantel beside a framed photo of a family sitting at a picnic table in a park. The woman resembled Morgan, only with shorter hair. The man, in his early thirties with light brown hair, smiled at the woman and held a little girl on his lap. The boy in the photo looked about two, and he had jelly on his chin and laughed with a huge smile. A nice looking family.

On the table, next to a brown leather couch, lay several books. One lay opened, face down to hold her page. School textbooks and paperback novels lined the shelves of a tall bookcase. Many of them looked well worn. He could see her sitting in the chaise, reading her books as the sun poured through the large bank of windows.

A rustic farm table with bench seats on both sides and a spindle-back chair on each end took up most the space in her dining room. The wrought-iron lamp over the table complimented the rustic feel of the house. Fresh flowers graced the room in several colorful glass vases. Some were large and others small. Their sweet fragrance filled the room. He knew she'd cut them from her flourishing garden. Pots of herbs lined the shelf in the window above the kitchen sink.

The house was homey. And quiet.

He hated thinking of Morgan here all alone. Day after day.

"Would you like to sit in the family room, or here at the kitchen table?"

"The table's fine." He took the platter of brownies from her and set them on the table. Jack had the pitcher of ice tea and they both waited for Morgan to arrange their glasses and take her seat before they took their seats.

Morgan brushed her hand over the smooth wooden surface and looked at him and Jack with a sadness that tore at Sam. He glanced around the huge room and imagined her there alone.

"You've never had anyone sit at this table with you."

Morgan's gaze locked with him. It hadn't been a question, but a softly spoken statement letting her know he understood her just a little. "I've been alone for a long time."

"I like all the flowers. Your garden is beautiful. You must spend a lot of time working out there."

She thought it nice he took the time to see her as more than just a psychic. He wanted to find out what else interested her. She hadn't missed his casual perusal of her home. She knew he took in every detail and tucked them away in case he needed them later.

"The garden is peaceful. It gives me a sense of accomplishment. I can go out there and work for a few hours and have tangible results. I can watch the flowers bloom and know I had a hand in their care. It's my way of giving back a little of what I take."

She wondered how he'd interpret that statement. Most people wouldn't think of that, or give of themselves in such a way. Others did it without thinking of it as giving back to their surroundings for what they take from them.

She's normal with a little something different about her, Sam thought. She wanted to be accepted and acknowledged as just another person on this earth, but she wasn't. She was different, and the difference made her special. You could see it in her eyes. She saw more than others. Right now, those eyes were a bright light blue. Outside she'd been cautious about meeting him, and they'd been shaded and just a bit dark.

"Kind of what I think about being with the FBI. I'm just one more good guy to go up against the bad. My own little balance on the scales of life."

"You want to fight the good fight and protect those that can't protect themselves."

He smiled. Every cop felt that way. The police motto was "To Protect and to Serve." It's what they did. It's what they were. At least, that's how it should be.

"I have to say, I'm a little disappointed there isn't a single crystal ball in the place. There aren't any pewter dragons or fairies sitting on toadstools." Those were the kinds of things he'd found in the murdered psychics' shops and homes. Again, Morgan was different.

"What kind of psychic are you?" He wanted to ease into the subject. A little levity might get them into the conversation without putting her on edge.

"The fairies are in the garden, of course. There aren't any toadstools. Fairies live in the lilies," she smiled. "They're like little balls of golden sunlight. They die if you say you don't believe in them, and when they think happy thoughts, they can fly," she said whimsically.

"As for the crystal ball, sorry to disappoint you, but I don't own one. I don't need it to do what I do. As for the cauldron, well, it's how I whipped up this batch of tea. You know, a little wing of bat and eye of newt. Poof and voilà, iced tea." She'd tried to keep her voice light, but a hint of annoyance tinged her words.

He was teasing her, but she wanted him to like her. She wanted to be accepted by him and everyone else in their family circle. She wanted to belong. She used to feel like she belonged, right up until she lost her connection with Tyler.

She didn't like people making her out to be something she wasn't. Like something bad or evil. She was just a person who'd been given an extraordinary gift. It had taken her a long time to get to the point where her gift was more blessing than curse.

She didn't trust him enough yet not to judge her. She probably already thought he had judged her and found her to be the witch everyone had called her as a little girl. Sam liked the whimsical way she spoke of fairies in the lilies, like a leftover fantasy from a childhood that had been anything but sweet and charming.

"Jack tells me you've lived here for about two years. I know you met Tyler in Texas. Where'd you live before that?"

"You have an interesting mind."

"Can you read my mind?"

"Sometimes. You have very good boundaries set up. It's what makes you a good investigator and undercover agent. What I mean is that you look at things like a puzzle. While I can't see the actual information you have, or what you're looking for, when I look at you as you ask me questions, I see floating puzzle pieces. I have a feeling that with each new bit of information I give you, you'll assign it a puzzle piece and fit it to its partner until you make the whole picture."

"Is that how you do what you do? You see images of things. I know the clues you give us are all abstract images or impressions. Is that how it comes to you?"

"Sometimes. Sometimes it's very specific, like a dream of what's happened or will happen.

"How to put it in simple terms?" She sat back and tapped her foot on the floor. "I might see a duck. Depending on the situation, or the person, the duck could mean simply a waterfowl, or look out. It could mean the person needs to let whatever it is roll off their back like water off a duck. What I see isn't always literal. It's taken me a long time to understand the things I see.

"To give you an example you can relate to, when I met Jack the first time, he rode up on his horse. When I look at that horse, I see a blue horse with a shield on its chest. Now, since you know Jack, you know his favorite color is blue. Blue, the horse, is his favorite and named for Jack's favorite color. The shield is a little harder to relate, unless you know Jack and Jenna. I can see a past in which Blue stood guard over her. He thinks of her as his to protect, hence the shield.

"If you and Tyler had a case and I told you I see a man on a blue horse who has a shield on its chest, you wouldn't know what to do with that information. Once you investigate and found out that the man rides a horse by the name of Blue and he protects his mistress it makes sense."

Jack laughed. "Is that really what you see when you look at my horse?"

"I see a lot more, but that just illustrates to Sam what I see and how I see it. It isn't simple."

Not simple at all, and he didn't need to hear the trace of irritation in her voice to know it frustrated her sometimes. He could just imagine having a picture in his head and not knowing what it meant. At times, some of his cases felt the same way. He had pieces of the puzzle and no idea what picture those pieces should make.

Now she was making him think like her. Creepy.

"Stop thinking I'm creepy. You and Tyler do that far too much, and I have to say, it's annoying. You'd think by now all of you would be used to me and what I can do."

Sam nodded at her in agreement and steered the conversation back to her past. "So, back to the question still on the table. Where did you live before Texas?"

"Ever the detective," Morgan mused. So he wanted

the details of her past. He must already know about her parents and her disappearance. Better to take the direct route than playing Twenty Questions. They'd wasted enough time. They needed to get to the heart of the conversation. That meant getting to the murders by way of her nightmare past.

Chapter Thirteen

"You know about my parents?"

Definitely a question. Sam had to stop assuming she knew everything he knew. Apparently, that wasn't the case. He'd seen enough TV shows and movies with psychics that he should know they didn't see everything. It worked more like a switch, either on or off. Morgan's switch seemed to be on more than anyone else's.

"I read the files and the newspaper accounts. Yeah, I know," Sam said.

Jack didn't know about this part of the conversation, so he kept his mouth shut and let Sam do his thing. If Morgan wanted to share, she would. She did things her own way, and he'd respect that.

"Does Tyler know?" She didn't necessarily want him to know one more thing about her that made her odd. Not everyone had a father who murdered their mother. Tyler would be angry she hadn't told him. Another thing she didn't share when he'd shared so much with her.

"Yeah, he knows the basics. I didn't fill him in on everything I've uncovered, since he's been gone and pissed me off."

She wanted to ask about his being gone, but she held her tongue. None of her business, even if she wanted it to be.

"Then you know my father killed my mother. They said he did it in a rage of passion when he discovered she was leaving him."

"That's what the police said. It isn't what you said."

"They didn't believe me."

"No, they didn't," Sam said sadly. "Instead they called you a witch and people protested outside the courthouse and chanted hateful things at you. Some even threw things when they brought you into the courthouse. The press fed the frenzy and the defense attorney made you out to be crazy. He tried to discredit you on the stand and advised the court you should be sent to an institution for *evaluation*. It's what your father wanted to do with you."

Jack let out a disgusted grunt, outraged for Morgan. He didn't like the idea of people treating her badly and Morgan appreciated his support and understanding.

"Oh, he didn't want to have me committed. He wanted to kill me. He started the cause to get the devil removed from his daughter's possessed body. After that, every religious zealot and fanatic came out of the woodwork. They didn't come to get justice for my mother and see my father pay for what he did to her. They wanted to see the witch, who could see things. Devil, demon, witch, crazy, psycho, I've been called them all since I can remember."

"What did you see your father do?"

"There's no mistaking the fact he killed her. It's the part where they called it a crime of passion and charged him with manslaughter instead of cold-blooded murder. That I couldn't let him get away with. He planned killing her. He thought everything through. Everything, except for me. He didn't count on me calling the police and having them show up minutes after he'd killed her."

She waited for the million-dollar question. They didn't disappoint her.

"Why didn't you call the police and tell them before he killed her?"

"Because I didn't know he planned to kill my mother before it happened. I only saw the murder and the events leading up to it minutes before he killed her. Without her standing between us, he'd finally have control over me. Standing up to my father wasn't easy, but when it came to me, she tried. She didn't want him using my gift and me.

"I was on my way home from school when it happened. I made the call to the police from a grocery store and ran all the way home. I arrived just as the end of the vision came true. I watched him kill her—twice."

A lot to take in, no one said anything for a minute.

"He used to play games with me. When I was really little, I thought it was fun. As I got older, and better at it, it wasn't fun anymore."

"What kind of games did he play with you?" Alarms went off in Sam's system. The little devils crawled up his back, his chest went tight, and he held his breath for what came next.

"Little things like, guess which hand I'm holding the coin in, or which card comes next in the deck. I was always right," she smiled.

Those were happy memories of a time when her father had been less angry at the world.

"He'd ask me to guess what number he was thinking. I wasn't always right on that one, but I got it most times. As I got older, the games got harder. He'd want to know something specific about someone. Like I've told you, it doesn't work that way. You can't ask me something like, 'What's Jenna's bank account number and her ATM secret code?'"

"So he'd ask you these questions, so he could use it to his advantage?"

"Yes."

"He was blackmailing people."

"You're sharp, Sam. It started off so innocent, the way it happened. The fun games we used to play turned into dark games. Then, they weren't games anymore, but serious business. To him anyway.

"I was about six. I asked why a friend of his was kissing another woman. I knew the man and woman in the picture in my mind. They didn't belong together. They were both married to other people. He took that information and got them both to pay him money to keep the affair quiet. An easy way to make money, it continued until I figured out his game."

She tried to tell herself she was young and hadn't understood the ramifications of what she saw. Sometimes she could accept that, and other times she blamed herself.

"When I helped him, he got his money and left me alone. When I got it wrong, or didn't know, I was punished. Usually, a slap and stuffed into the closet for a few hours. Other times, worse. He liked to taunt me and ask, 'Guess what's coming?' Even I could see a fist coming at me without being psychic."

Sam and Jack winced and sat further back in their chairs. Interesting, they did the exact same thing in unison.

"He killed my mother because I refused to help him with something he really wanted. My father wanted in on a scheme that made another man a lot of money, but he didn't know how the guy did it. I told him I couldn't see it. He went to my mother to get her to make me tell him.

"She'd denied her gift her whole life," Morgan said, looking into the past. "She'd learned as a little girl it didn't do any good to use her gift. She'd been ridiculed and teased. She simply put it on a shelf and ignored it. Whatever she saw or knew, she kept it to herself."

"Did she encourage you to use your gift?"

"She told me if I used my gift openly, I'd spend most of my life alone. My choice. I could hide my gift, lie, and have a normal life, always trying to pretend I'm something I'm not. I couldn't shut it off like my mother seemed to do. She was like other psychics I've met. I'm different even from them. Using my gift has certain drawbacks."

"What kind of drawbacks?"

"In order to do what I do, I have to open myself to

the energy around me. Imagine every experience and emotion you have is a ball of energy that circles you like planets in orbit. Now imagine someone like me connects with you. Some of those energy balls get thrown to me as a copy. I take in that energy and read it. Most are benign, or have a little punch to them. If it's a particularly happy memory, then I might feel that light, happy feeling. If the energy is rage, then it's like being hit by a hundred-mile-an-hour fastball."

"So you feel the emotion attached to the images."

"Yes. Most times. I like hanging out with Jack. He's usually a happy-go-lucky guy. That radiates from him. It makes me feel good. I don't have to keep any guards up to protect myself from something that might come at me from him. His energy is usually something happy or touching, especially when it's about his children or Jenna. She's very loved. I feel that, too."

Sam chuckled and Jack sat grinning, red faced.

"Now, imagine being around someone like my father. His energy is very negative. It can suck the life out of me. It's draining to be around someone who is always looking for the easy score, or how he can manipulate someone. All his energy is wrapped up in anger and frustration.

"Most people feel those kinds of things when they're around negative people. But for someone like me, it's magnified. Sometimes when I'm having a vision on one of your cases, it'll take all my energy. I'll just sit on the couch for hours, until I can focus on the room again, and then move that focus to the reality of the room around me. It's like I shut down until my energy can recharge, and the bad energy can dissipate."

"Are you telling me that it physically hurts you when you have a vision about a crime?"

"Not always. It's when the vision carries strong energy. That energy can be very bad, or very good."

Sam cocked an eyebrow, not quite understanding.

"A lot of people use the term *empath*, the ability to pick up on other's emotions."

She opened herself to him and right away she got a vision of him with Elizabeth.

"I can see your wife having Grace. I can feel the overwhelming emotions you have for that memory. You were happy and scared, in a good way, and nervous. When Grace arrived, you felt overwhelming love and joy. That kind of energy I can handle because it's good. It makes me feel a little euphoric. It's like food that nourishes the body. Bad energy is like junk food. Eat too much and you get a stomachache. Eat only junk food and it starts to hurt more than just your stomach."

"Okay, I think I get it. Let's get back to your father. You were saying he went to your mother when you wouldn't help with his newest blackmail scheme."

"This one wasn't about blackmail. He planned to kill the man and take over his operation. That's not important though. My mother wouldn't help him use me. He threatened, he trashed the house, and in the end he killed her."

"Wait, why didn't he ask her if she could help him?"

"Because he didn't know she could. She'd hid it from him their entire marriage. I know; you're going to ask why she married him if he'd only end up killing her. All I can say is that I don't think she knew. Or if she knew he'd be the man he turned into. Even I have a difficult time seeing my own future. I do know she got my sister and me out of the bargain. She told me all the time, I was the greatest gift she'd ever received. She used to say she knew I had important things to do in my life."

"Wait," Sam stopped her. "You have a sister? She isn't mentioned in any of the information I read about the trial."

"She didn't live with us. My mother sent her to live with an aunt when I was about three and she was six. They were having financial problems and she convinced my father it was one less mouth to feed until they got back on their feet. I think by then Mom knew my father's path led to destruction. For whatever reason, he let my sister go, but refused to let my mother send me.

"As it turns out, my sister lives outside San Francisco. I haven't seen her in a while, but I keep tabs on her from afar."

"The picture on the mantel is of her and her family. You two look a lot alike."

"You think so? I took that photo last summer without her knowing. I wanted to see my niece and nephew. They've grown so much."

Her sadness spoke volumes. She didn't have her parents. She didn't have her sister. "You don't talk to your sister," Sam said.

"She doesn't want me around. She blames me for mother sending her away. After all, they must have had their hands full with a psycho like me. Obviously, she didn't inherit the sight. Mother never told her anything about it, and my aunt didn't have it either. My aunt never understood my mother. They never got along. She filled Jillian's head full of crap about the long history of mental illness in the family. She told her it ran in the female line. My sister never considered that my mother sent her away to protect her.

"She grew up with my aunt, loved. She went to the best schools. She had a normal life. My mother did that for her. Jillian doesn't see it that way. She's never considered what her life would have been like had she lived with us. She's never considered what it would have been like to see her father kill her mother and endure the trial.

"I called her on my niece's first birthday. My sister was terrified her daughter inherited the family curse. She actually asked me if I heard voices and if they told me to do things." She laughed. It was actually kind of funny in a sad way. "I asked if she heard voices, because she was the one talking crazy. Then, I took a look at my niece and told my sister what she wanted to know."

"Is your niece psychic?"

"No, but she's going to give my sister a good run for her money when she's a teenager. She's a good girl. She'll be just fine. I made my sister wait a good five minutes for her answer. I paid my bills online and made out my grocery list while she sweated it out. As soon as I told her my niece didn't have any psychic abilities, she hung up on me. I haven't heard from her since. I respect her wishes. I let her know how to contact me if she needs me, or if there's an emergency through my PO box and my website. But I don't contact her, or the children, otherwise."

"You don't trust her with your phone number or address?" Sam asked, confused.

"Let's just say as much as I want to have a relationship with her, I see a darkness around her that gives me pause."

Sam couldn't imagine not being able to trust the people closest to you, your family.

"If your sister lived with your aunt, then where did you live after the trial? What happened after the trial?"

"I grew up and my mother's prophecy came true for the most part. Using my gift kept me apart from others. I couldn't hide it like she could. I've never met another psychic who can do what I do. They see what I see and know the emotion that goes with it, but I actually take on the vision and the emotion. It's hard to explain. They don't necessarily control what they do. I can to some extent. I can usually figure out what someone is thinking. In some instances, I can get into their heads."

"Like Tyler. He said you left his mind."

"Tyler is a special case. He and I became connected in a way even I can't explain. When I say I can get into their heads, I mean I can hear what they're thinking. Telepathy."

"So where did you grow up?"

"Here and there." At Sam's raised eyebrow, she gave in and elaborated. "When I left, I didn't really have a destination in mind. I took the money my mother hid away from my father. I boarded a bus and headed out of West

Virginia. I didn't want to wait around to see if the town folk resurrected the witch trials."

She stared off into the distance and remembered what it felt like to be young and scared. Nobody had ever understood her. Or even tried. Except her mother, and she was gone.

"I went to Atlanta. It didn't take long to figure out libraries are a great place to hang out. Churches are another safe and quiet place. People usually stay to themselves and you have a roof over your head. Some libraries are open seven days a week. Churches have long hours and lots of places to hide and catch some sleep."

"You've been on your own since you were twelve?"

"Yes. That's not to say that I didn't have some help along the way. A nun took a special interest in me. She helped me get my GED. Like I said, libraries are great places to hang out. I like to read, and I'm great on a computer. I studied for the GED and got it at seventeen. The nun hooked me up with a homeless shelter. I'd help out there in exchange for a bed. I'd go to street fairs and flea markets, set up a sign and a chair, and I'd give psychic readings for two dollars. I saved my money. I wanted to go to college, but I wasn't eighteen, I was hiding from my father and his lawyer, and I didn't have any money, a home, or any idea how to go about getting a school to accept me without transcripts.

"I like to read the newspaper. The financial section interested me, but I didn't know anything about stocks. I studied how people bought and sold them. I learned how to read a financial report and determine if a company was doing well or falling short. I came across several articles about people who bought and sold stocks as day traders. I studied and decided if they could do it, why couldn't I. All I needed was an account and a computer. Again, the library supplied the computer, and I set up an account at a local bank office and went online."

"So, how'd you do?"

"I paid cash for this house and land. What do you think?"

Sam looked around the house again and had new admiration for her. She had raised herself and managed to educate herself well enough to succeed in a field that most people didn't really understand, unless they had a financial advisor or their company's 401(k) plan.

"Do you pick the stocks based on a vision?"

"No, not really. That's a complicated question to answer. I do a lot of research on the company I'm going to buy. I have a kind of checklist of things I look for in a stock. Then there's the instinct factor. If it's a new company, I sometimes have a sense whether the company will do well or not. I've been wrong a time or two, but for the most part, between research and instinct, I've managed to make a good income. I have a place of my own now, and I can work from home."

"So, when you met Tyler in that restaurant, where were you living?"

"At that time, no place in particular. That was just a chance meeting. Something about him called to me. When I saw what might happen to his sister, I had to tell him. His life wouldn't have been the same. Your lives wouldn't have been the same."

"Why?"

"Because he would have burned out of the FBI after becoming disillusioned from his sister's death. He wouldn't have been there to help you with Elizabeth's case. That could have changed the events that happened. You might not have met Elizabeth and that was meant to be. Wouldn't you agree?"

Sam couldn't deny it. He nodded his acknowledgement.

Sam rubbed the back of his neck and tried to assimilate everything he'd learned. "Tyler is part of the reason I wanted to find you. He's headed down a road that will leave him unhappy. We can all see the train wreck coming and he insists on taking the train."

Sam watched for a reaction, something that would indicate how she really felt about Tyler. She didn't give anything away.

"He's doing what he thinks will make him happy. He's got his mind set on what he wants. He's determined to get it no matter what it takes, or who gets hurt. She's not for him. She knows it, too. They're both going down a path they shouldn't. Neither of them is willing to admit that being without the other would be a better choice than staying together and being miserable. Misery loves company, after all."

"If she's not for him, are you?"

"I don't know. Tyler and I have a connection to each other that runs deep. We're destined to cross paths again. That will happen very soon."

"It started with the press conference. It kicked everything off. Your name went out to the masses and this guy started killing people. Plus, your father contacted Tyler. He's trying to find you. He's been out of jail for a while. He's made it clear you're a priority. I've been trying to find you and warn you."

When she didn't say anything, Sam asked the one question that nagged at him. "Why did saying your name with Tyler's spark all this?"

"My father wants a reckoning. At least, that's how he looks at it. He feels I owe him the time he's lost. If I'd helped him, he wouldn't have done what he did. He's spent the last twelve years convincing himself I owe him. Jack and I have talked about this before. It's about life and time and events."

Whenever Jack saw her, their conversation and what she'd told him was never far from his mind. "You're talking about someone in the family being hurt. When you meet up with Tyler again, something will happen to someone in the family, and you'll stop it. It's more than that though. All of these events are connected."

Sam leaned in, ready to demand she explain.

Jack shook his head. "Don't even try it. She won't tell us who might be hurt, or what's going to happen. It could change what she sees if she does."

"What do you mean change it?"

Explaining herself and what she did was really time-consuming and frustrating.

"Sometimes, I can see future events. I've seen something happen, and I can intervene. The event will only happen the way I saw it if everything leading up to the event remains the same. Changing something could change the event, and then I won't be able to stop what happens. In this case, I've managed to keep the events lined up, so that I can intervene."

"Tell me how the press conference fits into this. You were upset about it," Sam said.

"There are several events tied together. If the press conference happened, then I know something else is going to happen. I'm brought to San Francisco for another event and that will lead to yet another event. Change one, and change them all. I can't risk one of the events, so I have to go along with the others."

"You can't risk the person who's set to be hurt," Jack said.

"No. I can't risk that." She smiled at him softly to reassure him. "There are several ways things could have gone. All I can tell you is that if my name hadn't been mentioned in the press conference, you wouldn't have the murders you do now. Also, the events that happen because of the murders wouldn't happen. I'd still be coming to San Francisco for a couple of reasons, but now those reasons are tied to the murders, too."

Confused, Sam's mind couldn't keep track of this event, that event, or the fact that they could happen or not. "You're talking in circles. So, if your name hadn't gone out to the press, the murders wouldn't have happened. Tyler won't like hearing that."

"So, don't tell him. He doesn't need to know in order to do his job. Besides, he didn't put my name out there. He did what he had to do to stop the men kidnapping women and using them as prostitutes."

"He already has an idea that it's because of him. The killer left Tyler a message. He's after you, Morgan."

"I know. I'll be his last victim."

The silence in the room was deafening. She didn't often get a glimpse of her own life. She could see other people's lives like movies in her mind, but not her own. Some kind of a cosmic safeguard. If she knew too much about her own future, then she'd spend too much time worrying about it rather than living her life for today. She'd had to learn that the hard way, through time and experience. She hadn't seen her mother's death coming until it was too late. If she had, she might have been able to stop it.

"I wanted to see you today to get you to stop focusing on finding me and get back to the case. I'll be there soon enough."

"When?"

"When the time is right."

Jack felt for Sam. "Don't even try to get her to tell you more. She's stubborn."

"I'm not stubborn. I can't jeopardize the vision I had. If we change the future, and I don't have another vision to tell me where to go, then I might not stop what happens to your family member. No one wants that."

"Help me with the case. Give me something to work with, because right now we don't have anything."

"You're looking for a man with thinning light brown hair. He's about five-foot-five, very thin, and deceptively strong. He works with his hands fixing some kind of machines. I think they're copy and fax machines. That won't help you though. He's good with computers and uses them to connect with people because he's not very good at talking to people one-on-one. He's a loner. He lives in an apartment that's cheap and shabby. The furnishings are old, but he likes them because they're his. There's something about that I'm missing. It's like I should know something connected to his sense of being on his own and having his own things. He has a sense of being independent and not answering to anyone. He's thirty-seven, so that doesn't make a lot of sense at this time in his life." She shrugged her shoulders. She could only explain what she knew.

"He uses a double-edged butterfly knife. You know the kind that people in movies flip around with their wrist and the blade is revealed. He likes it because it makes him feel like he's stronger and meaner looking than he is."

"Is there anything else, physically about him?"

"He wears glasses with dark rims. Brown eyes, pale skin, like he spends his time indoors a lot. His face is ordinary. His appearance is ordinary. He's the guy next door, who never got the girl, or played sports. He's coasted through life under the radar because he doesn't let anyone close, and he doesn't put himself out there. He thinks others don't understand him. Everyone else has what he wants. He feels like he's been held back. I don't know what it means, but when I see him, there's a great weight on him. Something is over him and holding him down. I think the weight is his conscience. He either feels guilty for the murders, or something from his past."

"Anything else."

For the first time, she noticed he'd taken out a small notebook and scribbled notes of everything she said. She'd never talked to him about the other cases. She'd kept her distance from him and Tyler on purpose. She found it comforting to see Sam taking his notes, completely focused on her. He believed everything she said. He had no doubts, reassuring her he'd do his best to put her information to good use.

"After he's killed each of his victims, I see a phonebook open on a scarred and stained coffee table. He lines out the name or ad for the person he's killed."

"You can see the name of the person he's going to kill?"

"No. I haven't actually seen any of the murders. I've only seen the phonebook. I think he commits the crime and goes home and lines out the name."

"He's not going in order. The victims aren't in alphabetical order." Sam took a moment to think about the store names. They weren't in order either. "Do you know what makes him choose his victim? Is there a reason for the order?"

She sat for a moment and settled her mind and opened herself to the question. Nothing came. This case had been the most difficult for her to get anything on because it was too close to her.

"I don't know."

"Anything else you can tell me?"

"He won't stop until all the names are marked off, or I get in his way."

"Will you get in his way?" Sam didn't know if he wanted her to say yes or no. He didn't want to risk her.

"It's inevitable."

He hated hearing that ominous prediction.

"I'll help you along the way. In the meantime, you have to do something. I don't think he'll stop, but it will make him pause and reassess what he's doing. Then, he'll make a choice."

"What choice?"

"To keep killing or stop."

"You don't think he'll stop though?" Sam said, doubtful.

"No, but it'll make him stop for a little while and that will allow time for other things to happen."

Sam looked at Jack for support. Jack shrugged and swallowed another bite of his brownie.

"She's only going to tell you what you need to know, and not enough for you to change anything. Get used to it."

"It's nice that you understand me, Jack," Morgan said, grinning.

"I'm trying."

"I'm trying, too. You aren't what I expected," Sam said with a sigh.

"No? What did you expect?"

"Someone weird. I've spent the last several weeks talking to a lot of psychics in San Francisco. They're weird. They talk about what they do in all kinds of mystical and metaphysical terms. Energy, vibrations, chakras, and whatever else they come up with. It all sounded so excessive. Not a single one of them sounded credible. Between their bizarre outfits and their dramatics, I had a hard time taking any of them seriously.

"You don't need any of that," Sam continued. "Either I believe you, or I don't. What you see and know is what you see and know. I met a couple people who I think had some psychic ability. Nothing like you, though."

"Thanks. I'm glad I'm not weird and you like my clothes."

He laughed. "Come to San Francisco with me. Help me with this case."

"Not yet. First, you need to have a story printed in the paper stating the FBI has contacted me and I don't know anything about the murders. I haven't seen anything. And specifically, I can't give you any information about the man. That part has to be stated as clearly as possible. This started with the press conference and the guy thinking I can ID him. Let's tell him I can't."

"Do you have a story ready?"

"No. I figured you'd take care of it."

"You could use the paper Jenna owns," Jack said. "The one we had make up the fake newspaper about her ex-husband. I think she still owns it. That way you can control what gets printed. It'll give the paper an exclusive, which will boost sales, and Jenna will love that."

"Good thinking. There's no telling what another paper will print, even if I write the article. This way we can be sure."

"Is there anything else?" Sam asked Morgan.

"No. That should do it for now. I'll contact you if I have more."

"Please tell me you're going to do something about Tyler and the woman he's seeing. He shouldn't be with her. You said it yourself.

"He's in love with you, you know. Hell, you probably don't. He doesn't even know it."

"Tyler's going to do what Tyler's going to do. He's got his mind set. I don't know if anything will change it."

He'd resisted his connection with her for so long, she had to accept that maybe he didn't want anything do with her ever again.

"Come to San Francisco. One look at you, and he'll change his mind."

True or not, she appreciated the kind compliment. She'd had too many people ridicule her.

"I'll be in San Francisco soon. Not to stop Tyler from seeing the woman, but for something else. That's all I can tell you."

Chapter Fourteen

TYLER SAT AT his desk doing one of the things he hated most—never-ending paperwork. He'd gone to the autopsy yesterday and hated to admit Sam was right. He couldn't look at the deceased and not think of Morgan. It could have been her. The killer had left him a message making it clear she was his ultimate target. It put a lead bowling ball in his gut that wouldn't go away. The urgency to find her and make sure she was safe intensified.

He'd spent hours going over the reports Sam had compiled on the case. Each murder another gruesome scene.

Four murders. Four psychics. Four women. Any one of them could have been Morgan.

It all started with the press conference. Before, actually. He'd set the ball in motion when he'd opened his mouth to Detective Stewart. It all started with him.

The only consolation, every psychic in the city bombarded Detective Stewart with a description and a vision they needed to share with him. Not a single one of them gave a similar description or shared the same information twice. Ninety percent of them were way out there. The other ten percent were scared to death they'd be next. Most of them said they saw a vision of the man coming for them and they wanted police protection. The police had stepped up patrols in the areas where psychic shops were located and in the neighborhoods where known psychics lived.

They were protecting people from a man they couldn't identify and had absolutely no leads. They couldn't even determine if they had his fingerprints. Every scene had multiple prints to sort and run through the system, hoping this guy was a repeat offender. He hadn't left any DNA. No hair, or blood, except for the victim's.

The press was going nuts over the case. The Psychic Slayer, Tyler thought, disgusted. Every newspaper in the city carried a story about the murders and made assumptions that in some way they were tied to Morgan, the FBI's secret weapon against criminals. Like she was some kind of superhero. She was just a woman. Okay, she was a special woman.

Sam came by and dropped a newspaper on his desk. The headline threw him for a loop.

FBI PSYCHIC BLIND TO PSYCHIC SLAYER

"What's this?"

"A little something I had printed last night and put out to the public this morning."

"I thought you were in Colorado last night."

"I was. How'd the autopsy go? Any new information?"

"Nothing. The coroner determined cause of death as strangulation, said the killer cut out her tongue postmortem and the glue used on her eyes was consistent with the other murder victims."

Tyler scanned the article. "Um, why did you have this story printed? It says Morgan has been in constant contact with the FBI, and she can't give us any information about this case. It says she hasn't had any visions about the murders, and she can't use her abilities at will. 'Inside sources at the FBI discredit her ability to provide accurate information on the cases that she contacts us about, despite claims by the San Francisco Police Department.'" He continued reading the article and the more he read the angrier he got. "This thing makes her sound like a complete joke, like we don't take what she says seriously. It makes it sound like she sometimes gets lucky based on public information. They made her look like a hoax."

"You think so?"

"Haven't you read this?"

"I wrote it," Sam said, sorting through the messages on his desk.

"Excuse me?" Tyler stood and faced Sam, angry Sam would do anything to hurt Morgan.

"It's exactly what she wanted it to say. It helped that Jenna owns the paper. A simple phone call, and I'm page one. Not bad, if I do say so myself."

"What exactly do you mean, it's what she wanted it to say? Have you spoken to Morgan?"

Sam wasn't ready to spill the beans completely. Morgan hadn't said anything about him keeping their meeting a secret. In fact, she knew Tyler would find out because of the article. Inevitable, some things couldn't be avoided.

"What'd you do last night?"

With a heavy sigh, Tyler answered, "Maria came over. We had a late dinner and caught a movie on TV. Why?"

"Did you tell her about your day yesterday? I imagine you were pretty upset after the autopsy and hearing those messages about Morgan. You must have liked going home to someone you could unload on. I know I took off on you yesterday, but you pissed me off, avoiding me for the better part of two weeks."

"I'm sorry about that. I just needed to step away for a while. Had I known this involved Morgan, I'd have called you back immediately."

"What does Maria think of all this mess?"

"We didn't talk about it. She prefers I leave my work at work."

He thought about that and last night. It was nice to have someone to share a meal with instead of eating alone. He couldn't remember half of the movie they watched. His mind had been on work and Morgan. He kept going over all the information and each time Maria laughed at something in the movie, he'd had to pull himself back, so she wouldn't catch him not paying attention.

He took her to bed, hoping for sex and a nice distraction from the case, but Maria fell asleep on her side of the bed. Truth be told, he let her because what he'd really wanted was not to be alone. He'd spent most of the night staring at the ceiling frustrated about the case, his relationships with women, everything in his life, and Morgan's continued absence.

"It makes me feel better talking to Elizabeth after a bad day."

Tyler didn't want to hear about Sam and Elizabeth and their great marriage. He and Maria had a good night together. He was satisfied with that. He'd only been up thinking about Morgan part of the time. His mind was on the case and she was part of it. Only natural he'd think about her.

He'd known her for more than five years. Missing her was natural, too.

"Tell me about the article. Why did you write and publish that Morgan can't help us with the case?"

"Because she asked me to."

"You talked to her. She called you."

"Yes. No."

"What?"

"Yes, I talked to her, and no, she didn't call me."

"Then, how did you talk to her?"

"I went to see her. Let me tell you, man. If I weren't married, I'd still be at her place right now begging her to keep me as her slave. That woman is gorgeous."

"You saw her. You spoke to her in person. Where? When?" Tyler fell into his chair, reeling.

"You're stuttering, man. I saw her yesterday. It's why I left. She wanted to see me in person. She had some things to tell me, and she wanted to do it face-to-face."

She didn't call him. After five years, he'd let her down so badly she didn't even want to see him. She'd rather see Sam.

"I thought you were going to see Jack."

"I did. She contacted him and he called me and told me to come."

"So you met her at the ranch. She went there to find Jack?"

"No. Jack and I are the only people who know where she lives. Actually, Jack's known for quite some time."

"Why didn't he tell us where she is?" The knot in his stomach drew tight. He fisted his hands, furious Jack would keep this from him.

"Because she asked him not to. She lives alone. She has since she was about thirteen. She's lived on the streets, in shelters, taken refuge in churches, libraries, anywhere she could find a safe place. She has a house now. She's worked really hard to make a place for herself away from everyone. She's alone, Tyler. Completely, one hundred percent alone. Jack is the only person she's seen in years. I gave her a hug and she held on to me like I was the only person who was ever nice to her in her whole life."

Sam waited a beat and let that sink in with Tyler.

"She has a sister, you know. She won't even see Morgan, or speak to her. She thinks she has the family curse. She thinks Morgan's insane—cuckoo," Sam said, and circled his finger in the air by his temple. "She thinks Morgan hears voices, and they tell her what to do. Can you believe that?

"She ran away after the trial. Her father wanted to

have her committed, so he'd know where to find her when he got out, so he can kill her."

"Why are you telling me all of this?" Tyler asked, annoyed.

"Why? Because that woman has only had you in her life for the last five years. You have been her sole connection to the world. Without you, no one would even know she exists. Well, no one who actually cared she existed. Her father wants her dead, her sister doesn't want anything to do with her, and you used her. She's reached out to you the only way she knew how after spending the majority of her life alone, and you turned your back on her."

"She left *me* the day of the press conference."

"That's right, *she* left *you*. You were never with her. There's the difference. When are you going to realize that and stop being angry with her?"

"I'm not angry with her."

"Now you're just lying. It pisses you off that she left. It pisses you off that you don't know where she is. It pisses you off to know I spent a couple of hours with her yesterday. It pisses you off that you care."

"Why didn't she call me?"

Sam shook his head. "Why would she? You've moved on with your life. You have Maria. You think she doesn't know that. You think she left you that day. She did, but then she tried to reconnect with you. She's tried so many times she's actually made herself sick a few times. You won't let her back in. You're the one keeping her away. She said sometimes she catches a glimpse of you when you're asleep and your guard goes down. She said it's like you sense her there and you lock her out again. She took the hint. You don't want her in your head, or in your life. You've decided what it is you want. She actually said, 'Tyler's going to do what Tyler's going to do.' She knows you very well."

Tyler stared at his cubicle wall, absorbing Sam's words and what they meant. Quiet. Everything about him went still.

"She gave me a description of the guy we're looking for." He handed Tyler his notes.

"Five-foot-five. Brown, thinning hair. Brown eyes. Wears glasses with dark rims. Pale skin. Wiry build. Deceptively strong. Thirty-seven. He's a loner. He probably works fixing copiers and fax machines. This could be anyone," he said in frustration.

"She said he uses a double-edged butterfly knife to kill his victims. Oh yeah, and then he goes home and lines out their name in the phonebook that's lying on his old junky coffee table."

"She sees the name before he kills the woman?"

"I thought that's what she meant, but no. Without her connection to you, she didn't know anything about the case until Jack filled her in the other day."

"Then why the article in the paper?"

"She wants some time. She said if I put the article out there, the guy would stop killing for a little while. It'll give us time to investigate the four murders without a new one happening."

"Did she say how long before he kills again?"

"No. She only said it would make him stop and think

about what he's doing. If he believes she can ID him, the article will tell him she can't and there's a chance he'll stop."

"She doesn't think so, though."

"No. She doesn't. Some other things are meant to happen and this will give her time for those things to take place."

"What events?"

"Yeah, if you can get her to tell you that, then you're better than me. I grilled her. She won't tell me everything she knows because it could change another event. Something to do with stopping something from happening. She basically said that if something in the other events changes, then this event could change, and she won't be able to stop someone from getting hurt."

"Who?"

"Someone in the family."

"Whose family? Yours?"

"I don't know. She thinks of all of us as a family. You, me, Elizabeth and Grace, Summer, Caleb and the kids, Jack, Jenna and the kids, Cameron, Marti, and Emma. To her, we are one family. It makes sense. Our lives are all tied together."

Tyler felt the same way. "So, someone in our family is going to be hurt, and she thinks she can stop it from happening. How?"

"Hell if I know. She might be beautiful and have an extraordinary gift, but under it all she's a woman, and she can be downright frustrating and stubborn."

"What else did you guys talk about?"

"We talked about how she grew up, her father killing her mother, and how she survived on her own. We talked about how she does what she does and the effect it has on her and her life. We talked about what she does for a living. We talked about her garden, things like that."

"You talked about her garden," Tyler said, surprised.

"Yeah, she says there are fairies living in her lilies. I think she was kidding, but then, who knows." He kept a serious face in place until Tyler scowled. Then he busted up laughing.

"She's just a normal person, who's not at all normal. I can't explain it. We sat at her dining room table drinking iced tea and eating brownies. Jack and I are the first people to ever sit at her table with her. You know how the ranch is isolated. Mostly that's because it's so big and there's all that land surrounding it. Well, Morgan's place is like that, too. Isolated. She doesn't have to see anyone if she doesn't want to. Sure, she goes to the store and does her shopping like everyone else, but she stays at her place most of the time. She works from home. Being around other people is hard for her because of her gift. She likes Jack because he's happy. It makes her happy to be around him. I'll tell you, man, she's had a hard life. Her mother warned her that if she used her gift in the open, she'd be alone. She was right. Right now, Morgan is as alone as it gets."

That hurt Tyler more than anything in the world could. How many times had she reminded him he wasn't alone? Not once had he reminded her that neither was she. He was with her just as much as she'd been with him.

That wasn't exactly true. Sam was right. He'd used her. It didn't make him feel good to realize it, especially when it was too late. She'd called Sam, not him. She'd seen Sam and confided things to him that they'd never talked about together. Well, she'd refused to tell him, but not Sam. He knew some things about how she saw the things she did, but Sam knew a lot more. He had a million questions he'd like to ask Sam. He wouldn't though. After five years, one stupid mistake, and being a heartless bastard to her, he didn't have the right to ask.

Sam had laid a heavy guilt trip on Tyler. He didn't really care if it got Tyler to wake up and take a look at what a mess he made of his life. His silence spoke more clearly than anything he could have said. Tyler gave up on Morgan and thought Maria was the answer. Too bad she was the wrong answer for Tyler.

He waited to see if Tyler would ask where she lived, or if he had her phone number. He did and could call her right now. He could send her an email. One word from Tyler and he'd do it. Tyler sat with his elbow propped on the arm of his chair and his thumb and index finger pressed to his bottom lip.

Sam gave up. He couldn't make Tyler get together with Morgan.

He and Tyler were better off working right now than discussing anything personal.

"So, we have some new information to work with. We'll have to keep it under wraps about how we got the information, since I've just let the world know Morgan can't help us. I'm sure we'll get a call from Detective Stewart this morning. That should be fun. I think we need to see if there's a connection or pattern to how he chooses the names from the phonebook."

"Did she say there was a connection or a reason for the order?"

She. He couldn't even say her name now. "*She* said she doesn't know. She tried to see, but didn't get anything. I think we need to get a phonebook and take a look at the page he's looking at. Maybe something will jump out at us. She can't see anything specific in the book, all she sees is that he uses a pen to line out the name or ad."

"Does she have any idea how many victims we're going to have?"

"She didn't say. She only said that she'd be his last."

Sam's last statement struck home, deep into his heart. Tyler had enough. He rubbed both hands over his face and leaned as far back in his chair as it would go. Then he picked up his pencil and threw it so hard at his bulletin board it stuck a half inch inside.

Chapter Fifteen

SATURDAY NIGHT, THE restaurant was especially busy. Tyler kept a firm grip on Maria's arm as they made their way toward the large table at the back of the room. The entire family would be together tonight for Marti and Cameron's baby shower. Marti was due to deliver their first baby in a few weeks. It had been too long since they'd all congregated as one group. He looked forward to seeing everyone, but his mind remained on work, the case, and the haunting thoughts of Morgan becoming the Psychic Slayer's last victim.

Over his dead body.

Emma remained on his mind. He'd taken her out for dinner and a movie a few nights ago. Cameron and Marti were worried about her health. She didn't eat well and slept even less. She dogged Marti's heels constantly, afraid she'd die because of the baby. Her own mother had died after giving birth to her, and she was scared the same thing would happen to her stepmother. She loved Marti like her own, real mother. Understandable the little girl was anxious, but Emma's health worried everyone.

He spotted the group sitting and standing around the table. He and Maria were the last to arrive. He and Sam had been going nonstop on the case since Sam returned from seeing Morgan two weeks ago. Maria saved his sanity, staying at his place most nights. He came home to dinner and company. He never got home at a decent time, but she'd adjusted, and they were in synch. Exhausted from working long hours and worrying about Morgan, he fell into bed and passed out, grateful he didn't sleep alone.

After Morgan left him and he'd set his mind to building his relationship with Maria, he'd bought her a ring. He'd thought to propose while they were on vacation in Hawaii. Every time he thought the timing and setting were perfect, something stopped him. When they returned home, he'd never found the right moment.

Maria had become a real part of his everyday life these last weeks. What was he waiting for?

He planned to ask her to marry him after dinner tonight. He showed the ring to Sam yesterday. Sam offered his congratulations, even though he thought it a mistake. Tyler knew what he wanted. A wife and children. Pretty soon, he'd have them. Well, they'd have children if he got his mind off the case and mustered up the energy to make love to her.

Maria seemed happy about the marriage idea. They'd

discussed it briefly. Her family wanted to see her married and settled, especially her father.

He'd met her parents. They were nice people and certainly approved of him. After all, he had a good job and would provide well for a family. That seemed to be their qualifications for their daughter's future husband. Her father seemed to disapprove of her working and living on her own. Tyler found that old-fashioned for the times, but Maria seemed eager to please her father and gain his approval. She'd practically put Tyler up on a pedestal, gushing about his job and accomplishments, making him uncomfortable, but he appreciated the compliments.

Tyler spotted Sam and Jack standing together, each drinking a beer. The twin brothers leaned into each other to say something confidentially. Tyler hoped they weren't talking about him and Maria. He wanted Maria to feel welcome.

Jack whispered into Sam's ear, "I thought you said she was coming."

"I talked to her yesterday after he showed me the ring. She said she'd be here. In fact, she already had her ticket."

"I could have sent the jet for her," Jack said and took another sip of his beer.

"It's fine. She'll be here," Sam said adamantly.

"I thought Cameron was stubborn when he wanted to marry that horrible woman who faked being pregnant with his baby. Tyler might take the cake for stubbornness if he asks Maria to marry him. She's nice enough, but she isn't for him."

"Once he sees Morgan in person, he won't go through with it."

"I hope you're right," Jack said and took another sip of his beer.

Cameron joined Sam and Jack. "What're you two whispering about?"

"Tyler and Maria. They just arrived," Sam said and tilted his beer in their direction.

"She's nice," Cameron said and glanced at the couple. "She came with Tyler to pick up Emma for dinner the other night. She didn't say much. I wouldn't peg her as Tyler's type, though. I thought he had a thing for his psychic ghost."

"He does. He just doesn't want to admit it. He won't have a choice tonight. Morgan's coming."

"You're kidding me." Cameron couldn't wait to meet Morgan. As president of Merrick International, he worked with Jack's wife, Jenna. He heard all kinds of stories from her about Tyler and his psychic ghost. What he didn't hear from Jenna, he got firsthand from Sam and Tyler. The woman was intriguing if nothing else.

Cameron had spent the last several weeks worried about his wife and daughter, Emma. He hoped tonight would bring some fun into their lives and all the gifts would make Emma interested in the baby and less fixated and concerned about the birth.

"I talked to Morgan yesterday," Sam said. "I told her we'd be here. Don't tell anyone else. I don't want Tyler to overhear. Here he comes."

They all greeted each other and spent time talking

and catching up. The children grew restless, so the menus were opened, the orders placed, and dinner served. They enjoyed their meal and each other's company. Everyone included Maria in the conversation. They added to the cacophony of the restaurant, and Tyler relaxed into the evening like he hadn't done in a long time. Seated next to Sam, who sat next to Jack, he noticed the two men look down the aisle and simply stare. Then he heard Sam say, "She's here."

More beautiful than Tyler remembered. He'd only seen her once and even that time had only been for a few minutes. Five years ago, her hair had hung down her back in a long braid. She'd worn old jeans and a well-worn navy blue T-shirt. Radiant tonight with her hair unbound. The thick mass waved over her shoulders and down her back. Lovely, it seemed to glow. Tall and slender, her white flowing blouse and blue floral skirt hugged her curves in all the right places.

Her eyes caught him off guard. Blue as the Colorado sky. They looked softly upon him and made him want. She simply took his breath away.

Five years spent talking on the phone and in his mind and she'd left him, only to come back into his life to torture him in person.

He wanted to grab her. To shake her and ask her why she'd come back tonight. After all this time, she'd returned on the night he planned to ask another woman to marry him, when all he wanted to do was take Morgan to his bed. His emotions were everywhere. Angry she'd left, happy to see her, he wanted to strangle her for calling

Sam and not him about the case. He wanted to beg her to stay and alternately push her away, so he could have the life he'd been carefully working toward with Maria.

She messed up his mind, and she wasn't even inside it anymore.

Morgan took a step back. So many emotions ran through her and came from the people in the restaurant and this group in particular. Her carefully constructed walls blocked out a lot, but with so much coming at her, they cracked.

Seeing Tyler rocked her.

The sadness hit Morgan hard. She couldn't feel anything but anger from Tyler. His dark eyes simply stared at her, no light in them. No joy at seeing her. It hurt to think that after all these years he'd completely closed her out of his life.

She knew why. The pretty woman sitting next to him radiated nice. The exact opposite in appearance as Morgan. Dark hair and eyes, her skin a lovely olive brown. She had a pretty figure and showed as little of it off as possible in her demure green dress. The dress color did show off her lovely skin tone, though.

Compared to Jenna, Elizabeth, and Marti, she felt like an ugly duckling. Tyler's girlfriend fit in far better than she, or so she thought.

She weaved her way to the table and stood behind Jack's wife, Jenna.

"Is it going to happen tonight? The event you warned me about. Who's going to be hurt? Can we stop it?" Jack asked in rapid-fire succession.

"Jack, who is this? Why are you so upset?" Jenna didn't like seeing her husband's distress.

Tyler answered the question for everyone by simply saying her name: "Morgan."

Morgan finally came to her senses and answered Jack's overflowing concern and urgency. "Jack, sit down. Everything is fine. We have some time. I came here for another reason."

Sam smiled and she directed her next statement to him. "He is not going to thank you for this."

Sam leaned forward in his chair. "It has to be done." She knew it, he knew it, and everyone at the table knew it. Even Tyler knew it. He just didn't want to admit it.

"Morgan. I'm Elizabeth, Sam's wife. You're the psychic ghost we've been hearing about for years. What brings you here tonight? It seems you and my husband have something cooked up."

"I came for a few reasons, actually." She should acknowledge all of the family members in some way. As much as she knew about them, in actuality, they'd never met. "It's nice to meet Tyler's family. I feel like I know all of you through him."

Tyler felt that one stab him right in the heart. She did know a lot about them because of him. He'd talked about them often, and she learned a lot more when they'd been connected mentally. He didn't know anything about her family, at least nothing he hadn't learned from Sam or the reports about her mother's death.

Emma liked the new person. Pretty, she had long

golden hair, longer than her own. It looked soft. "Are you really a ghost?"

Morgan stared across the table and focused on the tired, sickly looking little girl. No wonder they were all worried about her. The picture she had in her mind of the happy and laughing girl was missing tonight. This version of Emma wasn't a good one, and Morgan silently vowed to fix that right now.

"No, sweetheart. I'm not a ghost. I guess you could say I'm more like a witch. I have a special gift. And the reason I came today is to show *you* that gift. Would you like me to show you?"

Emma nodded. "I've never met a witch."

"Don't worry, I'm not a bad witch."

"That's what I was just thinking," she shrieked.

Morgan laughed and walked around the large oblong table toward the little girl. All the while, Tyler watched her every move.

"How come when I look at you I see a ladybug with a tiara of rubies on her head and sugar raining down on you? I have to say you make the most interesting and whimsical picture to me."

"Mommy calls me Sugar Bug and Daddy calls me Princess. I have a ruby necklace that I wear on my head sometimes. Mommy has an emerald one."

Marti and Cameron exchanged a shocked look.

"Well that explains her tiara when I look at her."

"What do you see when you look at her?" Emma liked this fun game, especially since everyone at the table watched her and the witch. Even her cousins, Matt and Sam, stared at her.

Morgan turned to Marti. At least eight months pregnant, if not more, she simply glowed. The image that came to mind was as unique as the woman. "I see a woman dressed like a pirate. She has a paintbrush instead of a sword, and an emerald tiara, like you said."

"Mommy's Daddy's pirate princess. She has a pirate ship."

"And the paintbrush?" Morgan asked.

Marti answered for her daughter. "I'm a painter and the granddaughter of a famous painter. Sophia Fairchild is my grandmother."

Morgan smiled and nodded. She liked this. She didn't often use her gift with people in person. It made her feel good to have the results confirmed. It offset the anger she felt rising in Tyler.

Emma didn't want the game to end. She took a handful of Morgan's long hair. She continued holding fistfuls of it and running her fingers through it. Morgan felt the little ripples of pleasure from Emma as she stroked the length of her hair. It felt good to be touched with such reverence. The golden locks fascinated the little girl.

"Do Daddy next."

Morgan laughed again, catching the little girl's contagious enthusiasm. "He's easy. He's a knight who slays corporate dragons with a gold Mont Blanc pen."

Cameron took the pen out of his pocket and held it up

to her. He simply nodded his agreement and flashed his mischievous grin.

"Do Aunt Jenna and Uncle Jack."

"Uncle Jack is another easy one. He's a cowboy with a heart the size of Texas. Jenna is a rabbit turned lioness. She loves her cubs and chews up whatever gazelle happens into her corporate den. Especially when that gazelle is an ex-husband. The hunted became the hunter."

Jenna held up her glass in salute to Morgan.

"Uncle Sam and Aunt Elizabeth next," Emma pleaded.

Morgan's gaze softened on Elizabeth. "I have never met anyone who is loved so deeply by their family and husband. When I look at you, I see a giant heart covered in chocolate."

Elizabeth mimicked Jenna's action and saluted Morgan with her water glass.

"Sam is as easy as Jack. They are the same in that they both have big hearts and care deeply for their family. While Jack is a cowboy in the truest sense, Sam is a cowboy with a badge. He looks like a marshal from the West to me. Little Matt and Sam are like their father and uncle."

"Now do Uncle Tyler."

Morgan ran her hand down the little girl's golden hair and looked into her hopeful eyes. She looked across the table at Tyler.

"Do you know the movie *Beauty and the Beast*, Sugar Bug?"

Emma liked it when she called her by her nickname.

"I know it. I like that one. The Beast isn't very happy, and he's kind of mean to Belle."

"That's what Uncle Tyler looks like to me. He's not happy I'm here."

Tyler didn't know what to say. She thought he was unhappy and mean. Great. He wondered what else she thought of him these days, but kept his mouth shut. He didn't have to ask though. Maria helped him out.

"That's very impressive. You got them all right as far as I can tell. I'm Maria, Tyler's girlfriend. I'm afraid I don't know much about you, except that you work with him at the FBI. Would you be willing to do me next? I have to admit, I'm fascinated."

Maria didn't point out being Tyler's girlfriend to stake a claim, or throw it in Morgan's face. She'd simply stated her own truth.

Morgan looked at Tyler to see what he thought. Still, that impassive expression and ever-present anger. Interestingly enough, she felt his fear. Then came the flash of a ring in his pocket. He truly intended to ask this woman to marry him. It would be the biggest mistake of his life. She couldn't change his mind, but she could enlighten him to his options.

"All right, Maria. It's nice to meet you, by the way."

"And you," Maria said and gave her a warm smile, making it that much more difficult for Morgan not to like her because she had a place in Tyler's life Morgan wished belonged to her.

"If you don't mind, I'll finish with Tyler first."

She looked at Sam and said, "This is going to go very badly."

"It has to be done," Sam responded, earning a glare from Tyler. Sam sat in a prime spot for Tyler to elbow him right in the face and break his nose. It'd be worth it if Tyler changed his mind about marrying Maria.

"Fine. It's part of the event, so let's go with it. Jack, so help me, be quiet."

Jack closed his mouth. He gestured with his glass of beer for her to continue.

"Emma, I told you when I look at Tyler I see the Beast. That's true because when I look at him I see an unhappy man who's trapped in a spell of his own making. He wants to have a wife and children like the rest of the couples at the table. He thinks he can't have that with a woman who is the love of his life because he thinks she doesn't exist. So, he's going down a path that will lead him to more unhappiness."

"Morgan . . ." Tyler tried to stop her.

"Let me finish," she coaxed. "The path you've chosen is the wrong path. Just like your sister took the wrong path once. You haven't even considered what that path will do to Maria.

"Maria, you asked me what I see when I look at you. I'll tell you. I see a woman who has spent her entire life trying to live up to the expectations of her father. I'm here to tell you that you will never make him happy. You already know that though. Going to the right school, getting the best grades, and having the right kind of job, suitable for a woman, hasn't made him happy. Marrying the right kind of man won't make him happy. Giving him grandchildren won't make him happy. He is destined to be who he is, and you have fallen into his trap. You have taken the wrong path in an attempt to gain approval from a man who will never give it.

"Would you like me to tell you what could be waiting for you down another path?"

At Maria's nod, she continued. "When I look at you, I see what could be. I see a lovely woman in a white lab coat with kittens on her shoulders and puppies at her feet. You have always wanted to be a veterinarian, and yet you never gave voice to that dream, or pursued it. You hide it away in the deepest part of your heart. You've been hiding that dream behind all the disappointment in your life. It is the treasure you take out and look at when you are the most down. It's still possible to make it a reality.

"Maria, that other path holds a love that will give you the acceptance you desire, but not from the man you've always sought it from.

"Tyler, don't you see. You are both headed down a road that neither of you particularly want. You want a wife and kids and you don't care if there isn't a deep love and passion with it, so long as you have the wife and kids. She wants acceptance from her family by marrying a suitable man and having children. Both of you look at the other and only see someone who fits the bill well enough to get them what they want and let the rest be damned. The only thing that will come of this is unhappiness."

Tyler couldn't believe she'd do this to him in front of everyone. His anger outweighed his patience. He couldn't let her be right, because then he'd have nothing left, not even Maria.

Sam and Elizabeth had both told him time and again they thought he belonged with Morgan. Looking at everyone at the table, he could see they all agreed with her. Not one of them believed he should marry Maria.

He pulled the ring box out of his pocket and held it up.

Maria's gaze locked on the ring, and she actually leaned away from it. She didn't want the ring. The last straw, he slammed the ring down in the center of the wide table and left it sitting between the two women in his life.

"Everyone here thinks this belongs to you."

Stunned by his rage, she took a step back.

"Morgan? Are you all right?" Sam asked.

She nodded yes, then leaned over the table and held the ring box under her hand and looked Tyler right in the eye.

"Take it. You've managed to ruin every relationship I've had in the last five years," he accused with barely controlled anger.

"You know, Tyler, this is only stones and metal. Without love, this symbol is meaningless. Look at the couples around you. You, of all people, should know that." She released the ring box on the table in front of him and stood tall next to Emma.

"Now, if you don't mind. I came here for a reason, and contrary to what you might think, you aren't it. Maria, my apologies if I've upset you. The veterinarian idea is blooming to life. Good for you."

She turned to Emma again and blocked out Tyler with supreme effort. Having him close was hard to block out.

"Now, Sugar Bug, the reason I came tonight is to see you about a certain baby. Your uncles, aunts, and your mommy and daddy are very concerned about you. You have a very big worry inside you."

"Are you really a witch?"

Big tears filled her eyes and Morgan felt the fear and sadness building inside of her. Morgan wiped the tears away and crouched in front of the little girl's chair.

"Some people call me a witch because I can do some special things that scare people."

"Like knowing all those things about everyone."

"Yes, honey, like that and other things. There's something very special I can do for you that will make all your worries go away. I can show you a picture of the future, and you won't have to worry anymore. Would you like that?"

"Yes. I guess so. Will it hurt?"

"It won't hurt you. I promise."

"Um, Morgan. Are you sure about this? How bad will this be for you?" Sam asked.

"Sam, can't you be quiet."

"How bad?"

"It'll be fine. Don't scare Emma." She turned to Marti. "I promise you, I will not hurt you, your baby, or Emma. I'd like to touch your stomach, and I'm going to touch Emma's hand. It won't hurt anyone. Do I have your permission?"

Marti looked to Cameron. He seemed torn between wanting to help his daughter and risking all of them. Cameron nodded his head in agreement and Marti nodded to Morgan.

"Okay, Sugar Bug. Now, I'm going to put my hand over your mommy's belly where the baby is sleeping. I'm going to hold your hand, and I want you to close your eyes. You'll see a picture in your mind, like a dream. It might seem scary at first, but I want you to concentrate on the picture of your mommy. Can you do that?"

Emma nodded and held out her hand. Cameron moved in close behind his daughter and watched Morgan with eagle eyes. If anything happened to his wife, daughter, or baby, Morgan would pay. She had no doubt.

"Here we go. Close your eyes."

Morgan put her hand on Marti's protruding belly and wrapped her fingers around Emma's hand.

"Keep your eyes closed, Emma. Here comes the picture."

Morgan made the connection and took Emma to the future image of Marti giving birth to the baby. She came in at the point the baby was placed on Marti's stomach. Cameron was beside her and they wore huge, happy smiles.

"I see them. Mommy had the baby. Ew, it's all gross and slimy."

"Keep watching, Sugar Bug."

The nurse took the baby across the room. Cleaned and wrapped, the nurse brought the baby back to Marti and Cameron.

"I see them. Daddy is by Mommy and the baby is so cute now. It's not crying anymore, it's sleeping."

Morgan took her hand from Emma and placed it on Cameron's cheek and gave him the last picture of him standing beside a tired but radiant Marti holding their child safe and sound.

"Oh my God."

Morgan broke the contact from Marti and Cameron and fell to her knees beside Emma's chair.

"Morgan, are you all right?" Sam asked after she dropped.

"It's fine, Sam."

"Sugar Bug, your Mommy is going to give birth to a beautiful baby, and she will be fine. You saw her. You have no need to worry. Okay?"

"Okay," Emma said and bounced up and down on her chair. She looked at all the amazed faces at the table. "I saw the baby born. It was yucky, but then the baby was so cute when it was sleeping with Mommy. It's okay. I saw it. Mommy didn't die."

Cameron looked at Marti and felt all of his worries vanish. "I saw the baby and you. You were both fine."

Marti put a hand on Morgan's shoulder. "Thank you. I can't tell you what a relief it is to have their worries taken away."

Morgan put her hand over Marti's. "She knows something about the baby that you don't. She can tell you if you want to know."

Marti's eyes lit up. "Emma, is it a boy or a girl?"

Emma looked at her mother. "Oh my gosh. It's a girl! They wrapped her in a pink blanket. I'm going to have a sister."

Marti and Cameron kissed as he put his hand over his wife's stomach. "A beautiful girl, like her mother."

Jenna couldn't believe it. "Darn, I thought you were having a boy. Sorry about your shower gift. It's all boy clothes. I'll take them back and exchange them."

Everyone at the table focused on Emma's transformation from tired and sickly looking to bouncing with energy, as if a weight had been lifted from her.

It took Morgan a minute to get up from her knees. She held the back of Emma's chair and met Tyler's gaze. For the first time since she arrived, she felt the door he'd slammed shut on her open a crack. She didn't feel his anger. His dark eyes went soft when he nodded to Emma and mouthed, "Thank you."

She gave him a soft smile and a nod, feeling good for helping a frightened little girl, and possibly Tyler if he changed the course of his life.

Morgan felt the shift in the atmosphere. Everyone's enthusiasm for Emma's return to her exuberant self helped replenish the energy she'd exerted to make it happen.

The real reason she came tonight walked in the front door.

"Everyone," she called to get them to stop talking over each other, "I need you to listen to me, right now. Since you have seen what I can do, I hope you'll believe me now. Something is about to happen, and I need all of you to stay in your chairs. No one can stand up. It's important."

"Tell us what you want, Morgan. Who's going to be hurt?" Jack asked, concern etched in every line of his face and laced in every word.

"I need all of you to stay seated. I mean it, Jack.

Remember what I told you about change one thing and I can't predict the outcome. The future can be changed."

"I hear you. We'll all stay seated. How long do we have?"

"Not long. Sam, Tyler, are you armed?"

"No. It's a family dinner, not a standoff," Tyler answered.

"You're wrong about that," she said. "Whatever you do, do not stand up. And for god's sake, do not identify yourselves as FBI agents. Let me do the talking, and I will make this right. If you don't do exactly what I say, someone will die."

That had everyone's attention, including Tyler and Sam's. They wouldn't risk their family.

"We'll do what you say," Sam agreed and clamped a hand on Tyler's arm before he argued further. "How bad will this be for you?"

"Fastballs, lots and lots of fastballs. When this is over, Sam, I need you to take me somewhere there are as few people as possible. Can you do that?"

"Yeah, no problem."

A commotion started at the front of the restaurant as the man made his way toward the back. She didn't have much time.

"Elizabeth, he's going to ask where the owner is. You are going to say that you're the owner, but you are not going to stand up. He knows who you are, so you'll have to talk to him. I'll take it from there. Understand."

"Yes," she whispered, fear in her voice and written on her face. Thinking of her unborn baby, she looked at Sam across the table. Much too far away to hold his hand for reassurance.

"Elizabeth, do what I say and you'll be fine," Morgan assured her.

Elizabeth nodded as the man came toward their table wielding a gun. A waiter got in his way and tried to stop his progress. The man yelled for the owner and waved the gun.

Morgan grabbed little Sam and moved him into his father's lap. Jack automatically wrapped his arms around his little boy and held him tight.

Everyone sat stunned when the sound of gunfire erupted. Sam clamped his hand down on Tyler's shoulder to keep him from getting up. The gun had gone off twice. Both shots screamed past everyone seated at the table and went into the back of Matt's chair. Luckily, Morgan had been fast enough to grab him from his seat.

The anger and rage coming from the man nearing the table almost sent her to her knees, but she held Jack's son Matt protected in her arms.

"Where is the owner?" he shouted. The gun wobbled in his hand. It only made it and the man more dangerous. Sweat beaded on his forehead, and his eyes were wide and wild. Everyone at the table recognized a man strung out on drugs and half out of his mind.

Elizabeth took a breath and looked toward the man and recognized him immediately. He'd recently applied for a job and she'd turned him down.

"I'm the owner." She remained seated like Morgan instructed. She kept her arms folded over her growing belly and felt overwhelming love when Jenna inched ever so slowly in front of her, blocking her view of the man standing only a few feet away from their table and obstructing his aim at her.

"Get up. You're going to open that nice big safe in your office." He waved the gun around, making sure everyone knew he meant business. He took care to point it at each man at the table. He didn't want any of them being cowboys. Funny, a couple of them looked like cowboys. They even looked exactly alike. All of them looked mean.

Morgan moved around the table and dropped Matt in Cameron's lap on the way. He wrapped a protective arm around Emma. Matt, none the worse for wear, curled up in Cameron's lap. Morgan kept moving around the table, grabbing a bottle of wine and hiding it behind her back. When the man took his gaze from Elizabeth, she seized her opportunity.

"Robert Parks, put down that gun this instant."

Robby looked at the woman coming toward him, and whether the drugs, the booze, or a trick of the light, he swore she changed from a beautiful blond angel into his grandmother before his eyes. He shook his head and tried to see clearly, but the pills he'd downed with half a bottle of tequila had left him bleary-eyed and flying high. Nothing could touch him.

That bitch hadn't given him the job he'd tried so hard to get. He'd sobered up and put on the cleanest clothes he'd had for the interview, and still she'd turned him down. Not enough experience. Hell, how much experience did you need to clear tables and wash dishes in a fancy restaurant? He could do that stoned and drunk, which is how he usually spent his days and nights. The tips from all the wealthy people who ate there would keep him high all the time, and he wouldn't have to resort to stealing and pick-pocketing.

He hadn't slept in two days and he was getting to the point where he'd have to take more pills to come down enough to sleep a few hours. He needed to score more drugs. To do that, he needed money. He'd seen the old-fashioned safe in the office. It reminded him of the old western movies where bandits stormed the bank and used dynamite to blast it open. He wished he had some dynamite. It'd be one hell of a show.

His grandmother came toward him and he took a stumbling step back and raised the gun to her. He leaned a little forward to get a better look at her. Maybe he was hallucinating. He hated it when he took too much and started seeing things.

"Grandma? Is that you? You're dead," he slurred.

"And you're supposed to be finishing school and getting good grades," Morgan said. "I taught you better than this. You come in here drunk, stoned, waving a gun, and scaring these folks. What's the matter with you, boy? Don't you have any respect for yourself? For me?"

Robby didn't know what to do. That safe had to be full of cash. He imagined it all stacked up. She wanted to stop him from getting all that money. His anger erupted and he took a step toward her and aimed the gun at her face.

"You're dead. You can't tell me what to do anymore."

"Boy, you best put that gun down, or I'll smack you into next Tuesday."

She would. He'd had her riled a few times when he skipped school and she'd shown him what for. Then she died and he wound up in a foster home. The woman didn't care about him. She only wanted to collect her check and watch daytime soaps. So he'd dropped out of school, started hanging out with some of the local guys, and they'd kept him busy doing petty crimes like stealing and shoplifting. One of the guys gave him some weed and another gave him some pills. Now all he thought about was making his next score and getting high.

"You died," he screamed, and spittle came out of his mouth with all the rage. "You died and you left me with no one."

Morgan's strength waned. He had the gun trained on her face, and although his hands weren't steady, at this range he wouldn't miss if he fired. The overwhelming sadness underneath the anger made her push on. This boy missed his grandmother. She'd been the only one to care about him. She'd kept him on the straight and narrow after his mother dropped him with her before leaving for parts unknown. He'd never known his father and couldn't be sure the man they thought had done the deed was for sure his dad.

"It's time for you to grow up, boy. You don't have me to keep you on the right path. You've got to do for yourself."

"I can't. I'm all messed up." He wiped the sweat from his brow with the back of his hand.

"Sure you can. Didn't I always tell you, you've got to

do for yourself? Ain't nobody gonna give you anything. You've got to work hard."

"I'll make her give me the money. Then, I can do for myself."

"She's done nothing to you, and here you are holding a gun wanting to hurt these folks. You don't want to hurt them. You put the gun down," she said softly.

He wanted to leave. He didn't want to see his dead grandmother anymore. He wanted to go back to that bug-infested apartment and sleep on his mattress on the floor. He'd let his mind clear and figure out what to do later. He just wanted to get away.

The sound of sirens and people shouting brought him back to the scene in the restaurant. He'd been there too long, and the lady hadn't even gotten up to open the vault. He'd never get away clean now.

"This wasn't how it was supposed to be," he yelled at his grandmother. "You aren't supposed to be here. I'm supposed to get the money and go." He shook the gun at her face with each word. The police poured into the restaurant and people directed them to him in the back. He didn't want to go to jail, or be killed.

Morgan feared he'd shoot. Exhausted, she wanted to shut down and block it all out of her mind. His rage and sadness were everywhere around her, like a thick blanket smothering her.

She took her chance when he glanced over his shoulder at the approaching police. She swung the wine bottle and knocked the gun out of his hand. It went flying across the floor.

"No." Robby grabbed the knife on his belt and slashed at the woman in front of him. His grandmother disappeared. He cut the woman across the arm before she swung the wine bottle at his head, and he didn't see anything anymore.

He dropped to the ground unconscious along with Morgan. She couldn't take any more. As she fell to the floor, she hoped Sam would keep his promise and take her somewhere quiet and isolated from others.

Chapter Sixteen

TYLER FELL TO his knees beside Morgan and carefully rolled her over, revealing the bleeding knife wound across her arm. The blood didn't particularly worry him, but the gray translucent color of her skin disturbed him. He opened one of her eyes. The vibrant blue had darkened to almost black. Her beautiful golden hair that always seemed to glow had gone limp and dull.

Her gift physically drained the life out of her. From the time she'd fallen to her knees after helping Emma see the future, and now, becoming a completely other person to a drugged-out boy, she'd given everything for them. He couldn't believe what his own eyes saw her do. Every time he'd tried to get up to help her, Sam held him down. She'd gotten right in the guy's face. He didn't understand how she managed to change her voice, or the way she spoke, making the guy think he was talking to his grandmother.

How did she do that? The crazy woman walked right up to a man with a gun.

Make that a boy. At first sight, he thought him a young man of about twenty or so, but as he approached the table it became apparent he was no more than sixteen or seventeen.

"You crazy woman. What the hell were you thinking?" His fear from a moment ago turned into anger as he leaned over her. She could have been killed. The thought sent a chill down his spine.

Morgan's skin broke out in a clammy sweat. Tyler brushed his shaking fingers over her cheek and leaned down and touched his forehead to hers.

"Wake up, sweetheart. Please."

Sam clamped a hand on his shoulder and pulled him upright. "She saved Matt's life."

Tyler stared in shock at Sam, and then down at Morgan's blank face.

"What?"

"Look at the two bullet holes in Matt's chair. They hit right about head level for the little guy. She's known about this happening for years. She's waited all this time, making sure nothing changed in the vision, not seeing you again until this night, all to save that little boy. He was meant to die tonight. She changed the future."

Tyler tried to digest she'd sacrificed being close to him, to any of them, in order to save Matt. Years she'd dedicated to helping him, but never getting too close in order to change that moment when a drugged-out boy pulled the trigger and nearly killed a child. The anger he'd carried with him all this time dissipated and turned to admiration—and guilt.

A shiver of fear rocketed through him as he glanced at the holes in the chair. The last five years had all led up to this night.

"If that crazed idiot had taken Elizabeth into the office and discovered the old-fashioned safe is unused and empty, he'd have killed her. She saved my wife."

"She's amazing, but we already knew that." Tyler brushed his hand over her hair. He didn't want to leave Morgan on the floor. He needed to get her out of there. She'd asked Sam to take her somewhere with few people. Seeing how she'd reacted to his anger, even unconscious, he needed to get her out of there quick. He put his arm under her head and around her back to pull her toward him, so he could pick her up. Scared and unsure, he touched his fingers to the wet burgundy carpet and pulled them away, wet with Morgan's blood. Not from her arm. He rolled her carefully to her side and swore.

He looked over his shoulder at the officer cuffing the boy who'd awakened moments ago. "Call for an ambulance. She's been shot."

Tyler pulled her torn skirt down and revealed the long gash across her lower back. The bullet left a furrow through her skin. Relieved the bullet hadn't gone directly into her back, but rather traveled along the width of it. He'd seen a lot of gunshot wounds in his line of work. Morgan would be fine. She'd have one hell of a scar, but she'd live and that's all that mattered. A half inch the other way and it would be a completely different story.

His tightly held emotions started to crack. He didn't want her to be hurt. He wanted her to wake up, so he could fight with her about keeping him in the dark, and tell her he was sorry for not understanding, and he wanted to kiss her. On second thought, maybe he'd kiss her first.

Sam smacked him on the back. "I've been trying to tell you about her gift. This has pretty much sucked the life out of her. I'll do as she asked and take care of her. You handle the cops. Detective Stewart arrived a few minutes ago. I don't want him anywhere near her."

"She's bleeding. I'll take care of her. It's my responsibility."

"Not going to happen. Tie up the scene here. Get rid of Detective Stewart and take your *girlfriend* and my wife home. *I'll* take care of Morgan."

Tyler wanted to argue, but he'd forgotten about Maria. He couldn't just leave her here. Besides, Morgan asked Sam to take care of her, not him. The hurt and guilt expanded inside of him until he could barely take a breath.

This night just kept getting better.

Emma broke away from her parents and came over to him. She put her hand on his shoulder and looked at Morgan with tears running down her face. "Is she dead?"

He hugged the little girl tight. "No honey, she's just sleeping. She's hurt a little, but she'll be fine."

Emma wiped at her tears. "Like when Mommy hurt her head on the ship, when she pulled me out of the water. She fell asleep for a long time."

"That's right. Here come the paramedics. They'll take

her to the hospital, so she can rest quietly. Okay? Go back to your Dad. I promise she'll be fine."

Emma leaned down and kissed Morgan's cheek. The simple affectionate gesture brought a touch of color into Morgan's cheeks. She'd reacted to his anger, and now she'd responded to Emma's love. No wonder she'd isolated herself.

"So, this is the infamous Morgan?" Detective Stewart asked. The paramedics strapped her to the gurney. "She doesn't look like what I expected."

"No? What did you expect, a black pointed hat and a wart on her nose? She's a woman. A very gifted woman, who saved your ass on that case by giving us the name of the ship where the women were being held. You repaid her by giving her name out to the press and opening her up to her murdering father and a madman, both of whom want to see her dead. I'll only say this once. Stay away from her."

"I'll need to get her statement about what happened here tonight. I'm getting conflicting statements from witnesses. Some of them say the boy thought she was his grandmother."

"He did."

"She's white. He's black."

"He's on something, completely out of his head and hallucinating. She kept him talking, until she got a clear shot and clocked him with the wine bottle. That's all you need to know. Talk to Sam. He'll give you the rundown. I can't talk to you right now."

Tyler walked away, following Morgan out to the ambulance, pissed off.

"What's his problem?" Detective Stewart asked Sam.

"You. And me."

Sam understood Tyler's anger. Outing Morgan to Detective Stewart set this whole thing in motion. Guilty. Angry. He wanted to make things right, but he couldn't even go with Morgan to the hospital because he still had to take another woman home.

"Did she save the little boy?"

Sam understood the skepticism. Detective Stewart believed in what he could see and touch, what he could prove. Morgan was something he'd never thought possible.

"Look at that chair, and you tell me. She knew just what to say to that boy to keep him from hurting anyone else, and she took him down by herself, while two FBI agents sat at the table behind her."

Stewart looked at the chair and at the two identical boys held by their parents.

"You'd think she'd have known about getting shot and moved out of the way."

"You assume she didn't know," Sam said. "Everything happens for a reason. She's known about this for years and she still came to stop it." That said it all. Sam couldn't make Detective Stewart respect Morgan, but he could give him something to think about.

Stewart didn't say anything, out of his element where Morgan was concerned. Used to dealing with the scum of society, who were only out for themselves. He had trouble believing someone would put herself in harm's way when she knew she'd be hurt in the process.

"I assume you won't mind writing up her statement for us."

That was as close as Stewart would get to saying he'd keep his distance.

"Yeah, I'll write up her statement. Right after she's stitched up and regains consciousness. I'd better not see her name in the morning paper, or on the ten o'clock news."

No less than three news vans were setting up outside the restaurant windows.

"How am I supposed to keep her name out of this? She confronted an armed man."

"I don't care. Keep her name out of it. Call her a friend of the family. We don't need the Psychic Slayer seeing her name on the news and trying to kill her. The only advantage we have over him right now is he doesn't know where she is. Maybe she can help us find him. I'd like to give her the chance to try before he comes after her."

"Can she help us with the case? I saw the newspaper report stating she couldn't *see* anything about this case."

"It isn't a matter of can she help us, she's already given us information. The clue about the phonebook and his description that we've been working with came from her. No, in this case, it's more a matter of if she'll help us."

"If she knows something, then she has to tell us. She can't keep her mouth shut about a multiple murder investigation."

"She can't? Why? If she came to you, would you believe her, or do anything with the information she provided?"

Stewart stood with his hands on his hips, staring at Sam, refusing to answer.

"If you know what's good for you, stay away from her," Sam demanded and ran to catch up with Morgan in the ambulance.

Something Emma said gave him an idea. He knew just where to take Morgan to be alone: Marti's pirate ship. He'd hide her away from the world for a while, and Tyler too.

Chapter Seventeen

JACK BOARDED *The World*, Marti's pirate ship she'd inherited from her grandmother. It had taken a while, but he'd finally gotten Jenna, Matt, and Sam out of the restaurant and home. They left the place in complete chaos while the police took statements, customers were given a gift certificate for dinner on Elizabeth at a future date, and the staff cleaned and closed up for the night.

The press came out in full force in front of the restaurant. A sensational story, especially when the president and CEO of Merrick International were inside during the attempted robbery. Not to mention the CEO's son had almost been killed. Add in the fact that Elizabeth was the daughter of federal judge John Hamilton and heir to the Hamilton fortune, and that two FBI agents were seated with them and did nothing to stop the events, and it was just another reason to splash the story all over the news.

Tyler had been in rare form. One minute he directed

the spectacle and the next he yelled orders and barked at the officers at the door to keep the press out. Maria sat patiently waiting for him. She'd been quiet, only asking Jenna and Elizabeth if Morgan could really see the future.

Jack found Sam sitting in a chair next to the bed in the master cabin below deck. Morgan slept with her bandaged arm propped on a pillow. Lying on her side, her long hair spread across the pillow and over the sheets covering her.

"How is she?"

"She's still out. How're the boys and Jenna?"

"Jenna's still shaken. The boys are fine. You know them. This was a big adventure. I don't think they really understand what happened. Matt didn't see the bullets hit his chair. Morgan turned around to protect him."

"I've been thinking about tonight. She threw Sam in your lap first. I don't think she knew which of them the bullets were headed for. She protected them both. If the bullets had gone into Sam's chair, you'd have been holding him."

"That's my feeling. She knew one of them would be shot, but she didn't know which, since they're identical twins."

"She saved Tyler tonight. I know he doesn't see it that way, but she did."

Sam ran both hands through his hair. He needed a haircut. He looked less like his twin, Jack, and more like one of the thugs he arrested.

"The last time we were on this ship, Cameron was being an idiot over Shelly when he was in love with Marti.

Have we really fallen into this scenario again with Tyler, Maria, and Morgan?"

"God, I hope not," Jack said. "You should have seen him tonight after you left. He didn't know if he should walk out and go after you two, or stay there and take care of everything."

"I'm glad he didn't come after us. In the last hour, I've finally seen the color bloom into her face and her hair looks like the shine is coming back."

"She didn't lie about her gift physically harming her."

"I don't think it's a single gift. I think she has several. She can see things like a psychic, but she has another kind of power. Empathy. She feels what other people feel, and she takes on those feelings somehow. That's why she referred to it as 'fastballs.' The anger coming from that kid hit her fast and hard. Add to that Tyler's emotions and she just shut down."

"How'd you get her out of the hospital?"

"I didn't take her in, but made the doctor come out to the ambulance and take care of her. They weren't happy with me, but I have an FBI badge and a gun. Works wonders on red tape and policy and procedure. The doctor cleaned and stitched her up, and I had the ambulance take us to the dock. Marti had already called the ship and Captain Finn was waiting for us when we arrived."

"Why didn't you just stay with her at the hospital?"

"Because before everything went down with that boy, she asked me to take her someplace where there weren't a lot of people. The hospital is full of people hurt, sad, anxious, and angry. You name it and they're feeling it.

I couldn't leave her there where all those things could make her worse. That's why you're here. When I came to Colorado, she said she liked being around you because you make her feel good. You radiate happiness and good feelings. I think you're the best medicine for her. She trusts you, and you aren't upset about anything."

Jack had to admit it was a good idea. They didn't have any other alternatives. Morgan couldn't tell them what she needed. "Why don't you stay with her?"

"Because I'm worried about Elizabeth and the baby. She had a pretty good scare tonight. I know she's tough, but someone violated her workplace and threatened her and her family. She's pregnant and her emotions are all over the map. I want to go home and see her. That, and I have a lot of things stored up inside of me with my work and Tyler. I don't want Morgan sensing those things. I think I have them under control, but I don't know if it's enough."

"Did the doctor say if anything else was wrong with her?"

"He didn't find anything. If she doesn't wake up by morning, we'll try something else. She said sometimes she needs a few hours to recover from a vision. I think to-night warrants at least a night of shutting out the world." He ran his hands over his face. "I don't know. I'm guessing here."

"Don't worry, Sam. I'll take care of her. If something changes, or she looks worse, I'll call you. Go see your wife and daughter. You'll feel better. I know I did after seeing Willow sound asleep and the boys sleeping peacefully in their beds."

"Whatever you do, don't tell Tyler where she is. He's the last thing she needs tonight."

"She's really got him tied in knots and standing on the edge of sanity. He's having a very bad night. I think Maria made up her mind to end the charade with him tonight."

"No matter what happens, we'll let Morgan decide if she wants to see him again."

"Absolutely. Go home to your wife and kiss your baby."

"I'll kiss Grace, too," he said jokingly.

Chapter Eighteen

EXHAUSTION HUNG ON Tyler like Spanish moss weighing down an old oak's limbs. He'd managed the scene at the restaurant among all the chaos of customers, police, and the media. He had to keep Morgan's name out of the press. For once, Detective Stewart willingly helped him along those lines. Sam must have given him what for about giving Morgan's name to the press again. After all, they had a serial killer out there targeting psychics, and Morgan in particular.

Elizabeth locked the restaurant and all but fell into the backseat of his car. She didn't speak the whole way home, and her silence unnerved him.

He escorted her into her converted warehouse and waited while she checked on Grace and paid the babysitter. He even went in and kissed Grace while she slept, relieved she and Willow hadn't been at the restaurant. Emma, Sam, and Matt safe and unharmed made him even more grateful to Morgan. He owed her more than he could ever repay for the lives of his sister and now Matt. Shudders rippled through his body just thinking about what could have happened tonight.

How in hell was he going to make it up to her?

Maria hadn't been quiet for more than a minute. She basically recounted the evening and asked him question upon question about Morgan. Some of them he'd answered and others he couldn't. The ones he couldn't answer hurt the most. It really got to him when she asked why he didn't know very much about Morgan when he'd worked with her for the last five years. He couldn't answer her because he didn't want to say out loud that he'd simply stopped trying when she shut him down. She'd insisted they keep things centered on him and his cases, but he should have seen what everyone else saw. If she was so interested in him and he in her, why did he give up so easily when he wanted her so bad? Like Elizabeth said, getting a woman had been easy for him. Morgan not falling for him hurt his pride and overinflated ego.

Their relationship may have been reduced to a working one over time, but he knew it went much deeper. At least he felt it had for him.

"Aren't you going to come in?" Maria knew he didn't want to talk. It had been a long night for everyone. From what she pieced together from the various conversations, and Morgan's assessment of her and Tyler's relationship, it was clear Morgan and Tyler had a history. A complicated one, at that.

She and Tyler needed to clear the air. True, they'd

talked about marriage, but somewhere in the back of her mind, she'd never thought he'd actually ask her. Seeing him pull that ring box out of his pocket had brought reality crashing down. All of a sudden, it didn't seem so important to be married and have children. Morgan showed her life didn't have to be planned based on someone else's expectations. She'd been thinking along those lines for years, but allowed herself to fall into her father's trap. She wondered if she'd spend the rest of her life trying to please the man, and why she tried in the first place.

After her parents met Tyler, they'd said he was nice enough and would provide a good life for her. They hadn't said anything about love or happiness. That stuck with her over the last week. They wanted her to have security. She appreciated that, but she wanted a lot more, and deserved it.

It all became so clear tonight sitting at the table with Tyler's family. They all knew she didn't belong. Not because they didn't like her, or thought she was beneath them or Tyler. No. They just saw what she and Tyler refused to see. They made good friends, but they didn't make good life partners.

She'd seen the bond between all the women and their husbands. Not hard to miss. She'd seen Marti look across at her daughter and smile at her husband when he'd made a joke. She'd watched Cameron hug his wife and daughter after the ordeal and the gentle way he'd put his hand over his wife's large belly. She'd never forget the reverence on his face when he'd touched her.

Jenna was a high-powered CEO of a huge corporation,

yet you couldn't mistake the love she felt for her family. They were her first and last priority.

Elizabeth was strong and independent, but Maria had seen how much it cost her to leave her husband's embrace, so he could go to Morgan. Before Sam left with Morgan in the ambulance, he'd turned back and simply stared at Elizabeth. She'd stared back, and in that moment a thousand silent words of love had been spoken.

Maria wanted that for herself and Tyler. It just wasn't something they'd share with each other. It wasn't something that would grow over time. It was either there, or it wasn't. She wasn't about to marry him and make his life miserable. She wouldn't let him do the same to her.

Morgan showed her the way. The path she'd wanted to take so many times, but was always too scared to try.

Scared or not, she was going to look into veterinary school first thing in the morning. She was going to make her dreams come true and let the rest work itself out.

First, she had to talk to Tyler.

"I'll come up for a little while. Are you sure you're okay? Tonight was traumatic for everyone. Morgan upset you."

They walked up the steps to her condo and went inside. She wanted to be alone with him, so they could talk privately. He hadn't liked the way Morgan talked about their relationship in front of everyone, and she didn't want anyone walking by unexpectedly while they talked on the sidewalk.

"She didn't upset me so much as opened my eyes. I think she opened yours, too. Marriage takes work, but it's a good thing when you love the person. We'd have worked and worked at it and still we'd have been unhappy because something would always be missing. Admit it. You don't love me."

His silence spoke for him.

"You deserve a great wife. You deserve the kind of wife Jenna is to Jack and Elizabeth is to Sam."

Which is exactly what he wanted, but couldn't seem to find. Standing in the middle of the living room, the rest of the house in darkness. The only light burned beside the sofa on a side table. It cast a soft glow over her that should have made her look soft and sultry. It didn't. She looked like just another woman. Nothing pulled at him to kiss her and unzip her dress and take her right there on the living room rug.

Damnit, Morgan. Why did you have to be right? I won't be satisfied with anything less than love and passion.

He'd made a huge mistake in trying to make a friendship into a lasting romance.

He struggled with what to say, and how to explain. After tonight, there wasn't anything left between them.

"You know, our getting married is nothing more than a square peg in a round hole," Maria explained. "They might fit together, but there's still a lot of empty space that needs to be filled. Morgan didn't do anything but call us a circle and a square. We don't fit together. I think you know it, just as well as I do."

"I'm sorry, Maria." He didn't know what else to say.

"No apologies necessary. We had a good time together."

"If you ever need anything, call me. I mean it."

"Thanks. Have a good life, Tyler. I hope you find what it is you're looking for. I hope you find love."

"I hope you do, too." He kissed her on the forehead and walked out of her place for the last time.

Once he got to his car, he made a call while he drove toward the hospital. He'd check on Morgan's condition, get her room number, and drive over to see her instead of spending another night alone.

Stopped at a red light, he slammed his hand against the steering wheel, pissed at himself for relying on Morgan to make him feel better. Right now, she needed him. He wanted—no, *needed* to talk to her and try to find out some of the things about her life she'd shared with others, but not him. This time, he wouldn't give up until they had a real conversation about her.

Nothing but a dead end at the hospital, they'd treated her in the ambulance in the parking lot and released her to Sam. Interesting.

He called Sam's cell.

"Go home and get some sleep, man," Sam ordered without so much as a hello.

"Is she staying with you and Elizabeth?"

"No. I'm just walking in the door."

Tyler heard Sam kiss his wife hello and tell her he'd be a minute talking to him.

"If she's not staying with you, and she's not at the hospital, where is she?"

"Someplace quiet and practically deserted."

"Where is that? This is San Francisco. There aren't many practically deserted places."

"You're telling me, but I found one."

"You left her alone. She wasn't in any shape to be left alone. Why didn't she stay at the hospital? She's been shot, for god's sake."

"Tyler. Man. Calm down. She's fine. I did not leave her alone. Jack's staying with her. She likes him. He has good energy. Happy thoughts, and all that shit. I couldn't leave her at the hospital because there are too many people there with bad energy. She wouldn't have healed there. She's better off where she is."

"Good energy. Bad energy. Sam, have you lost your mind? You're talking like one of those wacko psychics we've been interviewing."

"Wacko or not, it's the only way to explain what happens to her around people."

Tyler wished he knew more about what happened to her. He wished she'd confided in him about how she did what she did. Tonight had been an up-close view of her gift. Before, he'd only gotten a phone call with the details of her visions. He didn't know that she could pass her vision on to another person like she'd done with Emma and Cameron. He hadn't known she could become another person to someone and fool them like she'd fooled poor Robby. He didn't know what part the drugs had played in that scenario. He'd like to ask Morgan about it. He'd like to ask her about a lot of things.

"Where is she? I need to see her," he said softly.

"No." Sam poured a glass of milk and ate one of the cookies his wife baked. Chocolate chip with almonds, his favorite. The kitchen, and the entire house for that matter, held the sweet, delicious aroma of a bakery. Elizabeth baked when upset or trying to work something out. There had been times he couldn't see a countertop for all the baked goods. Great for her restaurant and café, but not for home. He could only eat so many sweets, certainly not twenty pies and twelve dozen cookies. The guys at work loved it, because he brought in the best treats in the city.

He didn't want tonight to be one of those nights, so when she put the last batch in the oven and turned to the mixing bowls to start on a pie or cake, he grabbed her and held her to him while he talked to Tyler. He felt better when she wrapped her arms around his waist, snuggling close with her head resting on his chest.

"Please, Sam, tell me where she is."

"Like I said, Jack's with her. She's still unconscious and needs her rest."

"I need to see her. Where is she? I won't upset her."

"Since she's out cold, I'm not worried about that. Listen, I'm not telling you where she is because I don't think it's a good idea for you to be around her right now. She needs time to recuperate. That's why Jack's with her. I'll see you on Monday." Sam hung up. He imagined Tyler yelling at him while he drove home.

"That wasn't very nice, Sam," Elizabeth said and held him tighter. She loved the feel of his arms around her, and right now she needed his strength.

"It's what he deserved. She needs time to come back to reality. She's out cold. When I left her, she was finally getting some color back in her skin."

"She was gray as death when they took her away."

"Don't worry, honey. She'll be fine. Jack will call if she doesn't start coming around."

His cell phone rang. Tyler, according to caller ID. Again. He pushed the button to send the call to voicemail.

"Let him see how it feels when your partner doesn't pick up. Come to bed with me, honey. I have a very big need to have you comfort me."

"Big indeed." She pressed her hips to his and slid her hands up around his neck and pulled him down for a kiss.

Chapter Nineteen

"Hi, Jack." Morgan's groggy voice broke the silence.

"Hi, sunshine. You gave us quite a scare."

"I did. Is that why you branded my back?"

"What?"

"My back is on fire. It feels like someone is pressing a hot branding iron against it."

"That's the bullet wound. You were shot. Do you remember what happened?"

She waited for the last of the fog to clear from her mind and glanced at Jack's expectant face. "I remember. Is he upset?"

"He was upset last night. This morning he was frustrated, and now I think he's pissed."

"Why is Matt so mad?"

"Matt?" Jack chuckled. "No, it's Tyler who is pissed. Matt didn't even understand what happened. He thought you were protecting him from the mean man. He didn't realize the bullets hit his chair. We made sure of it." He took her hand and sat on the bed next to her. "Thank you, Morgan. You saved him. He would have been killed. I don't know how to repay you."

"There's nothing to repay. I'm just glad I changed it. It isn't often I get to use my gift and see the results. It's very satisfying when it all works out."

"Yeah, well, regardless, I owe you, and someday I hope to repay the debt. Speaking of getting satisfaction from your gift, Cameron called a little while ago. Emma slept the entire night and even woke up late. She ate a huge breakfast and was working her way through a pizza for lunch. She's excited about the baby and asked Marti if they could go shopping, so she could get the baby a dress."

Morgan smiled. Nothing like a child's enthusiasm for something they really want. "I'm glad she's better." Morgan began to focus on her surroundings and realized she wasn't in a hotel. In fact, the room swayed. "Um, Jack, where are we?"

"We're on *The World*."

Of course they were on the world. What the hell was he talking about? "Excuse me?"

"*The World*. It's Marti's pirate ship. It's actually a very big sailing ship. She let us use it. She said you could stay as long as you like. Jenna is on her way with your luggage. We found the hotel receipt in your purse. She'll bring your things, and you can stay here as long as you're in town."

"That isn't necessary. The hotel is fine."

"No. It's not fine. There are too many people there.

You said you prefer to be somewhere a little more isolated. This is the best we could do. And after what you've done for us, the best is what you'll have."

"Really, I can stay at the hotel. I can put up blocks to keep everyone out. It's no trouble. I'm used to doing it."

"It must be tiring to constantly keep your guard up."

She wanted to lie and say it didn't bother her, but he knew it did.

"It's like being up all night. By morning, you're a little punchy."

"You won't have that problem here. Captain Finn is the only one on the ship right now. He's a really nice guy. I think you two will hit it off. He'll be happy to take you back and forth to the dock whenever you want."

"Wait. Back to the dock?"

"Yeah, it's about a half mile away. We're anchored in the bay." He laughed at her astonished face. "Sam did what you asked. He got you to a quiet and isolated place, so you could rest."

"Wow. You can't get much more isolated than this." No one had ever taken care of her like Sam and Jack. Her mother had tried, but her father had ruined all of her attempts to provide a safe and loving home for her daughter. She didn't know what to say. She didn't know how to tell him what it meant that they had taken care of her. She'd been alone for a long time. Too long maybe.

"I'd almost forgotten how nice it feels to have someone take care of you. No one's done anything nice for me like this, well, since I can remember."

"You saved my son. You made sure Sam's wife,

Elizabeth, and their unborn child weren't hurt or killed by that boy. I'd even go so far as to say you saved that boy, too. Drugged out of his mind, he might have done something stupid and pointed that gun at a cop. They'd have shot him dead. Watching over you while you slept was so little compared to what you did for all of us. I think you've been alone far too long. You have us now."

Overwhelmed, she swallowed back the lump in her throat. He meant it. Every word, he meant it to his soul. Part of their group. Part of the family. "Thank you, Jack. It's nice to know I have some new friends."

"You have that and more in all of us. You're part of our family. If you need something, we'll all be there for you."

Too much to take in, she couldn't speak.

She held back the tears. Jack couldn't fathom what it had taken for her to raise and educate herself and live all these years mostly alone, no family or friends to count on.

"Now, tell me what you're avoiding telling me about Tyler."

Jack sighed. He didn't want to upset her. She'd opened her eyes about an hour ago and just stared into the distance. He'd waited for her to fully come back. He didn't want to see her wilt before his eyes again.

"He's having a rough couple of days. You showed up out of the blue. That kind of threw him for a loop."

She smiled. He'd been really frustrated by her return. On the one hand, he'd wanted her to come, and on the other, he wanted her to stay away. After what happened, she wondered which part was winning.

"So, Tyler wants me to leave. Is that what you're trying *not* to tell me?"

"No. At least, he hasn't said he wants you to leave. He calls me every hour wanting to know if you're awake. He wants to see you, but his emotions are all over the place. We thought it best if he stayed away from you for a while. He needs to sort out his life before he sees you. I finally stopped answering the phone. He and Maria broke things off last night."

"Oh."

"Oh. That's it."

"What do you want me to say? His intentions are good. He wants a wife and a family. Who could blame him with such great examples as you've all shown him? No wonder he wants that, too." She smiled. "It's what we all want."

That made Jack smile. His parents had a great marriage. At one time, he thought he'd never find that for himself. Then he met Jenna. He knew almost immediately she belonged to him and vice versa. It had been a difficult road getting to the marriage vows, but well worth it. Sam and Elizabeth had gone through some difficult times when they first met. Actually, Sam fell in love with her while she was lying unconscious in the hospital after saving his life.

"Thanks. We're all happy. Tyler hasn't been happy in a long time. There have been women, but you don't want to hear about that," he said and looked away.

"It's okay. I know there have been other women, and he's been happy for a little while. He hasn't found *the* woman. That's what he thinks doesn't exist for him."

"We all think you're that woman for him."

"You do, huh. Well, I don't know about that."

"You can't see that in your future?"

She tilted her head. "I think it's some kind of cosmic balance. You know, too much information can sometimes be a dangerous thing. I prefer to let life happen. For the last several years, I've concentrated on helping Tyler and Sam with their cases and preventing what almost happened last night."

"And I'm so glad you did." He leaned down and kissed her on the forehead. Someone came in behind him.

"Jack Turner, I turn my back on you for one minute and you've already got a beautiful woman in bed, and you're kissing her."

Jack jumped up from the bed and took two large steps away from Morgan and stammered a bunch of nonsense. "I wasn't . . . I didn't . . . I was just . . ."

"Isn't he fun?" Jenna teased. She smiled at her husband and set down Morgan's luggage and a few things from Elizabeth.

"I bet you're starving. Elizabeth packed up dinner and some treats. You can't beat her cooking." She took out several covered dishes, a cardboard bakery box, and a plastic bag filled with cookies. "How are you feeling? It looks like I came just in time."

"Really, honey, I was just talking to her and thanking her for helping us last night."

Jenna smiled at her flustered husband and winked at Morgan. "Jack. I only meant it looks like Morgan just woke up." She turned her attention to Morgan. "You'd probably like to get cleaned up. Jack and I can take this food into the galley. On second thought, do you need some help?"

"Um, I think I'll be okay. By the way"—she looked down at herself under the sheets—"what happened to my clothes?"

"Sam probably undressed you after you got here from the hospital. Personally, I think it's his secret pleasure, he's seen all of us naked."

"He has?" She thought that odd, and wondered why he'd seen them all naked. Some kind of weird fetish?

"He saw me naked after my ex-husband beat me. He took the photographs for evidence. With Elizabeth, well, that's self-explanatory. Then, there's Marti. She saved Emma from drowning when she got pulled overboard. Sam had to get her out of her wet clothes and dress her. She was too cold to do it herself. Cameron wasn't happy about it, but he got over it. I'm sure Sam will give Tyler a good ribbing over this. It's all in good fun, I assure you."

She thought about being undressed by a man. It embarrassed her. She hadn't let many men close to her. There'd been one guy, a long time ago. She'd given herself to him, only to discover he couldn't deal with her ability. She irritated him every time she knew what he was thinking before he said it. If she didn't seem surprised when he brought her flowers, he got upset because he couldn't surprise her. She didn't always know something, but when she did, he didn't like it. She tried for weeks to hide the things she knew. In the end, she couldn't hide and lie to please someone else. It took too much energy to cover up her gift.

So, Sam had seen her naked. There were worse things. Besides, he'd gotten her stitched up at the hospital. She hadn't actually seen the wounds, yet, but she could feel the pull of the stitches on her skin.

"I guess there's nothing to be done about it now. I could cast a spell on him, or some kind of curse I suppose." Jack and Jenna went completely still. They slowly looked at each other and then her. She gave them a wicked grin. "You guys are fun." She mimicked Jenna's earlier comment about Jack. "Gotcha."

Jack and Jenna were still laughing when they left her alone to get cleaned up.

A phone rang down the hall as she came out of the bathroom refreshed and fully clothed. It had taken some doing to get her pants to ride low enough on her hips, so that the waistband didn't rub the wound on her back. She had to pull them down, and then be careful not to trip over the long hem.

Should she go home, or stay and try to help Tyler and Sam with the case? She'd play it by ear for a while and see how things went and how Tyler reacted.

A knock sounded on the door and Jack called to her.

"Are you awake? There's someone on the phone who wants to know."

Tyler. She'd put him out of his misery. She opened the door and spoke loud enough for Tyler to overhear. "Yeah, I'm awake."

Jack went along with the torture. "Wow, you look great. Jenna's got the food set out. Elizabeth and Sam just arrived. All the kids are with sitters, so it's grown-up night. We can eat and talk. Sam brought a bottle of wine. We'd all like to get to know you better."

Jack held the phone up so Tyler could hear them talking. "That sounds great. I'm starving. Do you think you could put the medicine on my back? I saw it on the counter in the bathroom. I got it on my arm, but I can't see my back very well."

"Sure. What'd you think of the stitches? Sam said there were dozens."

"Just a few, dozen that is. They're fine."

"Fine."

"Okay, they hurt like hell." She thought she'd put Tyler out of his misery, at least for a minute. "Is that call for me? I can't imagine who'd be calling," she said sarcastically.

"Oh, yeah. Do you feel like taking a call?" Jack dragged things out while leaning against the doorframe.

"Who is it?"

Jack almost burst out laughing. She had a good sense of humor. She wasn't going to give in easily to Tyler. He liked that about her. Tyler wouldn't be happy with a woman he could walk all over.

"It's Tyler. He seems to think Sam and I kidnapped you and are holding you for ransom."

"Looks like you guys get to keep me. I don't know anyone who'd pay to get me back." She made a grab for the phone.

Jack pulled the phone away before she seized it. "If someone really did take you, we'd get you back. Count on it. Count on us. We owe you. And more than that, we hope you'll count us as your friends and family."

"Oh, Jack. You don't know what that means to me."

"He means it," Jenna said as she came down the short hallway. "We all do. Come and eat. Sam and Elizabeth are waiting. Elizabeth and I want to pick your brain. Since you can read minds, we'd like to know what men are really thinking."

Without missing a beat, Morgan answered in her saddest voice, "Nothing. It's completely empty up there."

"Slander," Jack said and handed Morgan the phone.

Jenna laughed so hard, Jack had to take her by the arm and escort her back down the hall.

"Hello," she said to Tyler over the phone.

"Having fun," he said irritably.

"As a matter of fact. What do you want? Dinner's ready," she said, and realized she'd slept almost an entire day.

"I'd like to know where you are for starters." At the end of his rope, anger and frustration filled his voice.

"I'm with friends." That simple statement of truth meant so much to her. "Why? Do you want to come stand outside chanting, 'Kill the witch,' or perhaps you'd like to burn me at the stake?"

"I'd never do that to my best friend." Tears filled her eyes at his quiet statement. "Still, after everything we've been through, I didn't deserve the public humiliation. You told Maria we didn't belong together, and she's better off without me."

"You're wrong. I told her she made a mistake thinking that being with you would make her or her father happy. I told you that being with her would only make you unhappy because you wouldn't have the one thing you really want. If you want to blame me because you both decided to break it off last night, fine, it's all my fault. Feel better?"

"Do you always have to be right?"

He said it without any anger, but his voice held a trace of reluctant acceptance of the truth she'd given him. She wanted to believe he accepted her and her gift, but he'd second-guessed her for so long, she didn't quite believe his change of heart.

"I am this time, and you know it. I was trying to help out a friend. My dinner is getting cold. If I have anything on the Psychic Slayer case, I'll let Sam know, and he can tell you. Don't think I can't take a hint. I'll stay out of your life."

"Wait. I want to talk to you."

"About what?"

For the life of him, he couldn't put one complete thought together that would make any sense to her. His thoughts and feelings swirled around his head, never combining into a cohesive sentence that would tell her how he really felt. She'd completely thrown him for a loop telling him she'd stay out of his life. She'd been out of his life for over a month, and he was beginning to think he couldn't tell which way was up anymore without her.

He didn't know how to begin to tell her everything she meant to him.

Morgan had taken him off guard and thrown the ball in his court. He'd been expecting a basketball and she'd thrown him a curveball. She hated to do it, but he needed a wakeup call. He'd been living on impulse for the last few years and he needed to take some time to really think about what he wanted for his future. Alone now, disconnected from her, and he didn't have a girlfriend mucking up the mix.

"We've known each other for five years and you can't think of a single thing to say to me. Not even, 'How are you feeling after being shot and knifed?' How about, 'Gee Morgan, you must have been really scared you might not have gotten Matt and Sam out of the way in time?' Or, 'You must have been so frightened standing toe-to-toe with a man holding a gun in your face.' You might thank me for all the cases I've helped you solve."

"I want to know about all those things. But the question is, will you answer this time?"

"I had my reasons, and you had yours for keeping things simple."

"You never shared anything with me."

"If you really wanted to know me, all you had to do is look. The way I looked at you. You and I were connected, but you were too afraid to use that connection and the strange bond we shared to really see me. You didn't understand it or me, so you pushed me away."

"Morgan, I'm sorry."

"I am too." She hung up, something she'd never think to do to anyone, especially Tyler. He needed it though. Maybe someday soon she'd make things right with him.

She walked into the dining area near the galley and handed Jack back his phone. They overheard the conversation and sat in tense silence.

"He deserved it." She shrugged. Her stomach grumbled as the amazing food aromas hit her.

"You'll get no argument from us," Sam agreed for everyone.

That said, they went on with their meal and conversation. Reticent about her at first, it seemed they waited for her to predict gloom and doom. When they realized she wasn't going to start forecasting the future and talking about the flow of energy and how it related to the alignment of the stars, they relaxed. From there, it was like she'd been a part of the group all along. Sitting with friends, talking about their lives, and enjoying the wonderful food—definitely one of the best nights of her life.

Chapter Twenty

TYLER STARED AT the woman across the restaurant. Pretty, she sort of looked like Morgan. Shorter hair, a rounder face, but the family resemblance remained strong. He remembered Sam saying Morgan came to see her sister sometimes and something pulled at him to see her today.

Jillian, married with a daughter, three, and a son, almost two. A graduate from the University of California–Berkeley, she held a master's degree in education and taught at a local junior college.

An aunt in West Virginia raised her until she'd come west to attend college. She'd never returned. Instead, she'd taken the job at the college and married.

He'd followed her and her family from their well-kept three-bedroom ranch-style house in a nice track, close to an elementary school. He imagined they picked it because of its proximity to the school and low-crime neighborhood.

Unlike Morgan, she'd had every privilege and advantage. She'd grown up in a secure home with her aunt. She'd gone to one of the best universities in the country, gotten a great job right out of college, found the perfect guy, and proceeded to have two-point-five kids. He bet they had a family dog or cat. He hadn't seen one, but he imagined a family pet.

As they sat at their table across the cozy family-style restaurant, he knew they were one of those families people envied. They had it all, and here he sat spying on them, hoping Morgan would show up for a visit.

"I wouldn't want to disappoint you," Morgan said from behind him. She leaned over the back of his booth, and with her head next to his, said, "She's beautiful, isn't she?"

Surprised to see her, he'd also been expecting her to show up. After avoiding him for almost four days, and Sam enjoying every minute of harassing him about it, finally seeing her again made him happier than he wanted to admit.

"Yes, she is."

Morgan came around the booth, and instead of sitting across from him, she surprised him and scooted in next to him. She smiled when he made room for her and offered her a sip of his iced tea and some chips and guacamole.

"She's got it all, a husband, kids, nice house in a good neighborhood, a fancy education, and a good job. Everything a girl could want out of life. Her husband adores her. They're great with the kids. It's all so picture perfect."

She sat there staring at her sister. Jillian, so close and so far away. She wished she could go over to the table and say hello. She'd love to spend time with her niece and nephew. She remembered the family dinner Tyler had with the whole family and thought how sad she'd never have that with her own family. Her father hated her and wanted her in his pocket, or dead. Her sister hated her and wanted to forget she existed.

On the other hand, she liked sitting with Tyler when he was calm.

He took a sip of his drink after she passed it back to him. Intimate, and the first time they'd shared anything besides a conversation. He sat back and looked at Morgan's sister and her family. "That's just what I was sitting here thinking. Are you reading my mind?"

"No mind reading today. Besides, you won't let me anymore. You're all closed up. No trespassing signs posted everywhere."

"Is that right?"

"Yep. You've tucked away the anger. Are you trying to throw me off?"

He'd spent a lot of time over the last few days thinking about the past couple of years and wondering why he was angry with Morgan. She hadn't done anything to him, except come into his life unexpectedly and help him save his sister. She'd spent the last five years helping solve some tough cases, and she'd waited all that time to save Matt.

She'd always been there for him when he needed her, even when he hadn't realized he'd needed her. He didn't want to admit he'd needed a huge wake-up call where Maria and the other women in his life were concerned. He'd been going through the motions. If he wanted more, he'd have to give more.

He'd blamed her for things all his doing. What was the saying? Something about you hurt the ones closest to you. He'd spent far too much time hurting Morgan, instead of thanking her for everything she'd done for him.

She was right, their connection scared him. He'd never attempted to go down that rabbit hole and see if he could see and feel her the way she so easily did with him.

He'd made this mess. He'd have to dig himself out. He wanted a new start with Morgan, and he hoped she'd give him a second chance, because scared or not, he needed that connection with her.

"How about we start where we should have started in the first place?"

"Okay. And just where do you think that should be?"

He turned toward her in the booth, shifting his over six-foot frame, so he could look at her while he talked.

"My name's Tyler Reed. I'm an FBI agent. I believe in psychics, and I'm partial to a particular one, who has a habit of saving my family and friends from being killed. She's also really good at solving complicated cases for the FBI. She always knows when I need her, and I miss hearing her talk to me in my mind. It's nice to finally see you again."

He wanted to touch her. Sometimes, she didn't seem real. Like right now. Here she was, finally, and he had a hard time believing she wasn't a ghost.

"I should have said that to you at dinner last week. Instead I acted like a jackass. I'm sorry." He touched her cheek lightly with his fingertips and ran his fingers through her gorgeous blond hair. It felt like silk running through is fingers.

"I've been a complete bastard to you lately, and even worse, I never gave you back even half of what you've given me. You know a million little things about me, my friends, my family, and my work. You know my hopes, my dreams, and my life. I'd like a chance to know a million little things about you."

"Wow. Is that how you got Maria and the others into bed?"

Flip, and a little snide to comment on the superficial relationships he'd had, but he deserved it. Sure, he'd demanded she tell him where she lived, but that was more from frustration about her keeping secrets from him than a real wanting to see her. She wanted to be sure this was really how he felt, and not just words in an attempt to get her to forgive him.

"No." So she wanted him to eat crow. He deserved it. He'd done everything wrong with Morgan, starting with not being a good friend. He wanted more than that from her. He smiled and put his hand over hers on the table. "They thought I was sexy and mysterious. The FBI thing is a chick magnet, so getting them into bed was easy because that's all I was trying to do, really."

"Ah, so sexy guy plus FBI badge equals chicks between the sheets. I hadn't considered that equation."

"God, I missed your sense of humor." She was laughing at him. "You hadn't considered it for yourself, or that it's how I've been living my life?" he teased back.

He'd give his left arm for her to tell him all it took for her to be his was for him to look good and be an FBI agent. That was never going to work with Morgan. Even if it would, he'd be doing the same thing he'd done for years. It hadn't worked out for him so far, and he wanted things between them to be different. *He* wanted to be different with her.

"Random sexual relationships based on sex appeal and dangerous jobs aren't really my style. Besides, the whole psychic thing really turns guys off. Who wants a girlfriend who instead of asking you what you're thinking, actually knows without you saying anything. I'm great to show off at parties. It's always, 'Look what my girlfriend can do.' Isn't she creepy, strange, weird? Fill in the blank. I gave up on all that at nineteen."

"That's about the time you and I met," he said and sat up a little straighter and puffed out his chest.

She laughed. "Don't flatter yourself, sexy FBI man."

"You really think I'm sexy?" Her answer really mattered. He wanted her to think of him as a man, and not just the voice on the phone. Or worse, the asshole he'd been lately.

"What's not to like? You're the epitome of tall, dark, and handsome. It doesn't make up for your shitty attitude, or your lack of good judgment."

"Well, damn, honey. Don't sugarcoat it." At her dismissive shrug, he turned serious. "You're right. That's why, where you're concerned, I'm determined to redeem myself. So, tell me why you gave up on the male species."

Eyes locked on her sister's table, she answered, "You and I have a lot in common. We both think that"—she pointed to her sister and her family—"doesn't exist for us."

"We both know why I don't think that exists for me. Sam, Jack, and Cameron took all the great women, and you think I have a shitty attitude and lack good judgment. Besides, I have a job that consumes my life. No woman wants to come second to a murderer, or endless paperwork. Let's not forget waiting at home wondering if I'm coming home at all. So, why don't you think you can have a life like that?" He squeezed her hand and leaned closer. He didn't want her to think he was angry about her assessment. Hard to argue with the truth.

"Like I said, I'm a lot to deal with on a daily basis."

She didn't elaborate, so he waited her out. This time he wasn't going to let her get away with a short answer.

"It isn't easy to be around me all the time. How'd you like to take me out to dinner in a nice restaurant only to have to leave before dinner is served because I can't handle the other people? Or leave halfway through a movie? Maybe in the middle of an important conversation I completely blank out on you because I'm having a vision. You've got a glimpse of what it's like to have me in your life. You said it yourself: I know things about you, your friends, and your life. You got sick of it. You got sick of me."

"That's not true," he said adamantly. "I admit, having you talk to me in my head and always knowing what I was thinking or feeling was odd. But it never made me sick of you. In fact, I miss you." He took a deep breath. Opening up and talking about his feelings was not his way, but he needed her to understand. He didn't want to lose her again because he didn't speak up.

"The thing is, after you left, I felt like a part of me was missing, too. I still feel that way. I got used to you being in there, being a part of me. When you were gone, and I couldn't get you back, it made me angry. I want you back. Tell me how I get you to come back."

"That's just it, I don't know. I don't know how that happened in the first place. You're the only person I've ever connected with on such a deep level."

That revelation floored him. "I thought you could connect with anyone like that."

Jealous, he'd thought she might have that kind of intimate connection with someone else, which contributed to his anger when she left. Jealous. An emotion he only felt because of her.

"I thought you just didn't want to be with me anymore." Looking at her now, he could see that wasn't the case. She might hide her feelings as well as he did, but he could see she cared for him. That's all he needed to know, because he was beginning to realize just how deep his feelings ran for her.

He traced his fingers over the back of her hand. "You really can't connect with someone and talk to them in their minds like you did with me?"

"I sometimes know what people are thinking, but it's in the moment and when they're with me. It's a combination of body language, human response, and telepathy.

I'm not always right, but I'm pretty good. Let's say, it isn't my specialty. Five years ago, I saw you in that restaurant and something about you pulled at me. I needed to talk to you. I saw the vision of your sister, but there was more, something elemental about our meeting. Call it fate, meant to be, or whatever you want. We were supposed to meet. And during that meeting I connected with you on a basic level. Ever since then, you've been fighting yourself and me on it. You don't understand it, so you push it away. I guess the fight finally won. I can't hear or feel you anymore."

And it made her sad.

He'd been the only person in her life who accepted her for who she was and what she could do. Losing her connection to Tyler had been like losing a part of herself. Saying she missed him was too simple. She'd always felt alone because of her gift. Now, without Tyler, she was lonely, and it wasn't a feeling she ever wanted to get used to. Lonely is an emptiness that spreads through you, blocking out any ray of happiness.

Tyler missed her, and it was a loneliness he'd been feeling for too long. He wanted the connection between them back. The only way he knew how to show her how much was to connect with her on another level. He ran his fingers through her hair to the back of her neck and pulled her closer.

A simple touching of lips, soft and sweet. She hadn't expected the kiss, but she welcomed him. From the first touch, a slow warmth spread through him, replacing the gnawing loneliness.

She felt like home.

Her fingers dug into his shoulders, holding him close. She must feel it, too.

The kiss was short. Sitting in a public place, he didn't want to make their first kiss a spectator event. They began in a restaurant, and he felt like something new was happening between them again in this restaurant.

He wanted to keep kissing her, but knew he couldn't, shouldn't.

"I've waited more than five years to do that. I didn't realize it, until just now, but I wanted to kiss you all those years ago. I think the thing with my sister just overshadowed everything else. That, and you took off before I could even ask any questions, or thank you."

"You and your questions. I didn't want to have to convince you and waste time. I figured you loved your sister enough to investigate what I told you. I was right."

"Thank God, you were right." He held her hand and just stared into her bright blue eyes. It felt so good to touch her, to look at her. "You know, I'm going to have to kiss you again. I knew it."

Her eyebrow shot up. "You knew what?"

"That once would never be enough." His lips brushed hers softly and he sank into the kiss, thoroughly exploring her mouth. He could taste the iced tea, the salt from the chips, and something else uniquely her. A drug spreading through his system, she set fire to his nerves and inflamed his desire.

He'd never felt quite this way. The interruption from the waitress saved him from embarrassing both of them.

Past time they shared a meal and some normal conversation. He wanted to take the time to get to know her on a personal level.

Time to discover all those million little things he didn't know.

Chapter Twenty-One

MORGAN COULDN'T REMEMBER the last time she sat in a restaurant and had dinner with a handsome man. They talked. Well, she talked. He wanted to know everything about her. She explained about her website and how she provided answers to anyone she could help. She told him about how she educated herself and became a successful day trader. She surprised him with her knowledge of the stock market. At his puzzled frown, she knew she lost him a few times when trying to explain buying on margin and selling short. A complicated business, but she loved it, and if you studied and knew the rules, you could make a lot of money. She'd done well over the years and lived a comfortable life.

Side by side, they sat as they ate and talked to each other. For the first time in a long time she felt at ease, and they shared a true and equal give-and-take.

It all ended with the clatter of her fork hitting her

plate. She looked at Tyler next to her and wished she could freeze time. "Here comes a freight train."

Her words sent everything inside him to full alert. Her smile vanished, her eyes went from a crystal blue to a foggy gray, and her skin paled. He wanted to pull out his gun, push her behind him, and face whatever danger came her way. He needed to protect her, and knew if he had to, he'd lay down his life for her.

"What's wrong? Did you have a vision?"

She didn't answer. Couldn't. Her sister barreled up to the table, planted her hands, and leaned into Morgan's face.

"I told you to stay away from me and my family. I don't want you anywhere near my children."

Morgan sat back in her seat without realizing she scooted closer to Tyler.

"Hello, Jillian. This is my friend, Tyler."

Tyler heard the slight tremor in Morgan's voice and found it strange that in a matter of moments she'd gone from easygoing to completely on guard and hesitant to speak with her own sister.

Jillian stood steaming mad. "Freight train" was an apt description. She looked about ready to bowl Morgan down if she got in her way, and let out an earful of steam in the process.

"I'll take friend for now. We'll see how things progress," he said into Morgan's ear. He turned to Jillian. "It's nice to meet you. Morgan and I were just enjoying a quiet dinner."

"Sure you were. You just happen to pick the restaurant

my family and I frequent." She turned on Morgan and leaned in until they were less than half a foot apart. "I told you to stay away. I don't want you spouting off around my kids and spreading your brand of psycho." She turned her attention back to Tyler. "Has she told you that she sees things? She hears voices. She's crazy."

"He knows all about it, Jillian. Tyler is with the FBI. I'm not here to cause you any trouble."

"So, it's true. You're the Morgan who's working with the FBI. I knew it. You're the reason that maniac is killing anyone claiming to be a psychic."

Claiming to be a psychic, Tyler thought. She doesn't believe in her sister's ability. She thinks her sister is crazy, literally.

"Just a minute, Jillian. Morgan works with me on some of my cases. She's been one hundred percent accurate. She saved my sister's life. A few nights ago, she saved my best friend's son from being killed. She's psychic all right. Crazy? Not a chance."

"That's what you think. She's responsible for our mother's death."

People stared and all their curiosity disturbed Morgan. Their directed interest sapped her energy.

Morgan took a calming breath and tried to remember this was her sister, her blood. Morgan had a suspicion that her mother had known what was to come and done the only thing she could to save her eldest daughter. Jillian wasn't objective, she was angry. Buried under all that anger was a hurt little girl sent away by her parents.

"Jillian. I did not kill our mother. James killed her all by himself."

"James. You call our father James."

"I may have lived in that house, and thank God you didn't, but he was never a father to me, or you. Always out for himself, he wanted to make money fast and easy and spend it even quicker. He didn't care how he treated our mother, or me. He didn't care what he had to do to get that money. Blackmail, fraud. Mom refused to make me help, and he killed her to get her out of the way. He thought without her between us, he could control me."

"Even you admit it's your fault. He told me how you hypnotized him or something. You were in his head. You forced him to kill her."

"Why would I do that? I loved her."

"Because you probably had some crazy delusional episode. It's because of you they sent me away. Because of you, I barely got to see her as a child. Now, I'll never have a chance to know her."

"Mom sent you away to keep you safe and away from James."

Morgan didn't want to do it. She didn't want to give voice to the unspeakable things her father had done to make her give him information. She didn't want to validate Jillian's belief that it was her fault her mother died. She could have cooperated and given him the information. She didn't want to see other people get hurt. She hadn't wanted her mother to get hurt. She would have suffered at her father's hands a thousand more times if it meant her mother would still be alive.

"I'll tell you why. Because our father didn't care if he had to beat me to a bloody pulp to get the information he wanted. Sometimes, he'd lock me in a closet for days. He didn't care if I was hurt, or hungry, or scared. All the better to get what he wanted. Then, he figured out the best way to get me to talk. If beating me and the closet and starvation didn't work, hell, let's beat her mother to get her to talk. It worked every time. He hit her once, a slap across the face that sent her thudding to the kitchen floor. He never had to do it again. From that moment on, if he went for her, he knew he'd get me to cooperate."

Jillian went completely still and stared hard at Morgan. Tyler sat stunned, his hands balled into fists on the table beside her.

"He wouldn't have hurt me? I'm not like you."

"And you think that would have saved you. Do you really think he would have believed you can't do what I can do? Do you think he wouldn't have beaten you to be sure you couldn't help him get what he wanted? If you believe that, then you're stupid on top of being angry about something Mom did to protect you."

Morgan took a deep breath and tried to keep her carefully constructed walls in place. But they were crumbling. Fast.

"I'm glad you weren't there. I'd take your anger and hatred any day over knowing he hurt you because of me. I wouldn't wish one single day of my life with that man on you. I'm glad you had a good childhood. You have a great life. Be happy, Jillian. It's all I want for you and from you."

"It should have been you, not her. Why didn't he just kill you?"

"Because he wants to use me to get what he wants. He'll stop at nothing to make that happen."

Tyler broke free from his stunned reaction to Morgan's admissions. He couldn't believe everything she'd said. It was all so cruel and sad.

"Jillian, you said your father told you Morgan made him kill your mother. When did you talk to him? Has he been in contact with you?"

"He's written me off and on over the years from prison. Since his release, I've spoken to him a few times. He wants to build a relationship with me," Jillian said to Morgan. "He understands the injustice of my being taken away from him."

Morgan closed her dropped jaw, flabbergasted. "Do you really believe the man who killed our mother in cold blood deserves a second chance at being a father? Do you really think that's what he wants?"

Morgan didn't believe it for a second. James wanted something from Jillian. She meant to find out what that something was before her father ruined the life Jillian had made for herself. She didn't want her sister to get hurt. She didn't want James using her niece and nephew to get what he wanted either. The thought of those children suffering at her father's hands turned her stomach.

"Jillian, you can't let that man into your life or near the children. He only wants to use you."

"He's my father."

"He killed our mother."

"You killed her," she snapped. "It's your fault."

"But the children," Morgan pleaded, hoping her sister would see beyond her father's manipulation that he believed she'd been cheated and abandoned. Her father would feed Jillian's anger, bring her around to sympathize with him, and take everything from her without regret.

"You stay away from my children. They aren't any of your concern."

Morgan didn't know what else to say. She couldn't get Jillian to set aside her anger and hurt to see what their father really wanted. Jillian didn't want to believe he could be evil enough to do those terrible things. Much easier to believe her insane sister was to blame for everything.

She simply nodded her agreement to stay away.

Jillian may not want Morgan in her life, but she did want something from her. It broke Morgan's heart when her sister's misguided anger turned to selfish greed.

"You'll continue with the account."

Not a question. A demand, and one her sister expected Morgan to follow. Irritated her sister could be so consumed with hatred toward her and in the next breath demand she give the children money.

"The children will have their college funds. It's my gift to them."

"Yeah, you've made sure of that, since you're the only signer on the account. How do I know you won't change your mind?"

"You don't, and since my word doesn't mean anything

to you, I guess you won't know. When the time comes for them to go to school, I'll make sure they have the money they need. It's the best I can do."

"You could put the account in my name."

"Why?"

"Then, you don't have to be involved."

Maybe Jillian was more like their father than she'd previously thought. "I could, but what difference does it make who signs on the account, so long as the children get their money."

"You just don't trust David and me to take care of the money and investments for them."

Before tonight, she might have considered changing the signing authority on the account. Now a strange undercurrent rippled in the air.

"You know, you're right. I don't trust you. There's a reason you want access to that money, and it isn't so you can manage the account. I have a lot of experience with stocks, bonds, and mutual funds. I made all that money. Why do you want access to it? Are you and David having financial trouble?" As a teacher, her sister made an okay salary along with David. They lived a comfortable life, but extras were an indulgence they probably had to forego to meet their monthly bills, especially with two growing children.

No, she and David had a good, solid life. Jillian's request came from something else. Or, more likely, someone else. "Does this have something to do with your recent calls from James?"

"He said you'd refuse. The money belongs to us."

"It does? You didn't work for it, I did. The money is mine, until I pay the college of the kids' choice. You won't see a dime. It's for them."

She made sure Jillian understood the money would go to the school, not to her or the children directly. Encouragement for the kids to go to college. If she simply gave them the money, they may not go. She wanted them to have every opportunity. Money would come later if they had a good education behind them.

"Why would you tell him about the money?" Tyler asked, his mind working overtime, trying to figure out what angle her father was working this time.

"He wanted to know what you've been doing all these years. I told him about you playing the stock market and doing really well. He wanted to know how I knew that, and I told him about the money and investments you made for the kids. That's all," she swore, biting her bottom lip and glancing away.

"That's all? Hardly. You're hiding something. And it has everything to do with James."

Jillian looked around the room, nervous about something. Tyler had seen enough liars to read all the signs. She never met his or Morgan's gaze. She fidgeted with her purse strap. Her voice went high and she spoke too fast, the words tumbling from her mouth. "I have to go. My family is waiting for me. We'll talk about this another time."

Chapter Twenty-Two

"SHE'S A REAL piece of work," Tyler couldn't help pointing out, angry Jillian would confront Morgan in public and in such a nasty way. "She hates your guts and demands money all in the same breath." Pissed off, his anger seeped out in his words, though he tried to hold it back for Morgan's sake.

She'd been sitting there quietly for the last ten minutes. He'd given her the time she needed to settle down. In that time, she slowly transformed again before his eyes. Her sister sapped all the light out of her. When she left, the glow and vitality in Morgan slowly returned. Her eyes brightened, her skin returned to the warm, sun-kissed glow she'd had before, and her hair went from flat to bouncy once again.

Sam was right: people's anger physically harmed her. He imagined she reacted to anyone with a strong emotion. He wondered what she'd be like in the heat of passion. Just the thought sent a shaft of white-hot lust through his system, and he shifted uncomfortably.

Morgan came back to herself all at once at Tyler's words. For a moment, she'd completely forgotten about him, and still she felt like a part of her was safe knowing he'd always be there.

"I forgot you were here."

"You drifted away. I held your hand and waited for you to come back. Looks like you're almost all here now. Have a sip of your tea. It'll make you feel better."

It felt too good to have him care about her well-being. She took a sip of her tea and let out a big sigh.

"Let's get out of here. Where's the waitress? We need to pay the check."

"Already took care of it. She came by a few minutes ago," he said with an easy tone and smile.

"She did?" She didn't remember the woman coming by the table. She hated when that happened. Very disconcerting to blank out and not know what happened around her. She thought of her house in Colorado and the peace and safety she'd found there. She wanted to go home, and yet sitting next to Tyler felt almost as good.

"Yep."

She ran her hands through her hair and held her head between her hands and rested her elbows on the table. "She must have thought I was a complete space case. I'm so sorry I embarrassed you."

She looked so upset over something so little. He didn't care if she spaced out for a while. It gave him a chance to study her without her being aware of it. He liked looking at her beautiful face, the soft curve of her jaw, and the small pale freckles on her cheeks. She had the longest eyelashes. They swept up, a soft brown against the striking blue of her eyes.

"You didn't embarrass me. I told the waitress you were in shock because I told you I wanted to rip your clothes off and make love to you all night when we got home."

"You did not!"

"Sure did. She said if you weren't going to take me up on it, she'd be happy to take your place." Her shocked open mouth turned into a small grin. "That's just about the same smile you had when she said it."

"Oh, really."

"Yeah. I don't know if you were laughing at me or her."

"You're incorrigible. Listen, Tyler. You have to understand, I've been alone for a long time, and you and I have shared a kind of long-distance relationship . . ."

He stopped her right there. "We've shared a very one-sided long-distance relationship where you gave and gave and I took and took. Don't think for a minute I haven't figured that out. About the ripping off clothes and hot sex, it was just a joke to get the waitress to leave. Relax."

Her shoulders went lax and the intensity in her dimmed.

"Feeling better?"

She'd missed it. "You just did all that to take my mind off of that horrible scene with my sister."

"It worked. You're looking better every minute. Besides, we learned a few things about her and your father."

"He wants something from me, and he's going to use her to get it."

"Exactly. He knows there's money set aside for the kids. He'll probably be wondering how much he can get out of you based on how much Jillian told him you've set aside for them."

Morgan rolled her eyes. "I think my sister's thinking along the same lines as my father, only she'd like to get her hands on the children's account. He's probably told her that he can"—she made air quotes with her fingers—"*invest* the money for her and make her ten times as much. Then, she and her husband will have all their dreams come true," she said with a sarcastic and whimsical note and rolled her eyes.

"How much are we talking about?"

"In the kid's accounts?"

"Yes, and how much could he expect to get from you."

"He's not getting anything from me."

"What if he took one of the kids? How much would you pay to get them back?"

She put both her hands over her face. "He'd do it. He'd hurt one of them to get me to cooperate. I know he would."

Tyler hated to put the possibility to her, but she had to face what could happen. "How much?"

"All I ever wanted was to have enough money to live my life the way I wanted. I've worked really hard to put some money away and buy the property in Colorado. It's my sanctuary. I can be there and no one bothers me. I don't have to worry about the guy next door, or across the street. I don't have to put up blocks and guard myself, like I do when I'm here."

"If you don't want to tell me how much, then say so."

"It's not that. The first year I started, I took what little money I had and hoped I didn't lose it the first day. It turns out I have a knack for investing. Like I said, I wanted to make enough to live on and buy a home. I earned enough the first year to do both, though I didn't buy the property in Colorado for a few years. I rented a house in Texas before I moved. After that, I continued to work at it and set my goals higher."

"So, what are we talking about? A hundred grand? Several hundred grand?"

"And then some," she said and smiled sheepishly. She didn't want to brag, or seem like a snob about how much money she made.

Her evasion told him he wasn't even in the ballpark.

"Are you trying hard not to tell me we're talking in the millions?"

"A few," she said vaguely.

"What's a few? Two? Three?"

"About nine." She sat back in her seat and stared at the table. "I told you, I'm good at it. I've been doing it for the last five years. I have a lot of time on my hands. When I had enough for a house and to live on comfortably, I used the rest to invest. I figured if I lost it, I could start over with the money I make on the website. It isn't much, but it's enough of an income to cover my monthly expenses. Sometimes things go my way, and other times they don't. I turned a little bit of money into a lot. I set aside some money for the kids. It's some long-term investments that will grow and be enough for them to go to any college they want. Right now, there's about forty thousand dollars."

"Forty grand. That's a lot, but not enough for your sister to use without jeopardizing the kids' education."

"Forty grand each. There's eighty thousand all together."

"Damn, where are you sending these kids to college? Europe?"

"No." She laughed. "I want them to go wherever they want, and be whatever they want. What if one of them wants to be a doctor? That's four years of college, four years of med school, internships, and whatever else. That will take years, and that takes money. Law school would be the same. What if they want to get a PhD?"

"I see your point. I think I need to start saving now."

"You don't have any kids."

"If that's what college is going to cost me, I'd better start now." He smiled and liked that she smiled back.

He couldn't compete with her wealth, didn't know why he felt he had to. So she made more money than he did. It shouldn't matter. It didn't matter to Jack that Jenna had millions and ran Merrick International. It didn't bother Sam that Elizabeth came from an extremely wealthy family and was worth millions herself. Cameron was rich and Marti was even richer than him. They all seemed fine with it. He would be too. It would just take some getting used to.

"I just want to know what we're dealing with, so that when he calls me, I'm prepared."

"Why would he call you?"

"Because he knows I'm in touch with you. He'll try to get to you through me. Jillian will probably tell him she saw us together. Does she know where you're staying?"

"No. You don't even know where I'm staying."

"Why is that? Did you not want me to know, or was that all Sam and Jack's idea? You know Sam won't let me live down the fact he's seen you naked."

Pretty in her embarrassment, she turned a bright pink right before his eyes.

"It's not that I didn't want you to know, I thought you needed time to be alone and clear your head. Besides, I thought you didn't want to see me. When I got here tonight and saw you, I knew it would be impossible to avoid seeing you. How'd you know I'd be here?"

"FBI, remember. Sam told me about your sister. I figured at some point you'd come see her."

"You staked out my sister, so you could see me?"

"Is it so hard to believe I desperately wanted to see you? Besides, I thought seeing your sister and her family would teach me something about you. You're truly unique and special."

She turned her head and looked at the table instead of him. Uncomfortable, she changed the subject. "You know, I couldn't help it, Sam had to undress me. I was passed out."

He rubbed his hand over her back and shoulders and pulled her to his side. "I know. You were hurt. I should have been the one to take care of you. I'm sorry. How're the back and arm?"

"The stitches itch, but they're healing. They don't hurt anymore."

He kissed the side of her head. "I'm real sorry I wasn't more cooperative. You should have told me about what happened. Maybe I could have helped and made it less debilitating for you."

"You weren't in the mood to listen, let alone help me."

"I'm sorry. You're right. I didn't get my head screwed on straight until about four o'clock yesterday morning. Those late-night reflections of one's life take a lot out of a man. I finally straightened myself out and realized if there are things in my life I want, I have to work to get them, and that means putting in as much as I take out."

"Four o'clock in the morning, huh?"

"Honestly, I found it hard to sleep knowing you were out there somewhere." He gestured to the room and world at large. "Knowing you were close by, and I'd been the one to push you away, only made it worse. I wanted to hear you tell me I wasn't alone, like you used to. I needed to know you were all right. I wanted you to tell me we were back to being close. Instead, you were physically close, but I couldn't reach you. I tried really hard, but it didn't work. You know, you're really doing a number on me."

"You're doing a really good job of doing one on me, too."

"Really?"

"Yeah. When you start talking, you can really turn a girl's head."

"I like your head just fine. You're smart and funny and you do some pretty remarkable things with that pretty head of yours. What I'm interested in is a little further south."

"Oh, really." She raised her eyebrows, her eyes filled with disappointment.

She thought all he wanted was to cop a feel and tumble her into bed. That wasn't the case, and it stung to know that's all she thought he wanted. He had it coming, and he knew it. Now he needed to make her believe she was different. His friends had been trying to tell him for years, but now he got it. He felt it in every part of himself, deep into his soul. She was the one for him.

"Morgan, while I think you're gorgeous from the top of your head to the tips of your toes, the thing I'm interested in, besides your dirty mind, is your heart."

The unexpected truth, the sweet smile on his face, and the soft glow in his eyes when he looked at her melted her heart. What woman wouldn't simply melt when a man asked for her heart? Especially when that man was the right man.

She had no words to give him that would tell him how she felt. She turned in the booth and wrapped her arms around his neck and kissed him with all the love she had for him. She hoped he felt it.

"Wow!" Blown away, he didn't know a kiss could feel like this. He held her face in his hands. Her eyes came open and instead of seeing warmth, or even a sparkle, he saw the fog had rolled in again.

"Phonebook."

"It isn't exactly what I thought you'd say after a kiss like that. I know I have an effect on women, but never have I made a woman say *phonebook*."

"He's going to kill her."

And that killed the moment they'd just shared.

Chapter Twenty-Three

TYLER HELD HER close and practically dragged her out of the restaurant and into his car. Physically, she was there, but mentally she was trying to hold on to the images in her mind. She spoke softly to him and sat staring into space.

"She's alive. Something about her is keeping him from killing her like the others. She's sitting in a chair at a round table with a large crystal ball. It's just a prop. The room looks like so many of the other psychic shops, but the woman looks at the room and shop as ridiculous.

"That's what's different about her. She's got a real gift, and he knows it. He's keeping her alive for a reason. He wants something from her."

"Where, Morgan? Where are they?"

"I need a phonebook. That's how I've seen him in the past, crossing out the name or ad. I can't see the name, but I did see the size of the ad and where it's located on the page. If you get me a phonebook, maybe I can pick it out."

Tyler pulled the car over next to a line of shops, leaped out, and headed for the payphone outside a liquor store. He couldn't believe he'd actually found one of the endangered gadgets. He opened the phonebook holder. Empty. With a frustrated growl, he ran inside the liquor store, identified himself as an FBI agent, and asked the clerk if he had a phonebook. The clerk found one in the cluttered back office.

He slid back into the car, dropped the book in her lap; she immediately flipped through it, and he called Sam.

"Sam, it's Tyler. I'm with Morgan. She says our guy is holding a woman hostage. No, he hasn't killed her yet. At least, that's not what Morgan is seeing. She's looking in the phonebook, trying to get us a location."

Morgan found the listings for psychics in the city, and he sped away from the curb and headed in that direction.

"I'm not sure. This isn't the same phonebook. It's not laid out like the one the man is using."

"Just do your best. Do any of the ads look familiar? Is there something about the ad you see that is the same in one of the ads in this book?"

She leaned her head back on the headrest and cleared her mind of the speed of the car, the sounds of the road, Tyler sitting next to her, and everything else. She focused all her energy on the snapshot of the scene in her head. The open phonebook lay on the scarred coffee table. She hated seeing the names and ads already crossed out on the open page. Four murders, so far. She looked to the new, circled ad. He hadn't crossed it out yet. The ad showed a rose encased in a crystal ball.

She opened her eyes and focused on the listings in front of her. She didn't see it. She turned the page and scanned the ads. She tapped her finger on the one she needed. Smaller in this book, tucked in between several larger listings.

"Here. We have to go here. It's on Grant Avenue. Psychic Bloom. She offers spiritual guidance, in addition to the usual palm readings and astrological charts and predictions. There's a neon palm sign in the window and another neon crystal ball with a rose in the middle, like here in the phonebook."

"Sam, did you get all that? Yeah, we're on our way. Call the local guys and have them get down there. She's not dead yet. Maybe we can get to her before he kills her."

"Tyler . . ." She couldn't get the words out. Something stole her breath away and the woman's words echoed through her mind.

Morgan's coming for you!

"Morgan? Morgan? Morgan!" Tyler called to her, but he seemed so far away.

She floated through a dark tunnel and in the light at the other end laid the woman. The tunnel closed before her eyes, framing the woman's face. He was killing her, and as he did, the woman looked back through the tunnel and directly into Morgan's eyes.

"Morgan! He wants you. He's coming for you."

Her lungs burned and she tried to draw air that wouldn't come.

"Morgan. Baby, come on, breathe. Morgan!" Tyler rubbed his big hand over her chest above her breasts.

The tunnel closed completely as she took a deep shuddering gasp and her eyes flew open.

She grabbed Tyler's hand and held tight. "He killed her. He killed her," she sobbed, "and it's all my fault. He's coming for me."

"No, honey. It's not your fault. He doesn't know who you are, or where you are. You're safe."

"No, I'm not. They aren't. That's why he's going after the psychic shops and the women who run them. He's looking for me and trying to get them to tell him where I am."

"Then why is he cutting out their tongues and gluing their eyes shut?"

"He thinks all psychics can see something he doesn't want anyone to know. He thinks I know something about him."

She leaned her head against the side window and stared out over the hood and watched the road disappear under the car. She didn't see the traffic or the people outside. She didn't realize they'd entered the city, or the fact Tyler ran red lights and exceeded the speed limit.

They stopped in front of several buildings housing shops. Police cars lined the streets and people gathered at the yellow tape the police had strung up between the cars and buildings.

"Morgan, if you went in there, could you see more and maybe tell me more?"

Rousing herself, she considered his request. "It's possible. I don't know. This isn't what I'm used to. Usually, I get glimpses of the cases you're working on from you, and I have a vision. That's why the visions were so vague. You know, the green man."

"Yeah, he turned out to be a guy who worked in the green section of a flour mill and wore a green uniform."

"Exactly. This time, I can actually see the events more clearly. I have more information because I'm involved. The information isn't coming from you secondhand. It's coming from him, because he's connected to me somehow."

"What about your website? Could he have contacted you that way?"

"It's possible. I don't know. There've been lots of requests. I shut the site down after the press conference. I haven't opened it back up again."

"We'll have to look into the people who've contacted you that way. Maybe we'll get lucky and find something. Maybe if you open up the site again, he'll try to contact you. We can trace him that way. I'll have to ask the tech guys about it."

She looked terrible. It reminded him of the night she'd come into the restaurant and faced that drugged-up boy with a gun. Wiped out, her energy drained. He wanted to take her home and put her to bed.

He hated to ask her for help, but didn't have a choice. She was the best chance they had of catching this guy. "Honey, do you think you can go in there with me? If you can help us find this guy, I'd really like you to try. But I don't want you to get hurt."

"I'll go in, but I can't guarantee I'll see anything. In fact, this could backfire, and you'll be picking me up off the floor."

"Why? What do you mean?"

"Anger, hate, passion, and other strong emotions can linger in a space. You've seen what can happen. That boy laid me out for almost a full day. This could very well do the same thing, or worse."

"Worse? How worse?"

"Let's go inside."

He grabbed her shoulder and made her turn back to him before she opened the door. "Morgan, how much worse?"

She didn't want to explain again what it took to do what she did. Like talking rocket science to a kindergartner, they had no concept of how gravity worked and how to make a rocket overcome gravity to reach orbit. How could she explain energy and the give-and-take of her gift to someone who'd never experienced it?

"You know how sometimes you have a really long day, and you've used your mind so much that you're just exhausted. It can be more exhausting than running several miles, or working out for an hour. It can physically and mentally drain you to concentrate and focus for long periods of time. It takes energy from your body and your spirit to give that kind of concentration to something."

"Okay. I follow you. In order to do what you do, it takes concentrated focus. Is that what you're saying?"

"Yes. Now suppose that concentrated focus is like the light going through a magnifying glass. The light gets concentrated to a point that can burn hot enough to start a fire."

"Okay." He was starting to understand why she looked like she wilted when she was using her gift. She was the light going through the magnifying glass and her energy was what burned up. Or something like that.

"So, that's the concentrated focus it takes to do what I do. In the process, that focus burns up my energy, or better yet, that's the energy I expend in order to focus. Now, add in the energy that I absorb from the other person or event. In this case, imagine I'm an orange and the other person's energy, or the event's energy, is a hand holding that orange. Now squeeze. What happens to me, the orange?"

"Shit!"

"Actually, orange juice."

"Morgan, that's not funny. Are you saying this could really hurt you?"

"I'm saying there's a balance to things. When that balance is knocked off-kilter in my world, something's gotta give."

"I don't want that something to be you." He laid his hand on her thigh and squeezed. He'd have liked to kiss her, and take her home instead, but a lot of people milled around and many of the officers had already recognized him. He didn't want everyone razzing him over kissing a woman at the scene of a murder he was supposed to be working.

"I have some mental blocks I can use. I can block out a lot of what's coming at me, so long as it's nothing intense. Let's just go in and see what happens."

"I don't want anything to happen to you." He took her hand and brought her palm to his lips. He kissed her hand and her fingers pressed to his face.

She kept her hand to his cheek and said, "You're stalling."

"I'm stalling," he confirmed.

"It's a nice way to stall me, but we should go now. People have noticed you're here. Sam's waiting for us inside. He's getting antsy."

"You know that?"

"Yes. I know that." She stepped out of the car ready to face a nightmare.

Chapter Twenty-Four

MORGAN WALKED TOWARD the shop, and the crowd's focus shifted to her. The police officer guarding the yellow tape barrier lifted the tape and let her through. Evidently, he'd seen her exit Tyler's car and let her pass with Tyler on her heels. She wanted to get this over. She kept telling herself, *Just go in and get it done.*

"Morgan, wait up," Tyler called and ran up to her before she went through the shop door. He'd fallen behind putting the mask over his head to conceal his identity from the crowd and news cameras. "You can't just walk into a crime scene."

She realized that when a police officer blocked her entrance into the shop.

"Let's begin, so we can go home."

"I'm all for the second part of that," Tyler said and reached out to brush his fingers through her hair. Like before, she leaned into his touch, then stepped away and focused on the store.

Tyler showed his badge to the police officer at the door. Sam replaced him in the doorway while Morgan gave them her impressions.

"He came in this way. He stood out here for several minutes watching her inside, dusting the merchandise on the shelves. Soft music played in the background. Some kind of whimsical, enchanted instrumental." She swayed to the rhythm of the music in her mind. "When she noticed him through the window, he went inside."

Morgan jumped when her vision shifted to the outside world again, and Sam surprised her standing in front of her. Tyler thought she'd seen Sam come to the door. She'd simply been too focused on the scene in her mind to notice him. He'd have to remember to keep an eye on her. She already looked pale. He didn't want her passing out on him like she'd done in the restaurant. He'd also watch to make sure she didn't hurt herself when she lost focus on everything around her.

"Hi, Sam."

"Hi. How'd you know it was me under the mask? Never mind. Don't answer that. Are you actually going to come in here?"

"Yes."

"She thinks she can help," Tyler said.

"The coroner hasn't removed the body. The forensic guys are dusting for prints and gathering evidence. Tyler and I will bring you in, but I want you to stay between us. Don't touch anything."

"I won't. I'll do whatever you two tell me to do. I don't want to mess anything up."

Sam and Tyler just stood there. Neither one of them wanted to be the one to take her inside when they knew it might hurt her.

"Are you guys going to make me stand in the door all night, or should we go in and see what happens?"

Tyler and Sam exchanged a look and Sam preceded them in with Tyler coming in behind Morgan. They watched her as she stood between them. She didn't say anything. She just looked around.

Several other people worked scattered throughout the room, collecting evidence, taking pictures, and dusting every surface someone might have touched.

She'd spent much of her teenage years searching out places like this, hoping to find someone like her, someone who could explain the things she did.

This room didn't hold the answers she needed about the murder. It held the lingering energy of people who sought answers they already knew, if they'd only quiet themselves to listen to their inner voice. She knew the scenario well. She received most of the questions through her website.

The room held the lingering swirl of excitement and fun. The kind of feeling you got at an amusement park, that sense of anticipation and wonder. The tingly feeling of fear when there wasn't anything to really be afraid of, but you were, because you were headed into something unknown.

"There isn't anything in this room but what you'd

expect. People come in here looking for answers, and they're all tied up with conflicting emotions. Some are excited and others are afraid of what the answer might be. There's an overwhelming feeling of hopefulness. Some are hoping for confirmation and others are looking for validation. Many are looking for someone to tell them things will be different from what they fear."

She smiled. "It's kind of funny. People come in looking for magic. When they get it, some are excited and happy about finding something weird. Others go into some sort of denial, confusion, and anger. *She couldn't possibly have known that.*" She mimicked so many people who had said the same thing to her—Tyler and Sam included.

"Are you ready to go in the room off the back? There isn't much space, and she's still in there," Sam said, as much to prepare her as to stall for time before he took her back. No one needed to see the brutal murder, especially someone like Morgan, who might be able to feel the emotions of the killing.

She nodded her agreement and waited for Sam to lead her inside. Tyler stood so close behind her she could feel the brush of his jacket against her long hair.

They entered the room through a set of heavy purple velvet drapes, tied back with gold rope with tassels, like entering the tower of a castle. The walls were painted with a faux stone block pattern and wood planks worn smooth covered the floor. The owner had put a lot of thought into creating an old-world and mystical feeling. The soft glow of candles had been extinguished. The recessed lights burned bright, along with the flash of the camera.

Several shelves lined the walls. All held candles and crystal balls on pedestals in varying sizes and colors. In the candlelight, Morgan imagined the crystal balls would gleam and shine, casting light and shadow throughout the room.

She didn't want to look behind the square table draped in heavy dark blue velvet. The golden base for the crystal ball sat empty on the table. The large crystal ball lay on the floor next to a small bookcase. Cracked and chipped from crashing to the floor during the struggle.

"This isn't good."

"Murder usually isn't," Tyler said from behind her. He'd been taking in the entire scene while keeping a close watch on Morgan. So far, she seemed fine. Nothing out of the ordinary.

"That's not what I mean. There's no anger here. No rage. The two things you'd associate with someone strangling another person." Tyler moved to the side of her, and Morgan went still when she felt the cold air on the back of her neck, raising the fine hairs on end and replacing Tyler's warmth. Now someone else stood behind her, someone not of this earth.

He's coming for you, the breeze at the back of her neck whispered into her ear.

"Do you know who he is?" she asked the room at large.

Sam answered without even thinking. "You know we don't."

"How come you don't know?" Detective Stewart asked

as he joined them. "I thought you were here to tell us," he said sarcastically.

"I wasn't talking to you guys. I was talking to her."

Sam and Tyler exchanged glances. Detective Stewart rolled his eyes.

Tyler asked the obvious question. "Can you talk to her?"

"Yes. She's here."

"Yeah, right." Stewart wasn't going to stand around in the middle of investigating a murder and listen to some psychic witch spout off about a ghost in the room.

"Stinky Stewart, shut up. I came here because *you* involved me by giving my name to the press and the murderer. If you give me a few minutes, I'll tell you what I know. And then, I'll leave."

He hadn't heard that terrible nickname since grade school. He'd been an outcast even as a small child and always felt like an outsider and the other kids sensed it. They'd given him the nickname in the first grade. He'd hated it then, but not as much as hearing her use it now. It did, however, have the desired effect. She couldn't have known about the name unless she was psychic. He didn't comment, or acknowledge he'd even heard the name, except to keep his mouth closed and let her have her few minutes.

Tyler and Sam didn't say a word. Morgan's tone didn't call for comment, and neither did the implication that she knew something about Stewart he'd rather keep quiet. Everyone went silent when Morgan walked around the table and stared down at the body of the woman, whose ghost lingered.

Morgan sighed heavily. "The other psychics he's killed weren't as gifted, or gifted at all with the sight. She had a serious brain injury as a child. She woke up from a coma with the sight."

"Did you tell you this?" Tyler asked softly, unsure what to believe.

Morgan smiled. "Still have a hard time believing in me. Yes, Tyler. Remember the rose princess. She left you a gift after you found her. Is it so hard to believe this woman . . ."

Cheryl, she heard from behind her.

"Cheryl is here with us now, and I can hear her."

"Cheryl?" Detective Stewart asked. "We haven't identified her as of yet. We've only found information on Rose, the alias the woman used as part of her gimmick for the shop."

"Nobody wants a psychic named Cheryl when they're looking for fun, or spiritual guidance, so she used the name Rose for the shop. He came in and asked for a reading. He knew she was different because she charged more. You'll find a fifty-dollar bill underneath her. It'll be your best bet for the man's fingerprints."

She stood still as a statue, her eyes on the wall, opened herself, and in an unusual neutral voice she recounted the events as she saw them, like she was watching a movie on an imaginary screen.

"Cheryl brought him back here. They sat at the table. She asked him what he wanted to know. He told her he needed to find me."

"*I want to know where the psychic Morgan is. I want*

to know if she's coming after me. I want to know if she sees me."

Morgan didn't realize she spoke the words in an odd voice to everyone in the room.

Her voice changed again.

"Morgan seeks you out only to discover who you are. If you weren't seeking her, she wouldn't seek you. You started it, and she will finish it."

"Does she know me?"

"Cheryl looked up from the crystal ball and into the eyes of a killer. Calm, his eyes were black as night, and just as cold as winter."

"She seeks the killer that you've become, not the one you try to hide. She doesn't remember the past. It's the present and the future she seeks. She's coming for you. She'll stop you."

"No!"

"He leaped across the table and grabbed her around the throat. The chair fell back and they were on the floor. The crystal ball fell, and she watched it roll across the floor as her life left her body. She called out to me."

Morgan, he's outside. He's waiting for you. He knows you're here. The soft voice came from beside her, as if someone stood right there.

Morgan turned around abruptly, her eyes the darkest blue Tyler had ever seen them. She didn't see him. She stared through him. He didn't panic until she ran out of the room and toward the front door of the shop.

She yelled over her shoulder, "He's here. He's waiting outside for me."

She made it out onto the sidewalk before Tyler grabbed her from behind and hauled her body against his chest. People gathered behind the yellow crime tape. All of them stared at her and Tyler. She tried to break free and scan every face in the crowd. She dragged Tyler several steps out into the street. Reporters yelled her name and threw out questions. She didn't even realize they'd heard Tyler call out for her to wait when they arrived. Now, they knew she was here, and so did the killer. She just had to find him in the sea of faces.

She caught a glimpse of him as he turned from the group and walked away. Free of the crush of people, he ran up an alley.

"There. Blue jacket. He's over there."

"Stay here," Tyler demanded, and he and Sam took off through the crowd of people and went after the man they'd barely gotten a glimpse of as he ducked into the alley. Their only hope was that it was a dead end.

They ran between the buildings as fast as they could. They didn't see the man and had to take precautions not to walk right into a bullet, or anything else. Several shop doors lined the alley. All locked up tight. Dumpsters and trash provided several hiding places. They made their way, scanning every nook and dark crevice. They emerged onto a busy sidewalk and street with several other alleyways and streets leading off it. Their man got away, blended into the pedestrian traffic, disappeared down another avenue, or inside one of the many stores. The police would canvas the area, but both Sam and Tyler doubted they'd find anything. None of them had seen the man clearly.

"Morgan can work with a sketch artist, but it's going to take hours to circulate the picture. He's gone. For now," Tyler vowed.

Tyler!

"Morgan," he said out loud.

"What about her?" Sam asked, confused by his stunned outburst.

"I heard her. She just called to me." He turned and raced back to the shop, hoping he hadn't left her and the murderer had doubled back and taken her.

His panic only rose when he got back to the police barricade and she wasn't waiting for him. None of the officers knew where she went. Reporters called out asking to speak with her. He and Sam kept their faces covered with the lightweight ski caps. With FBI written across their jackets, no mistaking who they were. They needed to get out of there and preserve their identities. They worked undercover and couldn't afford to have their faces splashed all over the news. But where was Morgan . . .

They finally got their answer when they went back inside the building. The coroner had arrived. In the process of bagging the body, he informed them, "Stewart took her with him to work with a sketch artist after he saw the fifty-dollar bill lying under the body."

"How long ago did they leave?"

"Just a few minutes. She put up quite a fuss about going with him. She kept telling him she couldn't go into a police station. She said she wanted to wait for you two."

Sam and Tyler both knew why she wouldn't want to go into a police station. No one ever went there because they were happy about something.

"Shit!" Tyler said frustrated. "She can't go in there. When I get my hands on Stewart, I'll kill him."

Chapter Twenty-Five

"Tyler's going to wonder where I am," Morgan said nervously.

"He'll be here soon. He and Sam will tie up all the loose ends at the scene. That's their job. It'll take them a while to coordinate everything with my partner, Detective Rasmussen. That will give us time to do the sketch of the suspect. Maybe we'll finally have something to work with. If you're right," he added.

"I'll do the sketch, but I'm not going into the police station. You don't understand; that will only make things worse. I won't be able to function in there. It'll be too overwhelming."

Stewart rolled his eyes. "You'll be fine. I'll set you up in an office, and you'll do the sketch," he ordered.

They arrived and the closer they got to the door, the more she resisted. He finally clamped a hand over her wrist and dragged her up the steps and through the door, ignoring her attempts to pull free.

"Let me go. I can't go in there."

Several people waited in what could only be described as a reception area. An officer sat behind a short wall, typing on a computer, and ignoring the many people around him all asking for assistance. Several bench seats were pushed up against the walls, filled with waiting people. Some were just everyday people dressed in work clothes, a couple homeless people looking to get in out of the cold, and others who seemed to be the people most likely to be arrested. A couple prostitutes and a few thugs looked like they'd rather be anywhere than a police station. The odor of burnt coffee and unwashed bodies hung in the air.

The girl caught her attention. Of all the feelings of anger and desperation in the room, her despair washed over Morgan and took hold. She tried to pull away from Detective Stewart, but he wouldn't let her go and dragged her behind him. He walked her up to the man behind the wall.

"Is the sketch artist here yet?"

"Not yet."

"Detective Stewart, if you don't want me to find out other embarrassing things about you besides your nickname, you'll let me go. Now." Morgan didn't care about the sketch artist. She focused on the girl. About fifteen, she sat with her head down and her hands folded in her lap. She didn't lean back in her seat, but crouched over as if sitting in a pew praying. Morgan heard her prayer.

Someone, please help me.

"Who is that girl?" she asked the sergeant.

He looked up at the crowd, then back to Morgan. "I see the same people I see all the time. The faces might change, but the general array of characters remains the same." He nodded to the girl. "All, except her. She comes in all the time. Sits there for hours. She doesn't talk to anyone. I've seen her so many times before, now she just blends into the room.

"I think she needs a place to hang out while her parents are working, or something. She doesn't look like she lives on the streets. She's got good clothes and almost new shoes." He pointed to her feet with a pen.

Morgan frowned. This man could notice so much about the girl and not see what was right in front of him. She was scared to talk to anyone.

Morgan took two steps to go to the girl, but stopped short when Stewart blocked her path.

"We've got work to do. We aren't here to befriend little girls looking for a place to hang out. Why isn't she at the mall?"

"Because she came here for help."

The sergeant looked up from his computer. "She doesn't make any trouble, sits there quiet as a mouse, so I let her be."

"Did you ever ask her if she needed anything?"

"I did once. She just looked at me. She didn't say a word." He shrugged. "I'm not a babysitter to every young person who comes into the precinct. I have a job to do and taking care of wayward kids isn't one of them."

She wouldn't ask for help out loud. She's too scared to talk to a man.

Morgan turned back to the girl. She lifted her face and caught Morgan's eye. Morgan about fell to her knees when the visions hit her, one after another. Unspeakable abuse inflicted upon a fragile, innocent girl. Tears slid down Morgan's face.

Stewart saw the tears and let go of her arm. She walked across the room to the girl. Small, timid, about five-foot-one, dressed in jeans and a long-sleeve white T-shirt. Her brown hair tied back in a ponytail. Her sad eyes got to her. She looked at Morgan coming toward her like a lost puppy looks at its mother.

Morgan stood before the little girl and waited for her to speak. She didn't, and Morgan knew she wouldn't. She waited for someone to send her away. She didn't believe anyone would help her, though she sat praying for that very thing.

"My name is Morgan. I will help you."

All the girl needed to hear. She stood and wrapped her arms around Morgan and held on for dear life. She didn't want to let her go and find that she was there one minute and gone the next, as if she'd conjured her up in her mind like she'd thought so many times. She'd sat in that chair praying someone would help. She'd imagined someone would see her pain and make it all go away.

Today. Finally. Her prayers had been answered. This woman saw what no one else saw. This woman knew the unspeakable. This woman knew it without her saying anything, because she couldn't say the words.

The girl trembled in Morgan's arms. She might be a teenager, but she was all little girl. Frightened to the point she'd never matured into an independent and vibrant teen. Her world was filled with dark secrets, and an overwhelming demand not to speak the truth, for to do so held the threat of even greater pain. Her only teenage defiance was coming to the police station time and again hoping for help. If she were found out, it would spell disaster for her, and even the possibility of death.

Morgan turned the little girl's back to the sergeant and Stewart. She held onto the girl with a good grasp, though hers was much softer and more comforting than that of the little girl, and for good reason.

"Detective Stewart, would you please find me a female officer. We need someone who is soft-spoken, patient, and caring. This little girl needs our help." To prove her point, she lifted the back of the girl's shirt a mere two inches. The bruises and other marks were unmistakable. Both Stewart and the sergeant sucked in shocked breaths and understood immediately. Neither said a word as they went to get a female officer.

Morgan stood with her arms around the girl. She didn't speak. She didn't cry. She just held on and trembled with fear her head pressed to Morgan's chest over her breaking heart.

The three officers returned. The new blond officer, a woman, had a soft face. Her eyes were blue, and although she looked to be all business, when she smiled at the girl, she looked welcoming.

"I'm Officer McCormick. I understand you need my help."

Morgan liked her immediately. She'd said just the right thing to get the girl's attention and a chance for trust.

"Officer McCormick. I'm Morgan Standish."

"There's no introduction needed. We've all heard about you around here. It's a pleasure to meet you."

Morgan felt just as welcome, as if she'd been invited to dinner.

"This is"—she looked down at the girl in her arms and heard her say in her mind, *Leslie*—"Leslie." Morgan looked into the girl's eyes and waited for the questions to come. She asked one question. The most important one to Leslie.

Did God send you?

"Yes, he did, honey. I'm going to speak for you because you can't speak for yourself. Understand?"

The little girl nodded.

Morgan looked at the three police officers standing by waiting. She noticed others had been informed she was in the building. They stared with curiosity. Apparently, the infamous psychic had arrived.

"What did she say?" Officer McCormick asked.

No one actually heard Leslie speak, but Morgan heard her just the same. "She asked if God sent me. I think my being here was certainly meant to be. Leslie needs help, and I'm here to make sure she gets it."

"She will," Officer McCormick agreed. "Let's move into one of the rooms back here. They're quiet, and we can talk."

Officer McCormick led the way while Morgan and the girl walked behind her. Morgan never let go of the girl, and the girl never let go of Morgan. Though many people stared as they made their way to an interrogation room, no one said a word. They all made way for the psychic, who heard a little girl speak, even though she'd never said a word.

Chapter Twenty-Six

"MORGAN'S BEEN AT the police station for nearly three hours," Tyler said for the second time in ten minutes.

"She's helping out one of the officers with a child. I'm sure she's fine," Sam assured Tyler.

"I don't think she's fine. You don't think she's fine."

"Why do you say that?" Sam asked.

"Because you're doing fifty in a thirty-five zone. You're as anxious as I am."

Sam didn't deny it. Anxious, jumpy, they needed to get to Morgan and make sure she was okay. Stewart had been vague, avoiding Tyler's pointed questions about why he'd kept Morgan at the station so long. Still, Stewart's tone held an edge.

Tyler didn't trust the bastard. Stewart left something out. Something he didn't want them to know about Morgan and what was happening at the precinct.

They'd spent the last three hours directing the officers in a neighborhood canvas trying to find the murderer. Stewart managed to send them a copy of the sketch the police artist completed before Morgan assisted with the child. They'd been surprised to get one so quickly. Morgan had been right. The guy was ordinary. Nothing distinguished him from a thousand other men, although the sketch and her description were very good.

They parked, entered the precinct, and waded through the officers milling around the open lobby area. Many of them turned their interest to Tyler and Sam's arrival.

"That woman is the most amazing thing I've ever witnessed." The desk sergeant shook his head in disbelief, drawing their attention.

A strikingly beautiful woman, Morgan wouldn't be missed in a crowd of models. Something ethereal radiated about her, in addition to her physical appearance. The sergeant spoke about more than her appearance, and by the stares they received from the officers waiting around the precinct, Tyler and Sam both knew Morgan was doing her thing to everyone's amazement. They still didn't know what she was doing and exchanged a this-isn't-going-to-be-good look.

"What are you talking about? Where is she?"

"In interrogation room three. She's been in there more than two hours. She hasn't stopped talking for that girl. They're saying it's the worst case of child abuse they've ever come across. We never would have known if Morgan hadn't come in here. I tell you, that girl has sat in this lobby more times than I can count and never said a word to anyone. Morgan takes one look at her and the girl wrapped herself around her and never let go. Even now, she's in Morgan's arms and just sits there while Morgan tells all the bad things that ever happened to her. It's like listening to a horror movie that never ends."

"Morgan knew about the abuse?" Tyler asked surprised.

"I've never seen so many black and blue marks on a person. Cigarette burns, too. You'd have never known just looking at her in her jeans and long sleeve shirt. I don't want to even think about what else her clothes hid."

"Morgan's been in the interrogation room since then?" Fear for Morgan lanced through his gut.

The sergeant leaned back, apprehension and fear in his eyes as Tyler loomed over him. They could just imagine what happened to that little girl. They'd worked enough child cases to know what kind of horror monsters inflicted on a child. One case was too many in their book. To think Morgan was going through all those emotions and seeing all those horrors was bad enough, but Tyler and Sam also knew Morgan had been abused as a child herself.

"Yes. Everyone knows she's here. They've been taking turns listening from the adjoining room and watching Morgan and Officer McCormick go through everything. It's amazing and strange to watch. Morgan, she just keeps talking like she can't stop the words anymore."

The sergeant looked past them, anxious. "They're bringing in the father. That's what everyone is waiting to see. A couple of officers took him into custody earlier. He should arrive soon for questioning."

That's all Tyler and Sam needed to hear. They made their way through the doors adjoining the lobby past the many rows of cubicles. Most of the officers tried to look busy, but many of them stood, looking toward the interrogation rooms.

Tyler didn't want to barge in on Morgan and the child. He didn't want to scare her, or make her uncomfortable. He and Sam entered the adjoining room where people watched and listened through the two-way mirror. Tyler opened the door, surprised to see the room filled to capacity with officers. Stewart sat near the glass. He had a difficult time seeing into the other room because of all the people seated and standing in here.

Tyler didn't waste any time. "Stewart, what the hell is going on? Why is Morgan in there working on a child abuse case when she's supposed to be helping us with a serial killer?"

His tone and his question had the desired effect. Officers scrambled to get out of the room and back to their jobs. No one wanted to be in the path of Tyler's wrath, not to mention on the bad side of the FBI and their psychic.

Once the room cleared out, only Detective Stewart and a lieutenant working the Special Victims Unit remained. Morgan's voice droned on over the speaker in an ominous monotone recounting a terrible scene in which the girl had been beaten for not washing her dinner dish properly. She'd been dunked into an ice water bath and held down until her lungs felt like they'd burst. Tyler was afraid to look through the glass and see Morgan. Even he couldn't have prepared himself for the sight of her. He and

Sam both swore at the same time when they saw Morgan sitting in a chair behind a table facing the window. The officer in the room sat with her back to the mirror, but you could see most of her profile. She wrote out notes, along with the taping, holding a tissue and wiping her eyes constantly. Her devastated appearance got to them as much as Morgan's sad voice.

The young girl, a teenager by her physical appearance, appeared small for her age, timid, nothing but a scared child. Sitting on Morgan's lap with her head on her chest, her blank eyes stared into nothing. She didn't speak as she held onto Morgan's arm with both hands, as if Morgan were her life preserver in the middle of a hurricane at sea.

Tyler and Sam both growled out an expletive at the same time.

"This isn't my doing," Stewart said quickly. "She insisted the girl needed help. If you had seen the marks on that girl, you wouldn't have argued either. She won't stop. Look at her. I've watched her, I don't know, wither away before my eyes. Officer McCormick can't stop crying. Morgan just keeps talking. It's one unspeakable act after another and it won't stop. She won't stop," he said in a stunned monotone.

"Did you go in there and tell her to stop?"

"It's like she can't hear us. She just keeps talking. That girl won't let go of her, and Morgan won't let go of the girl. It's the most amazing and strange thing I've ever witnessed. Then, there are the stories, one after another. She started when the girl's mother died. She's recounting every incident with the father from about age six. She's almost finished, I think. She's recounting things from last summer. I don't want to listen anymore, but I can't seem to stop."

Tyler read Stewart's concern and horror at the situation. He'd only been in the room for a few minutes and just listening to Morgan talking about the girl being hit or punched or burned made him sick. The sound of Morgan's voice . . . No, wait. Not Morgan's voice. Another voice, like in the psychic shop and at the restaurant.

"Sam, it's like the restaurant. It looks like her, but it's not. Can you hear the difference in her voice?"

"Yeah. She doesn't look very good. She can't keep this up much longer." Sam stared through the glass.

"She told the girl she'd speak for her, since she couldn't. It's the only explanation any of us can come up with," Stewart said. "She's somehow talking for the girl. In the beginning, her voice was high and timid like a very young child. Eerie."

"I need to stop this. She can't keep this up. Look at her." Tyler ran his fingers through his hair and tried to think of the best way to stop her.

Morgan had dark circles under her eyes and pale skin. Her eyes had turned the darkest blue and remained completely unfocused. Although she held on to the girl, her head wasn't quite upright and every once in a while it bobbed like she was trying to stay awake.

"We've called the girl's aunt. It's one of the first things Morgan gave to us. The aunt lives in Tracy. She should be here by now. I guess with traffic and everything it's taking a while. She's the mother's sister. After the mother died, her father refused to let the aunt visit. Once she gets here, we'll turn the girl over to her."

No one noticed Morgan stopped talking. She'd turned in her seat, holding the girl tightly in her arms with her back to the door shielding the girl from the entry. The commotion outside the room, a man yelling about his rights and his daughter being questioned without a lawyer present, drew all their attention. He demanded to see his daughter. The officer escorting him opened the door and the man pushed past. Morgan wrapped herself around the girl with her whole body to protect her.

It happened so fast. No one had time to react. The man grabbed Morgan's hair with his shackled hand and yanked her back in the seat. The little girl held on to Morgan's arm with all her might.

"That's my daughter. Turn her loose. I won't have you filling her head with lies."

Officer McCormick rose out of her chair with her weapon drawn and inches from the man's head.

"Let her go, or I will shoot you." She meant it. For the first time in her career, she had her weapon drawn and wished the man would do something stupid, so she could pull the trigger. After three hours of listening to Morgan, she couldn't take any more. This man deserved a slow and painful death. A bullet seemed like a gift, but she'd take the shot if it meant the little girl would forever be safe.

Silence fell in the room. Morgan wanted to let the blackness that had threatened for over an hour take her

under. She wanted that deep sleep she'd had after the restaurant incident.

Tyler. Help me.

"I'm right here, honey," Tyler assured her, his own gun
held to the back of the man's head. "Let her go. If you so
much as pull one strand of hair from her head, I swear to
God, I'll kill you."

"She's my daughter," the man said defiantly.

"You're assaulting the woman I love, so you'll take
your hands off her before I forget the only thing stopping me from killing you is the badge I'm wearing. It says
FBI, by the way. You're under arrest for assault against
Morgan, as well as a multitude of charges against your
daughter beginning with child abuse."

Sam smiled from behind Tyler. He said he loved her.
About damn time. Morgan looked ready to pass out, and
they needed to end this quick. The girl whimpered like
a wounded animal. For the first time, tears fell from her
eyes. Tyler had the situation and himself under control.
Morgan might be in the shackled hands of this man, but
Tyler wouldn't do anything stupid. The guy couldn't hurt
Morgan seriously. He didn't have a weapon, his hands
were handcuffed in front of him. Tyler knew the score
and had his emotions under control.

"I never touched her. I only want to take my daughter
home."

"You won't go anywhere, if you don't let go of her,"
Tyler said with conviction. He nodded at Officer McCormick when she took a step closer, still with her gun raised
at the man.

"Let Morgan go, and we'll let you speak with your daughter. We'll see what she has to say," Officer McCormick tried bargaining.

Tyler, I'm going to pass out.

"No, you aren't, honey. You're going to focus on me."

No more sadness and anger. I can't take any more. I want to go.

He hated hearing her so down and sad. He hated even more that she sounded like she had nothing left. He didn't want to talk to her out loud anymore. He could finally hear her in his mind and he didn't want to lose the connection between them ever again.

Honey, I'm going to take you back to the ship. I promise you, I'll keep you safe, and you can sleep. I need you to stay with me right now. Find something happy in me. There's got to be something.

You said you love me.

Her words came as a soft whisper in his mind. "Yeah, honey, I do love you."

He spoke the words out loud unsure if it was because he was losing her, or because she didn't believe him. He'd never given the words to anyone else. He'd never felt like he did when he was with her, whether it was physically, or the way they'd been connected before and now. He only felt this way for her.

Her eyes rolled back and glassed over. If she passed out, he didn't know what the man would do, or the girl clinging to her as a lifeline.

I do love you.

That's good because I love you, too. I have for a long

time. Hurry, Tyler, I can't hold on much longer. There's still more to do.

"Last chance. Let go now," Tyler warned. If he had to, he'd clock the guy in the head with the butt of his gun.

The man let her go with a shove. Morgan's head whipped forward and she almost toppled along with the girl out of the chair. She managed to hold on to the girl and keep her seat while officers grabbed the man and shoved him into another chair. The small room filled to capacity with officers, the man, Tyler, Sam, and the three women.

He glared at Tyler, "Why the hell do you keep talking to her like she's talking to you?"

"She is talking to me," Tyler said and walked past the disgruntled man.

"You can hear her again?" Sam asked.

"Yeah, I can hear her." Tyler smiled at his partner and went to Morgan's side and kneeled down. He brushed his hand down Morgan's hair and kissed her on the temple.

"Thank God," Sam said, happy they'd finally found their way back to each other.

"Are you okay, sweetheart?" Tyler asked softly.

"Fine," she said and leaned her head against his chin.

"You're not fine. I'm going to take you back to the ship." He put his hand on her cheek and held her to him. It felt good to touch her, though her cool skin worried him. One more reason to get her out of there.

"No. Not yet." She barely managed to get the words out.

Sam agreed with Tyler. "Morgan, you're wiped out. You can't keep this up."

"Not yet. We have to finish this. I promised her I'd help."

"There's only one more thing we need," Officer McCormick said, and her lieutenant nodded in agreement and handed over the forms that had fallen from the table. "Leslie, is this the man who hurt you? You have to tell us. You have to say the words."

Morgan could feel the girl's reluctance and fear to speak in the chilled tremble that rattled through both of them.

"She won't say anything 'cause there's nothing to say. She's my daughter, and whatever lies she's told you, I'll deal with when we get home."

"That is never going to happen. The bruises and burns on her back are enough for us to call Child Protective Services. Her statement will allow us to charge you with multiple crimes."

"She's lying!"

Morgan sat the girl up on her lap, so they were face-to-face. She just looked at her for the longest time. Not even Tyler heard the words that passed from Morgan to the girl as they sat silently looking at each other.

I will keep you safe. Your aunt is on her way and will take very good care of you. I will be at the trial, and whenever you need me. I promise you, from this day forward you will have a life filled with happiness and love from your aunt. If I knew all the rest, don't I know that, too?

Unsure she'd gotten through to Leslie without her cooperation and her own words, the case would move forward, but make things more difficult for the prosecutor.

She'd have to find the strength to speak the unspeakable. Morgan had given voice to those acts already. The next time, Leslie would have to do it on her own.

She told her all of that and ended how she began, *I will help you. I opened the door, and now all you have to do is go through.*

Speak the words, and they'll set you free. You'll go with your aunt. You'll be safe. I promise.

Everyone, including Morgan, held a collective breath waiting to see what the girl would do.

Morgan didn't know what to expect, but the girl didn't disappoint. Hearing her first words made the last three hours worth it.

She spoke directly to Morgan. She knew they'd all hear, but she trusted Morgan, and so she spoke the words to her.

"That is my father. He hurt me. Everything you said is true. Those are my words. That is what happened to me. He did it, and I won't let him do it again."

"It's not your fault, sweetheart," Morgan said and knew Leslie believed her.

"God heard my prayer. He sent me you." She hugged Morgan.

The officers led her father out of the room. He'd been so stunned by his daughter's words, he didn't start declaring his innocence until halfway across the outer office. No one paid attention to him. They only had eyes for Morgan and the girl in her arms.

Officer McCormick cleared her throat. "Leslie, I'll need you to sign this statement. You have a long road ahead. You'll have to speak with the prosecutor, who's assigned to your case. There'll be a Child Protective Services representative assigned to you, and a whole lot more. I'll take you over to the hospital, so a doctor can look at your injuries. I'll make sure it's a female doctor, and your aunt and I will be with you the whole time."

Officer McCormick didn't know what else to say. After all those hours, she'd finally spoken and confirmed everything Morgan told them. They didn't need any further proof to confirm Morgan was the real deal. Morgan looked wiped out. Officer McCormick could only imagine what it had taken for her to do what she'd done. Completely whipped, she wanted to go home crawl into a hot bath and wash away this day.

"Sam, would you please go and get Leslie's aunt?" Morgan asked. "She's just now coming in the precinct. She's anxious to see Leslie and doesn't need to run into her brother-in-law."

"I'm on my way." Sam headed out the door as quickly as he could without running over the five people standing in the doorway looking in at Morgan. She'd become a celebrity in the precinct and everyone wanted to meet the psychic.

"Could I have a minute alone with Leslie?"

Tyler nodded for everyone to leave. He kneeled next to Morgan again. "I'll be right outside. I'll take you to the ship when you're done." He kissed her, holding his mouth to hers, letting her know in some small way he loved her, was proud of her, and needed her to be okay.

She reached up and touched her fingertips to his lips and nodded her agreement, too tired to do anything else.

When they were alone, she made Leslie take the chair next to her. They sat face-to-face and Leslie took on her usual posture of looking down at her hands in her lap. Leslie pulled away, afraid Morgan would leave her.

"Leslie, look at me."

Leslie met her gaze. "You don't look so good."

"Thanks," Morgan said and smiled. "I want you to listen to me. I'm going to make you a promise. I want you to see I mean what I say. I promise I will be with you every step of the way. I will be sitting behind you in court when they bring your father to trial. I will be the one you look at when you sit on the stand and tell your story. I don't want you to be afraid anymore. You know how I knew all those things about you?" Leslie nodded. "Then believe me when I say your aunt loves you and has waited a long time to see you again. Don't blame her. She tried to get you away from him. She tried more times than you realize. She'll be the mother you lost, and she'll keep you safe. Do you believe me?"

Leslie hadn't taken her eyes from Morgan. For the first time in more years and days than she could count, she felt hopeful. "I believe you. You'll help me," she said, and believed her own words too.

Morgan took a notebook out of her purse and wrote down her cell phone number and handed the paper to Leslie.

"Will you be okay going to the hospital with your aunt and Officer McCormick?"

"I'll be okay thanks to you."

Morgan took Leslie's hands and pulled her up with her

as she stood, and then she held her in her arms. "You'll be safe from now on."

"Thank you, Morgan. You're my gift from God."

"I'm glad I could help you. You've been a gift for me, too. If you open that door, you'll find your aunt waiting for you with Sam and Tyler. You can stand on your own now."

"Because you'll be there to support me if I need it."

Overwhelmed by this girl, she had such strength welling up and just beginning to bloom. When she blossomed, she would be a force.

"Yes, honey. That's exactly right. You've got me, and you've got your aunt. Lean on us when you can't stand on your own."

Leslie smiled shyly. "I think you should sit down, now. You look like you could use someone to lean on yourself."

Morgan caressed her cheek. She did need to sit down. "Go. Your aunt can't wait much longer to see you."

Morgan dropped into the chair and laid her arms and face down on the table as Leslie went out the door and into her aunt's arms. When she heard the happy hellos and the tears of joy, she blanked out.

Tyler and Sam found her that way, passed out with her head on the table.

"Did you two make up enough so you can take her back to the ship and stay with her until she recovers from this? Or should I call Happy Jack?"

"Happy Jack?"

"My new nickname for him since she likes him so much because he's always happy."

Tyler got the joke and the hint; don't take her to the ship if he was going to bombard her with anything but happiness and benign emotions. "I'll take care of her. We've worked out some things. Actually, I worked out a lot of things, and have finally realized I need her in my life. She's the one."

"We've been telling you that for years," Sam said and slapped Tyler on the back. "Get her out of here before anything else happens."

Sam turned to leave, but got blocked in by the half a dozen people behind them looking in the door at Morgan. "Back to work, people. She'll be fine. She's just drained."

Tyler scooped up Morgan into his arms and held her against his chest. Sam grabbed her bag and they walked out of the room. Tyler felt ten feet tall when Morgan wrapped her arm around his neck and buried her face in his neck.

"I've got you, honey," he said into her ear.

It's just so sad.

He held her tighter when he felt her finally give out and fall asleep in his arms. They were walking through the many cubicles toward the lobby when the officers stood and applauded Morgan. Sam and Tyler stopped in their tracks and turned around. Morgan was completely out.

Sam put his palm on Morgan's back and rubbed. "You feel that, Morgan. You did an outstanding job," he said for only her and Tyler to hear.

The officers knew how hard it was to get a child to tell what happened to them. Not to mention the fact they all knew at one time or another they might have passed the girl in the lobby without a second thought. The worst case of child abuse they'd ever seen or heard had been solved because Morgan came into the office and saw Leslie's secrets.

"Hear that, honey. I'm so proud of you." Tyler held her tight and kissed her head softly.

Police work took a toll on the emotions, especially when the case involved a child. These officers just wanted to acknowledge Morgan and her gift. Tyler and Sam nodded to them and left the station to get Morgan to the ship where she could recover. He had no idea if the acknowledgement from the officers had gotten through to Morgan. He hoped it had. Quite an impressive sight to see all those officers recognize Morgan in such a way.

Chapter Twenty-Seven

MORGAN WOKE UP with the most wonderful feeling of contentment. She hadn't felt this good in a long time. In fact, she couldn't remember ever feeling like this. She snuggled deeper under the covers and discovered why. Her head rested on Tyler's left arm and his right arm wrapped around her, holding her to his warm body. His rough whiskers tickled her neck as he kissed her and pulled her closer. Warm and wonderful pressed against the full length of her back and legs.

"Quit wiggling, or I'll forget to be a gentleman." His voice groggy from sleep, he nuzzled his nose into her hair. For the first time ever, waking up with a woman didn't bring on any anxiety, or worry about what was or wasn't happening between them. Waking up with Morgan in his arms seemed so natural, so right. Everything was perfect. He inhaled the fresh sweet scent of her and sighed.

"Gentleman? I'm half-naked under here."

"Sam had you completely naked when you got shot and he brought you back here. I'm a saint. I only took off your pants—without peeking, I might add. The room was dark. I swear. Cross my heart. You should be impressed with my restraint."

"Restraint, huh? What's pressed up against my backside isn't any indication of restraint." She wiggled her butt against his straining cock. She wasn't nervous or uncomfortable lying in bed with him. In fact, she didn't want to be anywhere else. Well, maybe closer.

He groaned and spread his big hand over her hip to get her to stop fooling around. "A man can only take so much." He sighed and hugged her. "Yeah, I took advantage and crawled into bed with you. I couldn't stop myself. You looked so wiped out after everything you went through yesterday. I just wanted to hold you and be close to you. You scared me. You looked so drained and lifeless. I thought if I held you close, comforted you, you'd know I was here protecting and watching over you and it would help."

Maybe he'd gone too far and taken too many liberties. Last night it seemed like a good idea. He'd needed to keep her close. Nervous and worried, he hated to think he might have jeopardized the tenuous bond they'd reconnected.

He hid a mischievous smile. "I told the truth though; I didn't look."

He wanted to, but he hadn't. At this point, nothing much escaped his imagination.

Her hips shifted and rubbed against his throbbing

cock. He squeezed her hip and she did it again. "Come on, baby, you gotta st—"

She cut off his words by rolling over and planting her mouth over his. She snuggled her body down his full length. Holding herself above him, her full breasts pressed to his hard chest, she looked down into his sleepy eyes and beard-stubbled face. "Is that *come on, baby* an invitation?" Her voice notched down into a deep sultry whisper.

Her eyes danced. Bright, the clearest softest blue he'd ever seen. Completely on top of him, her toes softly rubbed his shins. She gave him a bright smile, something mysterious and wonderful not quite hidden in her grin.

"Honey, you don't need an invitation. I belong to you. I'm the happiest man alive waking up with you in my arms."

"I can feel it." It wasn't his thick arousal that told her he was blissfully happy. The overwhelming sensations rippling off him crashed over her like a wave of joy. She'd never felt him this happy and content, and it filled her.

"That's not what I mean." He cupped her face, met her ice blue eyes. "I don't want you to think this is all about sex. Yes, I want you." Unable to hold back his intense response to her, he rubbed his throbbing cock against her soft belly, locked his jaw and clamped down on his baser needs. "I want you so bad, I hurt. But with you, I need more." For the first time, he knew they could be more together.

"Did you mean what you said last night?" Her smile softened, her words hesitant and so filled with hope. She needed his words as much as he needed to say them to her and make her believe. She had to believe, because he couldn't live without her.

Still holding her face, he pulled her to him for a kiss. Soft, tender, a brush of his lips to hers, he poured the overflowing feelings from his heart into the simple poignant touch.

"I'm sorry for being stubborn and selfish and stupid and pushing you away when underneath it all, I always wanted you here with me. With every fiber of my being, everything I am, I love you, Morgan."

"I feel it. Remember how I told you happiness can make me feel exhilarated? Your love makes me feel euphoric."

"You're glowing." His voice held the wonder he felt inside, looking at her radiating above him. He ran his hands down her shoulders and back, over her hips, only to circle back and repeat the long soft caress, pulling her T-shirt over her head.

He couldn't believe this was real. She's real. Here with him, in his arms.

"You feel so damn good against me. Your skin is so soft, and you smell so good." Her hair was like silk along his chest and shoulders. He traced his finger along the top of her shoulder, pulling the stands aside. He planted a soft, open-mouthed kiss at the base of her neck and she shivered in his arms.

He undid the bra clasp at her back and drew the straps down her arms. She willingly let it go without the slightest blush of embarrassment. Leaning over him, her hands planted on the bed by his shoulders, he had a perfect view of her lovely, full breasts. He cupped her pretty face and let his hands slide down her neck, fingers tracing the long column down to her chest. Warm, soft, he cupped her breasts and brushed his thumbs over her nipples, making them hard. She sighed and moaned at the intimate touch. He wanted to take them into his mouth, but took his time and explored, sliding his hands down her ribs to her slim, taut belly.

"I love you," she whispered in that husky voice he'd missed so much hearing in his head.

His desire to claim her, make her his forever, radiated heat through his whole body. His hands slid down her spine and over her hips, dipping into her panties; he cupped her bottom and pressed her down hard against his thick erection. They both let out a soft moan. He took her hips and pulled her forward. Their lips met, his tongue slipped in to taste and tease. He took the kiss deep and rolled her to the side and slipped her panties down her long, supple legs. With her hands free to roam, she spread her fingers wide over his chest and swept them down over his stomach in one long hot sweep. Propped over her on his elbow, she leaned up and kissed him again, trailing more kisses along his jaw and down his neck. He fell back onto the pillows and let her have her way with him, his hands softly tracing her skin anywhere and everywhere he could touch. She leaned over him, her breasts pressed against his chest, her lips and tongue driving him insane as she worked her way down his body to his stomach. Her hands traced a path over his corded stomach muscles to the hard length of him. Her fingers wrapped around, stoking up and down over his boxer briefs. He sank his head into the pillow and let out a gruff growl, enjoying every torturous moment. When her hands dipped inside his briefs and she took him in her warm hand, he nearly disgraced himself.

Impatient and wanting more, he gently pulled her hand away. She immediately tugged his briefs down and he helped her rid him of the last barrier between them. Lying on his side beside her, he stared down and took in her creamy skin and toned body, lush with soft curves that drew his eye and made him ache to be inside her.

"You are so beautiful."

"I love all your hard strength. The way you look at me with so much passion and need in your dark eyes."

"I want to be gentle with you."

"Just love me."

"I do."

"Show me."

He placed his palm on her stomach and leaned down and kissed her, sliding his hand down, fingers sliding past the soft folds to her hot, wet center. She opened her mouth to his tongue and spread her thighs wide as he dipped his finger into her slick sheath. Within moments, he had her writhing on the bed and his own need straining against his will to go slow.

Morgan took the reins, pushing him over onto his back as she rose up and straddled his hips. Glorious above him, her hair cascaded down her back in a mass of glowing golden waves. Her eyes danced with light. She gave him a soft, knowing smile and rocked her hips against his hard cock over and over. She leaned down and kissed him with a hunger and need that matched his own. He held her hips firm and thrust hard and deep. Mouths fused, bodies joined, they fell into the rhythm of their love.

Beckoned by her fire, he went willingly into the flames, and she made him burn.

What started off slow and sweet built to a passion he'd never felt. He kissed her neck, she caressed his cheek, and sank her fingers into his hair. He took her rose-tipped breast into his mouth, suckled, and made her moan. She held him to her, rolled her hips, and made him groan. And that made all the difference. For once, it was a mutual give-and-take. She gave a kiss and a caress of her tongue. He gave back her kiss and squeezed her breasts and reveled in her moan when he took her sweet nipple into his mouth again, suckled hard, feasted, savored, loved her.

She took him deeper, and he pushed her higher.

She sat up, rocked her hips, ground hers to his and he thrust hard. He marveled at the fall of her golden hair over her shoulders and down her back. The feel of it as it whispered over his thighs as she moved. Her eyes closed, her fingers dug into his chest, and she lost herself in the feeling and rhythm of their lovemaking. Her fingertips brushed over his nipples. She raked her hands down his chest. Lost in the spell, he sat up, wrapped his arms around her, held her close as she moved over him. He took her breast into his palm, licked, laved, suckled to his heart's content. She made those wild little noises and made him ache even more.

Lost in him, every touch of his huge hands on her body sent shivers over her skin and warmed her to her soul. The building heat and ripples spread from her center, tightening her core. She rode the waves, felt Tyler's passion swelling with hers. He fell back to the pillows, thrust deep, and pressed the pad of his thumb to her soft, wet center. The rising tide within reached a crescendo. Her head fell back and she moaned on a deep exhale, so filled with ecstasy she couldn't contain it.

He arched off the bed and buried himself deep inside her and let go of the world and knew only his love for her and the return of that love from her. She leaned forward and took his mouth, swept away by waves of pleasure. She trembled, her body rocked with aftershocks. She collapsed onto his chest with a cloud of golden hair raining down and draping over them.

Too spent to say anything, the soft hum of contentment and the brush of her lips on his shoulder told him the feeling was mutual. He wrapped his arms around her and held her tight, close. She snuggled into him; her breathing fell into an even, soft whisper against his heated skin. He closed his eyes and savored the feel of her in his arms as they both drifted on the cloud of bliss they'd created.

About to succumb to a deep sleep, the beeping of her cell phone jarred them both awake and alert again.

She groaned, lifted her head, and brushed her hair away from her face, dropping it over her shoulder. She kissed him and said against his lips, "I have to check that. I gave Leslie my number and email in case she needed me. I promised."

He gave her hips a squeeze, kissed her to let her know he didn't mind, and fell back onto his pillow.

Nothing, not even his satiated, sex-hazed lethargy, would stop him from watching the way her hair bounced against her back as she hopped out of bed. Beautiful, her skin a soft tan, the glow enhanced by the fall of golden hair down her back, reaching almost to her waist in long waves. His eyes traced the slope of her bottom and the sway of her hips as she walked to the corner table to grab her phone from her purse. She answered and turned toward him completely unfazed by his gaze on her naked body. His eyes locked on her upturned breasts, tipped with rosy nipples that tasted so sweet. She smiled and his heart turned over. Beyond lucky to have her in his life, to be loved by her, and finally feel the kind of love his friends felt for their wives within himself, he sighed his contentment.

She frowned while reading the email, then dialed a number. "Hi, it's Morgan. No, I haven't seen her."

Everything in him went still. The bright smile on her face fell, replaced with a look of concern and inevitability.

"She wouldn't call me. How long has she been gone? Last night. Where are the children? You have both of them." He felt her relief like his own. "Good. He did? Why didn't you just say that? Hell yes, he wants money. No, I'm not giving you the money for the kids. Just tell me what he said. Fine. Give me the number. I'll get her back. I said, I'll get her back."

She hung up. Tyler stood and zipped up his jeans. He pulled his shirt on over his head and grabbed his own phone and started dialing. She hated to see that gorgeous, strong body of his covered up. A sight to behold, all those rippling muscles and tanned skin with his dark hair and eyes made her want to crawl back into bed with him and forget the terrible things happening around her. They finally managed to come together, both body and mind. She hated to end the too new and fragile intimacy. Somewhere deep inside her, something whispered, *This is only the beginning.*

She held onto that precious promise.

She gave herself a mental shake and pulled on a clean pair of jeans and a turquoise blouse. She could fantasize about Tyler later. Right now, she needed to focus on her missing sister and getting her back from their father, James.

Did Jillian go with him willingly, or by force?

"Sam, it's me. Listen, Morgan's sister is missing. I presume James Weston's got her. He'll try to squeeze Morgan for money to get her back. Can you start digging and see where he might be?"

"How is she?"

"She's doing just fine. Full of energy this morning, she woke up happy."

"I'll bet you did, too," Sam teased.

He laughed. "Yeah, I did. Now, knock it off and help us out." He hung up and looked at Morgan. "What?"

"Are you reading *my* mind this morning?" Morgan winked.

"I already did that." He winked back at her. "Not hard to figure out what you wanted when you climbed on top of me. If you want to go again, you'll have to give me a little time to recover. When you wake up happy, boy, you wake up happy."

He pulled her up off the side of the bed, her sock hanging half off her foot, and kissed her because he wanted to and because he could. He'd lain in bed wishing for her to be with him more nights than he could count. Now that they were together, he didn't want to miss a minute of being able to touch her.

"It's not so much that I woke up happy, it's that you woke up happy with me. Happiness can make me feel a little high. It's like having a drink and getting tipsy. Mix your happiness with mine and add in some passion and you have ecstasy. That's just my assessment of this morning, mind you."

"Hell, honey. If we wake up like this every morning, I'll be dead in a month."

"It'll be a sweet death for both of us." She touched her fingertips to his lips.

He took her hand and pressed a soft kiss to her palm, placed her hand to his cheek, taking in her warmth. "Don't kill me yet. I want a long and happy life with you right beside me."

"I'd like that. Unfortunately, things are about to go from very good to very bad."

"Did you have a vision about this happening?"

"You and me? No. I have a hard time seeing things that will happen to my family, or me. I only see events with me in them when they have to do with someone else."

"Okay, so what did your sister's husband say?"

"It's like you told Sam. My sister is missing, or so it appears. Her husband is quite upset and blaming me for everything. The only good thing is the children are safe at home with him, for now."

Worry lines furrowed her brow. Their wonderful morning had certainly gone from good to bad. The concern and fear on her beautiful face told him she expected things to get a lot worse, especially with her father involved.

"You and I both speculated your father would try to get the money. I'll bet when he contacted your sister and found out you wouldn't turn over signing authority on the kid's accounts, he took her in order to get you to pay."

"If she isn't partnering with him," she added.

"I'm sorry, honey. I know how much you hoped someday she'd come around and accept you and you'd have a piece of your family back."

"I have you, and your family now."

"Always." He sealed that promise with a kiss.

The silence stretched for a moment, their gazes locked on each other's. They settled into their connection and let it surround them. She welcomed the familiar bond. No matter the distance, the pull between them would always guide her home.

She broke the spell, even though she wanted to block out all the rest and just be with him.

"Let's give him a call and see what he has to say."

She dialed and waited for her father to answer. Years since she'd heard his voice, she didn't want to hear it now, or ever again. She had a flash of him standing in front of her and slapping her across the face. She threw up her hand, blocking her face.

Tyler reached for her. "What's wrong?"

"Nothing. Nothing. I saw something. It's fine . . ."

Her father answered. "It's about time you called. I've been waiting."

"Where's Jillian?"

"She's in a time-out. I asked her to do one damn thing, and she screwed it up."

"You knew I'd never turn the money over to her."

"You would have if she'd kept her damn mouth shut. She shouldn't have told you that she and I talked. You owe me."

"I don't owe you anything. Nothing, and that's what you'll get." She caught a flash of a dark cramped space with someone curled up in a heap. Like a flash bomb going off in her mind, she put a hand to her head and tried to focus and get the picture back. An old memory of her in a closet, or Jillian wherever she was now?

"You owe me big-time, and it's going to cost you a cool million. That is, if you want your sister back."

"You just got out of jail. Do you really think I believe you'll hurt her and risk going back?"

"You know I'll do whatever it takes to get my hands on that money. I'm also not stupid enough to leave your sister where anyone can find her. If you won't pay for her, perhaps you'll pay to get one of the little brats back," he threatened.

She saw the smile spread across his face in her mind.

He enjoyed tormenting her, and he thought he had the upper hand. Just another sick and twisted game he thought he could win. She'd prove him wrong. Again.

"You think you can hide what you're doing from me. You should know better."

"You couldn't tell me what Jerry was doing with that business."

"Not couldn't. Wouldn't," she said to piss him off. "There's a difference."

"You bitch! Why didn't you tell me? I wouldn't have had to kill your mother if you'd just told me what I wanted to know."

Nothing would have stopped him from killing her mother. He needed her out of the way. She'd become too suspicious. If he took over Jerry's operation, he had no doubt she'd have left him and taken Morgan with her. He couldn't let that happen. Morgan was his ticket to getting what he wanted. Finding out other people's secrets and exploiting them was his bread and butter, so long as Morgan cooperated.

Now, he didn't have to do any of that. She had money and a lot of it. She'd pay to get her sister back. Then he'd make her continue to pay to keep him away. A simple plan, and one he had no doubt she'd fall in line with in order to keep him out of her life and interfering in other people's lives. She refused to see the potential her ability had in making them rich beyond belief. That's all he wanted. It's what he deserved, what he was destined for. He dreamed about sitting on a beach in the tropics, women and booze and a life of excess and leisure. He'd live the high life, the life he deserved. The life she took from him once, but not this time.

"You and I both know you planned to kill her long before you ever did. Don't put that on me. I won't give you what you want. I'll see right through you and find Jillian."

"I don't think so. Not this time. Prison provides a man a lot of time to think and read. I learned a lot about people who are psychic, and the way they do the things they do. There are books and books filled with information. They even give tips on how to hone what little skill most people have, and how to shield and put up mental blocks. I have a pretty good idea how to keep you from seeing into my mind. So, here's the deal. I want you to come to my place with the million dollars in cash. Unmarked bills. Don't think I don't know you're working with the FBI."

"And you think they're going to let me give you a million dollars, and you'll walk away without them coming after you? You must be really confident in your ability to make sure I can't see what you're doing."

"How many times did you tell me you couldn't see things in the people closest to you, especially when they involved you?"

"I lied before. What makes you think I didn't lie about that?"

"Because you didn't know I was going to kill your mother until it was too late. I've got your number, and you don't have a choice this time. Get the money, and maybe you'll get to your sister in time."

Tears spilled down her cheeks, but she wouldn't let him know how much it hurt that she hadn't seen what happened to her mother in time. She wouldn't let that happen again. She'd get her sister back, and she'd make her father pay.

"Where and when?" She'd get the money, and then she'd get him.

"I'll see you at my place at one. That should give you plenty of time to get my money. Come alone."

"The FBI won't let me come with a million dollars and no escort."

"They don't have to know," he said.

"They already do. My FBI contact is sitting next to me and listening to this conversation. They've already heard you say you have Jillian and are holding her against her will. Now, you've demanded a ransom. This is right up their alley."

Tyler put his arm around her. She was doing a great job and making sure she didn't have to face her father alone. He'd be with her.

"Then you know I've already considered their involvement and planned for it. You can bring your escort. I'm sure it will be that man you had dinner with when you met your sister. If I see any other agents, or they prevent me from leaving after the meeting, your sister will never be found. Once I've been allowed to leave, I'll contact you and tell you where she is."

"You and I both know you aren't going to tell me where she is."

"That's a chance you'll have to take, and one I'm sure the FBI will go along with because they're bound by rules and regulations. Taking me into custody will only ensure her death. Believe it. If they arrest me, I won't tell them where she is."

He didn't care if Jillian lived or died. He only cared about himself. Being arrested for kidnapping and murder wouldn't change his mind. He'd go to jail no matter what. This was his big score and he was either going to get his money, or take out another family member at Morgan's expense. She wouldn't let that happen. He knew it and counted on it.

He hung up on her. She sat and stared through the cabin window at the sea. A beautiful day, the sun shined bright and the water remained calm. She knew what she had to do. She couldn't let him win.

She pulled her laptop out of its bag and booted it up.

"What are you doing?" Tyler slid his hand under her hair to her neck. He rubbed softly, just to let her know he was there for her.

"I'm transferring the money out of my investments, so I can get the cash. Can you get a local bank to put the money together?"

"I'll make a few calls. You know you can't just give him the money and expect him to give you Jillian. He won't." He pressed his forehead to her temple, then kissed her softly on the cheek.

"I know." Morgan leaned into him and loved having him near. She didn't have to do this alone. She'd never be alone again. The truth in that thought gave her strength.

"I have a plan. I just need a little time to work things out."

Chapter Twenty-Eight

SAM WORKED WITH the bank to get Morgan's money. He had everything ready.

"She needs to make the transfer in the next ten minutes, so it can get to the bank in time. They've already started pulling the cash together," Sam told Tyler over the phone.

"I'm on it. What's the bank's routing number?"

Sam rattled off the digits and Tyler typed them into Morgan's laptop.

"Are you making the transfer?"

"Yeah, she left me with her computer and the code to get into her account and move the money."

Tyler hit enter and watched her bank balance fall a million dollars. It blew his mind to see all her accounts and investments lined up and totaled. Extremely organized. The rolling ticker tape at the bottom of the screen showing various stocks and their prices, along with whether they were up or down, mesmerized him. He'd seen the same kind of thing running across the screen during news programs.

"Hey, Sam. Can I ask you something personal?"

"Is there something you *don't* know about me?"

"I'm serious," Tyler said, trying to figure out how to phrase his question.

"Sorry, go ahead, shoot."

"Does it bother you that Elizabeth is wealthy?" Tyler thought he knew the answer, but needed to hear how Sam felt and thought about Elizabeth's wealth.

Sam didn't expect that question. He never really thought about Elizabeth's money. It was just something she had and they used. They lived a comfortable life, and nothing had really changed for them since they met and married. They didn't live a lavish lifestyle, but they could. There had been one moment where he'd realized she was different from him, when he'd looked at her and known he couldn't give her all the things she was used to.

Sam cleared his throat. "Do you remember the night of the charity benefit where Elizabeth trapped the Silver Fox?"

"That's a night I'd like to forget. You were kind of a mess when you shot her. Again," Tyler added.

"Thanks for reminding me. No, I'm talking about when I came to the house to pick her up. Jack and Jenna were with me and you were with Elizabeth."

"Yeah, she looked like a million bucks. I helped her get dressed," Tyler said wickedly.

"If you keep this up, I'm going to have to punch you."

Tyler laughed. He and Sam were best friends. Razzing each other was part of their friendship. "Fine. I remember that night. We surprised you with the benefit setup at the last minute."

"Do you remember my reaction when I saw her come downstairs in that dress dripping with diamonds?"

Tyler had to think about it, but yeah, he remembered. "You told her you'd just realized what being a Hamilton meant."

"Yeah, that night, I looked at her and saw dollar signs. She told me to get over it, she was just like everyone else and all those zeros didn't matter. After that, it never bothered me again. She loves me, not my wallet. I love her, not her bank account with all those zeros. That makes all the difference. If you love Morgan, all the zeros are just that, zeros. It's her that matters, not the money. If her net worth isn't important to her, then don't make it important to you."

"How do I know if the money is important to her?"

"You already know it's not. She gave you her password to her bank accounts. You could wipe her out with a few clicks of the keys. She's about to give a million dollars to her father without an absolute guarantee she'll get it, or her sister—who hates her—back. She's willing to take that chance."

"You're a smart man, Sam."

"Yeah, well, it's easier to see things from the outside. You're stuck in the middle, and you're blinded by a beautiful, golden goddess."

"She's golden all the way. I'm being stupid."

"Yes, you are. Where is she?"

"Up on deck. She's gone to another place. She's standing in the sunlight with the wind blowing through her hair. Her eyes are looking out at the horizon, but they're dark as night. She's not really there. The whole ship has this strange vibe. Even Captain Finn came down to ask if I felt it."

"What's she doing?"

"I don't know. Who can explain what Morgan does?" Even she had a hard time explaining how she did it. "She's doing her thing. She told me to wait and take care of the money. She wants you to be ready to leave."

"Where am I going?"

"I don't know. We'll have to wait and ask her when she comes back."

"That's just weird," Sam said. Though none of their interactions with Morgan had been normal. "She's up on deck and you're talking like she's left."

"I can't explain it. Her body is up there, but she's not. I can't say whether she's gone inside herself, or she's outside herself. She's there, but she's not."

"See, and you were on my case when I was talking about good and bad energy. She's got you doing the same thing now. So, you two worked out everything this morning."

"I thought we did."

"You didn't get mad at her again?"

"No. It's this thing with her father. It got me thinking about what you said concerning the Psychic Slayer and how she'll end that, too. She already knows. She won't tell me anything about it though. She said it has to play out the way she saw it."

"Like the way things played out with Matt in the restaurant."

"Right. So I got to thinking this guy must know her. When he heard her name on the news and discovered she really knows things, he must have connected her to the website. At one time, he must have sent her a request, and she told him something accurate enough to scare him into thinking she knew something about him he didn't want anyone to know. It's the only thing that makes sense."

"Okay, I follow you," Sam said. "That jibes with what I'm thinking."

"Well, since she's up on deck communing with the ether, I thought I'd look at her website files."

"Did she tell you you could do that?"

"She didn't say I couldn't."

"I'll go with that."

He'd used the same kind of logic many times in his line of work. It wasn't really crossing the line if you weren't told not to cross it.

"Find anything interesting?"

"She's anal about organizing her files. The stacks of papers and records in my home office will make her cringe. Anyway, she keeps a running log of the questions she answers on her website. The log records the person's question and the answer she sent along with the amount she charged, or didn't charge."

"She doesn't charge some of them?" Sam asked puzzled.

"Nope. She charges most of them, but there are times when the news is so good she just sends a reply and doesn't charge them."

"I think she thrives on good news, good vibes, whatever. That's why she probably doesn't collect a payment. She gets something and they get something. There's a balance there for her. The money isn't important. See, another confirmation on that," Sam said enthusiastically. "She holds more intangible things important."

"Thanks for the rundown, oh-wise-one. Now, tell me when you think this guy might have contacted her. Did this all start five years ago when she met me? That's when she knew about my sister, and possibly about Matt at the restaurant. She knew about you and Elizabeth a few years later. Where do I begin? And what am I looking for? Because I'll tell you, most of these questions are about relationships and wishes and just plain everyday stuff. There isn't a question listed where the person asks, 'Do you know I'm a killer?'"

"Well, damn. He couldn't make it easy for us."

Tyler went through several hundred entries in the log. Nothing stood out.

"There are several entries from law enforcement agencies. Most of them have to do with missing person cases. I wonder if she helped catch some guy, and he's coming back for retribution."

"That's possible. It sounds like there's a lot to check out and follow up on. Bring the computer to the office. We'll get the computer geeks working on it. Maybe we'll get lucky."

Morgan walked into the room, looking wiped out again. He didn't like it. He hated seeing her this way.

"Is that Sam?" Morgan asked, her voice raspy.

"Sam, hold on. Morgan is back." He pulled her onto his lap and wrapped his arms around her and rested his head against hers. "Are you okay, honey?"

"I'm okay. I just need time to recover. I haven't had to do something like that in a long time. Did you make the transfer?"

"It's all done. Sam talked to the bank. They're getting the money together." He looked at his watch. "We have about two hours before the meeting with your father."

She nodded and kissed him. Then she rested her forehead to his. "Do me a favor."

"Anything." He kissed her again, long and soft and sweet until she relaxed into him.

"Dial down the worry. It's a little overwhelming after what I just did."

"I'm sorry, honey. It's just that we've got your father to deal with and this serial killer. I've been looking through your website files. There's just too much to comb through. I'm going to give it all to the techs down at my office, so they can start sorting through it and . . ."

She put her hand over his mouth to stop him. "Stop. I can't do this right now. We have to go, and Sam has to go."

She took the phone from Tyler. "Sam, contact the local airports. He's leaving on a chartered jet."

"That narrows down his escape plan, but he's probably booked the flight under an assumed name. It could take days to figure out which flight."

"That's why you need to find the plane with the following ID number on it. Ready?"

"Have I ever told you how much I love it when you do this?" he said with enthusiasm.

"No. You guys usually call me names like *weird* and *creepy*," she said irritably.

"You sound tired. Did you fry your brain up on deck?" Sam chuckled.

"Just about. Here's the ID number: A16T432. It's a white plane with a dark blue stripe running along both sides. There'll be two pilots. I'd appreciate it if you'd let him get on the plane and think he's gotten away with this for just a minute. Once you have him in custody, you need to hall ass back to the police station we were at yesterday."

"What's going to happen there?"

"You have to keep Tyler from going ballistic, and yes, that's all I'm saying," she said to both men. "Tyler and I will drop off my computer at your office and go and get the money. We'll meet my father and find Jillian. You make the arrest, and we'll all meet up at the police station later."

"Don't I get to ask any questions?"

"No, you find that plane," she said and hung up. "Tyler, please. I can't play Twenty Questions with you right now. We have to go, or we won't make it on time. My sister needs to be found. That's our priority right now."

"You're my priority always." He cupped her face in his warm hands and held her still so he could kiss her.

She felt his love and took it in. She brushed her fingertips across the furrow between his eyebrows to smooth out some of the tension. "I can't change what's going to happen today. There isn't any way to stop it because if I do, things will be worse. I'm asking you to be strong for me today. I need you to trust me."

"Tell me what's going to happen, and I'll help you."

"The only way you can help me is by doing exactly what I ask. It's important. You aren't going to like it, but it's crucial. I have my reasons. Remember that when you think I've completely lost my mind."

"I trust you, but you have to trust me, too."

"I do, with my life. Have faith in me, and you'll know what to do."

He didn't understand exactly what she meant, nor have time to question it. She walked out of the room with her computer and purse.

In no condition to face her father, whatever she'd done up on deck had taken its toll. Time to go, but he wanted to call her back and make her stay safe on the ship.

Chapter Twenty-Nine

HE AND MORGAN had been in and out of the car over the last two hours. They dropped her computer with the FBI techs. They'd sort through everything, looking for a clue on the Psychic Slayer.

At the bank, she showed her ID, answered all the bank manager's questions, and counted the bundles upon bundles of money and stuffed them into duffel bags. She carried the heavy bags herself out to the car with him, escorted by two armed guards. He didn't think she even noticed the additional men. She dumped the bags in the back seat like they were her luggage for a trip, not a million dollars cold hard cash from her own bank account.

He hated using Morgan's money, but they didn't have a choice.

Agent Davies and Sam coordinated the other agents. They'd track James Weston once he left the small ranch in the hills.

Morgan remained silent on the ride, studying a map of the area surrounding her father's rented ranch house.

"Okay, we're here. What do you want me to do?" Tyler asked.

"What do I want you to do?" she mimicked his question. "I want you to drop me off and leave. I don't want you here for what's about to happen."

"No way in hell will you convince me to let you go in there alone, sweetheart."

Resigned, Morgan said, "Think of the worst criminal you ever went after and arrested. I want you to recall the cold, uncaring way he went about breaking the law and hurting people."

"Why do you want me to focus on that?"

"The person you know in your mind is the monster waiting for us in that house. He doesn't care if he hurts someone. He wants the money. His focus will be on me. You are insignificant in this charade. He believes he's outwitted the police, the FBI, and me, and can get away with this because he's got his ace in Jillian. He'll try to block me from seeing what he doesn't want me to see. I'm going to make him lose his concentration and his patience."

"How will you do that?"

"By playing a very dangerous game." She turned to him. "I need you to understand how serious I am. This situation will turn very ugly. I need you to trust me. I want you to walk in there with me because he expects you to, and then I want you to stand there and not say or do anything."

"Okay."

"I mean it. No matter what happens, you have to stand there and remain silent. It's important."

His eyes narrowed with concern and determination. "I'm not going to let him hurt you."

"Because you love me, this will be very hard for you. Please, Tyler. Do this for me. It's the only way to find Jillian. The clock is ticking down. We need to find her."

"Do you know where she is?"

"Not exactly. But he's going to tell me, if it's the last thing I do."

"I don't like the way you said that."

She slid out of the car and tried to ignore his words. She had to find Jillian. She couldn't have another death on her hands. How could she make him understand she couldn't live with herself if her sister died because she couldn't use her gift to find her?

"Morgan?"

"It has to stop. My mother, Jillian, the psychic women, it has to stop. Maybe my mother was right. If I use my gift, I'll be alone. People suffer because of me."

"No. This isn't your fault. This isn't because of you. And you'll never be alone again."

She stood with him next to the car, staying just out of his reach. If he touched her now, she'd break. She couldn't afford to be weak and let him take over the situation. Jillian needed her to be strong.

"I couldn't live with myself if something happened to you because of me and my gift," she explained, unable to put into words the depth of her love for him. "Don't you understand? I love you too much to let that happen. I'm going to stop this. All of it."

"Oh, honey. Please listen to me. This is not your fault. Nothing is going to happen to me."

"I know, because you're going to stand there and say and do nothing." She grabbed the bags out of the back of the car and headed for the front door of the house.

Tyler didn't like this, or her attitude. She couldn't tell him she loved him one minute, and tell him to stand there and be quiet the next. He went after her and caught up with her as she threw open the front door and walked in like she owned the place.

"Not even going to ring the bell." Tyler looked cautiously in the house and behind them before he followed her in. He didn't want to be taken by surprise.

"He's expecting us, and he knows we're here. Now, do what I asked. Here we go." She stepped into the family room. Her father stood behind the counter separating them from the kitchen.

He came around and stood in front of her. He didn't so much as look at her, but stared down at the two bags she strained to carry in her hands. The lustful look in his eyes, and the way he opened and closed his fists like he couldn't wait to get his hands on the bags, told her just how much he wanted them, craved them.

"Hello, Morgan. Looking good, I see."

"James." She expected the slap. Just like him to try to put her in her place right off the bat. The blow knocked her head to the side. She tasted blood from her split lip.

Tyler took a step forward to come to her defense and

kick James's ass into next week for touching her. She appreciated his instinct to protect her at all costs.

Stop. I need him angry.

At Morgan's words in his mind, he stopped himself from taking another step and stood behind her. He didn't like it, but he did it because she asked.

A little intimidation couldn't hurt, so he folded his arms across his broad chest and glared down at James, who stood at least three inches shorter. It wasn't much in the way of defense, but he'd follow Morgan's lead.

Thank you, she said, relieved.

That only made him glare more.

"I think you meant *Dad*," James said and leaned in close.

She stood her ground. "You lost that title a long time ago. Where's Jillian?"

"Oh, she's around."

"Here's the money." She dropped both bags at her sides, like they meant nothing to her. "Tell me where she is, and you can leave. You and I are finished."

"Finished. Oh, darlin', you and I will never be finished. You owe me. I plan on collecting for a long time. After all, isn't it the child's responsibility to take care of their parent when they get old? I have to say, since you sent me to jail, you owe me more than a stinky retirement home. I'm retiring to the tropics and living out my days in style."

He leaned against the side of the counter, a deck of cards sitting beside him. One of his favorite games to play with her when she was little. He found it fascinating to see she knew each card. The memory made her sad. Behind the attention he'd paid to her lay only manipulation and greed. He never loved her.

"I see you haven't changed. You still have a hard time believing I can do what I do. I will show you. I'm better now. I can do a lot more. I can control it a lot better."

"I have no doubt. Your sister told me you're working with the FBI. Said you helped them catch some really bad guys."

"You were my first. See, you taught me something."

He hit her again. Her jaw sang with pain, and in that moment she got a glimpse of her sister in a deep black hole, lying in mud and water. Scared to death and cold as ice, she lay curled into a ball.

Morgan needed more. She needed to know where to find that hole.

Tyler wanted to step in the second her head snapped back. He hated that he couldn't do anything about it. Her swollen lip bled. The angry red mark on her jaw would soon bloom into a vivid bruise.

Control your anger, Tyler. I can't have it coming at me from the front and behind.

I'm sorry, honey. I can't stand here and watch him hit you and not be angry.

Try. For me. For Jillian. I saw her. I just need a little more.

"I didn't teach you to betray your family."

"Sure you did. You betrayed Jillian and me when you killed our mother. And every time you broke the law and blackmailed someone. You betrayed us every time you used me to get what you wanted."

"I did it for us, but you wouldn't cooperate. I finally had the big score and you had to be Miss High-and-Mighty. Your mother got in the way. Without her, I could have made you tell me."

She caught another glimpse of her sister. His anger made him vulnerable, broke down his walls and let her inside his mind. Impressed with his ability to control his thoughts and build a wall against her, he was good. She's better. Time to show him.

"You know what I finally figured out back then? You liked to slap me around, beat me, and throw me in the closet. In the end, it didn't matter if I told you or not. You'd have done those things anyway, because hurting people is all you know how to do.

"When I saw what that man was doing, I got a glimpse at what would happen if you took over. You want to know what I saw. You had it all. Finally, you found the big score that would set you up for life." His anger built and she went in for the kill. "I couldn't let that happen, not when you treated my mother and me like dirt. That's why I didn't tell you."

He swung with his right to punch her in the face and hit nothing but air.

"I saw that coming. You underestimate me, *Dad*."

"I'm out of here. Find your sister yourself. *If* you can."

"Have no doubt, I'll find her." Before he took a step away from the counter, she continued. "Ace, king, queen, jack, ten of hearts. A royal flush."

He smiled a not-so-nice smile and turned each card over in the order she'd said. He'd set it up before she arrived to prove to her he had the winning hand in this million-dollar game.

"You're really confident you've won. Enjoy the money while it lasts," she said and kept her eyes on his. *I see your future and it looks very . . . gray.*

"Stop it. Get out of my head."

She showed him a picture of himself standing in front of a gray cinderblock wall—in a jail cell.

I wonder if this is your past, or your future. You can think about that when you leave here with my money.

"Stop it. Stop it." James hit at his head to try to push her out. "You're a witch. A real witch."

"Don't you forget it!" she yelled after him as he took off out the front door with the duffel bags. His pickup truck engine revved and the tires squealed. He took off down the long driveway and out of her life for good.

Rooted to her spot, standing there looking out the open front door, she forgot Tyler stood with her. He pressed a frozen bag of corn to her jaw and brought her out of her stupor. His other hand cupped her cheek, his thumb rubbed softly over her skin. She focused on his touch and the warmth of his hand.

"You knew he was going to hit you."

"He's predictable. Same as he always was. Nothing ever changes. He only thinks about money and what he wants. His thoughts all revolve around him."

"Did you find out where your sister is?"

"Not exactly. I didn't want to get hit again." She put her hand over his on the frozen bag. "Man, that really hurts. It's been a long time since he hit me. I'd forgotten how it feels to get whacked like that."

"It's more than him hitting you with his fist. You feel the anger that goes with it. I saw you. You took the blow, but the second hit of anger really did the damage." He brushed his hand down her head and through her long hair, hating that she'd been hurt. "I'm sorry, honey. I wish like hell you didn't know what it felt like to be hit like that."

"And it pisses you off that you just stood there while he did it."

"I'm that transparent, huh."

"You did a great job of looking intimidating and bored at the same time."

"How would you know? I stood behind you."

"Because that's what he thought of you. It's what I needed him to think of you. In my vision, you went after him when he hit me. He killed you with a knife from the butcher block."

Tyler stared at the knives on the counter and back at her.

"Thank you for believing in me and doing what I asked." Her fingertips rubbed a circle over his chest, around his heart.

He swallowed hard, unable to speak.

"He thinks he's in the clear. He's mentally high-fiving himself right this minute."

She pulled the bag of corn from her face and threw it into the sink. "Let's go. We have to get Jillian. Are the guys waiting outside?"

He pushed thoughts of his death by stabbing to the back of his mind and focused on the present and the future he still had thanks to Morgan.

"They should be coming up the drive any minute."

"Okay, let's go. We need to take the dirt road that leads out behind the barn and into the hills. He took her that way. We're looking for a well that's been boarded over. He used some branches and brush to camouflage it."

"Is she alive?" He hated to ask. This had to be eating her up inside. Even though they weren't close, and Jillian hated her, Morgan cared deeply for her sister. She'd worry about her niece and nephew growing up without their mother. After all, Morgan had grown up alone. She wouldn't want those kids to go through the same thing.

"She is, and she's scared. She's only been down there a few hours."

"A few hours?" He thought she'd been down in the well overnight. He thought time might be running out. If she'd only been down there a few hours, she'd probably be okay.

"He tricked her into staying last night by telling her I'd be here this morning with the money, so he'd stay away from me. She believed him," she said, disgusted with her sister's betrayal. "Let's go get her."

Chapter Thirty

MORGAN ASKED THEM to stop the vehicles on the dirt road and got out and stood looking across a pasture toward the trees. Impressed with the men Agent Davies sent to assist them, they respected Morgan and her gift enough to stand by their cars and wait. No one spoke. They gave her the time and space she needed to do her thing. When she walked off at a forty-five-degree angle from the road and headed for the trees, no one moved until Tyler started out after her. Tyler and ten other agents followed at a short distance as she made her way through a sparsely forested area.

Ten minutes later, they came upon a stone foundation for an old burned-down one-room building. Morgan continued past the crumbling structure and walked another hundred yards and came to a sudden stop. She swayed on her feet, what little energy she still had sapped away as she used her gift.

They reviewed a dozen detailed maps of the area, and none of them showed any wells. There could be one or a dozen out in the hills. The fact that Morgan knew the well had been covered by brush would only make it more difficult for them to find by searching the property on their own. Morgan was their best chance of finding Jillian.

She stumbled, turned to her right, and followed a path only she knew. He decided to try talking to her in his head.

Morgan, are you all right?

Almost there, she said weakly.

He didn't like the way she sounded. He could barely hear or feel her. Their connection to each other was tenuous. She used everything she had to find her sister.

She jogged down a small incline and dropped to her knees in front of what looked like a mound of boulders with several small bushes behind them. Deceptive, and a good cover for the well. When Morgan leaned over the boulders and threw several of the bushes aside, everyone saw they were just large branches broken from another large bush. Brittle, sun-bleached, well-worn wood covered the well. Anyone who happened to step on it might fall through and into the depths, maybe to their death.

As soon as Morgan and several of the men began removing the wood, Jillian called out, "Help me. I'm down here." Her voice nothing more than a gravely rasp. She must have screamed for a long time with no one for miles to hear her.

Without Morgan, they might not have found Jillian in time—or ever.

"Jillian, we're coming. Hold on," Morgan called to her.

"Help me! Get me out of here!" she screamed, but hardly anything came out of her sore throat. Scared and angry, she couldn't believe her father dumped her down this hole. Cold and wet, she twisted her ankle landing in the soft mud. It hurt so badly she couldn't stand on it. She probably broke it, and all of this was Morgan's fault.

Morgan waited while they lowered a man down on ropes. Twenty-something feet down, her sister cursed and pleaded in alternating tones of anger and misery. Morgan wished this hadn't happened, but Jillian brought it upon herself when she'd invited their father into her life. She should have left well enough alone.

As soon as she freed herself from the ropes, she turned on Morgan.

"Here comes the freight train," Morgan said softly to Tyler.

Tyler didn't have time to register Morgan's remark before Jillian managed to limp over the five feet to them, cock back her arm, and throw a punch toward Morgan's face. Morgan ducked in time and planted both hands on her sister's shoulders and shoved her back, making her stumble on her bad ankle. She squealed in pain, but kept the furious glare in place.

"I'll forgive you for that once." Morgan turned from her sister and walked away from everyone now staring at her. She couldn't take the added attention. Fading fast, she still had so much to do. She hoped Sam arrested her father.

"This is all your fault. If you'd just do what he asked,

none of this would have happened," Jillian screamed after her.

Tyler had enough of Morgan's family members taking shots at her. He grabbed Jillian's arm and spun her around to face him. She winced when she shifted her weight to her bad ankle, giving Tyler a little satisfaction.

"Leave her alone, or I'll arrest you."

"You'll arrest me. I was kidnapped and thrown down a well."

"You contacted your father and helped him set this up. You wanted the money just as much as he did. How much of a cut did he promise you?"

He waited to see if she'd answer. She didn't, but stood defiant, looking incredulous and guilty as hell. Unable to look at him, her eyes fell away.

"You wanted it just as much as your father does. A little quick cash and who cares who gets hurt. The fact that he double-crossed you hasn't even entered your mind. You just want to blame her because you're pissed he took off with the money and left you down that well."

"It's only a hundred grand. She won't miss it. She's rich, thanks to the family curse. She uses it to make all that money."

"You ridicule her for that family curse, and then you want to benefit from it. Well, let me fill you in on the kind of woman your sister is. She lived on the streets and in shelters from the time she was thirteen. She got her GED because a nun took an interest in her and helped her. She taught herself about the stock market and finance through hard work and studying her ass off. She doesn't use her *curse* to make money on the stock market. She uses her brain. And what difference would it make if she did use her gift? It's hers to use as she sees fit.

"Today, she used her money and her gift to find you. She paid your father one *million* dollars to get him to tell her where you were. A million dollars of her own money to get back a sister who hates her and would take her for every dime she has if you could."

She tried to get out of his grasp. The truth hurt, and she was going to listen. It was the only way he had to make up to Morgan for the fact that, again, she'd gotten hurt, and he'd stood by and done nothing.

"My father wouldn't leave me out here. He just wanted to be sure she gave him the money. That's all."

"You keep telling yourself that if it makes you feel better. The truth is, he took the money and left to catch the jet waiting for him at the airport. He never planned on giving you a dime. He meant for you to stay in that well. He didn't tell her where to find you. She did that all on her own."

He turned her so she could see Morgan. She'd fallen to her knees about twenty feet away, and one of the other agents helped her to sit down. She had her face turned to the sun and even from where he stood with Jillian, he could see her swollen jaw had turned an even deeper shade of red. Her lip had swelled and crusted over with dried blood. Her skin paled to ghostly white against the deep blue of her shirt. She looked lifeless, guarded by two agents.

"Look at her. That curse, as you call it, sucks the life

out of her every time she uses it, like she did today to find you."

"At least she wasn't down in that hole."

"I wonder how many times she was locked in the closet for days, not hours. I wonder how many times your father slapped her, punched her, or beat her until she couldn't move. Imagine it was your daughter down in that hole, or locked in a closet, or beaten. Hungry and hurt and scared. Your father could have just as easily taken your little girl and put her down that well. Morgan would have paid any amount and used her gift until she died if it meant getting her back. It's what she did for you today. It didn't kill her, but she doesn't exactly look like she got out of this unscathed. A bruised jaw, a busted lip, a million dollars gone, all to get you back." He turned her to face him. "What a waste, if you ask me. Don't contact her again. Stay away from her. If you don't, you'll answer to me."

"Who the hell do you think you are?"

He leaned into her face. "I'm the only family she's got."

Chapter Thirty-One

SHE FELT THE sun on her face and Tyler's strong body
along her back. They sat on the soft grass beneath a huge
oak, her body tucked between his long legs, her head
resting against his shoulder and chin. Her face hurt. She
turned her head and glanced around at the rolling hills.

"Tyler?"

"Yeah, honey?"

"Where did everyone go?"

"They left about an hour ago. They collected all the
evidence they needed."

"And my sister?"

"To my disappointment, they took her to the hospital.
Her husband and kids will meet her there. She maintains
this is all your fault."

"She won't be charged with a crime?"

"She should be," he said angrily. "But, no. Agent
Davies agreed he'd let her go. She didn't know your father

was going to dump her down that well. He used her. If you ask me, she got off easy. She wanted her cut of the money."

"He dumped her down a well," she said in defense of her sister.

"Yeah, and to thank you for paying to get her back and for finding her, she tried to clock you."

"Yeah, well, like father like daughter."

She gently put her hand to the side of her face. The throbbing pain ached like nothing else. Just talking hurt. She'd never again put herself in the position of being used by her father or sister. It saddened her to think that now she really was alone. She had no family, not like Tyler had a family. He had his sister and his friends. Her family was lost to her. She'd tried to be good to her sister and found it hard to accept that even though she'd tried, her family would never be what she wanted.

Let it go, she said to the universe and looked up to the sun, letting the warmth help to heal her broken heart.

"Let what go, honey?"

She'd forgotten he could hear her thoughts, but took comfort that she wasn't alone. Not when she had him.

"The dream that I was born into a family who cares about each other. My father and sister would rather curse me for my gift and exploit it to their benefit. I just have to let it go. I can't make them be something they aren't. I can't be something I'm not."

Her sadness radiated off her. He leaned forward and wrapped his arms around her. His wrists ached from leaning back on his hands, but he barely noticed. Morgan was all that mattered. He looked over her head at the land and the sun setting in the distance. "You picked a pretty spot to rest. I like it here."

"I didn't pick it so much as it picked me. I blanked out. The other agents must think I'm a nutcase."

"Not really. Impressed, bowled over by your ability, a little awestruck watching you work and find your sister. One of them wants to know if you'll help with a kidnapping case he's working on, and another wants to know if you can help them with a bank robbery scheme, something about a code they can't figure out."

"The girl ran off with the mechanic who fixed her eighteenth-birthday Beemer after she sideswiped a parked car on her way home from a club. They're in Fiji, spending her daddy's money. She's almost out of cash and will call home for rescue in a couple of days."

Tyler laughed. "I'll call the agent and let him know. Anything on the bank scheme?"

"Not now. I'm tired."

He held her tight. "I know. You're back, but you don't look like you've recovered."

"It's just been too much in such a short time. Between the attempted robbery at the restaurant, the whole confrontation in the restaurant with my sister, my father, and this mess, that poor girl, Leslie, and the serial killer, I haven't had enough time to rest and recover."

"Not to mention all the energy you expended waking up happy with me this morning," he teased and nuzzled his nose against her neck.

He wanted to make her smile. He didn't know how to

help her, except to keep her out here in the isolated hills. That's why he hadn't just carried her to the car and taken her back to the city. She needed the time alone.

"That's been the highlight of my week here in the city. I have to say, I much prefer you happy to mad. You're something when you're happy."

"Oh, yeah. I'll show you how happy I can be tonight." He nuzzled his nose into her soft neck and kissed her beneath her ear, making her giggle. "We need to swing by the office. You have some paperwork to sign on your father, and we have to get your million dollars back to the bank."

"Sam caught my father?"

"He did. He waited on the plane until your father boarded with the duffel bags in tow. Your father confirmed the flight plans with the pilots, asked the flight attendant to get him a drink, and sat back ready to gloat. Sam came out and arrested him after your father took the first sip of his celebratory scotch. Sam said he didn't take it very well."

"Is Sam upset about the eye?"

"How did you . . . never mind. He's fine. I should have warned him about your family's penchant for throwing a punch. Remind me never to make you angry."

"I'm more a lover than a fighter." She turned in his arms and pressed him back down to the ground. "Kiss me. I really need to feel something good."

He didn't have to be asked twice, especially when he'd been part of the trials she'd endured over the last few weeks. He cupped her face in his hands and pressed his lips to hers. Soft and sweet, he held the kiss, nibbled at her bottom lip and kissed the corner of her mouth. He used the tip of his tongue to trace her lower lip, and when she sighed, he slid his tongue inside and caressed hers.

She gave back the caress, and he buried his hands in the long strands of her hair and brushed them back over her head and down her back. He loved the feel of her lying down his body. He remembered what it felt like to have her lying on him naked that morning. He cupped her hips and pressed them down to his. A deep groan escaped up his throat.

She rocked her hips against his and continued kissing him. He really wanted to make love to her. It felt like if he didn't do it now, he might not get the chance to do it again. He kissed her cheek and her temple and forehead. When she rested her cheek against his, he wrapped his arms around her tight and just held her while they both calmed their need for each other.

He didn't care about lying in the dirt and grass. He only cared about the woman in his arms. She'd let go of her dream of having the ideal family. He'd let go of his dream of having the wife and kids at any cost. He only wanted Morgan, and whatever life they made together.

"We've got to get back," she said, but didn't move from her spot on top of him. He felt so good, and with his strong arms around her, she felt like she could relax and just be. She didn't have to put up any blocks or guard herself. When Tyler was like this, she could let go. It felt so good to have his warmth and passion and love wash over her. She wanted to draw it in and wrap it around her, around them, and forget everything else.

"Are you sure you're up to leaving this place? It's nice. No one's around but you and me."

"I can't hide here all day. We've got things to do. Sam is waiting for us."

He didn't have to ask how she knew that. He just helped her up and laughed when she turned him around and brushed off his backside. She gave him a few extra pats on the ass and surprised him by giving it a squeeze with both hands.

"Nice butt, Agent Reed."

He grabbed her and threw her over his shoulder like a sack of potatoes. He smacked her on the bottom and said, "Thanks. I like yours, too."

She patted his backside and he walked back toward the car with her over his shoulder. They both felt lighter and their laughter rang out over the hills. It was a good moment. One she'd hold on to.

"Let me down. You can't carry me like this all the way back," she grumbled and lost her breath from laughing so hard.

He pulled her back over his shoulder and let her body slide down his until her feet hit the ground. He held her to him and gazed down into her bright crystal-blue eyes. Her cheeks were flushed from the rush of blood to her head.

"You're so beautiful."

"Nothing like a woman with a split lip and a bruised jaw," she joked.

He wasn't in the joking mood. "You're beautiful," he said with all seriousness and kissed her on the forehead. He took her hand and headed to the car.

She didn't know what to say. The look on his face and the tone of his voice said more than his words. Her heart ached with joy and hope.

Chapter Thirty-Two

A LONG DAY for both of them, Tyler drove them down from the hills and back to his office. Morgan spent over an hour giving her official statement concerning her father, his abduction of her sister, and the ransom he demanded.

They returned the million dollars to the bank and transferred it back into her account. The bank manager had a fit when she simply walked into his office with the duffel bags, no guards, and asked to make a deposit. With guards posted at the office door, two tellers counted all the money, and she signed and received her receipt.

She didn't really care about the money. All she'd ever wanted was enough to live her life without having to deal with a lot of people and explaining her gift all the time. She had that in Colorado. Today, that life seemed so far away. She wondered if she'd ever get that quiet life back. Would Tyler be a part of it?

After the FBI office and bank, they met Sam at the police precinct for the task force meeting to go over the Psychic Slayer case and the latest results from the lab.

Sam waved them into a conference room. "What do you think, Morgan? We've got photos of each of the victims up on the walls along with a timeline and descriptions of evidence found at the scenes and the phonebook pages. Next to each dead woman's ad or listing, we've put a red sticker."

Morgan shivered. They stood out like drops of blood on the pages. An eerie reminder those women lost their lives to a man who wanted to silence and blind them. They died because they couldn't tell him how to find her.

She sat staring at those pages thinking about the murdered women and the ones who could be killed because a man ultimately wanted her. He thought she knew something about him. He wanted to make sure she didn't tell. And to make sure no psychic ever told.

Morgan listened to them talking about the case. Where they were with different pieces of evidence, what they thought about the man committing the murders, and when they thought he would strike next. No one wanted to say they all knew he was after her.

She must have had contact with the killer through her website. Living in Colorado isolated her from people. Sure, she saw people in town when she did her shopping, but the murders were happening here in San Francisco. There weren't too many psychic shops in the small towns close to where she lived, and she'd only visited Denver once.

"Tyler, have you heard from the guys at the FBI about my computer files?" she asked.

"Not yet. I checked in with them when we stopped by earlier. They didn't have anything conclusive. Why? Did you think of something?"

"Can you ask them to search the files in the last"—she paused to think about how far back they should go—"two years. They should look in my responses. If I saw something illegal this man did, I would have told him to turn himself into the police. Tell them to search the file for keywords like *police*, or *turn yourself in*. That might get us something."

"Do you have a lot of responses where you'd say that to someone?" Tyler asked.

"I can think of a few. There's something bugging me. I keep thinking I should know which one I'm looking for."

Everyone focused on Morgan, although they tried to hide it.

Tired all the way to her bones, being in the city and in the precinct gradually drained her. Keeping up her guard against the people in the station wore on her. She wanted this over. Only one way to do that. She'd have to find the man killing the psychics. Enough stalling, she knew what had to be done. She needed to find him her way.

"I'll call the office and have them search your files for the keywords you said. I'll be back in a few minutes." Tyler kissed the top of her head and walked by, his hand brushed across her shoulder and back as he passed. He'd make the call and get her out of here. Fading fast, he didn't want to see her blank out for hours again. She couldn't keep this up. He knew it, and Sam had already commented on it too.

He hated to admit she needed to go back home to Colorado. He didn't want to be separated from her, but he wanted her safe and healthy.

They had a lot to work out before they shared their lives. He wondered if she'd live with him in California. Not in the city or even the suburbs, but maybe they could find something more isolated. Someplace like where her father had been living. She'd done okay up in the hills. He'd have to start looking around for a piece of property. He had some money put away. Real estate and property were expensive in California, and especially in the Bay Area. It didn't matter. He'd find a place for him and Morgan, whatever it took to keep her safe and with him. They could use the property in Colorado throughout the year, or if she needed to get away. They'd work it out. He couldn't lose her. Not now. Not ever.

Chapter Thirty-Three

SHE WAITED FOR Tyler to leave, then stood, and with all eyes on her she went to the wall of pictures and details about the murders. She walked by each one and touched some of the pictures. Then she stood with her back to the group of men discussing the case and opened herself to the man who killed these women.

She tried to put herself in his home at the coffee table in his apartment looking at the open phonebook, looking through his eyes. A different experience for her; normally she saw her visions as if they were on a movie screen in her mind. In this case, she was the man sitting on the old sofa looking at the phonebook.

Once she had herself in that place, she mentally told herself to move away from him and walk around the room. It took all her focus and energy to make herself an active participant in the vision.

As soon as Sam saw her blank out, he silently signaled for everyone to leave. She needed her space. All of them focusing on her would only drain her faster. He'd watched her wilt when she shared a vision with Emma. This time, she looked like a leaf in fall withering away to a crisp death. He wanted to shake her out of whatever vision held her, but he feared what might happen if he touched her. He wished Tyler would come back. With his connection to her, maybe he'd know what to do.

She stood before the wall of pictures, not really seeing them at all. Her shoulders slumped with her hands and arms hanging at her sides. Her lively hair went as slack as her arms. The golden mass of waves now lay limp and lifeless. The golden glow of her hair tarnished and dulled. When she swayed slightly, he moved toward her and stood behind her within reach. If she collapsed, he'd catch her.

Morgan moved around the dingy room. From the small sitting area, she looked into an even smaller kitchen with scarred and battered cupboards. Many of the drawers hung at odd angles, unable to slide into place properly. Outdated, avocado-green refrigerator and countertops in a faded white-with-gold-flecks pattern.

Nothing in the space told her where this apartment was located. She glided to the door with the peephole, hoping to avoid getting trapped in a closet. She'd never done this before and relied solely on instinct. She floated through the door and almost laughed at the thought of Tyler being right. In this way, she could be considered a ghost. She found herself in a hallway with dark paneled walls and a threadbare, cigarette-burned, deep burgundy and navy carpet that long ago needed replacing. She didn't even want to consider the many stains. She turned and stared back at the door she'd just spirited through. Apartment 6D.

Tyler walked into the room. Sam stood behind Morgan. Although she stared at the gruesome wall of photos and evidence, she wasn't seeing any of it. She'd gone somewhere else. He quietly walked over to Sam and whispered into his ear, "Why is she smiling when she looks like she's fading?"

"I don't know," Sam whispered back. "She just said, 'Apartment 6D.' I'm guessing she's tracking down our guy using some kind of psychic spider sense."

"She isn't Spider-Girl. She doesn't have superpowers." Worried about her, she didn't look good, and seeing her this way ate away at his heart.

"I'm not so sure about that. She's got an apartment number. Let's see if she can get anything else."

"She's turning gray. We aren't talking pale here. Gray." He took a step toward her. He couldn't feel her with him. He couldn't hear her, even when he called to her in his mind. This wasn't like in the hills. This was different, like she'd gone somewhere he couldn't go.

Sam grabbed Tyler's arm before he touched Morgan. "Give her a chance. She went into this trance on her own. We didn't ask her to try and find out where the guy is. I think she wants to end this."

"Of course she wants to end it. People are dying."

"Yes. And she feels responsible because this started with her. She said this would end with her. Maybe this is it. Maybe she'll come out of this with the guy's name and where we can find him."

If she were anyone but the woman he loved, he would wait it out. So he stepped back and gave her some space. The smile had long since faded from her lips. They turned as pale as her skin. Her eyes were as dark as he'd ever seen them. He and Sam stood behind her just in case she collapsed. God, he hoped she didn't.

Morgan's sight was clearer, sharper than it had ever been. *This is important.*

Life and death.

She went to the window at the end of the hall and spirited her way through it and down the side of the building. The building and the neighborhood were in a state of decay. She found the front door along with a bank of mailboxes. She scanned them, found 6D, and read the red plastic label: *M. Tall.*

"That's a name you could never live up to. You were never tall in stature or in your life, but you've found a way to make yourself larger than life. You take it away. You've found a thrill in those women's deaths. Although you seek me, you'll continue to kill because you like it. You've been anonymous your whole life, and now you've found a way to make that anonymity work for you, so you can be hidden and seen.

"Everyone knows the Psychic Slayer, yet no one knows M. Tall.

"I know you, Mr. Tall.

"I'm coming for you."

Her words, haunting and whispered like a secret confessed in the dead of night, sent a chill down Tyler's back.

"Please tell me she isn't talking to him," Sam pleaded.

She'd given them his name. Now all they needed was an address and they'd get him. Progress. Finally.

She moved over to a map hanging on the other wall. She held up both hands and ran them over the map. Her right finger stopped and pointed to a spot. Sam and Tyler both looked over her shoulder.

"Twenty-three Windsor Street," she whispered.

Her finger rested on the street. The red dots indicating the murder locations spread out in an odd circle around the street she indicated. He'd picked the women, or the ads, based on the proximity to his own home. Close enough to walk to, most of them within twenty minutes from his apartment. Not so unusual for a serial killer to hunt in a familiar area.

Morgan leaned against the wall, hands spread wide. She knew who he is, knew where he lived, now all she had to do was find him and stop him.

Chapter Thirty-Four

SHE DISAPPEARED INTO the police station over an hour ago. He watched, waited, hid behind a dumpster in the back of the parking lot across the street, keeping the entrance and their car in sight. The anticipation made his gut tighten. He wiped his damp hands down his thighs.

Overwhelmed with excitement, she'd finally arrived, and he couldn't wait to get his hands on her. He'd waited outside the shop where he'd killed that woman, Rose. She'd known about him. She'd known about Morgan. Things she couldn't have known unless she was like Morgan.

The others were actors in a costume playing to their audience. He wished he'd kept Rose longer. He wished he'd had his special place ready, so he could explore the depths of what made her special.

Rose wasn't the one. He wanted Morgan.

At first, he'd thought her a witch out to destroy him.

He knew better now. She was the catalyst to his discovering his own power. Invisible his whole life, now he was somebody. People feared him, and others admired him for eradicating the imposters.

Ethereal and golden even in the night, she glowed like he imagined angels glowed with an inner light that shined through. Just thinking about her and the powers she possessed and controlled excited him.

Yes, she's his angel, sent to show the world who he really is.

The chill in the air seeped through his coat and goose flesh rose on his skin. The fog had rolled in with the setting sun and cast an eerie glow on the streets.

She'll come out soon, he told himself over and over again. He'd get his chance and she'd be his.

The wind blew, swirling the fog.

Someone tapped his shoulder.

He turned quickly, afraid he'd been discovered. No one.

Nothing behind him but trash and darkness. He thought he saw a transparent light blink out. Chills ran up his spine and a cold sweat broke out over his skin.

Scared to death, someone had just walked over his grave.

Chapter Thirty-Five

EVERYONE SCRAMBLED TO gather whatever information they could on M. Tall at 23 Windsor Street, apartment 6D.

Tyler led Morgan to a chair at the far side of the room and made her sit down. She'd done it. She'd gotten the information they needed. The fact that she looked like the walking dead didn't do much to make him happy about how they got the information. Eyes sunken, cheeks hollow, she'd shriveled before his eyes. Torn, he needed to get her out of there and back to the ship, but he also had to do his job and catch the bastard killing women and hunting Morgan.

"If she'd done whatever she did weeks ago, we could have saved time and *lives*," Stewart remarked.

Morgan didn't respond to Stewart, but sat as if she'd turned to stone, or fragile porcelain. Tyler lost it. He grabbed Stewart by the front of his shirt and propelled him across the room and as far away from Morgan as he could get the asshole. He shoved him against the wall of gruesome photos.

"She's done everything she can to help on this case and it's taking everything she has to do it. Do what you should have done at the press conference and shut the fuck up. If you don't, I'll see that you do. Got it?"

"Man, relax, I was only saying . . ."

Tyler slammed him against the wall again. "Not another word."

Stewart got his message and slipped free and left the room. Maybe now Morgan could have the space she needed to recover from all she'd done.

Tyler sucked in a deep breath and let it out on a ragged sigh, trying to pull himself together before he faced Morgan again. He didn't want to bombard her with his emotions.

He turned to her, but found nothing but her empty chair as everyone around him scrambled to do their job and not piss him off.

A spurt of adrenaline and fear rushed through his system. "Where did Morgan go?" Tyler asked, inwardly trying to sense her, but feeling nothing.

One of the officers getting ready to go serve the search warrant on the apartment spoke first. "The lady? She left a few minutes ago while we were going over the building layout. She didn't look so good. I think maybe she's sick."

Tyler and Sam looked at each other.

"I'm sure she's fine," Sam said. "She probably just needed to get away. Everyone is anxious and worried about the operation, she probably couldn't handle all the emotions."

Tyler wasn't convinced. "I wanted to take her back to the ship. She needs the isolation after everything that's happened. I thought maybe Captain Finn could come and get her and I'd meet her back there later."

"You want me to go look for her while you coordinate the teams?"

Distracted by his ringing phone, Tyler didn't answer Sam, who turned to answer a question from one of the officers.

"Reed."

"Got the information you requested."

"You found it."

"Two years ago. Martin Tall. He asked about getting a job, and she responded that he'd get it. She also told him she knew what he'd done, and he should turn himself into the police."

"Did she say what she knew?"

"No such luck there."

"Shit. Did he say the name of the company?"

"Mimitech."

"Perfect. Contact them and get his records. Dig up whatever you can on him. Start with the credit card he used to pay for the response and the business. I want this guy's history."

The noise in the room grew louder with all the officers talking and planning for the operation to find and take down the Psychic Slayer, aka Martin Tall.

Sam waited beside him for further explanation.

"You heard the bit about his request through her website about whether he'd get a job with a place called Mimitech. It's a copier repair service. Tech is doing the background now."

He turned around. Turned around again. Puzzled, he rubbed the base of his neck.

Sam grabbed his arm to stop him from turning again. "Who are you looking for?"

Morgan screamed in his mind. *Tyler!* The pain knifed through his brain, like the time she yelled *No!* during the press conference. He grabbed his head and grit his teeth.

Sam shoved Tyler into a chair. "What's the matter?"

"Mor-gan," he answered between clenched teeth, barely able to get her name out.

Tyler jumped up and ran from the conference room, Sam on his heels. They busted through the front door on the run like they were fleeing a fire. Officers and civilians stared after them. They searched the immediate area, but didn't find Morgan.

"You take the parking lot. I'll go around the other side of the building. Maybe she took a short walk." Even Sam didn't believe that, but said it in hopes Tyler would think it sounded good.

"She could barely walk ten minutes ago. I had to make her sit in the chair. She still seemed out of it, like she was still in a vision."

It hit him all at once. "Shit! She was still searching him out. She found him. He took her from right under our noses." He looked around again. "She came out here, stood right outside the police station, and he took her."

"You don't know that. She might have just gone for a walk to clear her head. Maybe she's too tired to get back here, and that's why she called out to you."

He shook his head. "No. She screamed my name because she's scared. Our connection broke again. I had her, but now she's gone again." He ran his hand through his hair and pulled on it in frustration.

They knew the guy's name and where he lived, but they didn't know anything else. They'd only had the information for half an hour, at most. The task force team worked diligently putting information together. Undercover officers remained posted outside the building, surrounding it. No one had spotted the suspect, and he wasn't at home. Now, it seemed, he had Morgan.

"Tyler, can you tell if she's still with you at all?" Sam asked the odd question, and yet they were both getting used to Morgan and her ways.

Tyler had to calm down, try to clear his mind, and sense whether she was with him or not. Angry she was gone. Unsure what to do next. Scared to death that bastard would kill her like all the others. He couldn't lose her now—before they'd ever had a real chance to live their lives together.

He sat down on the step, took a deep breath, let it out, and did it again. His eyes went up to the darkening night sky. He felt the breeze on his face, closed his eyes, and tried to empty his mind of everything but Morgan.

Morgan, where are you?

A splitting headache throbbed at the back of his head. He rubbed at the back of his neck to try to ease the tension and got a vision of Morgan curled up holding the back of her head.

"Shit! She's in the trunk of a car. He bashed her over the head, and she's hurting bad."

"She told you that?" Sam asked.

"No. I saw her. I don't know. It's like she sent me a picture. I could see her in the dark trunk curled up with her hands covering her head. Hell, the back of my head started hurting, but I lost the picture, and my head doesn't hurt anymore."

"Okay. This is good. She can communicate with us."

"Sam, she's wiped out, and she's hurt. For a few seconds, I could feel her. I actually felt what she feels. I don't know how to explain to you how empty she is. It's like every ounce of energy has been drained from her. Holding her head was like asking her to dig a six-foot hole."

"Bad analogy, buddy." Sam looked off in the distance, thinking things through, and turned back. "Okay, so we know who he is, we know he has her, and they're in a car. Did you see what kind of car?"

"No. I saw her as if I hovered a few inches above her." He considered the dark space. "She's not tall, maybe five-seven. She lay cramped in the trunk, so we're looking for a compact car, definitely not an SUV. No spare tire beside her, so there's either a compartment for it in the trunk space, or under the car. It's not a hatchback, but it's small."

Tyler's cell phone rang. He didn't want to deal with anything right now. He needed to concentrate on the picture she'd sent to him. Maybe he could come up with something else. He checked the caller ID, realized he couldn't ignore the tech at the FBI.

"Reed." He listened while the tech ran down the information he'd dug up.

"Shit!" He hung up and wanted to throw the damn thing across the street. Instead, he squeezed the phone until his knuckles ached.

"Is that your new favorite word?"

Sam didn't like seeing Tyler out of control and not thinking straight. It reminded him of what he was like when Elizabeth was in danger. Personal involvement made it hard to make the right decision. "Who was that?"

"The tech guy doing the background check on Mr. Tall. He checked the credit card used on Morgan's website. In the last two days, he's purchased things at a hardware store, a drug store, grocery store, and used a car rental agency, in addition to the various other charges that all looked like regular purchases."

They both knew what this meant. No telling what he'd purchased at a hardware store and drugstore. Nothing good if he planned a kidnapping. He had food and a vehicle and Morgan. He could go anywhere and do anything to her before they found her.

Tyler calmly walked back into the police precinct. Time to do some digging. He'd start with the rental car agency. He'd get the make, model, and license plate number. They'd scour the city for the vehicle. He wouldn't stop until he found her.

He walked into the conference room and stared at the wall of photos. Every single woman's face became

Morgan. Every photo of their death became a photo of Morgan's death. He closed his eyes. He didn't want to see it. He didn't want to think it.

The ache in his chest intensified. He couldn't breathe. He needed to find her. Now.

When he opened his eyes he saw the map. She'd stood in front of it and pointed out the street where M. Tall lived. By that time, she could barely stand. She'd put her left hand on the street and had to use her right to support herself.

Or had she? The vision came with a blast of pain that nearly sent him to his knees.

"Sam, what does this mean to you? I see the two bags of money. The cash is pouring out. Instead of a strap from one end of the bag to the other, there's a bridge."

"Are you seeing the duffel bags with the million dollars?"

"Yeah." Tyler didn't know why she'd show him a picture of the money. They'd already arrested her father. The money was safely back in the bank. The bridge seemed pretty obvious. Maybe she crossed one of the bridges. But which one?

"I wish I had a million bucks. I'd be rich," one of the officers said.

"Richmond Bridge," both Tyler and Sam said at the same time.

"Pretty good interpretation," Sam boasted. "No wonder she has a hard time figuring out those images. She did a good job of sending a picture we could understand. Is she still in the trunk?"

"I can't see her, or feel her." He didn't care if they all thought he was nuts. As excruciating as the vision felt, at least he knew she was still alive. And counting on him to find her.

Sam walked over to the map. "Okay, let's go with the Richmond Bridge. He's only had her for, what, a half hour at most. That's enough time to get across the bridge and into Richmond. We know this guy hasn't rented an apartment or hotel room, yet. His credit card would have shown it."

"Unless he paid cash," someone called out.

Sam shook his head, discounting the suggestion. "I don't think our guy wants to be anywhere with Morgan someone can see or hear them together. Besides, this guy doesn't have the kind of cash it would take to rent a place. He wouldn't take her to a hotel. Too many people. I think he's taking her someplace secluded, where he can keep her for a while and no one will see or hear them."

"A warehouse," Tyler said and grabbed the back of his head. "She's at a warehouse." He grabbed his shoulder. "She's out of the trunk. Oh God, he's dragging her by one arm across the pavement and her other arm and shoulder are getting chewed up. Her hair keeps getting stuck under her." He grabbed his head with both hands. "It's ripping right out of her scalp." He felt the pop as much as he heard it in his mind. Bone against bone, her arm came out of the socket in her shoulder. He grabbed his own shoulder and bellowed, "Shit!"

Sam had a hard time watching Tyler and the way this whole mess tore him apart. Everyone stood silent watching him, the pain in his face and wracking his body. They all knew it was nothing compared to what Morgan must be going through.

"Tyler, come on, man. Sit down."

"He pulled her arm out of the socket when he yanked her up a step. He didn't even stop. He's dragging her. She's in agony, and she can't do anything to stop him. She's completely worn out."

He took the seat Sam shoved him into and put his head in his hands and rested his elbows on his knees. He focused on his tenuous connection to Morgan. As much as he didn't want to feel or see what was happening to her, he had to. It was the only way he'd find her.

"Ask her where she is?"

It's the only thing he kept asking her. Over and over again, *Where are you?*

Three words she didn't have the strength to answer. He could feel her slipping away again. Then, when he thought he'd lose her, she opened her eyes and he saw through them. About to be dragged through a doorway into the warehouse, she looked down the length of her body at the surrounding buildings. In that moment, he could see everything she saw around her. She focused on the sign in front of an adjacent warehouse. Dragged into the building, he lost her.

"Contact Cantrell Commercial Real Estate. They have a sign in front of a warehouse that offers over twenty thousand square feet of space for lease or sale. She's across the street and over one building from that warehouse and sign. There are several warehouses around her.

None of them have lights on. The street is empty, except for a single white truck, probably from a construction crew, across the street. The warehouses we're looking for are under renovation and are being newly leased out. The one she's gone into hasn't been renovated yet. She's being dragged across glass and other debris."

He didn't want to think about her being cut, or scratched up. The shoulder was bad. Her head was in agony, and she was fading fast. He couldn't imagine what it was doing to her to be with a man evil enough to want to kill her.

One thought nearly sent him to his grave.

"Sam, we have a big problem. This guy doesn't know Morgan. He doesn't know anger and hate and other strong emotions hurt her. He doesn't know she's already used up her energy trying to find him."

Sam narrowed his eyes and nodded his agreement to Tyler's devastating revelation. "He could kill her without touching her."

Everyone in the room scrambled to get organized for the short trip to Richmond. At Sam's words, a quiet urgency settled on the group. This guy took the lives of five women. Morgan had helped the FBI on several cases, including the prostitution and abduction ring that sparked this whole mess. She'd saved Leslie from her abusive father. No one wanted her to be the Psychic Slayer's next victim.

Chapter Thirty-Six

EVERYTHING HURT, BUT Morgan's head and shoulder were the worst. Dumped unceremoniously in the middle of the floor, she'd lost consciousness. For how long, she didn't know. Regaining her focus, she caught a glimpse of the supplies spread out around them. A chair, a couple bags of groceries, a suitcase, and a sleeping bag. She didn't delude herself into believing she'd survive long enough for a good night's sleep. This man killed five women, and he liked it. She had no illusions she'd make it out of this alive.

A strange mix of happiness and elation mixed with a tremendous urge to feel the life drain from her when he strangled her like the others radiated from this man. The anger and rage she anticipated remained eerily restrained, like he had it locked behind a door. It pulsed, pushing against his restraint, giving her glimpses of its power around the edges. At any moment, he'd unleash it on her. The ebb and flow told her he didn't quite have control over it.

He remained conflicted as to what to do with her. A piece of him held her in reverence. She hoped that side of him won. Unfortunately, he had a taste for killing, and a growing hunger demanding to be fed. That side of him scared her to death.

"Wake up, angel," he whispered close to her ear. "Tell me my fortune."

He pushed her shoulder to wake her and her head rolled. Searing pain rushed through her shoulder and down her arm and back. She moaned and tried to remain still and minimize the agony.

She prayed for Tyler to save her. She'd done her best to connect to him. She had no way to know if it worked or not.

"Wake up, angel. Tell me my fortune. Remember, I asked you before about a job. You were right. I got it."

Then he remembered she'd also seen him end his mother's life. He'd been so careful, and only wanted to live his own life. She always demanded he be better, and in her next breath detailed how he didn't measure up. He couldn't take it anymore. When she'd become ill, she demanded he take care of her. After years of listening to her never achievable expectations and belittling remarks, it was even more demeaning to have to bathe her and change her clothes. He'd taken her back and forth to doctors. Every time they said she was well on her way out of this world, and still she'd linger.

She wouldn't just die, so he'd made sure she did after

the last visit to the doctor. They'd put her on a morphine drip with computerized dosing. Drugged up, she could barely speak or move.

She'd accused him so many times of being inferior and incapable of finishing anything. Well, he'd well and truly followed through on his threat. He told her if she wouldn't go on her own, he'd make her. He wouldn't spoon-feed her soup or change her bedpan anymore. He'd show her he was strong and powerful, not the weakling she'd always called him. He was a man, not a boy like she'd treated him his whole life.

"Wake up," he screamed and kicked Morgan in the side. He felt the thrill of satisfaction when she moaned and rolled over.

"Stop," she pleaded. "Just stop." She hurt. Awake enough to really see her surroundings, she was scared. What if Tyler didn't see where she'd been taken? What if he couldn't figure it out? What if they were too late?

"What's the matter with you? I saw you the other day. You were lit from within, an angel sent to help me. That's when I knew you were special. You can see things others can't. You can see the fakes, the impostors."

"Is that what you want? You want me to see if someone is an impostor. Because I can tell you right now, the only impostor I see is you."

She managed to sit up, but the backhanded slap across her face sent her backwards onto the floor again. She leaned to the side and spit the blood out of her mouth. She'd bitten her cheek and it made her mad. Tired of people hitting her, the anger gave her just the little bit of strength she needed. She struggled up to her feet and stood in front of M. Tall. Two inches taller than him, it didn't give her any extra confidence. He'd killed five women. His deceptive strength came from his rage in the moment he killed them.

"I know what you did. I told you before to go to the police. Now it's too late. The FBI is coming for you." She swayed on her feet. Bad idea to stand. She held her arm to her stomach, and still her shoulder felt like someone had set it on fire.

She closed her eyes and sent the scene to Tyler. Time to end this once and for all. She wouldn't let this man hurt anyone else. She'd be the last.

"DRIVE FASTER," TYLER demanded for the fifth time.

Sam drove as fast as he could. They all were, but traffic on the bridge made things difficult, even with the lights and sirens. It wasn't safe to excessively speed. If they got into an accident, they could be stuck on the bridge for hours at best, and at worst they could be killed, or kill someone else. Tyler understood that, but his need to get to Morgan overrode his good judgment.

"We'll get to her."

Tyler hadn't heard or felt anything from Morgan in the last twenty-five minutes.

They sped down the highway in silence and entered the industrial district close to the water and docks. Richmond Police had already been dispatched to the warehouse and surrounded the building. They couldn't see inside or get close enough to enter. Surrounded by windows, anyone inside would see them coming.

They listened to the police radio, the back-and-forth as officers gave out information on the scene and snipers took positions on the surrounding buildings.

Every radio call made Tyler more anxious. Almost there, he had his bulletproof vest on and his FBI jacket. Dressed and ready to do his job, only this time it wasn't just any person he needed to save. The woman he loved was hurt and dying. He could feel it. Somewhere inside of him, he knew she was dying.

It hit him all at once like being hit by a car. Her pain overwhelmed him.

Sam pulled in behind several police cruisers, but waited for him to get out. Unable to move, Tyler held himself completely rigid.

"What is it?"

"She's awake," he muttered. Difficult to talk with everything she was sending to him, she tried to keep the pain at bay, but didn't have the strength.

"He killed his mother. That's what she knew. That's what he's trying to hide." He waited. He could still feel her, trying to hold on to him.

Come on, baby. You can do this. I'm coming for you. I'm right outside. Tell me where you are.

He leaned back in his seat and the vision hit him like a sledgehammer. He saw the whole warehouse. He saw her, standing in front of him with her back to the front of the building. They were in the center of the open space with only a small camp light. She stood with her legs wide to

keep her balance. She had to hold her arm to keep the
pain under control. She might be standing now, but judg-
ing by the sway of her body, she wouldn't be on her feet
much longer.

He could go in through the south side of the building,
and they wouldn't be seen. They could take out the man
and get to Morgan. She needed them to get to her.

"Is the ambulance standing by?"

Sam hated that he had to ask. "Yeah, they're on the
next block."

"Tell them to come in on the south side slow and
easy. No lights. She needs them. Her shoulder is out of
the socket, her ribs might be broken, and she might have
a concussion. Her jaw is just throbbing. He must have
hit her. It pissed her off. That's twice today she's been
smacked in the face, and she didn't like it."

He tried to continue seeing the scene, but it faded as
he watched her struggle to get back up after falling. Her
bad arm hung limp at her side. She stumbled and cried
out a few times, making an effort to rise. Then she seemed
to look up at him before she stood up with conviction.

Tyler jumped out of the car, gun in hand. "We have
to go now. South Side. He won't see us coming. There's
only a small light. It's just him and her. He's losing it. He's
going to kill her," he said on the run.

At that point, he didn't care who followed him, or
didn't. He needed to get to Morgan.

Chapter Thirty-Seven

"THOSE WOMEN COULDN'T see like you can see!"

"Then, why would you kill them, and do those horrible things to them? They didn't know about your mother. They couldn't tell what they didn't know."

"They wouldn't tell me where you were."

"They couldn't," she yelled back.

He pulled out the butterfly knife and clamped his hand to her throat. He got right in her face, so she'd know he wasn't to be messed with. He was in charge. "They pretended and lied. Not you. You see the real me. No one else has ever seen me like you can."

Choking, the blade of the knife dug into her cheek. So sharp, it cut her skin and a drop of blood trickled down her face.

He saw the blood and pulled the knife away, but kept his hold on her throat. "See what you made me do?"

"I know everything you've done. I know what's going to happen next."

"Tell me! Tell me my fortune, angel."

"You want to know your future?"

"Yes, tell me. Tell me my future," he pleaded, excited like a child begging for a treat.

"You don't have one." She managed a small smile.

He squeezed tighter around her throat and watched her gasp for breath. He liked this part the best, holding someone's life in his hands. "What do you mean, I don't have a future?" He shook her hard and listened to her gasp and squeal in pain.

His grip weakened, allowing her to take a gasping breath. Tyler came into the light behind them and answered for her.

"Your future is in an eight-by-ten cell. FBI. Drop the knife and step away from her." He held his gun trained on the man's back. He tried not to look at Morgan. She'd distract him and he'd make a mistake. He couldn't make a mistake. Not with her life on the line.

Now he knew how Sam felt seeing the woman he loved in the hands of a madman and his own gun trained on both of them. Not a good feeling, and the thought of shooting Morgan made him sick. Just the sight of her made him hurt. Everything in him demanded he end this and get her to a hospital.

"I mean it. Let her go."

He had her, and he refused to give her up. He turned to face the agent and kept Morgan in front of him. His grasp tightened when he saw the man who'd carried her from the police station and taken her to the ship.

"Ah, so the boyfriend has come to get her," he said mockingly. "Well, you can't have her. She was sent to me. She's my angel!"

A blond agent stepped into the light, his gun trained on his head. Another moved in. No telling how many others were hiding in the shadows. He only knew he had her, and they wanted to take her away. He wouldn't let them. She belonged to him. If he couldn't have her, then he'd kill her.

He pulled her close. "You see me. You were supposed to see only for me. You're mine. You were sent to me," he said, his lips pressed to her cheek, his voice a whine of desperation and rage.

"I do see you, but I'm no angel. I'm a witch, and I belong to him." She tilted her head toward Tyler.

Tyler's heart ached at her words. He felt the wave of her love behind those words hit him. She belonged to him. And then, he heard her.

I love you.

Her face stung when he slapped her again and grabbed her by the shoulders. "You're mine," he screamed into her face.

The combination of anger from being slapped, yet again, and his hold on her shoulder unleashed something inside her. He shook her, and the searing pain that flashed through her body combined with her anger. Like a shock wave from an explosion, she let it fly, pushing him away.

The burst of energy came from her, throwing her to the ground and the man stumbling back. Astonished, Tyler had never seen or felt anything like it, and probably never would again. The wave of energy passed over them, putting them off balance too. When the man raised his knife to try to kill Morgan, he and Sam fired. Two rounds to the chest exploded into a blossom of blood as he fell backward.

Agents and police swooped in from the shadows. All of them with their weapons trained on the man lying dead on the floor. Tyler and Sam rushed to Morgan.

"I've never seen anything like that."

"It was like some kind of shock wave coming from her."

"How did she do that?"

The words and the voices swirled around Tyler, but he only heard the silence coming from Morgan.

"She's not breathing. Sam, get the medics."

He put his ear to her chest and listened for a heartbeat. Nothing. He cupped her bruised and swollen face in his hands and looked at her half-closed eyes. The blue went dark as the deepest ocean.

"No! Come on, baby. Don't you die on me." He gave her CPR and pounded on her chest. "Breathe, honey. Come on, breathe."

He gave her a breath, and then another and another. He pumped her heart and continued to breathe for her. If she couldn't do it on her own, he'd do it for her. For as long as it took, he'd do it for her.

"Come back to me, honey. Please. Come back!"

Chapter Thirty-Eight

THAT NIGHT BECAME the nightmare that haunted Tyler's every waking moment. Since he'd barely slept in five days, it was a constant agony.

He didn't remember everything once he and Sam shot M. Tall to death. He remembered Morgan lying beneath his hands as he pumped her heart and gave her air. Snapshots in his mind of police and FBI agents swarming everywhere, flashbulbs going off as they collected evidence, people talking and yelling orders.

He begged Morgan to come back to him.

He remembered Sam pulling him away, so the medics could get her into the ambulance and to the hospital. Sam drove and he stared at the back of the ambulance in front of them. She was in there, and he wanted to be with her. He wanted her to know how much he wanted her back. She couldn't die. She couldn't be dead.

After that, his days became a waiting game. He'd

waited outside the emergency room while they worked to get her back. He'd waited outside of surgery while they put her shoulder back in the socket and repaired torn ligaments and damaged tissue and muscles. They bound up her bruised and cracked ribs. They cleaned up all the cuts and scratches on her arms and torso from being dragged. Through it all, he didn't feel anything. He couldn't feel his own feelings, or hers. He wished, he prayed for her to share her pain with him again. Day after day, he waited, and nothing but the blip of her monitor slowly counting off the beats of her heart—that stopped more than once—entered his consciousness.

He sat beside her bed minute after minute, hour after hour, never leaving her side for more than a few minutes. He couldn't leave her.

Everyone in the family had come to see her at one time or another. Jenna, Elizabeth, and Marti wielded their collective power and made sure the rooms around Morgan were empty. The nurses and doctors kept their visits to a minimum. Everyone in the family understood Morgan's need to be isolated from the emotions of others, especially in her fragile state.

Five days, that's how long he'd been sitting by her bed, praying, begging, and slowly going crazy. He held her hand, brushed her hair, washed her, and he loved her. Most of all he loved her. She didn't move unless he moved her. Fed by an IV and constantly monitored. They'd tested her brain and confirmed his fears: she remained in a deep coma with very little brain activity. They didn't think she'd come out of it. He refused to listen to any of them. They didn't know Morgan and her exceptional abilities.

She breathed on her own now, and her heart rate remained steady. She just needed time. Hadn't she blacked out for almost a day after the incident in the restaurant? Well, this time had been more intense.

The family's hopefulness for him and Morgan helped to keep him sane. None of them believed she wouldn't come back. They all knew she would.

"How is she today?" Marti asked.

He hadn't heard them come in. He'd been watching Morgan's face. He thought she might look a little less pale today. Maybe. Maybe it was just wishful thinking on his part.

He glanced at Marti holding her new baby, sitting in the wheelchair Cameron pushed in. One of the only times he'd left Morgan for any length of time, he'd gone downstairs the other day to see Marti after she delivered a very healthy baby girl.

"She's the same." He tried to smile at his friends, but it fell short. Cameron held Emma in his arms and stood beside his wife. They made a nice picture, a new mother, a father, a young daughter, and the baby. He wanted that for him and Morgan.

"Oh, I don't know. She looks a little less pale today. Have you eaten?"

"When?" he asked, because he couldn't remember. He didn't care. Morgan hadn't eaten. She hadn't done anything for days. What he wouldn't give to see her eat. He remembered sharing chips and guacamole while they talked. She'd shared his iced tea.

"Well, if you can't remember, buddy, it's about time you did." Cameron hated seeing his friend like this. He understood though. He didn't know what he'd do if it were Marti lying in that bed, so still and pale.

The door opened and the rest of the family came in. Elizabeth, beautiful in her pregnancy. Sam holding Grace. Jack and Jenna with their boys and little Willow. Jack carried in a cooler, and Jenna and Elizabeth held bakery boxes from Decadence.

"We thought you could use a family brunch," Elizabeth said.

"Brunch," he said, confused.

"It's Sunday," Sam said. "The women said we're having brunch. Do what they say. Besides, you aren't going to turn down my wife's cooking, are you?"

Tyler's brain slowly started working. "Um, no. I guess it's all right."

"Sure it is," Jenna said. "Morgan would love a Sunday brunch with the family. We'll have a nice meal and some good conversation. Our collective happiness will help her feel better."

Jenna had a plan. She always did. She was right. Having everyone together would make Morgan happy.

Cameron set Emma beside Morgan on the blanket. "Why will happiness make her feel better?" Emma wanted to know.

Tyler answered. "Because she's special. Good feelings in others make her feel good. Bad feelings make her feel bad."

"Is that what happened? The bad man made her feel bad."

"She used her special gift to find the bad man. That left her feeling very tired. And then, yes, his bad feelings and her injuries made her not feel good. We're just waiting for her to feel better."

Tyler brushed his hand down Morgan's hair. His need to touch her grew more and more the longer she stayed away.

Marti stood up from her wheelchair and laid the baby down in the crook of Morgan's good arm. Her other arm lay across her belly in a sling. Tyler didn't stop holding her hand, even when she put the baby in Morgan's arm.

"What are you doing? She can't hold onto the baby," Tyler said, worried.

"It's fine. The baby is sound asleep and won't move much. If Morgan needs happiness, there's nothing more content than a sleeping baby. And nothing makes a woman happier than having a brand-new baby in her arms."

Elizabeth and Jenna agreed and looked over Tyler at the sleeping beauty.

Emma didn't look very happy.

"What's the matter, Em? You don't want the baby with Morgan?" Tyler asked.

"No, it's not that."

"Then what?" He hated to see her upset. Everyone in the room watched her as she studied Morgan's face.

"She's not a witch after all," she said sadly. "I liked the idea of knowing a witch."

"What do you mean? We know she isn't a witch. She's special."

"She's not a witch," she said excitedly. "She's something else even better. She's a fairy."

That got Sam's attention. "What do you mean, sweetheart?"

"She's a fairy. Like in the movie with Tinker Bell. If you're mean to her and say you don't believe, you kill the fairy. If you believe in fairies, then the fairy lives. They have to have happy thoughts in order to fly. She's a fairy."

"Oh, my God," Sam said and looked around the room. They'd all shared a collective laugh over the fact that they'd all brought Morgan lilies for her room. All the women had said they were happy flowers and they smelled good. Jenna brought her favorite: Stargazers, like the name of Jack's ranch.

"Jack, do you remember when we went to see Morgan at her house?" Sam asked. "She teased me about fairies in her garden."

Jack smiled. "I remember it well. One of the few times I've seen you nervous. You were disappointed she didn't have a cauldron, or a crystal ball."

"That's because she's a fairy," Emma said emphatically.

"You're right, Emma." Sam said. "She told us the fairies lived in the lilies." He waited a second while everyone noticed the flowers around the room. "She also said fairies are like little balls of golden sunlight. They die if you say you don't believe in them, and when they think happy thoughts, they can fly. Just like you said, sweetheart. She described herself."

Emma smiled at Morgan. "She does look golden with all this pretty hair." Emma ran her fingers through the soft silky strands.

Smart girl.

Tyler about jumped out of his seat. Everyone noticed his abrupt jerk.

"Morgan? Honey, talk to me again."

Pretty baby.

"Yes, honey. She is. Wake up and look at her."

Elizabeth couldn't take it. Tyler could hear her, and they all wanted in on it. "What did she say?"

Tyler kissed the top of Emma's head and leaned over Morgan. "She said, 'Smart girl.'" He looked at Marti. "Then she said, 'Pretty baby.'"

Marti smiled. "See. Every woman loves a newborn baby."

"Say something else, honey. Talk to me." He could barely feel her.

Love. You. She said it haltingly. She couldn't hold on to the connection anymore and slipped back into the empty space.

"Oh, honey. I love you, too. Come back. Don't go." He felt her slip away again. She'd come back. She just needed time. He'd had her for a minute. She'd fight her way back to him again. He kissed her on the lips softly and laid his forehead to hers. "Please, honey. Come back."

Everyone in the room got busy getting the food out and feeding the kids and themselves. Elizabeth went to

Tyler. They'd been friends for a long time now, and they had a special bond, like Sam and Jenna shared.

She put her hands on Tyler's shoulders and pulled him back from Morgan. He turned to face her and she wiped away the single tear that rolled down his cheek. "She will, Tyler. She's coming back. Give her time." She hugged him, and after a moment he hugged her back.

"Come on. Let's eat. You'll feel better. She talked to you. That's a good thing."

She coaxed Tyler over to the small table they set up. Everyone ate and talked and laughed together. Emma chatted with Morgan and even little Sam and Matt got up on the bed. They checked under Morgan's long hair to see if she might have wings. The little ones made up stories about fairies and the adults caught up on their lives.

Eventually, everyone left Morgan's room but Sam and Elizabeth. Grace slept peacefully at the foot of Morgan's bed.

Elizabeth held Morgan's hand while Sam and Tyler caught up on the office.

"The case is closed and all the paperwork is filed," Sam told Tyler.

"I hate paperwork," Tyler grumbled.

"Thanks to me, you don't have to do any of it." Sam studied Tyler. "Davies said you can take as much time as you need. You'll get your commendation for solving the case, and Morgan will receive a citizen's award. He said he'd come by to see you both."

"Yeah," Tyler said, his gaze on Morgan. Elizabeth stood beside the bed, stroking her hand.

Sam caught the sweet expression on his wife's face. "The baby kicking again?"

"Yeah. It's like a rolling ball of knees and elbows." She looked at Tyler. "We're supposed to have the ultrasound tomorrow. We hope to find out if it's a boy or a girl." She rubbed her and Morgan's hand over her belly where the baby kicked. She didn't want to let go of Morgan. She remembered lying in a hospital bed unable to move or communicate. Human contact was an anchor. Right now, she'd be Morgan's anchor.

It's a boy. J.T.

"Morgan." Tyler whispered to her.

"Did she talk to you?" Sam watched Morgan's face. She looked better after everyone had spent the day with her. He believed that happiness and contentment, family and love, had made her better.

"Do you want to know if it's a boy or a girl?" He smiled at them both.

"Yes," they said together. Sam drew closer to his wife and put his hand to her belly.

Tyler looked at them both, so in love and excited about their baby on the way. "It's a boy. J.T., she said."

"She knows his name. I mean, we talked about the names, but she knew. Oh my god, that's so amazing." She held tight to Morgan's hand. "Yes. It's a boy. He'll be J.T." She kissed Sam, so excited Grace would have a brother.

Ask her about the name.

"She wants to know about the name."

Not for me, for you.

"Oh, she wants *me* to know about the name." He

didn't know why she wanted him to know how they'd named their son.

"His name is Jackson Tyler," Sam said. "After Jack and you."

Taken by surprise, Tyler never expected this.

Babies are named after family. "You're family," she whispered and opened her eyes to look at Tyler.

Taken by surprise again, he nearly fell to his knees. "Morgan. You came back."

"I never left you."

Elizabeth and Sam silently signaled each other, *Time to go.* Elizabeth leaned over and kissed Morgan on the temple. "We'll come by and see you later. We have to take Sleeping Beauty, there, home."

"She's dreaming about puppies. She wants one."

Elizabeth laughed. "She's been saying *puppy* nonstop since she saw one in the park. We're thinking about it."

"I bet she gets one for Christmas," Morgan said on a sigh.

Sam came over to kiss her goodbye. "I won't take that bet. You've got inside information." She could barely keep her eyes open, so he kissed her goodbye, picked up his sleeping daughter, and took his family home.

Tyler and Morgan stared at each other. A wave of relief washed over her from him, along with his disbelief she was awake and okay.

"I'm fine, sweetheart. I promise."

"You scared me. I thought I'd lost you." He crawled onto the bed next to her. Not an easy task to scoot her over and move all the wires and IV lines, but he needed to be close to her. He put his arm over her and held her gently to him. Face-to-face, he leaned in and kissed her forehead.

"I feel better already." She leaned her head to his lips.

"Are you in pain? I can get the doctor to up your meds if you're hurting."

"I'm okay. It hurts, but you make me feel better."

"Oh God, honey. What happened?" He'd had a lot of time to replay the scene in his head. He had no idea, and neither did anyone else, what really happened that night.

She understood what he wanted, an explanation for the unexplainable. "I got slapped one too many times. He pissed me off. After that, I don't know. I wanted to push him away, and I couldn't physically do it. I don't know how I did it. It just happened."

"Now that you're okay, I have to say, it was awesome. Like being hit by a small explosion."

"I'm glad you enjoyed it," she joked.

He held her tighter and kissed her throat, and then her collarbone on her hurt shoulder.

"Honey, I hate to complain, but I'm not up to being seduced."

"I'm not seducing you. I'm just showing you how happy I am that you came back to me. I don't ever want to lose you again."

"You never lost me. I was always with you. I just didn't have the strength to tell you."

He laid his head on her pillow next to hers. All of a sudden he felt very tired. The last few days were finally catching up with him.

"Sleep with me," she said. He looked so tired and she felt his body relax next to hers. She had to admit, Tyler next to her was the best medicine.

"I thought you said you didn't want to be seduced," he teased.

She closed her eyes and snuggled up against him as best she could without hurting her shoulder or ribs. She waited for him to relax. When he did, she began to drift off to sleep.

Morgan?

I'm still here with you, she said and wanted to smile because he spoke to her this way—her way.

Will you marry me?

I thought you'd never ask, she answered on a giddy laugh.

Is that a yes?

Yes.

Epilogue

THEY'D MET IN a restaurant and today they married in one. Elizabeth graciously closed Decadence on a Saturday night three months after Morgan had been released from the hospital and recovered from her injuries.

Jenna, Elizabeth, Summer, and Marti went all out decorating for the ceremony and dinner reception. As if her garden exploded in the restaurant, everywhere you looked, bouquets of roses and lilies overflowed vases, their sweet scent filling the room.

They'd gone back to the house in Colorado for her recovery. Tyler took a two-week leave of absence to be with her. He'd surprised her with an engagement ring the day she left the hospital. He surprised her again by buying her a horse from Jack. Over the two weeks on her property, he taught her about horses and even took her riding. With her shoulder in a sling, she'd had to keep to a walk, but she was getting better and would soon be riding as well as Jack and the others.

Their new house in the hills near San Francisco was isolated as much as it could be near a big city. Their closest neighbor was over a mile away, and they'd paid dearly for the privacy. She'd have to work some serious magic with her stocks and investments to earn back what they'd spent for their home. She didn't care. Tyler could have his work, and she could have the space she needed away from others. They'd moved into the new house two months ago and furnished it with pieces they both picked out. Then they'd christened every room in the most outstanding ways. Her body still heated and tingled when she thought about some of the naughty things they'd done in those rooms.

Tonight, they'd been married with their collected family present. Even Tyler's sister, Agent Davies, and his wife joined their group for the wedding and reception. As she looked around the table, she had to sigh. All of these people where her family, maybe not by blood, but by choice and an abundance of love.

Sam, as Tyler's best man, gave the toast to the happy bride and groom. He'd wished them a long and happy life together and officially welcomed Morgan to the family.

Everyone sat, enjoying the food and the company. Morgan thought it the perfect time to give Tyler his wedding gift. She stood and held up her full glass of champagne. She'd only had the one sip after Sam's toast. She held it before her and cleared her throat to get everyone's attention.

"I'd like to make a toast and an announcement."

Everyone stared at her and the collective expectation and excitement from the group made her head spin. They were all so happy for her and Tyler. A far cry from the last time she'd stood before this group of people in this restaurant. They'd all been anxious and down about Tyler getting married then. Not this time. This time, they were ecstatic for him and her.

This time it was right.

"For a long time you fought the connection we shared." Tyler frowned beside her. She kissed it away and said, "Wait for it. It gets better."

"I already found that out," he answered, referring to the long wait they'd had to get to this moment.

"You asked me to explain it, but I never could. Now, I look around this room at the family you've made me a part of and I finally understand. We are connected in mind and heart and soul. To soul mates," she toasted, holding up her glass and using it to point to each of the couples around the table. Summer and Caleb. Jack and Jenna. Elizabeth and Sam. Cameron and Marti. She turned back to Tyler. "I love you."

"I love you, too, honey."

"I have a gift for you, but he won't be ready for several months," she said and ran her hand along his cheek and through the side of his dark hair as she stared into his love-filled eyes.

Her words didn't really register at first. "That's okay, honey, I can ... Wait. Did you just say *he* wouldn't be ready for several months?"

"That's exactly what I said. For a long time, all you wanted was a wife and children, family and love. You have them. Well, one child. We'll work on the rest," she teased.

He stood and cupped her beautiful face in his hands. He was going to be a father. The one thing he wanted more than anything besides Morgan.

"This, you, him, everything, it's exactly what I wanted and so much more. I love you." He kissed her and everyone cheered.

Their collective happiness and Tyler's overwhelming joy made her lightheaded and euphoric. She took it in and felt blessed in a way she could never explain, but cherished, along with her life with Tyler and their family.

Before Morgan sat down, Sam asked, "So, Mrs. Reed, do you have a prediction for the future?"

Oh, how she liked being called Mrs. Reed.

Everyone at the table held their breath, waiting for her to answer. The last time she'd come to this restaurant knowing the future, they'd all gotten a huge scare.

She gave them a knowing smile. "I see bright Colorado skies and smooth sailing for the Turner-Shaw-Reed family."

Tyler squeezed her hand. She'd described it perfectly.

I love you.

I love you, too.

Can't get enough of Jennifer Ryan's sexy Hunted Series?

You finally get the story you've all been waiting for!
For the first time, see how Caleb and
Summer fell in love
in the prequel Can't Wait
coming December 10, 2013, in the anthology

ALL I WANT FOR CHRISTMAS IS A COWBOY

If you loved CHASING MORGAN,
don't miss the rest of Jennifer Ryan's heart-stopping,
sexy Hunted Series!

SAVED BY THE RANCHER

Book One: The Hunted Series

FROM THE MOMENT rancher Jack Turner rescues Jenna Caldwell Merrick, he is determined to help her. Soon, he is doing more than tend her wounds; he is mending her heart. Jenna is a woman on the run—hunted down by her ex-husband, David Merrick, from the day she left him, taking part of his company with her, to the second she finds herself in the safety of Jack's ranch. More than just a haven, Jack's offering the love, family, and home she thought were out of reach.

Jack's support will give Jenna the strength she needs to reclaim her life. The hunted will become the hunter, while David gets what he deserves when they have an explosive confrontation in the boardroom of Merrick International. But not before Jack and Jenna enter into a fight . . . for their lives.

LUCKY LIKE US

Book Two: The Hunted Series

BAKERY OWNER ELIZABETH Hamilton's quiet life is filled with sweet treats, good friends, and a loving family. But all of that is about to turn sour when an odd sound draws her outside. There's a man lying unconscious in the street, a car speeding toward him. Without hesitation, she gets the man out of harm's way before they're run down.

Unwittingly, Elizabeth has put herself in the path of a serial murderer, and as the only one who can identify the FBI's Silver Fox Killer, she's ended up in the hospital with a target on her back.

All that stands between her and death is Special Agent Sam Turner. Against his better judgment, Sam gets emotionally involved, determined to take down the double threat against Elizabeth—an ex desperate to get her back, despite a restraining order, and a psychopath bent on silencing her before she can identify him.

They set a trap to catch the killer—putting Elizabeth in his hands, with Sam desperate to save her. If he's lucky, he'll get his man . . . and the girl.

THE RIGHT BRIDE

Book Three: The Hunted Series

HIGH-POWERED BUSINESSMAN CAMERON Shaw doesn't believe in love—until he falls head over heels for beautiful, passionate, and intensely private Martina. She's perfect in so many ways, immediately bonding with his little girl. Martina could be his future bride and a delightful stepmother . . . if only Cameron weren't blinded by his belief that Shelly, the gold-digging woman he's promised to marry, is pregnant with his child.

No matter how much his friends protest his upcoming marriage to Shelly, Cameron knows he has a duty to his children, so he's determined to see it through.

Will he find out in time that Shelly's lying and Marti's the one who's actually carrying his child? It'll come down to the day of his wedding. After choosing Shelly over Marti at every turn, will he convince Marti she's his world and the only woman he wants?

Give in to your impulses . . .
Read on for a sneak peek at three brand-new
e-book original tales of romance
from Avon Books.
Available now wherever e-books are sold.

THE GOVERNESS CLUB: CLAIRE
By Ellie Macdonald

ASHES, ASHES, THEY
ALL FALL DEAD
By Lena Diaz

THE GOVERNESS CLUB: BONNIE
By Ellie Macdonald

An Excerpt from

THE GOVERNESS CLUB: CLAIRE

by Ellie Macdonald

Claire Bannister just wants to be a good teacher so that she and the other ladies of the Governess Club can make enough money to leave their jobs and start their own school in the country. But when the new sinfully handsome and utterly distracting tutor arrives, Claire finds herself caught up in a whirlwind romance that could change the course of her future.

What would a "London gent" want with her, Claire wondered as she quickened her pace. The only man she knew in the capital was Mr. Baxter, her late father's solicitor. Why would he come all the way here instead of corresponding through a letter as usual? Unless it was something more urgent than could be committed to paper. Perhaps it had something to do with Ridgestone—

At that thought, Claire lifted her skirts and raced to the parlor. Five years had passed since her father's death, since she'd had to leave her childhood home, but she had not given up her goal to one day return to Ridgestone.

The formal gardens of Aldgate Hall vanished, replaced by the memory of her own garden; the terrace doors no longer opened to the ballroom, but to a small, intimate library; the bright corridor darkened to a comforting glow; Claire could even smell her old home as she rushed to the door of the housekeeper's parlor. Pausing briefly to catch her breath and smooth her hair, she knocked and pushed the door open, head held high, barely able to contain her excitement.

Cup and saucer met with a loud rattle as a young man hurried to his feet. Mrs. Morrison's disapproving frown could not stop several large drops of tea from contaminating her white linen, nor could Mr. Fosters's harrumph. Claire's heart sank as she took in the man's youth, disheveled hair, and rumpled clothes; he was decidedly *not* Mr. Baxter. Perhaps a new associate? Her heart picked up slightly at that thought.

Claire dropped a shallow curtsey. "You wished to see me, Mrs. Morrison?"

The thin woman rose and drew in a breath that seemed to tighten her face even more with disapproval. She gestured to the stranger. "Yes. This is Mr. Jacob Knightly. Lord and Lady Aldgate have retained him as a tutor for the young masters."

Claire blinked. "A tutor? I was not informed they were seeking—"

"It is not your place to be informed," the butler, Mr. Fosters, cut in.

Claire immediately bowed her head and clasped her hands in front of her submissively. "My apologies. I overstepped." Her eyes slid shut, and she took a deep breath to dispel the disappointment. Ridgestone faded into the back of her mind once more.

Mrs. Morrison continued with the introduction. "Mr. Knightly, this is Miss Bannister, the governess."

Mr. Knightly bowed. "Miss Bannister, it is a pleasure to make your acquaintance."

Claire automatically curtseyed. "The feeling is mutual,

sir." As she straightened, she lifted her eyes to properly survey the new man. Likely not yet in his third decade, Mr. Knightly wore his brown hair long enough not to be following the current fashion. Scattered locks fell across his forehead, and the darkening of a beard softened an otherwise square-jawed face. He stood nearly a head taller than she did, and his loosely fitted jacket and modest cravat did nothing to conceal broad shoulders. Skimming her gaze down his body, she noticed a shirt starting to yellow with age and a plain brown waistcoat struggling to hide the fact that its owner was less than financially secure. Even his trousers were slightly too short, revealing too much of his worn leather boots. All in all, Mr. Jacob Knightly appeared to be the epitome of a young scholar reduced to becoming a tutor.

Except for his mouth. And his eyes. Not that Claire had much experience meeting with tutors, but even she could tell that the spectacles enhanced rather than detracted from the pale blueness of his eyes. The lenses seemed to emphasize their round shape, emphasize the appreciative gleam in them before Mr. Knightly had a chance to hide it. Even when he did, the corners of his full mouth remained turned up in a funny half-smile, all but oozing confidence and assurance—bordering on an arrogance one would not expect to find in a tutor.

Oh dear.

An Excerpt from

ASHES, ASHES, THEY ALL FALL DEAD

by *Lena Diaz*

Special Agent Tessa James is obsessed with finding the killer whose signature singsong line—"Ashes, ashes, they all fall dead"—feels all too familiar. When sexy, brilliant consultant Matt Buchanan is paired with Tessa to solve the mystery, they discover, inexplicably, that the clues point to Tessa herself. If she can't remember the forgotten years of her past, will she become the murderer's next target?

She raised a shaking hand to her brow and tried to focus on what he'd told her. "You've found a pattern where he kills a victim in a particular place but mails the letter for a different victim while he's there."

"That's what I'm telling you, yes. It's early yet, and we have a lot more to research—and other victims to find—but this is one hell of a coincidence, and I'm not much of a believer in coincidences. I think we're on to something."

Tears started in Tessa's eyes. She'd been convinced since last night that she'd most likely ruined her one chance to find the killer, and at the same time ruined her career. And suddenly everything had changed. In the span of a few minutes, Matt had given her back everything he'd taken from her when he'd destroyed the letter at the lab. Laughter bubbled up in her throat, and she knew she must be smiling like a fool, but she couldn't help it.

"You did it, Matt." Her voice came out as a choked whisper. She cleared her throat. "You did it. In little more than a day, you've done what we couldn't do in months, years. You've found the thread to unravel the killer's game. This is the breakthrough we've been looking for."

She didn't remember throwing herself at him, but suddenly she was in his arms, laughing and crying at the same time. She looped her arms around his neck and looked up into his wide-eyed gaze, then planted a kiss right on his lips.

She drew back and framed his face with her hands, giddy with happiness. "Thank you, Matt. Thank you, thank you, thank you. You've saved my career. And you've saved lives! Casey can't deny this is a real case anymore. He'll have to get involved, throw some resources at finding the killer. And we'll stop this bastard before he hurts anyone else. How does that feel? How does it feel to know you just saved someone?"

His arms tightened around her waist, and he pulled her against his chest. "It feels pretty damn good," he whispered. And then he kissed her.

Not the quick peck she'd just given him. A real kiss. A hot, wet, knock-every-rational- thought-out-of-her-mind kind of kiss. His mouth moved against hers in a sensual onslaught—nipping, tasting, teasing—before his tongue swept inside and consumed her with his heat.

Desire flooded through her, and she whimpered against him. She stroked his tongue with hers, and he groaned deep in his throat. He slid his hand down over the curve of her bottom and lifted her until she cradled his growing hardness against her belly. He held her so tightly she felt every beat of his heart against her breast. His breath was her breath, drawing her in, stoking the fire inside her into a growing inferno.

He gyrated his hips against hers in a sinful movement that spiked across her nerve endings, tightening her into an almost painful tangle of tension. Every movement of his hips, every slant of his lips, every thrust of his tongue stoked her higher and higher, coiling her nerves into one tight knot of desire, ready to explode.

Nothing had ever felt this good.

Nothing.

Ever.

The tiny voice inside her, the one she'd ruthlessly quashed as soon as his lips claimed hers, suddenly yelled a loud warning. *Stop this madness!*

Her eyes flew open. This was *Matt* making her feel this way, on the brink of a climax when all he'd done was kiss her. *Matt.* Good grief, what was she thinking? He swiveled his hips again, and she nearly died of pleasure.

No, no! This had to stop.

Convincing her traitorous body to respond to her mind's commands was the hardest thing she'd ever tried to do, because every cell, every nerve ending wanted to stay exactly where she was: pressed up against Matt's delicious, hard, warm body.

His twenty-four-year-old body to her thirty-year-old one.

This was insane, a recipe for disaster. She had to stop, now, before she pulled him down to the ground and demanded that he make love to her right this very minute.

She broke the kiss and shoved out of his arms.

An Excerpt from

THE GOVERNESS CLUB: BONNIE

by Ellie Macdonald

The Governess Club series continues with
Miss Bonnie Hodges. She is desperately trying
to hold it together. Tragedy has struck, and she
is the sole person left to be strong for the two
little boys in her care. When the new guardian,
Sir Stephen Montgomery, arrives, she hopes that
things will get better. She wasn't expecting her new
employer to be the most frustrating, overbearing,
and . . . handsome man she's ever seen.

When he reached the water's edge, Stephen stopped. Staring at the wreckage that used to be the wooden bridge, he was acutely aware that he was looking at the site of his friends' death.

Images from the story Miss Hodges had told him flashed through his mind—the waving parents, the bridge shuddering before it collapsed, the falling planks and horses, the coach splintering, George's neck snapping, and Roslyn—God, Roslyn lying in that mangled coach, her blood pouring out of her body. How had she survived long enough for anyone to come and see her still breathing?

Nausea roiled in his stomach, and bile forced its way up his throat. Heaving, Stephen bent over a nearby bush and lost the contents of his stomach. Minutes later, he crouched down at the river's edge and splashed the cold water on his face.

From where he crouched, Stephen turned his gaze down

the river, away from the ruined bridge. He could make out an area ideal for swimming: a small stretch of sandy bank surrounded by a few large, flat rocks. Indeed, an excellent place for a governess to take her charges for a cooling swim on a hot summer day.

Stephen straightened and made his way along the bank to the swimming area. A well-worn path weaved through the bush, connecting the small beach to the hill beyond and Darrowgate. The bridge was seventy meters upstream; not only would the governess and the boys have had a good view of the collapse, the blood from the incident would have flowed right by them.

No wonder they barely spoke.

Tearing his gaze from the bridge, he focused on the water, trying to imagine the trio enjoying their swim, with no inkling or threat of danger. The boys in the water, laughing and splashing each other, showing off their swimming skills to their laughing governess.

Stephen looked at the closest flat rock, the thought of the laughing governess in his mind. She had said she preferred dangling her feet instead of swimming.

His mind's eye put Miss Hodges on the rock, much as she had been the previous night. The look on her face after seeing his own flour-covered face. Her smile had been so wide it had been difficult to see anything else about her. He knew her eyes and hair were certain colors, but he was damned if he could name them—the eyes were some light shade and the hair was brown, that he knew for certain.

And her laugh—it was the last thing he had expected from her. He was in a difficult situation—not quite master but regarded as such until Henry's majority. For a servant, even a governess, to laugh as she had was entirely unpredictable.

He shouldn't think too much about how that unexpected laughter had settled in his gut.

The image of Miss Hodges sitting on the rock rose again in his mind. The sun would have warmed the rock beneath her hands, and she would have looked down at the clear water. She would laugh at the boys' antics, he had no doubt, perhaps even kick water in their direction if they ventured too close. Her stockings would be folded into her shoes to keep them from blowing away in the breeze.

Good Lord, he could almost see it. The stockings protected in the nearby shoes, her naked feet dangling in the water, her skirts raised to keep them from getting wet, exposing her trim ankles. The clear water would do nothing to hide either her feet or her ankles, and Stephen found himself staring unabashedly at something that wasn't even there. He gazed at the empty water, imagining exactly what Miss Hodges's ankles would look like. They would be slim, they would be bonny, they would—

Thankfully, a passing cart made enough noise to break him out of this ridiculously schoolboy moment. Inhaling deeply through his nose, Stephen left the swimming area and made his way back for a closer look at the ruins.